D1521117

Contents

Books By Nesha

Standalones:

Envy Me
Fraud
You'll Always Be My Baby
We Could've Been
Lucid Dreams
Stay Schemin'
Twisted Lies- (Collaboration)
Jokes On You-(Booklovers app)

Series:

Bambi 1-3
The Carter's Holiday

Catching Flights
Catching Feelings

Spin Offs

Here We Go Again
Emotionally Scarred

This book has been rated Nesha

Messy Asf
Excessive inappropriate language
Sudden laughing fits
Unapologetically Urban

Snakes aren't always strangers. They come in the form of family and friends with trusting smiles and familiarity. Those bites hurt ten times worse because you can't see it coming.

Prologue

"Nigga, what?!" Duke howled, stretching his hands in the air. "Janet Jackson is fine, but she don't have shit on Toni Braxton."

"Fuck is you saying?" Bruce countered, twisting his face in disgust. "Toni Braxton sounds like she gargles rocks. Ole deep ass voice. That's not even including that manly ass haircut."

"Rah, tell this man he snorting dope." Duke looked to his best friend for help.

"I'm more of a Keke Wyatt guy myself," Rahlo smirked, looking up from his notebook. "Not only is she fine ass hell, but her voice has range. When I make it big, I'm going to put her on a track."

"Nigga, please," Duke snarled, waving him off.

"Don't trip," Rahlo responded. "When I'm big everybody is gon' be on my dick.... including yo spiked-haired ass mama."

"My mama is a crackhead. Give her ten dollars and she'll stay on your dick, record deal or not."

"This nigga!" Bruce cackled out loud.

It was no secret that Duke's mother was a crackhead and if the price was right- actually the price didn't even matter- she'd suck the skin off your dick for five dollars, let you fuck for ten.

"You stupid," Rahlo chuckled and returned his focus back to the notebook in his hand. He jotted a few words down but closed the notebook when he spotted a crowd of people walking towards them. From the bats and various weapons in their hands, he knew it wasn't a friendly visit.

"What the fuck you do?" Bruce quizzed, glaring at Duke, who was already on his feet. He removed the wife beater he was wearing and folded his arms across his bare chest. Rahlo sat his notebook down and stood next to his friend. Whatever they were accusing Duke of, he did it, but Rahlo wasn't going to stand by and watch him get jumped.

"Lil nigga, you stole my cousin phone?" The leader Qu barked while pointing the wooden bat at Duke.

"What kinda phone was it?" Duke cocked his head to the side with a playful grin displayed on his face.

"The Samsung, nigga."

"What model?" Duke interrogated as if he really had to think about it. He knew exactly what phone they were talking about. Currently, it was sitting in a pawn shop with a promissory note attached to it that Duke never intended to fulfill. With the stolen phone, he was able to buy noodles for the week, a loaf of bread, peanut butter, and a dime bag of weed.

"You think this shit a game?" Qu stepped forward, prompting his crew to do the same. Duke had terrorized many of them, so they were ready for whatever. If he wasn't stealing their things from the basketball court, he was shaking them down with black pantyhose concealing his face.

"This city is crawling with crackheads, petty thieves, and hoodrats. It could've been anybody," Duke said with a lift of his shoulders.

"It was you 'cause I saw you going through my bag!" The victim stepped forward. He was a skinny kid with big glasses and a chili bowl fade. His father was a doctor and his mother was a nurse, they had money to burn, and the phone Duke stole could easily be replaced.

"Special Ed, please, you wear them thick ass glasses and still can't see. I didn't touch your bag. The phone was sitting on the bleachers."

"So you got it?"

"Nah, I *had* it," Duke admitted, never one to shy away from his wrongdoings. "I sold it though. I can give you the ticket number if you want to buy it back."

"Beat this nigga ass," Qu hissed, pointing the bat.

On cue, the crowd of boys charged Duke, trying to rip his head off his shoulders. Like a bunch of hyenas, they clawed at his shirt and yanked his hair.

"Get the fuck off him!" Rahlo jumped in, slinging people left and right until he reached Duke, who was in the center laughing as if they weren't trying to kill him.

"Aye, this ain't got nothing to do with yall," Qu said loudly, but his words fell on deaf ears. Bruce and Rahlo started swinging to defend their friend. It didn't matter what Duke did, Rahlo had his back, and Bruce had Rahlo's.

"Break this shit up!" A deep voice roared. Almost immediately the fighting came to a halt.

"Chef," Qu tried to reason. "He stole my lil cousin phone."

"I don't give a fuck, take yall ass on." Chef waved his hand. "Duke, get yo thieving ass from around here."

"I'll see you around pussy." Qu threw up the east side with his hands.

"Fuck outta here. Yo whole crew cripple. Leader of the east side my ass, nigga you leader of the hazmats," Duke taunted. "Next time tell that lil nigga to put his shit up."

"Rah, let's go," Rahlo's older sister Esha called out.

"Aight," he hollered back. "Bruce, make sure this nigga get home." Rahlo gave his boys a pound and picked up his notebook. He hoped Esha hustled up enough money to get them something good to eat. For the past two weeks they had been eating noodles and hotdogs. Rahlo wasn't picky, but if he had to consume another hotdog, he'd probably start fasting. There was only so much pork wrapped in casing he could digest.

"Nah, this nigga talk too much." Bruce shook his head.

"Hush it up, fat boy." Duke grabbed Bruce's stomach and dodged the fist that flew in his direction.

"Stop playing before I call them niggas back to beat yo ass."

"In your dreams, Biggie Smalls."

"Aye," Chef called out, thumbing his nose. "Let me talk to you, Rah."

"Sup, big homie?" Rahlo stalked over to him.

"Where yo mama?"

"I don't even know." Rahlo hunched his shoulders. His mama was a local rolling stone. She was never too far but never close enough.

"Yall straight?"

"We good," Rahlo assured him. His pride wouldn't allow him to willingly take anything from another man. It was bad enough that Esha had to buy all of his clothes, shoes, and draws. At fourteen, Rahlo felt like he could've been doing more, but Esha made it clear that his focus was school and nothing more. It didn't matter that she was only a few years older than him. With a mother like theirs, Esha assumed the position of the parent in their household.

"Aye, Esha, can y'all drop me off?" Duke asked.

"Even if I was driving the answer would be no. Get your shit startin' ass on." She gave him the finger. Duke wagged his tongue out at her and started his hike. Night would fall soon and he would be locked out if he didn't make it home. His grandma didn't play. She honestly didn't want him staying there, but since his mama was in the streets, she took him and his sister in. The checks she received from the state softened the blow, yet it still wasn't enough for her to display any type of emotional support.

"You be careful with that one." Chef nodded his head in Duke's direction.

"That's my boy," Rahlo defended with an arched eyebrow.

"Yea, I get that and I love your loyalty, but it can also be a downfall."

"I hear you, big homie, but I gotta go."

"Be easy." Chef dapped him.

"How we getting home?" Rahlo asked Esha once he was at her side.

"The bus. I have a few dollars and I was going to get a pizza." She grinned, knowing that he was going to be happy.

"Thank God," he exhaled. "You heard from Emory?"

"Nah." Esha shook her head. "But I'm going to do a couple of heads tomorrow and I'll be able to go grocery shopping and get you an outfit."

"If I make it, I'm going to take care of you, Esh."

"When you make it, nigga!" She bumped his shoulder. "I'm not doing this shit for my health."

"Yea aight."

"Now spit something for me," Esha demanded.

"You gotta pay for this show, sis."

"Keep playing and you'll be eating hotdogs tonight."

"Oh hell nah." Rahlo shook his head. It only took him a few seconds before words started to flow from his mouth. Esha bobbed her head, knowing that her brother was something special and it was only a matter of time before the world caught wind of how dope he was.

Chapter 1

"Bring out all top shelf bottles," Rahlo boasted, slipping into the booth, followed by a couple of groupies who were hanging on to his every move. Neither of them was his girl, but they wanted to be for the night. They wanted one night with an upcoming rap star and the ten minutes of fame that came with it. Even if it wasn't good attention, it was still some attention.

"How many?" the hostess asked, trying to keep her composure. Rahlo wasn't a regular nigga and there he was sitting in her section just as cool as a fan.

"Shit, bring about four." He grinned. A drink was the last thing he needed because the back-to-back blunts he smoked in the limo already had him feeling as if he was floating. His normally tense shoulders were slumped and the mean mug he always sported had vanished minutes before he stepped into the club. Although it was dark, *Cartier* sunglasses shielded his sleepy eyes. The last thing he needed was for the paparazzi to catch him in his laxed state. They would swear he was snorting dope or, worse, shooting heroin.

At only twenty-five, Rahlo had just signed with Eastwood Entertainment and was guaranteed to make more money than he could spend in a lifetime. The moment was surreal and he was still having trouble wrapping his head around it. For two years, labels all over tried to persuade Rahlo to sign with their company with promises of luxury cars, gated homes, and exclusive trips to private islands. Those same labels also tried to give him bullshit contracts that most people would have glossed over. They wanted him to sell his soul, and if they had offered it to someone else, they would have jumped on it. Not Rahlo though. He combed through their contracts with a fine-tooth comb and questioned them every step of the way. What he didn't understand, he Googled until he felt comfortable enough to move on. By the time he was done, they didn't even want him on their team.

Mixtapes and shows had been his bread and butter for years, so there was no way he was settling for anything. Being an indie artist had its benefits, and if labels weren't willing to give him his worth, Rahlo walked away from the table, tossing their business cards in the trash on the way out.

Eastwood Entertainment was different. They appreciated his attention to detail and willingness to negotiate. With the help of his manager, Terri, Rahlo walked away with one of the best deals the company had to offer. That alone was cause for a celebration and Rahlo's entourage was along for the ride. Even before the deal, Rahlo was generous, and they knew now that he had just signed a multi-album deal, it would be payday for them all.

"You're Southwest Rah, right?" The hostess lustfully licked her glossy lips.

"The one and only." He grinned, checking out her thick frame.

"In that case, the first bottle is on the house. I'll send over one of my best girls to take care of you. Congratulations on your deal." She winked. "The city is proud of you."

"Thanks, baby, I appreciate that." He nodded coyly. Rahlo didn't think he'd ever get used to the love and recognition he received on a daily basis. If someone wasn't asking for an autograph, they wanted a picture or simply to congratulate him on his success.

"Now chop chop, hoe. Stop dick riding and go get us a bottle." Rahlo's best friend, Duke, snapped his fingers. The hostess rolled her eyes and walked off. She was already on her second strike due to throwing candle wax at a guest the week prior. While the asshole rightfully deserved it, management had to comp his four thousand dollar bill and pay to get his jewelry cleaned.

"Chill out and let lil baby do her job. I'm trying to relax tonight, no bullshit," Rahlo warned.

"You know this nigga don't know how to act outside of Southwest," Rahlo's security guard, Bruce, chuckled. Bruce grew up with them so he knew Duke just like Rahlo. He was sure before the night was over he'd be breaking up a fight or trying to prevent a shootout.

It was no secret that Duke was a hot head. Since the young age of fourteen, he had been in and out of juvenile detention because of his *fight first, ask questions never* motto. His rap sheet was so long that the word criminal should have been stamped across his forehead. On his last stint in jail, his family gave up on him. They didn't write, visit, or put money on his books. If it weren't for Rahlo, Duke would have went crazy. His best friend made it his business to write him, even if it was only a few lines, Duke appreciated him. Rahlo put money on his books faithfully and was there to pick him up when the iron gates opened.

"Aight, I'ma chill," Duke promised, posting up next to Rahlo as if *he* was the bodyguard. As if it was his job to protect

Rahlo from hating ass niggas and schemin' hoes.

Duke's transition back into the free world wasn't easy. Since he'd been gone, Rahlo had blown up. It was one thing to hear about it from behind bars, but to witness it in person was another thing. Duke watched Rahlo easily drop twenty bands on a new wardrobe for him and even put money in his pockets. Rahlo's circle had even changed. Besides Bruce, everyone else was a stranger, and Duke wasn't feeling it.

∞∞∞

Across the crowded club, Taylor pushed her way through the sea of people until she reached the employee lounge. Her feet were aching, and she was more than ready to go home and soak in the tub. She was supposed to leave after the lunch rush but promised to help out since the club was packed. Everybody wanted a bottle they couldn't afford and stale wings cooked in fish grease. The club had the worst food, but the drinks, music, and pretty waitresses made up for it.

"Wait, where are you going? I know you not leaving," her best friend, Kiki, asked, watching her remove the apron from around her waist.

"Uh, yes, I am," Taylor confirmed, plugging up her work tablet and kicking off her shoes.

"Wait, I thought you were staying to help."

"And I did. I been here since nine this morning and it's going on midnight. I'm about to go home, soak and take my ass to bed."

"Tayyyy, it's a full house. I need you," Kiki whined.

"And I understand that, but I'm tired."

"Just do one more table for me. I told them I would get the best and you are the best." She batted her long mink lashes.

"Bitch, don't try to geek me up."

"I'm dead ass."

"Go get Nelly," Taylor insisted.

"Now you know her funny looking ass ain't the best shit. Plus, they look like big tippers!"

"Ugh, who at the table?"

"Southwest Rah!" Kiki cheesed.

"Who?" Taylor arched her eyebrow, not recognizing the name.

"Southwest Rah, bitch! Don't act like you don't know."

"I don't. You know I don't listen to all of that rap shit, but judging from your excitement, he's someone important, and you know I don't serve famous people. They are too arrogant and I'm not trying to lose my job tonight."

"Come on, he's sweet. One of the guys with him is a piece of work, but Rah himself was nice. Please," she begged.

"Fine, but I want next weekend off," Taylor groaned, sliding back into her black Airmax.

"You really the best," Kiki cheesed.

"Shut up!" Taylor rolled her eyes. "What section are they in?"

"A1."

"How many?"

"It's about ten of them. Take the order and I'll have one of the busboys make the order. See, I'm making it easier for you. He wants a mix, but find out exactly what he wants. I'm not about to resend shit."

"You owe me."

"And I got you. Oh, can you see if he'll sign a napkin or something for me?"

"Absolutely not, bitch." Taylor waved her off and retrieved her tablet before twisting back out onto the floor. Stopping at the mirror, Taylor removed her lip gloss from her apron and gave herself a touch-up. Running her hands through her short blonde mane, she took a deep breath and headed to the floor.

At 5ft8, Taylor was a solid 230 pounds, and she rocked the shit out of it. Her perky c-cup breasts were full, soft, and juicy. She took pride in being able to prance around without a bra. Her hips were wide and sharp and her ass was fat and round. The extra weight she carried around her midsection was simply extra cushion. Taylor had the kinda body Drake rapped about. Her presence would either make you uncomfortable or turn you on. Her cashew complexion mixed with black silky eyebrows and full lips were a whole experience. Besides having a dope ass body, she had the personality to match. Taylor was sweet, but once you rubbed her the wrong way, there was no coming back. The Gemini in her wouldn't have it any other way.

Working at Top Notch wasn't a dream, but the money was good. Kiki put her on two years ago and swore that she was going to make good money…which she did. The tips alone paid for her brand-new jeep and the last minute trips she loved to take. Taylor's family hated that she worked at a club, but they gave her the freedom to make mistakes. While they preferred she went to college, they respected her decision not to. As long as she was taking care of business, they had nothing to say.

Maneuvering through the crowd, Taylor made it to the section and wanted to turn right back around. Either Kiki lied to her, or Rahlo had invited the whole damn club to his section. The women easily outnumbered the men, but no one seemed to mind. The thick smoke made her feel like she was stepping into a smoke chamber, and the flashing lights made her think she had just stepped on the red carpet.

"Uh, who is Rah?" she asked, clearing her throat.

"Bitch, don't bring yo disrespectful ass up here asking who Rah is. Go Google it and then come back and say sorry," Duke rudely responded with a frown. Women in the section snickered while the men shook their heads.

"Bitch?" Taylor snaked her neck. "The only bitch around this muthafucka is your tight pants wearing ass. Do the whole club gotta know you got on Versace draws? That's broke nigga shit, so I know you ain't Rah."

"Hoe, who the fuck you think you talking to?" He jumped up, knocking the girl on his lap to the floor.

"And what the fuck you think standing up is going to do?"

"Chill out, nigga," Rahlo spoke up. "My fault, sweetheart, I'm Rah."

"Hm, talking all that shit and you just a fucking leech," Taylor spat in Duke's direction.

"You better watch your fucking mouth," he gritted.

"Nigga, sit down," Rahlo warned. Giving Taylor one last glare, Duke took his seat and pulled the same girl he knocked on the floor back in his lap.

"What can I get for you?"

"I told baby girl to mix it up."

"You sure?"

"Positive. I'm not going to drink all that shit and these niggas drink whatever."

"Anything else?"

"You want something else?" Rahlo asked, looking at Duke. Taylor glanced at him and smirked. He talked all that shit and another man was footing his bill.

"Nah, what you ordered is enough."

"That's it, sweetheart," Rahlo told her.

"Ok, I'll be back."

"Nah, send somebody else. I don't like you," Duke snarled.

"Good, because I don't like your leeching ass either." She twisted away.

"You bet not tip that hoe," he spat, watching her disappear in the crowd.

"You just mad because she called you out. I been telling you to pull up your pants." Bruce frowned. "I told you that shit wasn't cute."

"Neither is all them fucking rolls. Shut yo fat ass up."

"Can you beat me though?"

"Fuck outta here, I'll knock your big ass out," Duke promised.

Rahlo chuckled at their banter. Bruce was probably the only one who could put Duke in his place. Growing up, they'd go back and forth until the jokes became too personal and the laughs turned into fistfights. Bringing up someone's mother was a no-no and they crossed the line every time.

Fifteen minutes later, Taylor returned with one of the busboys pushing the cart of liquor, ice, and chasers. She tapped on the tablet a few times before passing it over to Rahlo to insert his card.

"The bottle of Dom is on the house," she told him as he whipped out the fresh Amex with his name written across the front. The card with no limit had been swiped so many times in the last five hours that his accountant called to ensure it wasn't stolen.

"All this shit needs to be on the house," Duke muttered, still pissed at how Taylor played him.

"Which bottle you paying for?" she snapped, glaring at him. Unbeknownst to Duke, he had the right one. Taylor grew up in a house full of men and backing down from one wasn't on her resume.

"I'm not-"

"I know. Yo broke ass ain't paying for shit, so can you please stop talking to me?" Taylor popped at her wits end with his shit talking ass.

"You better ask about me. I've slapped hoes for less," Duke gritted.

"Boy bye. You walking around with your ass hanging out of your pants like it's a mating call and you think you put fear in my heart. I'll slice yo funny looking ass from ear to ear."

"Nah, none of that, baby," Rahlo chuckled. He was surprised she was going back and forth with Duke. His ruff appearance was usually enough to scare people, but not the thick hostess. She looked like she was ready for war the moment she stepped into the section.

"Thanks, sweetheart." He handed her back the tablet. "You wanna stay for a minute? Have a drink with me?" Rahlo flirted, causing a few of the women to suck their teeth.

"Hell nah, this bi- mean ass broad fucking up my vibe." Duke snatched a bottle of champagne from the bucket.

"Boy, shut up before I dump this ice on yo wannabe hot boy ass. Rah, have a good night." Taylor stuck the tablet in her apron and twisted away. Any other time he would have tried his hand at her, but Rahlo wasn't in the space to chase pussy when the section was full of thirsty women.

"We got Detroit's own Southwest Rah is in the fucking building!" The DJ shouted, causing the women to scream out. The lights went crazy as the DJ dropped one of Rahlo's tracks.

"Detroit in this bitch!" he shouted. With a grin on his face, Rahlo sat back and watched the section rap the lyrics to his latest release, *Trouble*.

On YouTube, the song had been streamed over three

million times and was sitting at number one on other platforms. Everything earned from that song was his being that he signed after he dropped his mixtape. Not only were YouTube and Apple Music paying him, but other artists were also contacting him to do features. To say he was proud was an understatement.

Duke lifted the bottle to his lips and stopped mid-sip. His glossy eyes were fixed upon the figure standing across the club like shit was sweet. Duke had been combing the streets for his old running buddy Gee, and he knew damn well he wasn't sitting in the section across from him popping bottles like he didn't owe him money. Like he wasn't the reason for him spending the last five years of his life behind bars.

What was supposed to be a quick smash-and-grab turned out to be anything but that. Gee came up with the genius plan for them to run in the Gucci store and snatch as much as they could while the security guard was in the bathroom. Gee swore the girl at the counter was in, and he even borrowed a crackhead's car so it wouldn't trace back to them. The plan was solid. However, anything that could go wrong did go wrong.

When they got in the store, the chick who was supposed to be at the counter wasn't. In fact, she called off and there was an older white woman there. Against his better judgment, Duke still went along with the plan. The clerk must have alerted security the minute they stepped inside the store because before Duke knew it, the store was flooded with rent-a-cops. Instead of aborting the mission, Gee started snatching everything he could, and like a fool, Duke followed suit. They ran out of the store, dropping shit along the way. They would have gotten away, but when Gee started the car, it stalled. As if that wasn't bad enough, the passenger door got stuck and Duke couldn't escape. He literally got caught red handed and Gee got away.

"You straight?" Rahlo asked, noticing the shift in his

demeanor.

"Nah. You see that bitch ass nigga over there popping bottles like I won't smash one across his head," Duke gritted. Rahlo and Bruce both followed his hard stare and already knew what time it was.

"Aye chill. I already told you I can't be in no shit. Fuck that nigga."

"That's easy for you to say. You didn't spend five years behind bars. I did!" Duke slapped his chest.

"I get that, but there is a time and a place for everything."

"Aight man, on the strength of you, I'll chill." He mugged Gee once more and turned the bottle up to his lips. Rahlo sighed but still told Bruce to get the car ready.

"We love you, Rahhhhh," a group of women shouted outside of the section.

"I love yall too," he winked, standing to his feet.

"Can we get a picture, daddy?" One flirted.

"Yea, bring yo fine ass up here," Rahlo motioned. The girl squealed in excitement and quickly moved through the crowd to get to him.

While Rahlo entertained his fans, Duke sat there stewing in his anger. He had never been the type to let shit go, and as far as he was concerned, he wasn't about to start. If Gee had been solid and dropped money on his books or even came to see him when he touched down, shit would have been different. The fact that he was sitting there draped in designer clothes and popping bottles had him in his feelings. He came up off their hard work and Duke wanted what was owed to him.

"Nah, it ain't going down like that." Duke shook his head and jumped up. The liquor and drugs in his system wouldn't have it any other way.

"Where you going?" Bruce asked, snatching the bottle of

liquor out of his hand. Duke shrugged him off and angrily stomped out the section and down the stairs. Rahlo didn't notice because he was standing in a sea full of women signing titties, stomachs, and a couple of bras.

"Yo, Rah!" Bruce hollered over the music. Lifting his head, Rahlo glanced over at Bruce and did a doubletake when he didn't see Duke sitting there. Scanning the club, he noticed him heading straight to Gee's section.

"Fuck," he cursed.

As soon as the word slipped from his mouth, all hell broke loose. The piercing sound of gunshots caused the club to go into a frenzy. Quick on his feet, Bruce pushed through the crowd of people to get to Rahlo, who was making his way to Duke. Grabbing him by the shoulder, Bruce tried to push him in the other direction, but Rahlo snatched away. He wasn't leaving without his best friend.

"I'll get the nigga, just go!" Bruce hollered. He loved Duke, but his job was to protect Rahlo at all costs.

"Fuck!" Rahlo was angry, pissed that for once Duke couldn't just listen to him and chill. Now, right after signing a deal, his name would be in the media connected to a nightclub brawl.

Taylor snatched her purse and keys from her cubby as the police started to storm the club. People were getting trampled over, fights had broken out, and it looked like a scene from Fight Club. Slipping out the employee exit, Taylor hopped in her car and was about to pull off when the passenger door was snatched open. Her eyes bucked at the sight of Rahlo slipping in her passenger seat.

"What are you doing?" she screeched.

"Aye, just drive," Rahlo ordered, sliding down in the seat.

"Are you out of your fu-"

"Look, just shut the fuck up and drive," he snapped.

Taylor clamped her mouth shut and put the car in drive. Pulling out the parking lot, she saw everyone standing outside the club as police officers instructed them to back up so that the paramedics could get inside.

"Fuck fuck fuck!" Rahlo slapped the dashboard as Taylor pulled away from the scene.

"Aht aht, don't be hitting on my baby like that."

"What?" He frowned.

"My car, nigga. Don't hit on her like that."

"My fault."

"It's ok," Taylor assured, looking in the review mirror as they drove further and further away from the club.

Rahlo looked out the window, wondering why he didn't follow his first mind. Instead of going clubbing, he wanted to go home and vibe with a few bad bitches. He wanted a minute to himself before his life drastically changed. Sure, the people in Detroit and surrounding states knew him, but after the deal he had just signed, the world was going to know him. Foolishly, Rahlo allowed Bruce and Duke to hype him up. Their intentions were pure, but he knew deep down shit was going to go bad.

"Uh, where am I taking you?" Taylor asked, glancing over at him.

"I don't even know. Give me a minute," he groaned, looking down at his ringing phone. Like clockwork, text messages from his manager started to pour in, back-to-back calls from his sister and a few numbers he didn't even recognize. Taking a deep breath, Rahlo tried to ignore his thumping heart and watery mouth. All of a sudden, he felt sick and couldn't breathe.

"Fuck!" he cursed.

"You ok?" Taylor whispered, glancing over at him.

"I'm straight," Rahlo lied, looking down at his ringing phone. He wasn't surprised to see his label's number flashing on the screen. Rahlo knew without a doubt that the night's events were all over social media. His new PR team was going to be pissed. They had warned him that the second the ink dried on the contract, he wasn't just a regular person anymore. That the world would be watching his every move.

"Don't you think you should at least answer the phone to let someone know you're okay? I mean, they probably think you're dead."

Rahlo glanced at her and then back down at the vibrating phone in his hand.

"Yea?" he answered. Taylor couldn't make out what the person on the other end was saying, but from the look on his face, she knew it wasn't anything good.

"I know, damn," Rahlo sighed into the phone. "I'm on my way to the crib. I'll call you in the morning," he promised and then ended the call.

"See, don't you feel better?" She smiled.

"I know you just heard me get cursed out." Rahlo cut his eyes in her direction.

"I mean, it's better than being dead or in jail, right?"

"Right," he scoffed, staring out the window.

"What happened?"

"I didn't follow my first mind," Rahlo sighed. Taylor opened her mouth to ask him to elaborate, but he answered another call.

"Where the fuck you at?" Duke yelled as soon as he picked

up. Taylor rolled her eyes. She recognized his loud ass voice.

"Gimme the phone, nigga." Bruce snatched the phone from him. "Aye, you good?"

"Yea, I'm in the car with-"

"Aht aht, don't be telling people you with me. I might be driving with a murderer for all I know," Taylor interrupted him.

"The fuck, I didn't kill nobody." He frowned.

"Tell her to drop you off at the gas station on 8mile and Livernois," Bruce said with a chuckle.

"Aight." He hung up and turned to her. "You heard him?"

"Yea," Taylor responded. "I thought you just told somebody else you were going home."

"You a nosey one, huh?"

"This is my car and I'm entitled to listen and dip in all conversations."

"You funny," Rahlo chuckled.

"That's what they say, I'm just being me."

"What's your name?"

"Why?"

"Damn, a nigga can't get your name?"

"Hell nah. What if you need a witness or something and they call me to stand? I'm snitching."

"Snitching on what? I didn't do shit."

"I bet it was your big mouth friend, huh?" Taylor twisted her lips.

"Why you say that?"

"Because he looks like the type to run his mouth and get everybody in trouble."

"What do I look like?"

"Like you choose to be loyal to the wrong people."

"Damn, tell me how you really feel."

"And is. But I'm just saying somebody just told you to go home, which sounds like the right thing to do, but you about to meet up with your crazy ass friends at the gas station. Sounds like trouble if you ask me."

"Nah, nothing like that. I'm going to the crib."

"Mm-hmm," Taylor pursed her lips. Rahlo chortled at the expression on her face and sat back.

The twenty-minute ride was smooth. He listened to her sing off-key to HER and Summer Walker. Taylor didn't know half of the words and he thought it was funny that she hummed through the parts she didn't know. While she drove like he wasn't in the car, Rahlo checked her out. It was dark in the club and he couldn't get a good look at her, but now that he was up close, Rahlo was impressed with her smooth complexion. Even in the dark it glistened and he could almost bet it was as sweet as it looked.

"What?" Taylor asked, cutting down the radio.

"You're a whole vibe."

"What do you mean?"

"You just in the zone, singing, dancing, all that shit like I'm not even in the car. Most women would be trying to suck me up while I drive their whip."

"Why? Because you're a superstar?"

"You Googled me?" Rahlo smirked.

"I did. My best friend loves your music, and I decided to see what the hype was about."

"Were you impressed?"

"You'll never know." Taylor winked, whipping into the gas

station next to the only truck in the parking lot.

"Thanks, I appreciate the ride."

"You're welcome. Stay out of trouble."

"You wanna give me your number? Maybe you could help me stay out of trouble."

"Nigga, come on. I got a boatload of hoes waiting for us at the Marriott," Duke yelled out. "We about to be swimming in pussy all night."

"Nah, go entertain your boatload of hoes." Taylor put the car in reverse. "Take care of yourself, Rahlo."

"Damn, you calling a nigga by the government name."

"Is it a problem?"

"Nah, I'll give you that."

"Take care."

"So you not gone tell me your name?" He licked his lips.

With his glasses off, Taylor finally got a good look at his face. It was easy to see why Kiki was crazy about him. The man was fine. He possessed a deep brown complexion with pretty, thick lips. His dark brown eyes were big, but because he was high, they were low, as if he was struggling to keep them open. Rahlo had one dimple in his left cheek that women couldn't get enough of, claiming it was his best side. His Detroit fitted hat was turned to the back, showing off his thick eyebrows and trimmed beard.

"My name is Taylor," she finally gave in.

"Aight, Tay baby, it was nice meeting you." He grinned, causing the dimple to cave into his cheek. "Do you need gas money?"

"No, I'm ok. Be safe, Rahlo."

"Chop chop, nigga! I'm trying to run through these hoes like dirty clothes." Duke clapped his hands.

"You be safe too, sweetheart." Rahlo winked, swaggering off to where his friends were waiting.

Taylor glanced at him one more time before pulling onto the dark street.

Chapter 2

Taylor rolled her eyes for the umpteenth time as she explained to her boyfriend Jasper how Rahlo ended up in her car. Somehow, a picture of them pulling out of the club's parking lot was floating around the internet, and people were calling her Rahlo's new flavor of the week. Jasper already wasn't thrilled about her working at the club, and now hearing that she was a getaway driver for a rapper wasn't sitting right with him.

"So you took him where?"

"Omg, Jasper! I already told you to a damn gas station. Why do you keep asking like I'm going to change my story or something?" Taylor snapped with her hand on her hip.

"Because out of all the cars in the parking lot, he just happened to hop in yours?"

"YES!"

"And then what?" Jasper calmly asked, trying to find any holes in her story. He found it hard to believe that a rapper just jumped in her car for safety.

"I took him to a gas station," she stressed for what seemed like the millionth time.

"What did yall talk about?"

"Nothing really. Why are you acting so insecure?"

"Aye, watch that shit," Jasper warned, raising his eyebrow in her direction. "I'm not insecure about shit. I know who the fuck you belong to. It's the principle of the matter. Niggas at work talking about a rapper nigga took my girl."

"Fuck them broke ass niggas. Don't project your trust issues onto me."

"Nah, I think it's time you find another job. I'm not okay with you working at the club anymore. The news said somebody got shot and everything."

"Jasper, please." Taylor waved him off. "They are shooting up churches, schools, and concerts. It doesn't matter where I am, shit happens everywhere."

"You heard what I said."

"Are you going to pay my bills?"

"Mannnn, you know I can't-"

"Right, you can't, and until you can, you *can't* tell me where to work."

"Wow, so my feelings don't matter?" Jasper stood back and crossed his arms. Taylor bit her tongue. She wanted to say hell no but decided to spare his feelings. It seemed like the picture had already done a number on his pride and her smart mouth wasn't going to help it.

"Baby, I love you and you have nothing to worry about. I dropped the man off and came right over here to you."

"Are you trying to shut me up?" he questioned, cocking his head to the side.

Instead of answering, Taylor pushed the covers back and slowly crawled to the edge of the bed. Pulling him closer by the belt loop, she unzipped his pants and looked up at him with a smirk on her lips.

"Yep." Taylor licked her lips and lowered her head to meet his already hard dick.

"Shit." Jasper closed his eyes and softly stroked the back of her head. Without gagging, Taylor inched his dick down her throat until it was completely covered, just like he taught her.

"Fuck yea," he grunted, enjoying the excess slob dripping down his sack. On her knees, Taylor effortlessly swallowed him whole, causing chill bumps to prick through his skin. With the chokehold her throat had him in, Jasper prematurely shot his load in the back of her throat, and Taylor happily swallowed it before releasing him from her grasp. Spinning, Jasper held onto the wall to catch his breath. Out of the corner of his eye, he watched Taylor roll out of bed and switch into the bathroom as if she just didn't snatch the soul from his body.

The first time Jasper laid eyes on Taylor, she was sitting at the bar taking shots with her friends. From where he was sitting, Jasper could see it was her twenty-first birthday, and she was partying like a rockstar. All night he watched her dance like no one was watching and sing at the top of her lungs like she was Beyonce. Taylor was so in the zone that she didn't even notice half of the men in the club lustfully watching her. They didn't care that her singing sounded like nails on a chalkboard. Her seductive dance moves made up for the damage her unpleasant voice caused. To his surprise, when he worked up the courage to approach her, Taylor accepted his dance invitation. Jasper could barely keep up, and his homeboys taunted him, but he didn't care. He had convinced the prettiest girl in the club to dance with him.

After months of dating her, Jasper decided she was the breath of fresh air he had been craving. Being that she was younger than him, Taylor had him at clubs, concerts, and taking trips at her every request. The start of their relationship was just the distraction he needed from his failed marriage. Taylor was outgoing and very adventurous, whereas he was closed off and often followed her lead.

"What time do you have to be at work?" Taylor asked when he stepped into the bathroom. She was standing in the mirror with a towel around her thick frame. Thanks to the oversized towels from Target, Taylor could move around without it falling.

"Around three, why? You trying to spend some time with me?" Jasper grinned, eyeing her curvy body.

Taylor was only twenty-four and Jasper was sure she had the baddest body on earth. Two years ago, she shaved her hair into a fade and dyed it blonde. Now that it was growing back, it stopped below her ear and was normally pushed to one side. The style meshed well with her blemish-free skin and perfect eyebrows. Not only was Taylor fine, but she could also dress her ass off. Being a big girl had never been a problem for her, and whatever she couldn't fit, her best friend was a designer and could mimic any outfit she wanted.

"Actually, I'm about to go home for a minute, and then I'm meeting Kiki for lunch and a trip to the mall."

"What about me?"

"I'll be here when you get home."

"Aight, man," Jasper sighed as she hopped in the shower. "Damn, I wish I had something to give you." He patted his pockets like it was a magic move to make money appear. "When I get my profit-sharing check from work, I'm going to spoil you."

"It's cool. I did good last night. I made over three grand in tips and they paid me double for staying over," she told him, leaving out the part where Rahlo tipped her two bands.

"Got damn! Maybe I need to get a job up there. They hiring?"

"Boy bye. You wouldn't last a day and they only tip women like that. Are you getting my baby this weekend?" Taylor inquired, referring to Jasper's eight-year-old son Jalen.

"I think so."

"Ok, let me know. I wanted to take him and my little brother to the movies and Laser tag. I promised Trooper that I'd take him."

"Ok, will do," Jasper agreed, pushing off the wall. "You want something to eat?"

"No. My granddad is making breakfast. I'll eat when I get home."

"Aight," he responded, carefully lifting her phone from the counter and slipping it into his pocket.

Jasper sat on the edge of the bed and fidgeted with Taylor's phone until it opened. Thanks to his son begging to play games on her phone, it only took him a couple of tries to get the pattern right. His first stop was her DMs. Because Taylor was attractive, her DMs were always jumping. Clubs asking her to host, men asking her on dates, women asking her for fashion tips. Everybody wanted a piece of his girl and that irritated Jasper to the max. After deleting a couple of thirsty niggas from her page, he moved on to Twitter, Facebook, and Snapchat to repeat the process. By the time Taylor was out of the shower, he was in her text messages.

"You find anything interesting?" she asked, walking back into the room drying her body.

"Yea, why you posting thirst traps and shit? You like these niggas all in your face, huh?" Jasper scowled in her direction.

"Jasper, please. I am not your slut ass ex-wife. I'm capable of communicating with the opposite sex without spreading my legs."

"I know, man, but damn," he sighed, tossing the phone on the bed. Jasper mulled over her words. She was right. Taylor was nothing like Sherri, but he couldn't help it.

Jasper sat on the bed watching Taylor move around the room, unbothered that he had just swept her phone like the FBI. She truly had nothing to hide, and everything he thought she was doing was in his head. Jasper often projected Sherri's unfaithfulness onto Taylor, and he hated it. In three years, Taylor showed him more loyalty than Sherri had in their ten-year marriage. Not only did she cheat on him, but she got pregnant and tried to pass the baby off as one of his own. It almost worked until the other man wanted to be a part of his child's life, forcing Sherri to come clean. Jasper was heartbroken and his confidence was shattered.

"I'm about to leave. I love you. Get some rest and call me later," Taylor announced, snapping him from his thoughts. Jasper glanced up at her attire and fought the urge to tell her to change.

Dressed in a pair of distressed jean shorts and a Bob Marley crop top, Taylor easily challenged society's rules of what was considered acceptable for a big girl. Shamelessly, she strutted past him and slipped into her Tory Burch sandals before picking up her phone off the bed.

"You don't think those shorts are too revealing?" he asked, pulling at the loose strings.

"They're distressed, they're supposed to be revealing."

"And you think it's appropriate for you to dress like that while you're in a relationship?"

"Jasper, miss me with all that. Nothing is wrong with my outfit. I've been dressing like this for years."

"That's the problem," he mumbled but dismissed the conversation to keep the peace. "You coming back tonight?"

Jasper asked, pulling her between his legs.

"No, I haven't been home all week. I miss my guys." She kissed the top of his head.

"You can visit them and then come back. Honestly, it's time you thought about moving in."

"Jasper, as much as I love being here with you, I need space. You can be overwhelming sometimes."

"How?"

"Are you for real?" Taylor gawked.

"I am. Besides going through your phone, what do I do?"

"Popping up at my job, my people house, Kiki's house, tracking my phone," she listed. "And look, I know you haven't had the best experience with women, but I'm not her. I'm loyal to you and have been since the minute I let you slide between these thick thighs."

"I know."

"Good." Taylor kissed the top of his head. "I'll call you later."

"I love you." Jasper buried his head in her stomach.

"I love you, too." She attempted to pull away from him, but he grabbed her wrist.

"Be good, Tay," he warned.

"I'm always good."

Taylor waited until she was in her car before rolling her eyes. Being with Jasper was exhausting at times. Somewhere along the way, things changed. Jasper became clingy, and at times, he was overbearing. If she wasn't constantly reassuring him in their relationship, she was into it with his old, dramatic wife. Their seven-year age gap didn't help the situation either. There were times when Taylor wanted to pop out with her friends, but Jasper wanted to lay up and watch movies. For him to be so young, he acted like he was in his fifties. Jasper hated her social media presence, so she tried to keep it low-key for him, but with over a million followers, that was hard to do.

Just as she was pulling into traffic, her phone started to vibrate in the cup holder. Without looking down, Taylor knew exactly who it was. Kiki's name flashed across the screen in her Jeep, confirming what she already knew. Taylor smiled. She was surprised Kiki waited so long to call her.

"What up?" she answered.

"You bihhh. Let me find out you slid off with my man."

"Girl bye! Your crusty lil man hopped in my truck on some demanding shit."

"Oh my goddd," Kiki dramatically groaned. "I wish he would have waited five seconds. I was literally right behind you. Tell me everything. What did he smell like? What did yall talk about? Where did you drop him off at?"

"Eww, you sound like a stalker," Taylor giggled.

"Bitch, I am. You know I like Rah," Kiki bucked. "I would have been trying to swallow his babies while he drove my car."

"Ok, don't make me tell Mike you out here trying to slut yourself out for a few backstage passes."

"Tell him. Shit, if Rah let me suck him up, I'll tell him my damn self."

"Where are your morals?"

"I don't have none, hoe. Now where you at? I want to shop before we eat."

"I'm on my way home. I stayed with Jasper last night."

"Lord, I know granddad was mad as hell. You all over the blogs this morning," Kiki tittered. She knew firsthand how jealous Jasper could be. There had been plenty of times when he camped out outside the club waiting for her to exit.

"He has no choice but to be chill." Taylor shrugged. "I'm

about to pull up at home. Let me kick it with the guys and I'll see you at 1."

"Ok, don't be late."

"I'm never late."

"Bitch, you a never ass lie," Kiki grumbled before hanging up.

Taylor dropped her phone in the cup holder and cut up Rah's newest single. Since dropping him off, she had been listening to his mixtapes back-to-back. His videos sucked, but lyrically, he was a genius. His raps were more than guns, hoes, and violence. He rapped about real life shit and Taylor could vibe with that any day.

*"I can see them haters coming from a mile away, but I'm too busy stacking paper fa dem rainy day*s." Rah's raspy voice filled her car speakers and blessed her ears. Thus far, *Snakes in the Grass* was her favorite mixtape.

When she approached a red light, Taylor replayed the song and rapped into her phone while recording a video on Snapchat. Instead of posting the video, she sent it to Kiki, who sent her a laughing emoji and a message.

Bitch your rapping is as bad as your singing and I'm posting this.

Taylor laughed and sent her back the middle finger emoji. She couldn't sing for shit, but it didn't stop her from having random outbursts. Whenever Coco Jones or Tink came on, it was only right for her to sing along.

Twenty minutes later, Taylor pulled up at home. It had been days since she'd seen her guys and she knew trouble awaited her on the other side of the door. Grabbing her purse and overnight bag, she slipped out of the car, stuffing the keys in her back pocket.

"Tay baby, come fuck with me," her neighbor's son, Kool,

called out.

"Kool, please. How long are you out for this time?" Taylor asked, never breaking her stride.

"I'm chilling this go round," he swore. "I need a girl like you to keep me out of trouble."

"Boy bye. You like to fight and I'll fuck around and stab your ass. We'll both be in jail."

"I like that violent shit though," he called out after her, stroking his dick through his pants. "Shit is a turn on." Taylor was exactly the type of woman he needed, but she'd never give him a chance, and Kool knew that.

"I know you not out here flirting with her bald-headed ass," his baby mama squeaked, peeking out the window.

"See what I mean. Get yo girl before I sit on her boney ass," Taylor warned.

"I'd pay to see that shit." Kool licked his lips. "Matter fact, I'll pay you right now to Rikishi her ass."

"KOOL!" his baby mama yelled.

"Aye, shut the fuck up and go lay down or something. Them dishes better be clean before my mama get home," he fussed, going into the house and slamming the door.

Taylor shook her head and pushed the front door open. Immediately, she was greeted by the smell of cigars and cedar. Before she could make it any further, a pair of small arms wrapped around her waist.

"Tayyyyy," her younger brother, Trooper, sang the moment his big sister crossed the threshold.

"Trooperrrr," Taylor squealed, dropping her overnight bag on the floor. She turned to swoop him in her arms and proceeded to plant kisses all over his face. He allowed her to shower him with love until reality sat in.

"I haven't seen you in this many days!" he angrily snatched away from her, holding up his fingers.

At eight years old, Trooper was identical to his older sister. They shared the same cashew complexion, the same oval eyes, and the same non-tolerance for bullshit. Taylor taught him to speak his mind, and from the moment he could talk, he had been doing just that.

"I'm sorry, Troop. I was working," she explained, poking her lip out.

"Don't let her lie to you," Taylor's grandfather, Papa, grunted, walking past them with a cup of coffee in his hand. "She was probably laid up with that no-good nigga, and where are the rest of your clothes? Back in my day, we called girls like you night crawlers."

"Good morning to you too, Papa," Taylor snickered, following him into the living room where her father Von was sitting on the couch. "Good Morning, Daddy," she cooed, falling on the couch into his side.

"How are you this morning, baby girl?" he asked, placing a kiss on her forehead.

"She's good, coming in here slut-walking," Papa answered.

"What's a slut-walk?" Trooper quizzed, scratching the top of his head.

"Nothing, Papa is just being a grumpy old man," Taylor snickered. "Daddy, you just gon' let this old man talk about your daughter?"

"What he gon' do? I'm his father," Papa bucked, blowing his coffee before taking a sip.

"Old man, chill and leave my child alone," Von said, peering up from the TV. "I need you to keep Trooper tonight."

"He has a *dateeee*," Trooper mocked. He wasn't too fond of his father dating. It was bad enough his big sister was dating and spent all her time away from home. Trooper couldn't afford to lose his father's attention, too.

"He needs a date. No grown man should be alone as much as he is. It's about time he got out there and showed them women the power of the Williams men."

It had been over four years since Von entertained a woman. There were a few he messed around with to get his rocks off, but none he took seriously. After the death of his wife, he couldn't see himself in a relationship. Tanya was the sun, the moon, and the stars. There wasn't a woman on earth that could fill her shoes, and Von wouldn't expect any of them to.

Tanya's sudden death left a crater sized hole in their hearts. In the middle of the grocery store, the aneurysm she had been carefully tiptoeing around for most of her life ruptured. It was quick, painless, and unexplainable. By the time Von made it to the hospital, Tanya was gone. There was no time for goodbyes, advice on how to raise their baby boy alone, or how to help Taylor navigate through life without her. She went out to shop for Sunday dinner and two weeks later they were burying her.

"I don't like it!" Trooper stomped his feet before running off.

"I wish you would whoop that boy's ass. He has too much range. When you were his age, I used to pop you upside the head off GP," Papa snorted. "Then again, don't do that. Maybe that's the reason you a little slow."

"Papa, please," Taylor giggled. "Is there some more breakfast left?"

"Yea, I put you a plate up. Go wash up and I'll warm your plate up," Von said.

"Will do, and I want to hear all about this date."

"Me too, and I hope it's with a real person." Papa glanced over at his son. "I was watching *Dateline* and you'd be surprised how many men like freaking on dolls."

"Dad, stop it." Von frowned at his father.

"I'm dead ass. They call them plastic lovers."

"I assure you I have enough game to pull a real woman."

"That's right, because my daddy is handsome." Taylor smiled, rubbing the top of his bald head.

"Of course you'd say that, you look just like his funny looking ass," Papa grunted.

"And we all look like you," Von retorted. Papa couldn't deny it if he wanted to. His genes were strong and he passed his complexion, curly hair, and witty comebacks right down to his son and grandkids. He swore he had Indian in his blood and no one argued against him. What Papa said was law.

"Tay, can I have yo blue card?" Trooper asked, floating back into the living room with his phone in hand.

"For what?" She furrowed her eyebrows. Since Trooper found out what a credit card was, he associated it with unlimited funds, and because of him, all the kids in his class thought Taylor was rich.

"Roblox, duh."

"Watch your mouth before I pop you in it. I'll cash app you. Use your debit card."

"Thank you," he exclaimed, bouncing back to his room.

"That's why he spoiled now. Boy gets anything he wants and still talks all crazy. Couldn't be my kid. He'd have a dent in his chest." Papa snorted.

"He's a good kid," Taylor swore.

"And you're a good church-going girl," he shot back.

"I am."

"And a liar. Lord, son, what kinda kids are you raising?" Papa asked Von.

"Free spirited ones," he answered.

Taylor followed her father into the kitchen and washed her hands in the sink before taking a seat. She watched him warm up her food with a smile on her face. Von was the reason Taylor thought the sun rose and set on her. Since the moment she was born, he doted on her. Nothing was too good for his baby girl. He was her first experience with love and showed her how a man was supposed to love a woman. Before his wife died, Von took them on trips, picnics, concerts, and random shopping sprees. Neither one of his girls had to touch doors or do any heavy lifting.

In return, Tanya taught Taylor how to take care of home. Tanya could cook her ass off and she happily passed those skills down to her daughter. At the age of nine, Taylor was frying chicken and peeling greens. Tanya made sure her daughter knew the fundamentals of taking care of the home, but only when it was deserved. She instilled that it was ok to be submissive, but only for the right man. All men didn't deserve the royal treatment.

"So, who is this woman?" Taylor asked as Von sat the plate of hot grits, fish, and biscuits in front of her. Lowering her head, she said her grace before digging in.

"Just a woman from Trooper's school. She's been asking to make me dinner for a while, and I finally agreed," he coyly answered, moving around the kitchen. "You want orange juice or lemon water?"

"Lemon water, please," Taylor answered, scooping up a forkful of grits. "What lady?"

"I think she's the music teacher, Ms. Riley."

"See, Daddy," she popped a piece of fish in her mouth. "I told you to stop wearing them jogging pants to drop him off. You out here looking like a snack and then showing the goods."

"Tay, stop it. I wear those because they are comfortable."

"Um-hm, now Ms. Riley is trying to play with your flute," she teased.

"Watch it," Von warned. "It's just dinner."

"Make sure you stand on that. Don't be easy, Daddy."

"Shit, he needs to be easy as Sunday morning," Papa grumbled, strolling in the kitchen to refill his cup. "Lay down and let that girl ride until you remember yo last name."

"Old man, please," Von waved him off. "Tay, don't forget I need you to keep Trooper tonight."

"I won't. I'm going to the mall with Kiki and then I'll come back and get him," she promised.

"You staying over at Jasper's house tonight?"

"No, I'm coming back. He's being too clingy and I need some space." Taylor rolled her eyes.

"Hm, you need more than space, you need to dump his old ass," Papa complained. "Go get you one of them corner boys or something."

"Did you really just tell my baby to get with a drug dealer?" Von frowned.

"That or go stand on the campus at Wayne State. Anyone is better than that overbearing piece of a man."

"Tell me how you really feel," Taylor snickered.

It was no secret that her grandfather didn't like Jasper, and he never tried to hide it. To Papa, Jasper was too old to be liking on his granddaughter. A divorced man with a child had no business wanting to be with a young woman like Taylor.

"I just did," Papa declared, backing out of the kitchen.

"He has a point." Von refilled her lemon water.

"You just worry about Ms. Riley and your flute," Taylor teased.

42

"Watch it."

Chapter 3

Rahlo sat at the head of the table with a blank expression on his face. His manager, Terri, was going off, but he was too hungover to comprehend the words that spouted from his mouth at the speed of light. Although he had every right to be upset, Rahlo was over the rant.

"Aight, I get it," he finally spoke up.

"I don't think you do, Rah. I told you to go home and it was for good reason. We have deals and brands on the table. These companies are not going to fuck with you if they think you're a liability. We've come too far to mess up now," Terri preached.

"Damn, nigga, loosen up. It was just a bad night. Nobody got hurt." Duke frowned, pulling off his glasses. He, too, was tired of Terri's rant. The old Rahlo wouldn't have went for that shit and Duke couldn't figure out why he was just sitting there taking it.

"Chill," Rahlo expressed.

"Why are you even here?" Terri glanced in his direction.

"Nigga, who you talking to?"

"I don't think I stuttered. I'm trying to change his image and you are determined to keep him in the hood. If you want to see him make it, then support the move."

As of right now, Rahlo was Terri's only client. Fresh out of the school of business, Terri studied under big hitters in the music industry until he was ready to branch out independently. He rubbed shoulders with top producers, engineers, and artists, so the transition from apprentice to manager was a breeze.

On one of his many scouts, he ran into Rahlo. It was ten in the morning and Rahlo was standing in the middle of a busy intersection passing out flyers to his show. From afar, Terri watched him interact with people. He flirted with the girls and still thanked the few who refused his flyer. Something about the moment felt nostalgic. There weren't too many people pushing their business on foot during the era of social media, but there he was by himself, doing whatever it took to get his name out there. Terri appreciated his hustle and took the flyer but kept it moving. He didn't plan on attending the show but made a mental note to look the kid up later.

As luck would have it, Terri ended up at the show with one of his friends, and when Rahlo performed, he was blown away. It wasn't the new age rap. Rahlo rapped clearly and on beat. To say he was impressed was an understatement. Terri waited until the show was over to approach Rahlo, but a fight broke out and Terri was led out the back door as Rahlo ran the other way. It took Terri almost five months to track Rahlo down, and while he had love for him, he hated the company he kept.

"Fuck you, lil dog. You don't know shit," Duke roared. "I been holding him down, nigga." Rahlo glanced at Bruce, who tapped Duke on the shoulder.

"Let's take a walk. Let this man handle business. I'll be outside when you're ready," Bruce informed him.

"Aight. I need to check on some shit anyway." Duke stood

and pulled his sagging pants up. Terri waited for them to close the door before he turned to Rahlo.

"I don't like him."

"He aight." Rahlo waved him off.

"Look. We have to move differently. You can't be out getting into club fights and hanging around thugs."

"Thugs?" He hiked his eyebrows.

Rahlo knew they came from two different worlds, so while he appreciated Terri's business savvy mind, he didn't care for his judgmental opinions. Duke was a handful and often put him in messed up situations, but he was his best friend, and if nothing else, he was loyal.

"You know what I mean. When you know better, you do better. I understand Duke is your friend, but riddle me this.... how much of a friend is he if he's putting everything you worked so hard for in jeopardy?" Terri lifted his brow and tilted his head to the side. "You want pussy? I can give you the numbers to some of the baddest women who don't mind being slutted out. You want to party? I'll bring it to you, but there is a certain way we do things," Terri stressed. "You aren't independent anymore, your image affects the label as a whole."

"Like I said, shit went left and I'll make sure it doesn't happen again," Rahlo repeated.

"You can't guarantee that though. You are building a brand, a legacy, and you can't do that while keeping the same mentality. I need you to think different, to talk different, and walk in rooms like you own the muthafucka and not hungover." He nodded toward the bottle of water, Gatorade, and empty packs of BC.

"Aight," Rahlo gritted.

"Good, now go sleep that shit off and head to the studio about nine," Terri finalized, standing to his feet. "Oh, and your mother called me about paying your aunt's mortgage. Did you authorize that?"

"Nah," Rahlo shook his head. His mother's house was his next stop. "Go ahead and pay it though."

"You know-"

"I know," Rahlo cut him off, not wanting to hear another lecture.

Picking up his phones off the table, Rahlo grabbed another bottle of water and chucked Terri the deuces. Bopping out of the office, he ignored the lustful stares of women in the lobby. The throbbing in his temples had him ready to crawl under a rock and pass out.

"Can I get a picture, Rah?" A soft voice asked. Rahlo inwardly groaned but turned around with a grin on his face, trying to hide his annoyance. Being social was part of the superstar package he signed up for.

"Sure can, sweetheart." He stretched his arms out. The girl squealed and quickly ran to him before he changed his mind. With one hand wrapped around his waist, she held her other arm in the air and started snapping a few pictures of them.

"Oh my god!" she exclaimed. "Thank you so much! I'm a huge fan. I've listened to all of your mixtapes and I can't wait to see what's next."

"I appreciate that, sweetheart."

"I'm a dancer and if you ever wanna use me for a video... or anything else," she licked her lips. "Here is my card."

"I'll give it to my people," he assured her.

"Thank you, Rah. Can I tag you?"

"I'm not on social media," Rahlo said as the elevator doors closed separating them.

Sliding the card into his pocket, Rahlo leaned his head back on the wall and let out a deep sigh. Terri got on his nerves, but he was right. He had been thrusted into a different tax bracket overnight, and being smart was a must. His fame and fortune didn't come easy, but he could lose it in seconds with one wrong move.

"Did you get in trouble?" Duke asked when he strolled out of the double doors and into the summer heat.

Leaning against the truck with a blunt hanging from his lips, Duke acted as if he wasn't in Downtown Detroit. As if the felony painted on his back wasn't already a red flag. As if he needed another reason for the police to fuck with him. Bruce noticed the irritated expression on Rahlo's face and shrugged. He told him to leave Duke at home, but he wanted to tag along.

"Put that shit out," Rahlo gritted. Duke dropped the blunt and smashed it with his foot. "I know you trying to adjust, but you need to chill."

"I told you to leave the ugly ass nigga at home." Bruce shook his head, walking around to hop in the driver's seat.

"And I told yo fat ass to go on a fucking diet." Duke gave him the middle finger, sliding into the back seat. "What the nigga say? Why you look like you just got in trouble by yo daddy?"

"Aye, on some real shit; if you can't keep it together while I handle business, then I'm going to start moving without you," Rahlo said, looking in the rearview mirror.

"The fuck did I do?" Duke feigned innocence, hunching his shoulders.

"The shit with Terri and then smoking in the front of the building. We are Downtown driving in a car that's worth more than most people's salary, and you don't think the police will lock all our black asses up?"

"Fuck Terri ole dick in the booty ass and fuck the police."

"He gay?" Bruce asked, pulling into the street.

"That man's sexual preferences has nothing to do with me," Rahlo proclaimed. "As long as he's taking care of business, I don't give a fuck what he does in his spare time. Swing by my mama's house," he directed, slouching down in the seat.

"Yo weak liver ass can't hang with the big dogs," Duke jeered.

"I'm straight, I'm just not fucking with yall niggas no more," Rahlo promised, cutting up the radio as Tee Grizzley flowed through the car.

∞∞∞

Thirty minutes later, Bruce pulled up in the heart of Southwest Detroit. Smart and McDonald was the center of all the action, and at any moment, something could pop off, but neither of the men in the truck was worried. The tattered blocks would be considered the trenches for some, but for the trio in the truck, it was home. Per normal, kids flooded the streets, some playing hide and seek, others jumping rope and playing hopscotch. A group of teens stood on the corner selling overpriced bottles of cold water while the ice cream truck slowly rode down the block playing everything but the normal annoying bullshit that was custom. *Cash Shit* by Megan Thee Stallion blared through the bullhorns on top of the truck, gaining the attention of young girls who couldn't resist rolling their hips to the beat.

Once the kids noticed Rahlo's truck was on the block, they all started running in his direction. Whenever he was around, he gave them money for snacks, bought out the ice cream truck, and even gave them tips on rapping and perfecting their crafts. Unlike others who came before him, Rahlo poured back into the streets that raised him. It was nothing for him to give out school supplies or donate to projects happening around the community.

"Here come these bad ass kids," Duke snorted, looking out the window.

"Don't start yo shit," Rahlo warned, sitting up.

"Fuck these kids. I let Connie slut ass suck me up and her bad ass kids stole my fucking wallet."

"Say word," Bruce laughed. Connie was twenty-five and had six kids. The way they terrorized the neighborhood should have been a crime. Connie allowed them to roam the streets, shaking down other kids and robbing her company's pockets when they went to sleep.

"Word. Lil thieving ass fuckers bought pizza for the entire hood and reloaded their google play cards on my fucking dime," Duke said with a frown.

"What Connie do?" Bruce chortled, finding the story hilarious. He fucked Connie too, but he left his wallet in the car and hid his keys on top of the refrigerator. When he left that next morning, her kids were sitting on the couch grimming him.

"Talking about they misunderstood. I almost knocked that hoe stained veneers out of her crooked ass mouth."

"That's payback for all the bad shit you used to do," Rahlo said, unbuckling his seatbelt.

"If I recall, you used to spend them stolen food stamps with me."

"Sure did," he admitted, exiting the car.

For a minute, Rahlo chopped it up with the kids and ended up buying three cases of water for triple what they cost in the store. He only took a couple of bottles for himself and had the boys take the rest inside his mother's house. They did as he asked and went on about their way with a pocket full of money.

"Rah, can you buy me a ice cream?" A little girl asked and

then placed her thumb back into her mouth. With all the silver caps on top of her front teeth, ice cream was the last thing she needed, but he couldn't say no to the curly haired cutie pie.

"I'll tell you what-" he dug in his pocket and fished out two fifty-dollar bills. The girl's eyes lit up. "Bring me back a strawberry shortcake and you can keep the change."

"For real?" she exclaimed, taking the money from his hands.

"Yep, buy some for your siblings too."

"Aye, and get me a Choco taco," Duke said as he rounded the car.

"Nope, cause my mama don't like you and neither do I." She twisted on her heels and ran down the street, waving the money in the air.

"What did you do to her mama?" Rahlo asked, looking over at his best friend.

"Ate all her kids' snacks while they was at school. Lil brats came home crying about their fruit snacks. I fucked around and fell asleep and left the wrappers all on the floor."

"Nigga, yo dick gon' fall off. You been fucking everything that ain't nailed down."

"You ain't shit," Bruce chuckled.

"Shut up, big boy," Duke joked.

"That's what yo mama call me, nigga."

"I bet her crackhead ass do," he muttered.

Rahlo ignored his bickering friends and walked up the sidewalk leading to his mother's house. Per usual, she was sitting on the porch with a cup glued to her hand while Rahlo's older sister, Esha, stood over the grill. The smell of the seasoned meat and charcoal caused his stomach to growl, reminding him that he hadn't eaten.

"Brotherrrrr," Esha screamed, dropping the fork on the side of the grill and running to him. Rahlo wrapped his arms around her shoulders and kissed her forehead. It had only been a week since he last seen her, but it felt like forever. Esha was his best friend, and they didn't go days without talking, let alone a week.

"Sup, sis?"

"Nothing, over here doing what I do," she beamed. "You want a plate?"

"Of course." He rubbed his stomach. "Make one for these niggas too." Rahlo tossed his head to the side.

"I'll make Bruce one, but Duke can kick rocks." She rolled her eyes before turning back to flip the rib.

"Nigga, don't nobody like yo black ass." Bruce shook his head.

"Ask me do I give a fuck," he snorted, looking up from his phone.

"You can cry if you want to."

"Fuck outta here. I'm about to walk around the block. Scoop me when yall ready." Duke bopped off without another word.

"Here go my famous ass son," Emory greeted with a wide grin spread across her face. "My fine ass son," she praised. "Ain't my son fine?" Emory glanced over at her friend.

"Is and if I was a couple of years younger-"

"You still wouldn't have a chance," Emory cut her off.

For a woman in her late forties, Emory was the definition of black don't crack. Her flawless skin was free of any signs of aging. There wasn't a pimple, wrinkle, or dent in sight. As always, her hair was hidden under a custom 30-inch lace that fell over her shoulders and down her back. Emory's long nails were decorated in loud colors with jewels and charms. Thanks to Rahlo, her wardrobe was top-notch. Even if the designers didn't match, Emory rocked it. Dressed in a Gucci short set with Prada sandals, Emory was the shit, and she dared anybody to contest it.

"What's up, Em?" Rahlo pulled her into a hug, inhaling the pungent alcohol that lingered on her breath.

"Nothing, superstar. Did Terri tell you I asked him for a debit card? I don't wanna have to keep calling you every time I need something. I think he should just add me to your account and call it a day."

"I pay all of your bills and give you money for spending, what else do you need?" he asked, releasing her.

Since sixteen, Rahlo had been paying all the bills in the house. Emory didn't care where he got the money from, as long as he was cashing out on her every other day, she was satisfied. Emory was even bold enough to go into his shoebox and take what she needed. It didn't matter if he was stacking up to buy studio time or get his tracks put on CDs, Emory was taking it, not caring if it set him back. Somewhere along the line, his willingness to help around the house created a sense of entitlement in his mother. When he told her no, Emory locked him out of the house until he gave in to what she wanted.

"For whatever I want, duh. Was I asking you what you needed food for, what you needed lights or clean clothes for?" she snapped. Rahlo stared blankly at her, unmoved by her apparent attitude.

Emory's guilt trips weren't new to him. Whenever she couldn't get what she wanted on the first try, she started throwing stuff in his face. Most of the time to avoid arguments, he caved, but in reality, he wanted to express all the fucks he didn't have to give. It was her job to take care of him, so the shit about lights, food, and shelter went in one ear and out the other.

Emory did the bare minimum and expected to win Mother

of the Year. She acted as if going missing for days at a time was normal, as if making them call her Emory was the motherly thing to do. Yet even with all her flaws, Rahlo loved her. He silently hoped that he could fix all the problems created before he came along, but trying to fix Emory was like trying to fill a basket riddled with holes.

"I'll talk to him," he sighed.

"That's my baby." She hugged him again. "Esha, you making my baby a plate?" Emory slurred.

"It's right here." Esha walked up behind him with two plates. One filled with ribs, a burger, and hot sausage, and another with greens, mac and cheese, fried corn, and deviled eggs.

"And when you get a minute, go by your aunt's house. I paid her mortgage with that emergency money you left here, but she still needs a little help. Maybe you can give her a couple of dollars. Your cousin lost his job and I know you don't wanna see her out on the streets," Emory said, picking up her drink from the table. Esha rolled her eyes. To keep the peace, Rahlo nodded.

"See, that's why you're the star of this family. You are going to take us to the top," she cheesed, swaying her hips. "Yall hear that," Emory shouted to no one in particular. "My son is a star.

Esha rolled her eyes and waited for Emory to go in the house before she pulled a chair up next to her brother. It was bad enough that Rahlo had been paying all of her bills, but asking for a debit card attached to his account was another story. Esha didn't care how much he loved their mother, her grown ass needed to get a job and stop depending on them for everything.

"You better not put her on your damn account," Esha whispered.

"I'm not. I actually was going to set up an account for both of yall," Rahlo mentioned with a mouthful of food.

"Eww, chew your food." She frowned, turning her nose up at him. "And I work, unlike your mama, so I don't need your money."

Unlike her mother, Esha worked and had been holding down a job since she was fourteen. From running errands for the neighbors to walking their dogs, she was born to hustle. In contrast to what she was taught, Esha believed in getting up and making her own moves versus holding her hand out and waiting for a man to fill her palm. Esha graduated from P&A Beauty School and worked out of their basement. From braiding to lace fronts, she could do it all and was steadily adding new styles to her resume.

"You came over here bothering me." Rahlo shrugged, stuffing another bite of the greens and macaroni combo in his mouth. "And the account isn't optional. If you don't want to use the card, don't, but you'll still have it in your possession for emergencies."

"Ok," Esha gave in, knowing he wasn't going to budge. "I guess I'll put it up for rainy days."

"Do whatever you want with it, Esh." He looked up at her. "You should really think about opening a shop. I can set you up with my accountant and I know Terri will hook you up with a few big name clients. All you have to do is say the word."

"It's that easy, Rah?" Esha twisted her lips.

"Don't act like I haven't been saying it for years, Esh. When I win, you win."

"But-"

"But nothing. I'm not going to keep pushing it on you. When you're ready, you know where to find me."

"You know I love you, little brother."

"Ain't shit little about me, Esh. I'm a big nigga out here in these

FINALLY FAMOUS

streets."

"Yea, but you're still the same pissy ass little boy who used to steal money out of my piggy bank."

"You ain't gone ever let that shit go, are you?"

"Nope, and when you have kids, I'm going to tell them before you were a superstar, you were a snotty nose little boy who peed on everything."

Rahlo bit into his hot sausage and chuckled. Esha was spot on. From birth, it had been his mission to drive her up the wall. At seven years apart, Esha might as well have pushed him out herself because the moment Emory brought Rahlo home, she pushed him into his sister's arms. Having a baby didn't slow Emory down one bit. She gave birth on a Monday and was back out in the streets by Sunday.

It was Esha who fed her brother, bathed him, and changed his diapers. Emory kept Rahlo when Esha went to school, and even then, she would find someone to babysit until Esha got out of school. The only time Emory paid attention to her kids was when it was time to renew her Section 8 or food stamps. Other than that, she ran the streets, leaving them to fend for themselves.

"That's fucked up, sis." Rahlo bumped her with his shoulder.

"Aye Rah!" the neighborhood homeless man, Chef, called out.

"Hey Chef." Esha waved. "You eat today?"

Chef hit a quick 1-2 step and then spun around, removing the top hat from his head and tilted it in her direction. Dressed in a black tuxedo with a dingy white button-up and shiny black shoes, Chef gracefully moved through the dirt path as if it was a runway and he was accepting an award for best dressed.

"Sure did, sweet thing." He winked. "Always looking out for old Chef. You nothing like your gold-digging mama."

56

"Nope," Esha agreed. She wasn't offended in the least. Emory was a gold digger and she wore the title proudly.

"Sup, old man?" Rah sat his plate down and wiped his lips.

"Put me on a track," he demanded, snapping his fingers. "I might can teach you a thing or two."

"You can't rap," Bruce taunted, sucking the bar-b-que sauce off his rib.

"And yo big body ass can't run," Chef rebutted.

"Bust a flow." Rah blew into his closed fist, creating a beat with his mouth. Chef nodded and then a grin spread across his face before words flowed from his mouth.

"I used to be the man until I tried crack," he rapped, sending everybody in earshot into a laughing fit. *"I lost everything and now my stomach touch my back."*

"Chef, that's not funny," Esha scolded.

"They call me a zombie because I'm like The Walking Dead, and if you got enough dollars, I'll give you head."

"Brooooooo," Bruce belted, holding his stomach from laughter. Rahlo and Esha fell over each other, tickled that Chef could always make light of his situation. He reasoned life had already got the best of him and there was no reason for him to be down on himself.

"How I do?" He grinned.

"Uh yea, stick to your day job," Rahlo said as the front door opened. Emory locked eyes with Chef and instantly a scowl covered her face.

"Well, well, well," Chef snapped his fingers. "If it isn't my number one client," he teased.

Before he was Chef the crackhead, he was Chef the dope dealer and Emory's first love. Chef was the man. He had the money, the bitches, the cars, and everybody wanted a piece of him. His dope was top-notch, and unlike many of his competitors, Chef's shit was pure. One hit of his product would have you running down the street ass naked without a care in the world.

Emory was only seventeen at the time and she was head over heels in love with Chef. She had just given birth to Esha, and although it wasn't his baby, Chef helped out like she was produced from his sack. He moved Emory out of her mother's two-bedroom apartment and into a condo on the other side of town. Chef took care of all the bills and gave Emory money whenever she held her hand out. Emory was young but not naïve. She knew Chef did his thing when they weren't together, but she was happy to have a piece of him. A piece of Chef was better than not having any of him.

Thanks to his hood status, she was accustomed to all the attention being on them. Whenever Chef took her to the hood, Emory was draped in designer, and Esha was in the backseat dressed just like Chef. People swore she was his daughter, and Chef never denied it. For a while, it was all good, but like the old saying, nothing good lasts forever.

The more money Chef made, the more hoes he accumulated, and the more niggas fought to take his spot. Bullets and panties were thrown his way left and right. Emory tried to act unphased, but her feelings were hurt. Chef started clubbing without her and then he simply stopped coming around and moved on to the next fine girl. He still provided for Esha, but Emory was on her own.

To prove a point, Emory moved out of the apartment he set her up in and went back to her mother's house, hoping Chef would come get her, but he never did. She started popping up at the clubs with different niggas and acting a fool when Chef ignored her. Emory went as far as fucking with other niggas on his team, but Chef laughed in her face, claiming she went from the boss to the workers. Emory was a joke and he treated her as such.

It wasn't until his blunt was laced with the same crack he sold did his life change. Chef's fall from grace was slow and painful. It started out with him continuing to drop pieces of crack on his blunts to him simply firing up the pipe. The same people he sold dope to became his friends, and soon he was just another nigga who lost it all by getting high off his own supply.

"I told yall about feeding strays." Emory glared at Chef.

Even though he was a full-blown crackhead, it wasn't hard to see why she fell for him. He still had dimples and clear skin, and when he cleaned himself up, Chef looked good, and for that, Emory despised him. She prayed on several occasions that Chef would turn into a bum, but he always caught himself before he hit rock bottom.

"If I'm not mistaken, I used to be your stray," he teased, sticking his tongue out at her. "Member this?" Chef rolled his tongue and started thrusting the air with his hips. "I used to have you climbing walls."

"And now look at you," she snorted. "A pipe sucking nobody."

"Emory, chill." Rahlo frowned.

"Boy, fuck this dope fiend." She gave him the finger and went back in the house. Rahlo shook his head and turned to apologize to Chef, but he was halfway down the street tipping his top hat at everyone who passed him.

Chapter 4

"Get the door," Taylor groaned, rolling over on her side. It was seven in the morning, and she knew it wasn't nobody but his disgruntled ass ex-wife. Jasper's phone had been vibrating on the nightstand all morning and Taylor thanked God when it finally fell on the floor.

"J," she moaned, bumping him with her booty. "Get the door." Jasper shifted in his sleep, throwing his arm around her waist, but he didn't attempt to get up. Taylor wanted to slap his ass out of his peaceful slumber but decided against it. The next time he wanted to pick her up in the middle of the night, she was going to tell his ass to kick rocks.

Rolling out of the bed, she slipped his shirt over her head and strolled to the front door just as another round of impatient knocks were released. Snatching it open, she was met with both an angry glare and a big smile. Jalen's little arms instantly wrapped around her waist, and with a smug grin, Taylor hugged him back while shooting daggers at his mother.

"Tay! You're here," he exclaimed.

"I'm always here, baby," she cooed, getting under Sherri's skin.

"Where is Jasper?" Sherri frowned, eyeing the young girl from head to toe. She hated that her son was so attached to another woman, but because of the court order, there wasn't much she could do.

Sherri wanted to front and say she didn't know what Jasper saw in Taylor, but it would be a lie. Taylor was stacked, pretty, and from what she knew, she was smart. It didn't help that Jalen swore she was an amazing cook. It was always Tay this, Tay that, and since Sherri couldn't tell her son to shut the hell up, she gnawed on her bottom lip and listened to him excitedly talk about another woman. Every time Sherri saw Taylor, she looked like she stepped off a runway. Her hair was always dyed to perfection, and her lashes, eyebrows, and nails were flawless. Even now, just rolling out of bed, Taylor was still all of that, and Sherri hated it.

"He's asleep. Can I take a message?"

"No, but you can go tell my husband-"

"Ex-husband," Taylor corrected her.

"Girl, please. Jasper is going through a phase. We've been together since middle school, you think just because we're having marital problems, he's going to take you seriously?"

"Are you delusional?" Taylor cocked her head to the side. "Last time I checked, divorce was more than marital problems, sis. That's the end of the road if you ask me."

"We might be divorced, but I promise he knows where home is," Sherri smirked but quickly stopped as Taylor stepped forward. She knew the young girl was wild and would mop the floor with her ass.

"Is that some slick way to say yall still fucking?" Taylor

cocked her head to the side, ready to knock Sherri's head through the screen door and kick her lumpy body down the steps.

"What's going on?" Jasper asked, walking from the back rubbing his eyes.

Taylor and Sherri were both temporarily captivated by his presence. Jasper had always been in shape, but after his divorce, he threw himself into the gym. Simply dressed in a pair of Polo boxer briefs, Jasper's semi-hard dick was on display as well as his toned six-pack and neatly trimmed pubic hairs. Sherri almost shitted bricks when she saw Taylor's name etched across his chest. She used to practically beg him to get a tattoo. Hell, she used to beg him to work out, to get haircuts on the regular, and even dress a little nicer. Everything that he was for Taylor was everything Sherri prayed he'd be for her. It nearly killed her to see Jasper being the man of her dreams to someone else.

"Put some damn clothes on!" Taylor snapped, noticing his dick playing peek-a-boo.

"Op, Tay said a bad word," Jalen snickered, coming up behind them with his tablet in his hand recording them.

"My fault, baby." He shielded his print as if Sherri wasn't the prior owner. "Thanks for dropping him off, Sherri, but you can go," Jasper dismissed her while picking up Taylor's robe off the couch and putting it on. Jalen laughed at his father in the pink robe, but Taylor smirked. He knew better than to play with her. She'd happily collect all her shit from his house and leave him there with his funny-looking ex-wife.

"Nah, run that lil slick shit back for him." Taylor snapped her fingers. "Tell me where his home is at again."

"Baby, what are you talking about?" he questioned, rubbing her back in an effort to calm her down.

"I'm going to go." Sherri stepped out the door. "I'll call you when your little guard dog isn't around," she said when she was a safe distance away from Tay.

"Sherri, gone with all that." Jasper waved her off, locking his arms around Taylor's waist.

"Nigga, you need to follow her. That's where home at, right?" Taylor pulled away from him, not caring that she was threatening to put him out of his own home. "That's what the silly hoe said."

"She was talking shit. You know my heart resides wherever you are." He closed the door as Sherri laughed in the distance.

"For your sake, it better be because I promise if I find out you're creeping with that bitch behind my back, I'm going to snatch your heart out of your chest and make you eat it," Taylor warned, poking his nose with the tip of her stiletto nail.

"I believe you, too," Jasper tried to grab her hand and kiss it, but Taylor snatched it away and turned on her heels.

"You should because I don't make idle threats," she shot, walking back into his bedroom with Jalen on her heels.

Taylor's plan was to sleep in 'til noon, suck Jasper's dick until his sack was empty, and then make them breakfast. Those plans went right down the drain when he neglected to mention that Sherri wildebeest looking ass was bringing Jalen over. While she loved Jalen dearly, Taylor didn't play that last minute shit, and she wasn't going to rearrange her day to babysit.

"Tay," Jalen called out, watching her repack her overnight bag.

"Yes, baby." She stopped moving, giving him her full attention.

"I'm a spy now." He gave her a toothless grin.

"You are?"

"Yep, and I spy on everybody."

"You can't be invading people's privacy, baby."

"Even if it's bad because my mommy-"

"Where you going?" Jasper interrupted, stepping into the room and cutting Jalen off.

"Home," Taylor replied, turning to finish packing.

"I'm working tonight. You taking Jalen with you?" he asked, pulling the shirt out of her hand.

"No." She snatched the shirt back, stuffing it in her bag and moving around him.

"No?" Jasper cocked his head to the side.

"N-O," Taylor slowly spelled out. "I have plans tonight and you didn't even tell me he was coming."

"Sherri had something to do and asked me to keep him."

"Then call off and keep him because I'm not doing shit for that strong back bitch."

"Watch your mouth," Jasper warned.

"Your child is sitting right there on the bed with those headphones on, nigga. Don't tell me how to talk."

"So, you not gone watch him for me?"

"No, I'm not. Didn't I just tell you I had plans?"

"Your plans are more important than me going to make money?" he quizzed.

"Money that I don't see though."

"Tay, don't be like that. You know I'd look out if I could."

"I know, but Jasper, I'm not about to cancel my plans because you agreed to switch days with your bitter baby mama."

"So you're not going to watch him?"

"You should've thought about that before you agreed to do

a favor for a bitch that cheated on you," she snapped.

Taylor knew it was wrong to throw Sherri's indiscretions in his face, but they both had her fucked up. She didn't know what lie Sherri told to trick him, nor did she care. As far as Taylor was concerned, Jasper could call off or drop Jalen off over his people's house because she wasn't switching up shit to accommodate a bitch she couldn't stand.

"You're so fucking selfish, man," Jasper grunted.

"I'm in my twenties. I have the right to be selfish if I want to, and you're not about to guilt trip me like ole girl did you."

"Whatever, man, gone."

"Oh, you putting me out?" She raised her eyebrow, standing back on her legs.

"No," Jasper quickly answered. "I'm just saying you were about to leave, so gone on."

"Yea ok, Jasper."

"And since you taking all your stuff, I guess that means you're not coming back tonight."

"Hmph," Taylor scoffed. "Look at you using your context clues," she sassed, tossing the bag over her shoulder. Leaning over, Taylor kissed Jalen's forehead and strolled out of the room without an ounce of remorse.

"Give me the beat back," Rah requested in the microphone.

The producer sat back in his seat and replayed the beat. In the booth, Rah bobbed his head with his eyes closed. Although the beat was sick, he couldn't formulate the right words. Normally, he was able to annihilate any beat at any time, but at the moment, he couldn't do it. Frustrated, he pulled the headphones off and dropped them on the stool before locking his hands behind his head.

"What do you need, Rah?" Terri asked, tapping the intercom. From the stress lines on Rahlo's forehead, he knew something was wrong, and whatever it was, he wanted to fix it.

"He need some hoes," Duke responded, pushing off the plush couch. "It looks like a fucking funeral home waiting room in this bitch. Where the hoes? Where the bottles? Where the weed?" he ranted. "I'd be depressed too."

"Nigga, this ain't no fucking movie." Bruce glanced in his direction just in time to see Terri take a deep breath.

"Shit, maybe it needs to be because this shit is lame. Hell, I almost fell asleep."

"Please," Terri begged, "I'd bring an air mattress in here if it'll get you to shut up."

"Nigga, who the fuck you talking to?" Duke stepped forward just as the booth door opened. Rahlo stepped out with his phone glued to his ear.

"We out." He bypassed the men in the room. Bruce followed and Terri looked at him with a confused expression.

"We paid for eight hours of studio time. We've only been here two," he reasoned.

"I paid for eight hours," Rahlo corrected him. "Plus, ain't shit popping. I need to go get my mind right." He glanced at the producer. "You gone be around?"

"How long you gone be?"

"I'm about to hit the strip club. I need to smoke and see some ass. Shit, I need to loosen up. I'll be back in about three hours."

Rahlo wasn't used to recording in such a prestigious studio. His most popular hits were recorded when he was high out of his mind and surrounded by naked women. It was nothing for his sessions to turn into a club scene, but once he stepped into the booth, the world around him became obsolete. The beat intoxicated his veins and the words flowed from his mouth like water. The studio they were currently standing in seemed so cold and impersonal, but Terri claimed it was the best, filled with top-of-the-line equipment, and if they wanted to win New Artist of the Year, he needed to be the best.

"Hell yea!" Duke clapped. "I told them it's boring in this bitch."

"Yea," the producer nodded, "I'll be here."

"Aight, I'll be back," Rahlo told Terri and bopped out of the door.

"Don't get into no trouble!" he called after him.

"*Don't get into no trouble*," Duke mocked.

"Yall might as well kiss and make up," Bruce teased.

"And you might as well terminate your Planet Fitness membership because your fat ass ain't losing shit but your hair."

Rahlo ignored their banter while he texted the club owner. He didn't have much time and wanted his section set up before he arrived. Terri wanted an award-winning album, and Rahlo needed inspiration. It was balance.

Two hours later, Rahlo, Bruce, Duke, and half of the strippers were in the VIP section making a video. Rahlo was high as fuck and standing in the middle of the floor, rapping into the mic while dancers shook their asses on him from every angle. Big bills littered the floor, and all three men had a bottle of top shelf liquor in their hands. The diamonds on

Rahlo's chain danced under the wild light scheme and bounced around on his chest whenever he moved. He was almost sure the video was going to go viral.

Shakin all that ass, but can you ride it?

Don't put yo lips on me, hoe you tried it!

"Southwest Rah in this bitch!" the DJ shouted over the mic.

Envious eyes glared in their direction. Just three years ago, Rahlo was hustling dime bags and pills. He didn't have the latest gear, and when he was grinding, his appearance was unkempt. The man on the mic rocking diamond chains and iced-out grills was nothing like the scrub they were used to, and it stung. To watch Rahlo glow while they remained in the same spot put a bad taste in their mouth. On top of that, he took all the bad strippers leaving them with the out of shape, non-twerking ass dancers.

On the other side of the club, Taylor and Kiki sat in a section with a couple of the other hostesses- Candi and Shani- who worked at the bar with them. A dancer was on the stage in front of them, and just like the men, they made it rain on her. They slapped her ass and even climbed on stage next to her to showcase their skills.

"Aw shit." Kiki stood up. "My boo is here." She ran her fingers through her long weave.

Kiki knew she was all that, and if given the chance, she could have Rahlo or anyone for that matter. Being a plus-size woman worked in her favor. She had ass and hips for days, small breasts, and a pretty face. Not only was Kiki fine, but she was talented and kept a pocket full of money. Her own money!

"Girl, please." Taylor playfully rolled her eyes while placing a couple of twenties in the G-string of the dancer with her legs spread in front of her. It was the least she could do since her coworkers were getting their rent paid in Rah's section.

"I'm about to go over there." Candi picked up her purse. It

was cool chilling with the girls, but Rah's fine ass was in the building, and she wanted parts.

"Me too. I don't even need Rah." Shani applied lip gloss to her lips. "That fat nigga he be with can get the pussy. I know he got some money. Fat niggas love to eat and take naps, that's right up my alley."

"You coming?" Kiki asked, peering over at Taylor.

"Nah, I ordered lamb chops." Taylor shook her head. "I'm not trying to eat all pretty and shit."

"Suit yourself." Candi hunched her shoulders, stepping out of the section with Shani right behind her.

"I guess I'll stay here with you." Kiki sat back down.

"Don't let me stop your fun. I'll be ok," Taylor assured her.

"Bitch, please. When do we ever leave each other alone?"

"You not worried about Beavis and Butthead taking your man?"

"I'm not worried." Kiki waved her off. "Rah only has eyes for me."

"Bitch, you're delusional," Taylor snickered.

"Plus, Candi's breath smells like she got old meat stuck between her teeth. I know my man has higher standards than that."

"You stupid, but her breath do got that lil bite," Taylor agreed as the waitress brought them over another drink.

Never the ones to need a large crowd or group of bitches, Taylor and KiKi took shot after shot while rapping the lyrics to damn near every song the DJ played. They didn't throw anything larger than a ten, but their section floor was covered in dollars, and the dancer assigned to the section was very appreciative.

"Don't play wit' it, don't play wit' it, come on baby, don't play

wit' it," Taylor rapped, throwing money at the camera while KiKi recorded her.

Rocking her hips, Taylor squatted down while sticking her middle fingers up. In rare form, she rolled her hips like a dancer, never messing up the lyrics to one of her favorite songs. The short leather shorts allowed her butt cheeks to make a brief appearance while showcasing the dimples in her lower back.

"I'm on demon time taking niggas soul. He say I'm a pretty bitch, I know," Taylor rapped in her fake New York accent, making KiKi giggle.

"I hope you rap my shit like that," Rahlo's voice boomed over the music. KiKi damn near fainted. She had been close to him at Top Notch, but this was personal. Rahlo was all in their section like he wasn't that nigga. Taylor stood up and smirked at him. He knew damn well she literally just got hipped to his music and still couldn't recite a whole song.

"Boy bye, you know Lola on your head," Taylor teased, taking in his appearance.

Dressed in a pair of black jeans and a crispy white tee, Rahlo's outfit was simple, but the jewels flooding his neck, ears, and wrists told a different story. The lights reflected off his dark skin, creating a blue illusion while making his diamonds shine. When he smiled, she caught a glimpse of the grill that covered his bottom teeth. Rahlo had no business being that fine, and Taylor tried hard to hide the temptation that danced in her eyes.

"That's how you feel?" He cocked his head to the side while running his tongue across his lower lip.

"I'm just saying." She looked away from him, not being able to handle the way his eyes shamelessly roamed her body.

"Introduce me, bitch!" Kiki bumped her hip.

"Oh, my bad," Taylor snickered. "This is your future baby

mama and my best friend, KiKi. KiKi, this is the love of your life, Rahlo," she introduced them.

"Love of my life is far-fetched. He's the love of my right now," KiKi corrected her. "But how you doing?" She batted her mink eyelashes at him.

"Yall funny," Rahlo chuckled, making the one dimple cave into his face. "And how she my baby mama when I've already claimed you as my wife...I mean, unless you're into that kinda thing."

"Um, eww. I'm not. Plus, I'm taken."

"Fuck that nigga," both Rahlo and KiKi said in union.

"Both of yall can shut up. Don't do mine." She playfully waved them off. "Why you over here anyway? Your section looks like a BET uncut video."

"Honestly, because I walked by and saw that ass in them shorts," Rahlo flirted. "Come fuck with me."

"Nope, I can't be seen with you."

"Why the fuck not?" He squinted his eyes at her.

"Because being seen with you comes with attention that I don't need."

"Humor me," he requested as he stepped closer to her. Kiki stepped away, giving her friend a minute to chat with the star. She guessed if anyone had to have her future ex-husband, it could be her best friend.

"Are you oblivious to your status?"

"My status?" He raised his eyebrow.

"Yea, nigga. You're a freaking rapper. Not just any rapper, according to Google."

"What Google say?"

"That you are the hottest thing since J. Cole," she bucked. "That you have a bright future, and if you play your cards right, you can be one of the greatest."

"Google said all that?"

"I might've added a little bit," she snickered. "But the point is you're not regular."

Before Rahlo could respond, Duke ambled in their direction with his pants hanging off his ass, displaying the Gucci draws that covered his narrow ass. With a bottle of liquor in his hand, he stepped into the section.

"This don't look like the bathroom," he slurred, walking up behind them. When his eyes landed on Taylor, he frowned. "I know you didn't leave our section to come see this-"

"Finish that sentence if you want to and these dollars won't be the only thing laying on the floor. I'm not at work, nigga, so I'd advise you to tread lightly," Taylor warned.

"The fuck you gone do?" He chuckled, amused that she thought she could really beat his ass.

"Fuck around and find out," KiKi co-signed.

"Oh hell nah. All these bad bitches in the club and you find the most aggressive ones." Duke looked both women up and down.

"Chill out before they jump your ass and I'm not going to stop them," Rahlo snorted. Just the thought of them jumping his best friend tickled him.

"Fuck all that." Duke waved him off. "I got a couple of Hot and Ready's we can take back to the studio."

"Who 'cause I know you not talking about ole girl in the yellow?" Rahlo frowned. Taylor and Kiki snickered. They knew exactly who he was talking about.

"Yea, her breath a lil tart, but you not gone smell it if her mouth on yo dick. Duh, nigga," Duke reasoned.

"Nigga, no! Fuck around and get gingivitis on my dick."

72

Rahlo's face twisted in disgust. "Matter fact, they coming with me." He threw his head in the direction of the duo.

"Hell nah, leave Thelma and Louise right here."

"First of all, I'm not going nowhere with you. I could have sworn I said I had a boyfriend," Taylor reminded him, ignoring Kiki's bucked eyes.

"I could have sworn I said I don't give a fuck," Rahlo reiterated, raising his eyebrow.

"Well, I do, and second, what makes you think I wanna be around your broke best friend? I bet this nigga picking up money off the floor to throw."

"He what, friend?" Kiki laughed out loud.

"His broke ass probably throwing quarters at these girls," she continued, this time Rahlo joined in. Taylor matched Duke's energy and it was entertaining.

"You talk a lot of shit for a bitch with a muskrat on top of her head," Duke tossed back, eyeing her from head to toe. He actually liked her hair but wouldn't give her smart mouth ass the satisfaction of knowing that.

"And you walk around with your pants hanging off your ass like it's an entrance sign above the muthafucka," she countered.

"Ugly ass," he muttered.

"I could have snot running down my nose and I'm still badder than any bitch you'll ever pull."

"Period." Kiki gave her a high five.

"So you not rolling with me?" Rahlo pouted, causing his dimple to cave into his face.

"Nope, I'm about to eat my lamb chops and take my ass home to my bed," Taylor said as Candi, Shani, and Bruce joined them. "But good luck with your session."

"Can I at least get a good luck hug?" He stretched his arms out. Taylor didn't have time to think about it because Kiki pushed her into his arms. Rahlo chortled, catching her. Taylor tried to give him a church hug with her ass sticking out, but he wasn't having it. Raising her arms, he placed them around his neck and slipped his around her waist, closing the space between them.

"Damn, you feel good as fuck in my arms." He hugged her tight, causing a moan to slip from her mouth. When he nuzzled his head in the crook of her neck, Taylor pulled back.

"I'll let yall go." She cleared her throat, uncomfortable with the way her nipples hardened at his touch.

"Bout time." Duke clapped his hands.

Rahlo licked his lips and checked her out once more before turning to walk away, leaving Kiki with her mouth ajar and Taylor swooning with butterflies. Candi and Shani were both happy that Taylor declined the invite. It wasn't hard to see that the superstar had eyes for the girl.

"Aye," he called out, stroking his beard.

"What?" Taylor answered, gathering her composure.

"Tell ya nigga he's on borrowed time." Rahlo winked. "I gotta have your soft ass next to me every night."

Chapter 5

"Yesss, baby," Taylor moaned, throwing her ass back into Jasper's face. "Eat this pussy," she encouraged, feeling the nerves in her stomach shoot to the tip of her clitoris. Taylor's toes curled as Jasper sucked and lightly pulled at the bud while his fingers worked her G-spot. The lethal combination sent Taylor over the edge, damn near drowning him with the sweet juices that released from her body.

"Hmmmm," she cried out as the orgasm coursed through her insides, causing her to clamp her legs closed around his neck.

"Damn, girl," Jasper gasped, wiping her juices from his mouth. "I almost died between these thick ass thighs." He broke free of her hold.

"It's a good way to meet your maker," Taylor exhaled, pulling the covers over her body. Cumming back-to-back had her feeling weak and she needed a nap to recharge.

"Nah, get up." Jasper pulled the cover right back off of her. "You know my mama cooking."

"You can go without me. I don't have time to be sitting in her face. You know your family is fake as fuck."

"Damn, you just gone keep dogging them out?" He laughed.

"Now you know damn well they fake as hell. They talk all that shit about Sherri, but every time you go to an event over there, she's right in attendance, cooking with your mama and joking it up with your sister," Taylor expressed, rolling out of the bed. Jasper was temporarily distracted by her booty jiggling. He couldn't help but reach out and stroke the fat muthafucka.

"Let me get a little more." Jasper grabbed his dick, stroking it through the boxers.

"No, we gotta go, right?" She slapped his hand away. "Let's go visit your fake ass mama, funny looking sister, and desperate ass ex-wife."

"You want them to hate her? Sherri been around for over twenty years."

"Ugh, I forgot yall from the ice age," Taylor cracked and then laughed at her own joke.

"Haha," he mocked her, not finding her old age joke funny. "Just because I moved on don't mean they have to, baby."

"You're right, but at the same time, they shouldn't talk about her when I'm around but kiss her ass when I'm not. If you're going to be anything, be consistent. I don't like the bitch and I stand on it every time I see her. You'll never catch me smiling in her face. I don't like the slick mouth hoe."

Jasper nodded his head in understanding. Taylor had a valid point. His younger sister, Jada, loved Sherri and had formed a relationship with her outside of her brother. Sherri called his mother Ma and walked in the house without knocking. It didn't matter that she cheated on Jasper. His mother reasoned that marriages went through obstacles, and he should've fought a little harder for his.

When Jasper brought Taylor around, she instantly clicked with his sister. They were almost the same age and into a lot of the same things. His mother was leery of the young girl, but it was easy to see her son was in love, so she let it go. For a while, everything was all good until Sherri came around. She walked around the house like she was the queen bee and almost got her ass whooped more than once. Taylor didn't care that it was his mama's house, she didn't tolerate disrespect. The tension in the house was usually so thick that Taylor always ended up leaving. It wasn't hard to read the room, and she didn't need a pick me ass bitch on her side.

"Can't we all just get along?" Jasper asked, following her into the bathroom.

"I'm cool, but if your ex-wife is there, then I'm leaving." Taylor closed the door in his face. "Cause I'll drag that hoe all through yo mama house with a smile on my face."

∞∞∞

Two hours later, Taylor was dressed in a black sleeveless maxi dress that hugged her curves. She paired it with her Tory Burch sandals, sunglasses, and Glamaholic bucket bag. Simply running her fingers through her hair, Taylor applied a thin layer of lip gloss to her full lips and met Jasper at the door.

"You look good, baby," he complimented, pulling her into his arms. "How did I get so lucky?"

"I ask myself that every day," she jested, walking out the front door.

"Yea, ok." Jasper slapped her on the ass as he held the door open for her.

In the car, Taylor pulled out her phone and turned on Rah's mixtape. The day after she saw him in the strip club, he went into the booth and went off. According to a post on social media, he stayed in the booth for five hours remixing every popular song to date. Her favorite was the remix he did to Chris Brown's *Under the Influence*. His voice was way raspier than she remembered, and the words made her pussy thump.

Shorty got a man but who care

Tell his ass to get the steppin' cause baby I'm here

Shorty got a man but who careee

I'm about to stretch that pussy out right here

"Turn that shit off." Jasper frowned.

He used to like Rahlo's music, but now he detested it. Especially the song that Taylor was playing. You couldn't tell him that Rahlo wasn't talking about his girl.

"I like this song," Taylor pouted.

"Then listen to the real version. This nigga on here crying and shit. It's annoying."

"Let me find out you hatin'." She grinned.

"And let me find out he made this shit for you," he rebutted, glaring at her.

"What you gon' do, daddy?"

"Fuck around and find out." Jasper gripped her thigh. "That nigga will be on the Shaderoom for getting knocked the fuck out."

"I hear you talking," Taylor giggled and changed the song.

The ride to his mother's house was smooth. She lived in Westland, and normally, Taylor hated the long drive, but today she laid back and listened to the music while the wind whipped through her hair. Every so often, Jasper would reach over and stroke her cheek or kiss her lips.

When they pulled up, he was happy to see Sherri's car wasn't in the driveway. It was his day off and all he wanted to do was chill with his girl and visit his mama without all the extra bullshit. Getting out of the car, Jasper ran around to Taylor's side and opened the door for her. Once she was on her feet, he wrapped her in his arms and began placing kisses on her face and neck.

"Stopppp," Taylor giggled, trying to pull away from him.

"I can't help it. You smell so fucking good. Let's go get this over so I can take you back home and get some more of this pussy."

"You acting like a crackhead."

"And you're my pusher." He slapped her on the ass.

"Stop, nigga." Taylor pushed him and started making her way up the driveway.

From the porch, she could hear the loud laughter and knew right off the day wasn't about to go as planned. Sherri's car wasn't outside, but her trout mouth ass was in attendance. Irritation instantly filled Taylor's veins. There was nothing more irritating than a bitch who didn't know when to let go.

"Mama!" Jasper called out as he entered the house.

"Back here!" she called out from the kitchen. Taking Taylor by the hand, Jasper led her through the house until he reached their destination. As soon as he dotted the doorway, he peered back at his girl, almost begging her to behave.

"Hey, baby," Etta greeted her son and then smiled at Taylor. "How you doing, sweetheart?"

Instantly, the energy in the room shifted. Sherri was sitting at the kitchen table with his mama and sister. They were drinking wine and looking at old pictures. From the empty bottles on the table, Jasper could tell they were all buzzing.

"Hey, Ms. Etta." Taylor waved with her free hand. Jasper was still holding her other hand.

"What's up, Mama? Why you ain't tell me she was here?" He nodded toward the table.

"Her car is in the shop and Jada picked her up. Is there a problem?" Etta asked, knowing damn well there was a problem. Taylor laughed under her breath.

"*She?*" Sherri sucked her teeth. "You know my name, boy."

"Was I talking to you?" Jasper snapped.

"Look, we are all family. You know we love Sherri, and I don't see a problem with her being here."

"It's not, but don't invite me and my girl over if she's going to be here."

"I didn't know little ole me made her feel uncomfortable," Sherri taunted, making Jada laugh under her breath again. This was the fake shit Taylor hated. Jada was laughing at Sherri's pettiness, but they were both sadly mistaken. Taylor was Queen Petty, and she didn't do the shit for kicks and giggles. She hurt hoes' feelings.

"Baby, can you tie my sandal?" Taylor sweetly asked. "It feels a little loose."

Without question, Jasper dropped down and did as he was asked. Sherri shifted in her seat and Jada stopped laughing.

"While you're down there, can you please put a little lotion on my ankle? I think I missed a spot." She handed him her clutch. The women watched Jasper remove the lotion, rub it into his hands, and then apply it to Taylor's ankle.

"That's good?" he asked, gazing up at her.

"Yep, thanks, baby." She patted the top of his head. "Oh shoot, I left my lip gloss in the car. I don't want it to melt on your seats."

"I got it." Jasper turned on his heels and ran out the door. With a smirk on her lips, Taylor addressed the room.

"Don't you just love a man who does whatever you ask without question?" She teasingly smiled in Sherri's direction. "You had one, right?"

"Lil girl, please." Sherri rolled her eyes. "Ain't nobody thinking about you or Jasper."

"Oh no, does it make you uncomfortable to see the man you exchanged vows with jumping at my every request? Shit, if you think this is something, you should see what he does in the bedroom, but I'll spare you the painful details. We both know what he's working with." Taylor winked.

"Come on now, ladies," Etta sighed.

"So it's okay when she shoots shots, but a problem when I do it?" Taylor questioned, turning to face Etta.

"I'm just saying we're all family," she reasoned.

"I keep forgetting you just left third grade. Tit for tat is a child's game, right?" Sherri sniped, still testing her luck.

"Don't think because we're sitting in Ms. Etta's house that I won't snatch that loose ass lace off your head. Find you something safe to do because I'm not it."

Sherri shifted in her seat but didn't reply. She was all talk and no bite, and the theory had been proven more than once. Etta cleared her throat as Jasper stepped back into the kitchen empty-handed and out of breath.

"You might've dropped it because it's not in the car."

"Sorry, baby, it was right here." Taylor innocently smiled, holding up the lip gloss that had been in her hand the whole time.

"Tay!" Jalen greeted, bouncing in the kitchen with his iPad in his hand. Per usual, he was recording everything. Focusing the camera on Taylor, he did a fit check video. Taylor placed her hand on her hip and smiled as he recorded her.

"Told yall Tay be flyyyy," he sang and then told his

imaginary followers that he'd be right back.

"I like your hair," a little voice spoke shyly. Taylor glanced at the pretty little girl and smiled.

"Member my sister?" Jalen asked, pushing Jamie forward.

This was another thing Taylor couldn't get behind. She didn't give a flying fuck how long they knew each other, there was no way Sherri should have still been able to come around and bring her daughter at that. It was nothing against the baby because she was innocent, but Sherri, on the other hand, had balls the size of Texas. In Taylor's opinion, Etta was flat out wrong. The woman was basically rubbing her affair all in Jasper's face, but because Sherri was considered "family," she was forgiven without so much as a beat down by his sister.

"I do." Taylor pinched her cheek. "She's such a cutie."

"Can I come with you?" Jalen asked, wrapping his arms around her waist, pressing his face into her stomach.

"Me too. Can I go with you?" Jamie questioned, looking up at Taylor with hope

"No!" Sherri squeaked before Taylor could answer them. "I mean, I thought we were going to the zoo," she cleared it up. "We'll get ice cream too."

Taylor thought it was funny that Sherri was trying to bribe her son to stay home. Normally she was pushing Jalen into Jasper's arms, but the moment Jalen showed interest in Taylor, Sherri damn near had a stroke. Either way, it didn't matter to Taylor. She loved Jalen, but she wasn't going to compete for his love or time. If he wanted to come, cool. If not, she'd see him when it was Jasper's weekend.

"I wanna go with Tay, plus you always say your back and legs hurt every time," Jalen whined. Going to the zoo with his mother was a bore. She didn't let him get his face painted like Taylor did and she spent more time on the phone versus telling him fun facts about the animals.

"I wanna go too," Jamie fussed, grabbing Taylor's hand.

"Can my sister come?" Jalen begged, pulling on Taylor's arm.

"Aww baby, you know your mama is a little older. Maybe she needs a wheelchair?" Taylor cracked, making Jasper chuckle a bit.

"Like the ones she uses at the grocery store?" Jalen cocked his head to the side, further embarrassing Sherri. Even Jada had to stifle her laughter.

"Yep, just like those." Taylor nodded.

"Boy, hush, and yall let that girl go. Did you even speak to your father?" Etta spoke up. "You act like Taylor is the only one in the kitchen. You didn't even hug me like that," she fussed, getting up from her seat. Jamie released Taylor's hand at the command but folded her arms with a pout on her lips.

"He doesn't ever speak to me when Taylor is around." Jasper rubbed the top of his son's head.

"Cause Tay my favorite," Jalen told them, standing at her side. "So, can I go?"

"Yea, go get your bag," Jasper told him. Only then did Jalen detach himself from Taylor.

"Can I go too?" Jamie asked, peering up at Jasper.

"Uh, maybe next time," he lied. Even if he wanted to take Jamie with him, his pride wouldn't allow it.

"Ok," she pouted and turned around to follow Jalen out of the kitchen.

"Didn't I just say I was taking him to the zoo?" Sherri snapped when Jalen was out of earshot. "Plus, it's my weekend."

"Since when does that matter? We have him the majority of the time anyway. So, drink ya little wine and chill."

"Jasper, please don't act stupid in front of your little friend."

"You know what-" Taylor turned around and placed her hand on Jasper's chest. "I'm going to wait in the car because the last thing I want to do is knock your ex-wife's head off her shoulders, and I have a taste for seafood, so after you grab Jalen, come out."

"You got it, baby." Jasper kissed her lips.

"Enjoy the rest of yall day." Taylor waved as she switched out of the kitchen and then the front door.

Etta shook her head at the lovesick look on her son's face as his eyes followed Taylor out of the house. She had seen him in love, but never like this. Jasper reminded her of a boy who got his first piece of pussy. He was so far up Taylor's ass that if she farted he'd bottle it to spray on his pillow when she wasn't around.

"You just let that girl run all over you." Etta shook her head in disgust.

"He's a simp, Ma," Jada added.

"A simp, no. A man in love, yes. I've never experienced anything like this, so excuse me if my glow bothers yall." Jasper held his hands up in defense like his words didn't shoot daggers into Sherri's chest.

"Really?" she gawked. "I mess up one time and now I'm this awful woman?"

"One time?" Jasper bucked his eyes in her direction. "You cheated, got pregnant, and tried to pass the kid off as mine."

"It was a mistake, Jasper!" she yelled, allowing the wine to get the best of her. "We were together for so long and I just, I don't know. I just wanted to try something new."

"Something new, huh?" Jasper rubbed his chin. "Well, on your quest to try something new, you lost something old. Tell my son I'll be in the car."

Sherri's eyes filled with tears as she watched the love of her life walk away. One drunken night cost her not only her family but her best friend. Jasper was unforgiving, and no matter what she said or did, he couldn't let it go. By the time they started marriage counseling, Jasper had already checked out of the marriage, and Sherri's loneliness sent her back into the arms of the other man.

"Don't cry, Sher." Jada rubbed her back. "He'll be back after he's done playing house with her."

Sherri nodded, but she didn't know how true that statement was. From where she was standing, Taylor was there to stay.

∞∞∞

In the car, Taylor pressed the phone to her ear, trying to convince Kiki that she didn't need to pull up. Fucking with her best friend was a guaranteed one-way trip to stomp a hoe town and Sherri's ride was well overdue. Her snide comments and shady behavior were begging for a beatdown.

"Turn your location back on!"

"No, fool. Jasper should be coming out right now," Taylor snickered. She had been friends with Kiki long enough to know she was with the shits.

"It's ok. I'm going to catch that hoe at Krogers and drag her ass up and down the deli aisle," Kiki promised.

"You gone have to catch her first. According to Jalen, her big ass be riding in the motor carts."

"I know you fucking lying! I can't stand it when people ride on them carts. Like get yo big ass up and walk. Ugh," Kiki groaned. "Now I really wanna beat her ass."

"Girl! Their whole situation is giving Mama Dee and Shay because ain't no way."

"These mamas be choosing, but fuck all of them. So, are you coming or not?"

"Not," Taylor answered.

"Whyyyyy? It's a studio session with Rah. Food, liquor, smoke. What's better?"

"It's about to be nothing but half-naked hoes up there."

"And I'm trying to be one. Plus, Rah is sweet on you. He might put us in a video."

"I can't just ditch Jasper. I did just make him leave his mama's house."

"Then start an argument and send his old ass back in there," Kiki said matter of factly. "I wanna go to the studio, but not by myself. I'm shy."

"Bitch, you a shy lie, but I'll let you know in a minute. Jasper is on his way to the car."

"Start an argument and ditch his ass," Kiki said before hanging up the phone. Taylor laughed and removed the phone from her face as Jasper got in the car.

Jasper tried not to question her, but his insecurities got the best of him. The thought of another man trying to climb between the thighs he claimed as his own sent his heart plummeting to his feet. Reaching over, he attempted to grab her phone, but Taylor popped his hand. She needed to delete the texts of her calling his mama a bald head tramp before he started going through her phone like he paid the bill.

"Who was that?" he asked, running his tongue across the front of his teeth.

"Kiki. I'm going to go to the studio with her tonight."

"Studio?"

"Yea. A few of the girls from the bar were invited to Rah's studio session and she wants me to tag along."

"Well, you can't," Jasper opposed. "We're about to take Jalen and Trooper to Sky Zone and then to get pizza."

"And after that, I'm going to hang with my friend."

"So what about me?"

"What about you?" Taylor furrowed her eyebrows. "We're doing something with the boys and when we're done I'm going to get dressed and leave. Trooper can stay or I can drop him off. Either way, I'm going out."

"So it's fuck me?" Jasper scoffed, trying to keep his composure.

"I didn't say that, but it's Saturday night and I'm going to hang out with my friend."

"In a studio full of niggas."

"I mean, there might be niggas there, but if you trust me, then it shouldn't be a problem. Do you trust me?"

"Yea, man," he sulked, knowing she was about to hit the streets anyway.

"Then we shouldn't have a problem. Open the door for your son." Taylor lifted her chin toward the house. Bent over, Sherri's breasts spilled from her top as she attempted to kiss an eager Jalen goodbye.

"Desperate ass hoe," Taylor snorted, picking up her phone to text Kiki.

I'm coming out.

Rahlo reached across the couch and grabbed his phone. He

was twenty minutes late for his studio session and Terri was having a fit. Rahlo had every intention of being there on time, but due to an unexpected guest, he was running behind. Now that her head was buried in his lap, Rahlo wished he would've dismissed her.

"Uh, everything ok?" Lexi raised her head, wiping the corners of her lips.

"Nah, you need to start drinking more water. Your mouth can't even produce enough saliva to wet my dick." Rahlo peered down at her and then back at his phone. "Plus, I told you I was straight on all this anyway."

"Yet you opened the door and allowed me to suck your dick," she snapped.

"I let you in because you was standing there looking all stupid and shit. I told you I was about to dip, and as far as sucking my dick, that's a little far-fetched. I mean, you used to nick my shit, but now you're trying to give me second-degree burns."

"Oh my gosh, you're such an asshole." Lexi pushed up from the floor. "Let me find out that lil fame and money got you acting different."

"And let me find out you hating. Ain't shit little about me but the amount of nonsense I accept from hating ass muthafuckas."

"Wow, so now I'm a hater. Don't forget I knew you before the fame," she scoffed. Rahlo dropped the phone in his lap and peered over at her.

Growing up, Lexi's family lived down the street from Rahlo's grandmother Norma. Being that Emory liked to run the streets, Rahlo and Esha spent most of their summers in the vibrant streets of Detroit. Esha was normally babysitting kids for extra money or running errands. The money she made, she'd give her brother a few dollars and save the rest.

By the time school rolled around, Esha had enough money to go school shopping for them and get Rahlo a haircut. Emory would give her a couple dollars, but that was chump change compared to what Esha spent.

While his sister hustled, Rahlo ran the streets with Duke, Bruce, and a few of the other neighborhood boys. When they weren't riding their bikes up and down the street, they were at the park until the wee hours of the morning. Norma really didn't care what he did as long as he didn't bring any drama or babies to her house. Most days, Rahlo hung with his boys, studying music videos and memorizing legendary rap battles. Out of all his friends, Rahlo was the best. Thanks to his sister, he had an expanded vocabulary and could mix words and form verses that put grown men to shame. At twelve years old, he was rapping better than half of the men in the game, and with time, he'd only get better.

Nightfall is when he hung out with Lexi. Since her parents worked overnight, Lexi invited all the boys over to her house to chill with her and a few girls from her class. They started off watching movies, and then Duke would suggest they play *Hide and Go Get It* or *Spin the Bottle.* Unsupervised, the adolescents played in the dark, recreating acts they'd seen in movies or from their older siblings. Lexi hid in the same spot every time, making it easier for Rahlo to find her. They started with kissing and then his mannish hands would find their way into her gullible panties. For him, it was simply the pathway into manhood, but for Lexi, it was the beginning of a toxic relationship with her first love.

"So you think I'm a hater?" Lexi asked, planting her hand on her hip.

Throughout the years, Lexi had filled out. No longer was she the stick figure who used to get fingered in her mother's closets. She gained a little weight, but Rahlo wouldn't say she was thick. At a size five, Lexi was slim and shaped like a

Coke bottle. The glass ones, to be exact. She had a little waist, perky breasts, and petite booty that fit in the palm of Rahlo's hands. She had always been a pretty girl, but over the years, Lexi perfected makeup application and made weekly trips to the salon. Her shoulder length hair was bone straight and her lashes were perfect. Lexi knew her eyebrows could use some work, but she wasn't tripping. She was the perfect replica of the girl next door.

"Any time you put *lil* on anything concerning someone's accomplishments, you're a hater." Rahlo glanced over at her.

"You know I wasn't saying it like that."

"That's how I took it, but look, it was nice seeing you, but I gotta go." He started toward the door.

"Can I come?" Lexi asked, running behind him.

"Nah. I'm going to the studio and you know how you get."

"How do I get?" She cocked her head to the side. The question was redundant because they both knew she didn't have any act right when it came to him. It didn't matter that years had passed since they had been a couple. Whenever Rahlo was surrounded by other women, Lexi's claws came out.

"All possessive and shit."

"So. You think I want hoes in your face while I'm sitting there with your dick on my breath?"

"Barely," he muttered. His dick was still irritated from her dry ass mouth.

"Don't be an asshole, Rahlo. You know I've always had a problem putting your whole dick in my mouth."

"Then just suck the tip like I've been telling you for years and save us both the embarrassment."

"Shut up!" Lexi hit him. "I'm coming."

"And the first time you start acting stupid, I'm going to

have Bruce put yo ass out."

"Whatever." She waved him off. "All I have to do is wave a jelly donut in his face and his fat ass will forget all about little ole me."

"You heard what I said," Rahlo warned, locking up his loft.

"Besides, you said it's a bougie ass studio in Browns-town. You know these hoodrats don't know nothing outside of Detroit city limits," Lexi jested, following him. "Can I ride with you?" she asked once they were outside.

"Nah, I need time to reset," he answered over his shoulder, stopping her in her tracks.

Rahlo didn't have to turn around to know that she was shooting daggers at his back, and he didn't care. Rolling her eyes, Lexi walked over to her car and pulled up beside him.

With his studio session on his mind, Rahlo sat down in the driver's seat and removed a neatly rolled blunt from his pocket. Placing it between his lips, he fished his pockets for a lighter and sparked the tip. Inhaling deeply, Rahlo pressed play on his steering wheel and allowed the allegro beat to serenade his ears. When the beat dropped, a grin etched across his face as words formed and flowed from his mouth with ease.

"Are you making love to a beat again?" Lexi yelled, impatiently waiting for him to pull off so she could follow him. "I can't believe you still do that."

Rahlo opened his eyes and glared at her. He was already regretting his decision to let her tag along.

"Shut up, cotton mouth," he spat before pulling off into traffic, leaving her sitting there with her dry ass mouth wide open.

Forty-five minutes later, Rahlo pulled up to the studio and nearly blew a gasket. The parking lot was full of cars that he didn't recognize. Women were half dressed and standing in line as Bruce picked out who could enter and who could get to steppin.' Terri was leaning against the building with steam coming from his ears. The once bougie studio now looked like a scene from a Ludacris video and it screamed Duke.

"About time you made it here. Do you see this shit?" Terri ranted as Rahlo exited the car. "I'm going to get a fine because your friends are trying to turn this session into a freaking *Girls Gone Wild* episode."

"More like a Uncle Luke classic," Duke corrected him, strolling out of the building. "I like my chicken rinsed and seasoned, if you catch my drift."

"The fuck is all this?" Rahlo quizzed, peering around the parking lot at all of the half-naked women.

"Last time we went to the booty and this time I brought the booty to you." Duke stretched his arms out toward the array of women. "Now I know how picky you are, so I checked their teeth, nails, and toes."

"I can't deal with this today." Terri shook his head. "Get rid of this line and please don't have people in the lobby. This isn't a damn club."

"Honestly, you need to take one of these hoes to the back and let them loosen you up," Duke suggested.

"And you need to get a real job. I'm sure being a homeboy doesn't pay much," Terri shot.

"Can yall both shut the fuck up, damn," Rahlo interjected. "Duke, clear the parking lot. Terri, I got it from here. I'll let you know when the session is complete," he said, walking away. Their bickering was fucking up his flow.

"It's a wrap on the set!" Duke hollered, causing a few women to suck their teeth. "Oh, hell nah," he scoffed. "Who invited Lexi clingy ass?"

"Shut up, jailbird." She flicked him off, bypassing the line of waiting women.

"Oh, hell nah. I know if her flat ass can get in so can I," a woman hollered out.

"How about you take that gray ass weave out of your damn head. You shouldn't be in a hurry to get old sis because that big ass booty you bought gone start sagging soon," Lexi retorted, bypassing Bruce. "What's up, big boy?" she teased, rubbing his stomach.

"Not those eyebrows. Are they supposed to be uneven?" Bruce countered, causing the smirk to slip from her lips.

"Nope, her shit fucked up," a girl yelled out from the line. "If you get me in, I'll fix them for you, sis."

"You wish," Lexi spat. "Stay yo musty ass in line." She flicked her wrist as she stepped into the studio. Rahlo stifled his laughter, watching Lexi twist through the door throwing her hips a little harder than she needed to.

"We love you, Rah!" A few women shouted out as he passed by them.

"Not as much as I love yall." He winked, licking his lips. The dimple in his cheek sunk into his face, sending the women into a screaming fit.

Inside the studio, Taylor rolled her eyes for what felt like the umpteenth time. When Kiki invited her to hang out, she knew there would be a lot of people, but this was simply too much. She was sitting on the edge of the couch with half her ass hanging off. The liquor in her system wasn't strong enough for her to ignore the woman on the arm of the chair that kept bumping her or the toxic smell coming from Candi's mouth. Taylor offered her gum, mints, and even a shot, but nothing worked. The foul smell mixed with the loud music had her head spinning.

"I'll be back." Taylor patted Kiki on the back as she stood.

"Where you going?"

"Outside for some fresh air. If Candi laughs again, I might die from suffocation. You need to tell her to pull that fuckin tooth."

"You wanna switch places?" Kiki giggled.

"No, I'll be back," Taylor practically yelled, already halfway across the room. As pretty as Candi was, Taylor couldn't believe she walked around with her breath smelling like a garbage disposal, and any man who entertained her was desperate as hell.

Rummaging through her purse, Taylor blindly walked out of the studio and headed down the hallway. She was in dire need of fresh air and a bottle of water. Just as Taylor raised her head, she collided with a hard body, sending her tumbling backwards. A pair of tatted-up arms caught her before her body hit the ground, and Taylor was thankful.

"Damn, girl. If you wanted another hug, just say that." Rahlo grinned, wrapping his arms around her waist.

"Boy, hush," she giggled, backing out of his grip.

"Where are you rushing off to?" he asked, allowing his eyes to roam over her from head to toe.

Per usual, she was dressed to impress. The jean shorts tightly gripped her waist and thick thighs while the graphic tee struggled to contain her breasts that spilled over the top. Braless, he watched her titties jiggle as if they had a mind of their own. On her feet were a pair of red Chucks with a gold anklet. Rahlo tucked his bottom lip into his mouth, thinking about all the ways he could twist and turn her body while she nutted back-to-back on his dick. Just the thought caused his member to stiffen.

"Uh, out of here." Taylor looked away from him. Rahlo's

stares were just as intoxicating as that dimple in his cheek. "There are way too many people in there and not enough breathing room." Taylor turned her nose up as if she caught a whiff of Candi's breath.

"Come keep me company in the booth," Rahlo suggested, not ready for her to take off on him just yet.

Cocking her head to the side, Taylor folded her arms and stared at him. The smirk on his face caused her to roll her eyes.

"You know I have a boyfriend, right?"

"So." Rahlo furrowed his eyebrows. "That nigga let you out of the house half-naked and smelling good. His fuck up is my come up."

"Ain't no coming up tonight, my boy. Good night." Taylor stepped around him, but Rahlo grabbed her wrist.

"Please come chill with me." He poked his lips out.

"What would my boyfriend say?"

"Tell that nigga to get used to it." Rahlo stepped forward. "I like the view."

"You swear you can take me from him."

"I can," he confirmed, stepping closer to her. "And when I do, I'm going to make your ass wear dickie jumpsuits and church clothes."

"Don't tell me you're the jealous type," Taylor teased.

"Nah, I'm the pluck a nigga eyes out of his head if he staring too long type," Rahlo warned. "Now come in the booth with me and give me some of that good ass energy that's oozing from your pores." He stuck his hand out.

"I know how to walk. I don't need you to hold my hand." She bypassed him. The last thing Taylor needed was for someone to take a picture of them holding hands and post it on the internet. Jasper would swear up and down they were fucking.

"Oh, hell nah!" Duke's loud voice rang out when he saw Taylor enter the room with Rahlo. "How the fuck yo mean ass keep finding us?"

"Us?" She squinted. "Ain't nobody looking for your crusty ass."

"I swear I don't like yo tight clothes wearing ass," he swore.

"Good because I don't like your scrub ass either." Taylor stuck her tongue out at him.

To defuse the situation, Rahlo placed his hand on her back and escorted her to the booth. Lexi watched from the other side of the room with a scowl covering her face. She had no idea who the girl was, but Rahlo had her fucked up. She was literally walking around with his dick on her top lip and he was flaunting a fake booty bitch all in her face. Lexi didn't care that their relationship ended before it ever really started. Rahlo was her first and only love if she had anything to do with it. With her sight set on the booth, Lexi took a couple of steps forward, but her path was blocked before she could cross the room.

"Don't start no shit," Bruce warned, reading the expression on her face.

"Who is that bitch?" Lexi snarled.

"I don't know and I don't care. I'm being paid to keep the peace. If you start cutting up, that's fucking up the peace and fucking with my money."

"So it's fuck me?" she questioned in disbelief. "We were just together and now he got another bitch in there skinning and grinning."

"That's on yall, Lex, but don't act like you didn't start this back-and-forth shit. You left. You went off and started this new life and came back pregnant by another nigga with your heart in your hands."

"So I'm being faulted for going to make a better life for myself?"

"Not at all, but don't think time stood still because you left."

"Whatever! You're always on his side. You are my friend, too."

"I am, but I'm also his security," Bruce told her. "So you can either sit down or leave."

"I'll sit," Lexi decided, knowing he was right.

When she decided to go upstate to college, Lexi packed up her old life and focused on starting a new one. She wanted more than what her city had to offer. Most of her childhood friends already had kids, and others were locked up or pushing up daisies. Lexi hated that for them, but with limited resources, they were only walking the path society deemed fit.

Her decision to leave wasn't an easy one because not only was she leaving her parents, but she was also leaving Rahlo. Leaving wasn't an option for him since he had a little buzz around the city. Even if it was, Rahlo swore college couldn't teach him skills that came naturally. Once fall rolled around, Lexi moved on campus and cut off all contact with anyone from her hometown for three years.

"Ugh," Lexi grunted, watching Rahlo stare at the mystery chick in a way he never looked at her.

In the booth, Rahlo dimmed the lights and pulled the stool to the middle of the floor. Taylor leaned against the wall, watching him set the tone for his session. She didn't know why she suddenly had butterflies, but between watching him like a creep and Kiki texting her, Taylor was nervous as hell, and according to the text on her phone, it showed.

Kiki: Bitch loosen up! You standing there like a damn statue. Unclench your cheeks!

Taylor glanced through the window and Kiki was wiggling her shoulders.

I'm nervous, she replied.

Kiki: *I see! It looks like you have to shit.*

"Op," Taylor laughed out loud and it caught Rahlo's attention. "My bad." She pressed her finger to her lips.

"You good, my baby. You comfortable?"

"I am," Taylor nodded. "It's a lot better than being out there with your loudmouth friend."

"So you just gone keep talking shit to that nigga?" Rahlo chortled.

"Uh, yea," Taylor bucked. "My daddy didn't raise no punk and I can tussle with the best of them."

"Well, ain't no tussling today," he assured her while adjusting the mic.

"It's not gon' mess up your sound with me standing in here?"

"No. Just do me a solid and put your phone on DND."

"Can I record you?"

"Nah, but you can snap a few pictures. The music I'm working on is for my album and I don't want any leaks."

"So I'm getting an exclusive preview?"

"Yep, does that mean I can get a kiss?" he flirted.

"No, superstar."

"Nah, I'm just Rah, sweetheart."

"Hm. Well, lay some tracks just Rah," Taylor said, picking up her phone.

Kiki: *That's better! Show them pearly whites!*

Snickering, Taylor glanced at Kiki and then did as she was told.

Sitting on the floor against the wall, Taylor watched Rahlo

tell the producer where he wanted to start. Once the beat started to flow, Rahlo closed his eyes and began bobbing his head. In a zone, he blocked out the outside world and thought about the rap he started in the car. Once he had it down in his head, Rahlo opened his eyes.

"Run it back for me," he told the producer.

Glancing over at Taylor, he grinned at the intrigued expression on her face. Like everyone else, she was waiting to see what type of magic he was going to add to the track. Once the beat dropped, Rahlo had an out-of-body experience as the words effortlessly slipped from his lips.

In awe, Taylor and the rest of the studio bobbed their heads watching Rahlo in his zone. As if he was the only one in the room, he rapped his verses with ease and then went back over them to plug in adlibs. By the end of the song, he had everybody on their feet trying to recite the catchy parts of his song.

She gon get dis hard dick

While I'm rubbing on that pussycat

Fuckin in the studio

Cuz music get her pussy wet

Bae I know you feeling me cuz I swear I'm feeling you

Might as well call that nigga cause whateva yall had is thru

"That made your pussy wet?" he asked, gazing over at Taylor, who was still stuck in his trance.

"No!" she yelped, lying through her teeth. Her pussy was drenched and she prayed there wasn't a wet spot on her ass. While the lyrics were fire, it was the muscles in his neck for her. It was the way his tongue glided across his beautiful front teeth that made her pussy wet. "Look, I know I'm fly and all, but the only thing I have to offer is friendship."

"I don't want it."

"You don't wanna be my friend?"

"No," Rahlo sternly replied.

"I'm in a relationship, so I can't offer anything more than that. I can give you my friendship, but that's about it."

"And like I said, you can keep that let's be friends shit because I'm never going to pretend I don't wanna get to know you on a personal level. I won't ever front like my end game isn't to get between those thick ass thighs and land a place in your heart underneath all them titties."

"Boy," Taylor laughed.

"I'm just letting you know what it is, baby girl." Rahlo winked, putting the headphones over his head. "Oh, and order us something to eat. We're going to be here for a while."

"How do you know I'm about to stay here with you all night?" She cocked her head to the side.

"You leaving me?" Rahlo gazed back at her. His eyes pierced her soul, daring her to lie and pretend she wasn't enjoying what was brewing between them.

"No." She swallowed the lump that formed in her throat.

"Good."

Chapter 6

Early the next morning, Rahlo pulled onto his mother's block and parked in front of her house. She had been calling him all morning, claiming she missed her only son, but Rahlo knew it was a ploy to get him over to her house. According to Terri, Emory ran through the money in her account and wanted him to refill it like it was a water dispenser. Rahlo told him he'd handle it first thing in the morning. He was used to Emory's money-hungry ways and knew that since he was making more money, her hands were going to dig a little deeper.

"What up doe, Chef?" Rahlo greeted, getting out of his car. "You out and about early, huh?"

"What up doe?" Chef did a quick one-two step, removing his top hat.

"Nothing much, old man. What you doing out here this early?"

"Looking for a quick buck to fill this pipe up," he rhymed, tapping his shiny dress shoes on the pavement.

"Chef," Rahlo frowned. Chef was someone he looked up to as a kid and seeing him out in the streets dressed like a Michael Jackson double would never sit right in his heart.

"Aye, that's my drug of choice. As long as I'm not stealing and killing to get the monkey off my back then I'm smooth."

"You eat?"

"I had an egg sandwich with a side of pussy this morning," Chef cackled, wiping the corners of his lips. "You'd be surprised at how many of these women like fucking crackheads. My mind might be gone, but this dick still lethal."

"Nigga, too much information." Rahlo shook the image from his head.

"You ever wonder why they used to call me Chef?" he continued, disregarding the disgusted look on Rahlo's face.

"No."

"Because I was out here serving dick and dope. If the pussy was hitting, they got a lil head too. They used to call me the one-stop shop."

"Ch-I don't even wanna call you that shit anymore." Rahlo dropped his head. It was too early and he was too sober to mess with Chef. "I'm about to go talk to my mama."

"You do that, but in the meantime, bless my hands."

Rahlo hated the thought of contributing to Chef's drug habit, but he also hated the thought of him begging a stranger for pennies even more. Reaching into his pockets, Rahlo pulled out a stack and peeled off a few twenties.

"Make sure you eat something," Rahlo reminded him. "Real food." Chef simply smiled and tap danced down the street with the thoughts of getting high on his mind.

After collecting his thoughts, Rahlo bopped up the stairs and pulled the door open. Instantly, he was greeted with the smell of fresh biscuits, bacon, eggs, and a few other delicious aromas. Rahlo opened his mouth to make his presence known, but when he heard all the voices in the kitchen, he was tempted to turn around.

"Don't even think about it," Esha said, coming up behind him. "If I gotta get drug out the bed to deal with her nonsense, then you do too."

"Who in there?" Rahlo whispered.

"Yo begging ass mama, her begging ass sister, yo non-rapping ass cousin, and his non-dancing sister."

"The fuck she call me for?" Rahlo snorted. Esha gave him a knowing look, and before she had time to help him escape, Emory pranced around the corner, looking like she was about to go to church on Easter Sunday. A hat, tight fitting dress, and gloves completed her look. Emory looked like the first lady who never stepped foot in a church.

"There goes my babyyyyy," Emory sang, stretching her arms out to hug her son. Rahlo shot Esha a look and she shrugged.

"What's going on?"

"What do you mean? I'm cooking for my baby." She released him.

"Em, you can't boil water, so I know you didn't cook." Rahlo stepped back, giving her a once-over. Emory had never been the cook a meal, bake a cake, tuck her kids into bed type. She was the leave a note on the back of the bill, don't leave out the house until I get home type. Esha was the reason Rahlo ate breakfast, lunch, and dinner.

"Boy, fuck you. I know Terri told you I took cooking classes." Emory twisted back into the kitchen where everybody else was waiting like Rahlo was the prize goose.

"And he told me they kicked you out after you threw water on a grease fire."

"Terri talk too much."

"That's his job," Rahlo reminded her. "How you doing, Auntie?" He walked around the table and placed a kiss on her forehead.

"I'm good, superstar. Thank you for helping out with my mortgage. Your cousin is between jobs, but we'll pay you back when I get my check on the first."

"Girl bye, that's chump change to my baby." Emory waved her sister off. Even if she did fork over the money, she was going to need it right back to pay bills.

"We family, Auntie." He rubbed her shoulder. "Sup, AJ, Aja," he greeted his twin cousins.

"Shit." AJ eagerly slapped hands with Rahlo. "I been working on my rhymes and when you ready, I want you to jump on my track."

"That's right!" Emory clapped her hands. "We about to have a family full of superstars. I'm going to be his manager. All you need is a catchy beat and know how to mumble with style. Rahlo can connect you with a few people."

Looking around the kitchen, Rahlo searched for a hidden camera crew because they couldn't be serious. Instantly, his temples started to throb. Not only was Emory reducing his craft to dust, but she also showed more interest in AJ's rap career than she ever showed in his. He could count how many of his shows she attended on one hand but always had her hand out when the check cleared.

"I know damn well you didn't get me over here with this fake Betty Crocker act because you think this man can rap." Rahlo glared in his mother's direction. He didn't mean for it to slip the way it did, but it would be a cold day in hell before he ever hopped on a track with his cousin. AJ rapped like he was struggling to breathe and had the nerve to rap fast and use rhyming words with comparisons that didn't make sense.

"Rahlo!" Emory hissed. "He's your cousin and he has a nice flow. All you have to do is sit him in front of the right people."

"Are you tone deaf or are those heavy ass earrings affecting your hearing?"

"You think you all that because you signed a contract and got a lil money?" AJ snarled.

"Nah, I'm all that because I can afford to pay your mama's mortgage before the deal and after. You damn near forty and talking about a feature," Rahlo scoffed"How about you go to Target and ask them for a feature? I heard the greeters got a raise."

"Are you calling my brother slow?" Aja scrunched up her face.

"He raps like you dance. Slow and offbeat. If anything, the nigga can make a TikTok and go viral for rapping like he gargling water."

"Rahlo! That's enough now. Your cousins just need a hand, and I thought since Terri helped you, he could help them." Emory nodded toward the twins.

"The only thing Terri can help them with is tickets to *America's Got Talent*. They always looking for bloopers and Tweedledee and Tweedledum are memes waiting to happen."

"Rap something, nephew," Emory encouraged, ignoring her son's obvious disinterest.

"Gimme a beat." AJ started bobbing his head. Aja did as requested and started knocking on the table without much rhythm.

"Uh." AJ bobbed his head up and down. "*Uh, my flow like water, the shit just flow and I'm the nigga with all the bitches call me G.I Joe*," AJ rapped.

"Make it stop," Esha laughed, now standing at her brother's side. Emory was standing behind him, nodding as if she resonated with the nonsense spilling from his mouth. In her tight dress, she dropped her hips to Aja's struggling boombox. The entire scene was hilarious, and if he didn't have a headache, Rahlo would've recorded them.

"These niggas can't see me, they wearing bifocals and I'm the type of nigga that will leave you driving in circles. Purple. That's the color of the dank and I only smoke good weed and that's something you can take to the bank," AJ finished, folding his arms as if he had just delivered a flawless speech.

"Yea, it's way too early for this shit." Rahlo caressed his jawline while staring at his family.

Since a kid, he had been big on family, even when family wasn't big on him. Since Emory was considered the wild child, she and her kids were rarely invited to cookouts, parties, or any other special occasion. They knew it was nothing for Emory to get drunk and start telling people how she really felt. There had been plenty of instances where she had to be dragged out with her kids in tow.

The only time Rahlo saw his aunt was when her hand was out. The twins only came around when Rahlo was giving out free tickets and Christmas gift cards. Besides that, he rarely saw them, and Rahlo was okay with that. He just hated it when Emory wanted to act like she had the power to make him put people on.

"Nah, I'm straight. Auntie, you have a good day," Rahlo said, turning on his feet.

"Wait!" Emory ran after him. "We have all of this food and-"

"And it don't mean shit." Rahlo spun around, making Emory's short frame run right into his chest.

"You better watch your damn mouth," she scolded.

"I came over here because I thought you really wanted to have breakfast, but I walk into *American Idol* auditions. Why every time I come over here it gotta be something? You need this, that person needs this, help this person."

"You better lower your tone." Emory hiked her eyebrow. "Since when do you have a problem with helping family?"

"Since I became the sole provider for muthafuckas' households. And what's this shit about you being a manager? You can't even manage to pay your own bills, how the fuck are you about to help that nigga?"

"For one, it's your job to repay the favor! I am your mother and you owe me for giving you life." Emory pointed her finger in his face. "And I'm a good manager, we just need a little help."

"Help?" Rahlo thumbed his nose in frustration. "Seems to be a running joke around this bitch. Tell me how many mixtapes did you help me sell? How many studio sessions did you pay for, and how many concerts did you attend? You want me to help everybody, but who was helping me?"

"Wow." Emory stepped back. "When did you get so bitter?"

"Around the same time you started treating me like your bank account versus your son," he snarled, stalking out of the house and slamming the door behind him.

Jasper punched into work and went right to his line. He hated working at Pieces factory, but the money was good and the job provided an ample amount of overtime. Being that child support took half of his check every week, he picked up every available shift. Sitting his lunch bag and jacket underneath his table, Jasper grabbed his orange safety jacket and goggles before hopping on his Hilo.

"Sup J!" His homeboy Nerd spoke.

"Another day, another dollar." Jasper stopped the Hilo to kick it with him for a minute.

"I'm surprised you here today. I thought for sure you'd be up Tay's ass right about now."

"Nah, I'm trying to surprise her with a trip to Ohio next week. She wants to take Trooper and Jalen to Cedar Point."

"That's what's up." Nerd nodded. "You better do something because ole boy on her ass."

"Who?" Jasper arched his eyebrow.

"Southwest Rah. He had some kinda party at a studio last night and your girl was there. They went live and the shit was rocking. I'm talking about liquor, weed, hoes twerking!" He clapped his hands for emphasis. "I wish I could get in with his niggas. They be having all the bitches. You think she can put a good word in for me?"

"Taylor is a good girl. I don't have to worry about no rapping niggas taking her when I have her wrapped around my finger." Jasper nonchalantly tossed his head back. He didn't want Nerd to know how badly his words affected him. The man was bothered and he needed answers.

"You might wanna check out the video. The nigga was all in her face and ya girl was smiling. I'm talking about ear to ear, all 32 teeth showing ass grin. If the nigga didn't hit it, from the way she was grinning, it won't be long. You talking about Ohio, you might need to dig a little deeper if you trying to compete."

"Fuck outta here." Jasper snorted as his stomach churned. "That's my bitch, the fuck I gotta compete for?" he barked. "Taylor not like the rest of these bitches."

"Yea, well I just thought you should know." Nerd hunched his shoulders. It was clear that Jasper put Taylor on a pedestal, and if he thought she was perfect, who was he to argue?

"Good looking." Jasper tossed him a head nod, putting the Hilo into drive. He couldn't get to the bathroom quick enough. Taylor swore that all they did was listen to music and vibe. She didn't mention a party, and she damn sure didn't say anything about being in Rahlo's face. Parking, Jasper jumped off the machine and hastily walked to the bathroom with his phone clutched to his side.

"Damn, nigga," someone called out. "You ate them gas station taco sticks again?" The person joked, but Jasper didn't have time to reply. His mind was elsewhere.

Once in the bathroom, Jasper locked the door and leaned against the sink. Signing into his fake Instagram page, he went right to Taylor's page. Unbeknownst to her, Jasper had a fake page and followed her on all platforms. He told her that social media was for young people and declared he didn't have enough time to check pages all day, but it was a lie. He stayed on Taylor's page, watching her every move and reporting pictures that he thought were too provocative. He commented about how she was too big to wear certain clothing and hoped that she'd delete the pictures, but she never did.

Clicking on her last post, it was a picture of her and Kiki standing in the studio. There were people in the background, but nothing jumped out at him. Switching gears, he went to Kiki's page and damn near had a heart attack. Taylor was sitting in the booth with Rahlo. They were looking at one another in one picture, and in the next, Taylor was laughing out loud and Rahlo's bottom lip was tucked into his mouth as if he was admiring the face that stayed buried in his lap.

The video took the cake. Taylor was dancing in the booth while Rahlo rapped. She wasn't twerking, but with her body, a simple two-step was sexy. Rahlo kept looking back at her with lust in his eyes, and Jasper was livid. The fact that Taylor was in the booth alone with him pissed Jasper off the most. Like she had special privileges or some shit. Taylor had him royally fucked up. She preached all that trust shit but was practically fawning over another man like hers wasn't working hard to take her on a trip. Deciding that he'd seen enough, Jasper stuck the phone in his pocket and took a deep breath before exiting the bathroom.

"You good, nigga?" Nerd asked, seeing the sick look on his

face.

"Nah, let them know I had to leave. I don't feel too good," Jasper answered truthfully. He was miserable. Seeing Taylor laughing and living it up with a rap star had him sick to his stomach. It was like dealing with his ex-wife all over again, only this time he wouldn't give up so easily. Jasper loved Taylor more than his next breath and living without her wasn't an option.

"Aight. Take care, bro."

"Same," Jasper shot over his shoulder, basically running out of the building without punching out or grabbing his belongings.

∞∞∞

Taylor rolled over and grabbed the vibrating phone. She knew it was Jasper because he had been calling her since he left. Even when she told him she was still asleep, he insisted she wake up and talk to him until he made it to work. Annoyed, Taylor resorted to balling up paper to create static on the line and then hung up. When he called back, Taylor told him her call dropped and she'd call him when she left out of the house.

To her surprise, this time it wasn't Jasper.

"What?" she answered.

"Eww, you still sleep?" Kiki yelled into the phone.

"I'm trying to, but Jasper been calling me all morning."

"What granddad want?"

"Recaps of last night, girl. When I got here this man was sitting up in the living room waiting like he was my daddy." Taylor rolled her eyes. "Mind you, I didn't get in until like four and he had to be at work for eight."

"Tell him to rub some Bengay on his aching ass knees and go to bed."

"Hush."

"He's getting a little too possessive for my liking."

"Jasper wouldn't hurt a fly," Taylor swore.

"A fly, no, but a woman that he's in love with? Yes. Especially if you're making moves without him."

"Does he get upset? Yea, but I'm grown, and he knew I was a social butterfly before we even decided to be serious. As long as I'm not out here fucking on another nigga then we're good."

"You sound just like the women on *Dateline* before the crazy niggas pop out the bushes and chase them down the street with a knife. I'm just saying don't take that jealous shit lightly. Women have lost their lives over it. It's cute for a minute, but Jasper takes the shit to another level," Kiki warned.

"I got Jasper," Taylor repeated. Jasper was a lot of things, but abusive he was not. He might've raised his voice, but he was as soft as cotton and the least of her worries.

"If you say so, but anyway. What's on the floor tonight?"

"Nothing. The fuck!" Taylor gawked. "I'm on the schedule later and after that I need to go check in. Trooper about to replace my ass."

"Awe, Troop Troop," Kiki cooed. "What my lil boyfriend been up to?"

"Sending me Cash App requests. I don't know who is worse, him or Jalen."

"You a good step-mommy."

"Bitch, don't call me that." Taylor rolled her eyes.

"So, are you ready to talk about Rah?" Kiki asked, getting to the real reason she called. "Yall looked real cozy in the booth."

"We were vibing."

"Vibing?" Kiki sucked her teeth. "Bitch, I was vibing. Yall was in there with stars in yall eyes and shit. I mean, the nigga was escorting you to the bathroom and everything."

"It was nothing," Taylor denied. Admitting that there was a spark between her and Rah would be admitting that another man had her attention.

"Girl bye! I can hear you smiling through the phone."

"I am not!" she lied, falling back on the pillows.

"Try again."

"Ugh. Ok, I think he is so fine, and girl, if I was single, I would've fucked him all over that studio," she moaned into the phone. "And then he was rapping to me. Bitch I don't even like rap, but I was about to bust a flow of my own for that nigga."

"So much for being loyal, huh?" Jasper gritted, damn near making Taylor jump out of her skin.

"What the hell! Why are you spying on me?" She held her chest. Taylor wanted to kick her own ass for even talking like that in his house.

"He's back?" Kiki whispered as if Jasper could hear her.

"What was all that trust me shit and you out here acting like a fucking hoe? Is that what trust looks like?" He advanced toward the bed.

"Jasper-" Taylor started, but he held his hand up to halt her.

"Shut up."

"Who the fuck his old sore back ass talking to? Mike! Find my shoes," Kiki hollered out. "Tay, you need to leave."

"I'm good. I'll call you back," she said and hung up without waiting for an answer. "Jasper, what are you doing here?"

"It's my fucking house, but the better question is, what would you do if you were single?" he quizzed. Taylor watched his jaw clench and the vein in the side of his neck throb. Jasper was pissed, and he had every right to be, but talking to Jasper while he was mad was like talking to a brick wall.

"It was girl talk, Jasper, and if you weren't sneaking up behind me, then you wouldn't have heard me." She rolled out of the bed.

"Then I'm calling your fucking phone and you in this bitch talking about fucking another nigga. In my bed!" Jasper yelled angrily as Taylor moved around the room like he wasn't talking to her. "Sit the fuck down!" He snatched the bag from her, breaking her nail in the process.

"Ouch," Taylor cried out, examining her bleeding finger. "Why would you do that?"

"Then sit down while I'm talking. That's the problem. You don't fucking respect me," he barked, jabbing his finger in her face.

"Jasper, move! My damn finger is bleeding."

"How the fuck you think my heart feels after hearing that shit? Got niggas at work showing me pictures of my bitch and another nigga." He pushed her. The hairs on the back of Taylor's neck stood up.

"Jasper, stop putting your hands on me," Taylor warned.

"The fuck you gon' do?" Jasper mushed her. "Call your daddy?" he taunted.

Ignoring his comment, Taylor picked up her bag off the floor and walked around him. Things were going left, and she hated to admit it, but Jasper was scaring her. It didn't matter how mad she made him, Jasper never put his hands on her, and she wouldn't sit around waiting to see how far he'd go. Grabbing her phone off the bed, Taylor wiped the tears from her eyes and slipped on her Crocs.

"Where you think you're going?" Jasper squinted,

following behind her.

"Home." She picked up her keys off the coffee table. "I'm not about to sit here and let you manhandle me."

"Stop being dramatic. All I did was push you."

"And that's enough!" Taylor yelled.

"You not leaving this house." Jasper pinched the brim of his nose in an effort to calm himself down. He knew he was overreacting, but he couldn't control himself. All he saw was the Sherri situation all over again and his heart couldn't handle it.

Taylor picked up her purse and headed to the door. All the blood in Jasper's body went cold as he watched her reach for the doorknob. In a flash, he was on her ass. Grabbing the bag, he yanked it off her shoulder, making Taylor drop everything on the floor. When her keys hit the ground, they both raced to pick them up, but Jasper was quicker.

"Give me my keys," Taylor sternly demanded, reaching for them.

"Didn't I just say you're not going nowhere? Go lay down."

"Jasper, give me my keys. I'm going to leave so you can calm down. This is not what we do, and if you put your hands on me, it's going to be a problem."

"Fuck calming down!" he roared. "You set this shit in motion and now you want to cry."

"Then let me leave!"

"For what? So you can run to that nigga?"

"Fine." Taylor wiped her face and turned to open the door. "I'll take an Uber."

Infuriated, he reached out and grabbed Taylor by the back of her shirt, slinging her onto the couch. He hopped on top of her when she was down, pinning her arms above her head.

"Let me goooo," Taylor cried out in frustration, but her cries fell on deaf ears. The man holding her down wasn't the Jasper she loved. This was the ugly version of him Sherri's deceitful ways created.

"Loyal my ass. Always wanna walk all over me." He gripped her wrist, digging his knees into her side. "Wanna cheat on me like I'm some soft ass nigga."

"I didn't cheat on you!"

"Might as well! You want to!" His grip became tighter, pressing the pandora bracelet into her wrist.

"Jasper, you're hurting me," Taylor cried, unable to break free.

"When I let you up, go lay the fuck down, and we'll talk about it when you calm down. Ain't no leaving. Do you understand?"

"Jas-"

"Do you understand?" he repeated.

"Yes, Jasper," Taylor replied. Kiki might've been right. A *Dateline* exclusive was probably in her near future.

Chapter 7

Rahlo leaned against his car with a bottle of water attached to his hand. It was a little after midnight, and instead of being at home, he was in the middle of Gratiot surrounded by intoxicated people, loud cars, and police waiting for someone to make a wrong move. The liquor store he was posted in front of served as a meet-up spot for partygoers who had left the club and weren't quite ready to call it a night.

Bruce was posted to his right with a mean mug on his face. He hated being on the scene, but since Rahlo was there, he was there. Duke, on the other hand, loved it. The hood, the women, the drugs, and gambling were his serenity. Duke was a hood nigga through and through and he wore it with a badge of honor. He was a few feet away, kneeling with his red cup in his right hand and dice in the other. A blunt hung from his lips as he talked shit every time the dice rolled in his favor. Hell, even when it didn't hit, he was still talking shit. It was actually his idea to hit the streets after Rahlo's studio session. Now that they were there, Rahlo knew it was the wrong call.

Niggas he once hustled beside were now looking at the

thick diamond chain around his neck like a meal ticket. It didn't help that their women were lustfully gazing in his direction. A few had even been bold enough to blow him a kiss. Rahlo, on the other hand, didn't pay them any attention. They couldn't be loyal to the nigga they were standing next to, what the fuck were they going to do for him?

"I'm ready to dip," Rahlo told Bruce. There was nothing out there for him, and with an interview, photo shoot, and a studio session just mere hours away, going home was the best move. Partying all night then getting up early to work was getting the best of him, and the last thing he wanted to do was be burnt out before he really started.

"Duke, we out," Bruce bellowed without hesitation.

Before Duke could reply, one of the men who had been watching Rahlo loudly scoffed, causing a few people to peer in his direction. All night, he kept stealing glances at Rahlo, waiting for an opportunity to say something slick. Never one to back down, Duke gave the man the attention he requested.

"Something in your teeth, my man?" Duke stood to his feet, stuffing his winnings in his pocket.

"What?" the man sneered.

"You got a problem?"

"Not you, ya mans." He grimed Rahlo.

"Damn, I thought you was checking a nigga out," Rahlo chuckled. He was low-key, but there wasn't an ounce of bitch in his blood.

"The fuck you say?"

"I'm saying it's bad enough your bitch been watching my every move, but you being all my grill don't sit right with me. I'm not into none of that three-way shit unless it's two bitches trying to take a nigga down."

"Time to go," someone shouted, knowing how the

situation was about to play out.

"Nigga, fuck yo wanna be Lil Wayne ass. How the fuck you go from trappin' to rappin'?" he snarled. "You think you Nipsy or something? Think you about to save the hood with your fucking toy drives and back-to-school events? This my hood, nigga! We don't need your help."

"Your hood?" Rahlo thumbed his nose before he let out a low chortle. "Nigga, you only making money because I found a better hustle. Don't act like you don't know how I get down. I'm still the same nigga that ran in ya mama house and made you run ya pockets. Ain't shit changed but the amount of zeros my accountant clear."

"Talk yo shit then!" Duke instigated. "We been running shit, the fuck you broke niggas thought."

"Nigga can't even rap for real." The man ignored Duke and continued to focus on Rahlo. It was clear who he had the problem with.

"Let me find out you jealous." Rahlo cocked his head to the side.

"Of what, nigga?"

"Of the fact that if I wanted yo bitch to suck my dick in front of all these people, she would. I think it might be the ice that got her pussy hot, but then again, the dimple drive the hoes crazy," Rahlo smirked. "Which one is it, sweetheart?" He glanced at the woman standing next to Mr. Loudmouth.

"Nigga, I'll-" he stepped forward, but about ten niggas standing behind Rahlo reached for their waistbands.

"You not gone do shit but move the fuck around if you wanna keep walking. I got a lil money now so I don't have to get my hands dirty. I got niggas who'll willingly do it for me. Luckily for you, I don't want your bitch. The bottom of her feet dirty and every time she laugh I see the cavities in the back of her mouth. Yall out here in matching Louie sets, but shorty needs a dental plan."

"I'll see you around." The man shook his head up and down.

"Bitch ass nigga." Duke moved through the crowd, pulling the gun from his waistband and pointing it in the man's face. "See him now, bitch!"

Whap!

The gun struck his face.

"Threatening my brother like I don't have a few screws loose."

Whap!

"Duke!" Bruce roared, snatching him in the air.

"Southwest Rah Bitch!" Duke ranted, throwing up gang signs as Bruce carried him to the car.

Rahlo shook his head at all the people recording them, knowing that the press and Terri were going to have a field day.

"Fuck!" he cursed, getting in the truck as Bruce stuffed Duke in the back.

Bruce started the truck and pulled off as Duke popped shit in the back. He was the only one who couldn't feel the tension and it was partly because he was drunk. For a few blocks, he was oblivious to the fact that he was the only one talking -and loudly at that.

"Yooo! I haven't seen you clown a nigga like that in a while!" Duke excitedly pounded his fist into his open palm. "I was starting to think them Hollywood ass niggas made you soft."

"Pull over," Rahlo gritted, clenching his jaw. Without question, Bruce pulled over onto the side of the road and Rahlo hopped out. Duke was confused until his door was snatched open and he was met with an icy glare. Knowing how things could end, Bruce slid out of the driver's seat and rounded the car.

"The fuck is up?" Duke frowned. Rahlo rubbed the back of his neck in an effort to stay calm. The last thing he wanted to do what fight his best friend, but just like everybody else, Duke had him fucked up.

"Let's get something straight...ain't shit soft about me. I pick and choose what I want to respond to because everything and everybody isn't worth my time and attention," Rahlo calmly stated. "I'm still the same nigga that will pop a grimy ass nigga between the eyes and then go to church and pray for mercy on his soul. Just because I'm not in the streets anymore doesn't mean them muthafuckas didn't raise me."

"Aight, nigga, back up." Duke stretched his arm out, but Rahlo slapped it away.

"I put myself in fucked up situations because I allow our friendship to cloud my judgment. I don't be in fucking clubs unless I'm being paid, and I damn sure don't hang around niggas that can't afford to buy my fucking shoestrings."

"So what, you too good to hang around the same niggas that we grew up with?"

"Yes!" Rahlo bellowed. "I outgrew all that street shit. I'm focused on making money and seeing the world. I'm Southwest til the death of me, but this shit is old."

"Outgrew the hood, huh?" Duke scoffed, getting out of the car, pushing past him. "Then I guess you outgrew me too?" He snorted, backing away. "If you don't wanna fuck with a nigga then just say that. No need for this long drawn out speech."

"I've never been one to sugarcoat shit. If I didn't want you around then you wouldn't be."

"Aight, boss man. I'm going to take the hint and move around. Everybody can't be a bodyguard like big ugly over there."

"The fuck I do?" Bruce held his chest.

"Duke, I'm not about to chase you, nigga. You not my bitch," Rahlo called after him.

"Good. Don't chase me, hoe. I'm going back to the hood. You know…where the broke niggas like me reside." Duke chucked them the deuces and bopped away without another word.

Taylor glanced down at Jasper's hand and rolled her eyes. It was going on one in the morning and they were still laying on the couch with his arms wrapped around her body and his head nuzzled in her neck. Every so often, he'd kiss her cheek and whisper in her ear. If it had been any other time, Taylor would have loved the affection, but he was literally making her sick. The feel of his breath on her neck made her skin crawl. Jasper had even went as far as getting her a ginger ale and crackers, not knowing he was the cause.

A week had passed since their big blow up and he had been up her ass worse than a thong. Jasper claimed they needed a little alone time to overcome their disagreement, so he lied to his job and told them his grandma died. The lie got him four bereavement days and tons of sympathy cards and flowers from his coworkers. When they asked about the arrangements, Jasper told them the funeral was in Texas. Taylor damn near died. She couldn't believe they simply trusted his word without so much as an obituary, death certificate, or anything else to prove he wasn't lying.

"Let me up." Taylor tried to roll off the couch, but Jasper kept her in his grasp.

"Where you going?"

"To the bathroom, damn Jasper."

"You need help?"

"No, nigga," she hissed.

Jasper damn near followed her all around the apartment, and leaving out of the house was out of the question. He apologized repeatedly but still wouldn't let Taylor out of his sight. Jasper wasn't stupid and knew that if he let her go, it would be like pulling teeth to get her back.

"You still feeling sick, baby?" he asked, sitting up.

"A little," Taylor hollered out before closing the bathroom door for a little privacy.

Sitting on the toilet, she checked the time on her Apple watch and sighed. She was supposed to be at work, but Jasper's clingy ass wasn't letting up. Pulling up her text messages, she shot Kiki a quick SOS text and flushed the toilet.

"You might be pregnant," Jasper proclaimed, tapping on the bathroom door.

"I doubt it," Taylor denied immediately. "I take my pill like I take my next breath."

"Damn, you acting like it would be a bad thing." Jasper shifted on his feet. Taylor pulled the door open and wanted to laugh in his face. She'd run into oncoming traffic or jump off the Eiffel Tower before ever having his baby. Jasper was clingy without any permanent attachments. Having his baby would be like signing her life away.

"I'm not ready to be a mother. I still have some living to do," she replied instead of telling him she'd be at an abortion clinic with bells on. As soon as they opened, Taylor would be lying on their table with her legs spread wide open.

"Whatever, man." Jasper sucked his teeth and prepared to call her on her bullshit, but the vibrating of her phone caught both of their attention. Taylor reached for it, but Jasper beat her to the punch.

"Do you have any other friends?" he asked, answering the

phone.

"I would say do you have a life, but I already know the answer. Your old ass is hanging on by a thread. I wish you'd just croak so my friend can be rid of your old shriveled up ass."

"That's the problem, you want her to be a hoe like you," Jasper snarled.

"And you want her to be old and miserable like you."

"Jasper, my phone, please and thank you." Taylor stretched her hand out, and Jasper reluctantly gave it to her but blocked her path so she couldn't move.

"Hey boo," Taylor cooed into the phone.

"He by you?" Kiki whispered.

"Yep."

"You ready for your way out?"

"Depends."

"Look, I'm outside and I have a plan. I moved your car with my spare key and I flattened all his tires."

"Bitch, you didn't," Taylor tittered, staring at Jasper, who was trying his best to listen to their conversation.

"I did. I'm about to break his window. When the alarm goes off, slide out the back door."

"No!"

"Too late, the shit already in motion. Five, four, three, two-"

Crash!

"What the hell?" Jasper jumped up from the couch and ran to the front door. Seeing his lights flashing, he grabbed his keys and ran outside.

"Run bitch!" Kiki hollered into the phone. Not putting much thought into the situation, Taylor jumped up from the couch, snatched her car keys off the end table, and ran out the back door without shoes.

"Where you at?" Taylor whispered in the phone as she ran through the complex storage area.

"I'm parked by the pool."

"Wait, who messed up Jasper's car?"

"Girl, Mike. You know my plush ass wasn't running no damn where," Kiki exhaled, tired from the idea of even vandalizing a car and then running to the other side of the complex without being caught.

"Oh my gooddd," Taylor cooed, getting in the car. "You saved me." She reached over the console and wrapped her hands around Kiki's neck.

"Of course I did. I just had to get Mike on board." She hugged her back. "Let me look at you." Kiki cut on the light. "Did he hurt you?"

"No, just all up my ass."

"You sure? Because I'll have Mike's cousins run in is shit."

"I'm sure. I can't believe he agreed to be a part of your crazy ass plan."

"I sucked his dick and swallowed his balls," Kiki shrugged, pulling off. "That nigga would've signed over his lungs if I asked. Now, where to?"

"Take me home," Taylor sighed.

Jasper wouldn't dare pull up at her granddad's house looking for her. Papa would shoot him and swear it was self-defense. For the first time all week, Taylor took a deep breath and sat back in her seat. She could just imagine the look on Jasper's face once he realized she dipped on him and only then did a smile form on her lips.

∞ ∞ ∞

"You gone be ok?" Kiki asked once they pulled up to Taylor's house. Sighing, Taylor looked over at her best friend and nodded. She was both mentally and physically exhausted. A hot bath and her queen-size sleep number bed were hollering her name.

"I'll be fine."

"Ok, text me when you're up to talking. I'll have Mike bring your car home tomorrow."

"Thanks again."

"No worries. You know how I'm coming behind you," Kiki said matter of factly. "He lucky I didn't bring the strap. I've been wanting to use my bedazzled nine."

"I thought Mike took your gun."

"He did, but I gave him some sloppy toppy and he handed it back fully loaded."

"Lord." Taylor shook her head. "It's a shame how whipped he is."

"That's what this good pussy do." Kiki tooted her glossy lips. "Bye bestie."

"Byeeee."

Taylor hoped to slip into the house unseen, but Kool and a few of his homeboys were sitting on the porch drinking beer and talking all loud like it wasn't damn near sunrise. As soon as she exited Kiki's car, Kool's nosey ass leaned over the railing trying to focus. When he noticed it was Taylor, he grinned and sat the beer down.

"I thought you moved on us, girl."

"Nope, I still live here," she assured him.

"You good? Where your shoes and shit at?" He examined her.

"I kinda left in a hurry."

"Anything I need to know?"

"Yea, if you see Jasper lurking, give me the heads up."

"Heads up?" he grunted. "I can do you one better. If I see the nigga I'll beat his ass and send him back to the other side of the tracks," Kool promised.

"Who we pulling up on?" his friend Rio slurred. "I'm really about that life the niggas rap about. I bust heads and asses all day! Point them out, Tay!"

"Nigga, pipe down. You drunk and know damn well you can't fight," Kool hushed him. "I'm with the shits too though, Tay baby. That nigga come over here if he want to, I'll light his ass up like it's New Year's Eve."

"No need for all of that," Taylor snickered. Kool would love to flex on Jasper, but those were problems she didn't need or want.

"Aight, on the strength of you, I won't leave that old ass nigga gasping on the pavement like he need a oxygen machine," Kool promised. "Get yo fine ass in the house, you too cute to be walking around barefoot. Got those lil piggies on the nasty ass ground."

"Kool! Stop flirting with that girl before I slap you," his girlfriend yelled out the window.

"How about you slap some edge control on your barely there edges? You got bionic ears every time I'm talking to a female, but when I tell you to get a job, you can't hear."

"She what?" Rio laughed out loud.

"Deaf as fuck. Bitch put her resume on Indeed and spelled her own name wrong. She needs to focus on that instead of what I got going on."

"Fuck you, Kool!"

"Stop cussing in my mama house!"

"Goodnight, Kool!" Taylor giggled, using her key to unlock the door. She glanced back at Kiki and mouthed thank you before sliding inside the house.

Chapter 8

Rahlo stood in the middle of the stage with beads of sweat rolling down his forehead. He tried to keep it conservative, but the longer he bopped across the stage, the hotter he became. When Rahlo removed his shirt, exposing his tatted-up stomach, the girls went wild. Some tried to hop on the stage; others tossed him business cards, pictures with their names and phone numbers, and even their worn panties and bras.

The concert hall was packed and Rahlo was on a high that drugs or alcohol could never match. The amount of love he was receiving was overwhelming and Rahlo thanked the man above for blessing him with such a gift. Recording in a studio was cool, but performing live was the shit. Half of the time, all he had to do was stand there and the crowd rapped the song to him.

"I done came too far to quit now, I'm on a everlasting high," Rahlo rapped and then held the microphone toward the crowd so they could finish.

"Fuck chasing fame and paper, I just want the peace," the crowd finished the verse.

"Fuck chasing fame and paper, I just want my peace," Rahlo repeated. "I fucking love y'all Detroit!" He bellowed into the microphone.

Once the beat ended, Rahlo thanked the crowd as they begged him for an encore. At the moment, he had nothing left to give. He was sweating like crazy and out of breath. Passing the mic to the host, Rahlo strolled off the stage with a small team behind him. Bruce was to his right, Lexi to his left, looking like she was ready to jump on his dick at any second. Esha, along with a couple of her friends, were near the end of the stage clapping and showing out.

Terri lagged behind, tapping on his phone and talking into his AirPods. While Rahlo was performing, he was off to the side, recording him with one phone and streaming on Facebook Live with the other. Rahlo didn't know it yet, but Terri started him a YouTube channel to generate another source of income. When he told Rahlo he was going to take him to the top, Terri meant it in every way possible.

"My brother did that!" Esha clapped her hands. "Literally, tell me who better, I'll wait." She popped her shit, knowing that her brother was the hottest in the game.

"He did that," Esha's friend agreed, licking her lips. She wanted nothing more than to lick the sweat off Rahlo's chest, but Esha made it clear that if they tried to fuck her brother, they couldn't hang with her anymore.

"You did so good," Lexi cheered, possessively placing her hand on his shoulder. She wanted it to be known that he was leaving with her.

"That's what I'm talking about," Terri praised, walking up behind them. "That right there is what I'm talking about. No bullshit, straight art! You see how much the crowd loves you, how much they soak up the energy you pour onto the stage. Tell me what new age artist is moving the crowd like this?"

"Nobody," Esha answered for her brother.

"That shit was lit huh?" Rahlo lazily grinned.

"Lit is correct!" Terri clapped his hands. "I just posted the video of your performance on YouTube and it's already at 10,000 views. And over 250,000 subscribers."

"Since when am I on YouTube?"

"Their platform is one of the most lucrative moneymakers in the game right now. Fans love to get a glimpse into the lives of their favorite celebrities. I know rapping is your thing, but you need to expand. I've made you a couple of social media accounts-"

"Aye, I don't have time to be changing status and liking pictures." Rahlo shook his head no. Thus far, he had done a good job dodging social media. Word of mouth and physically promoting himself had gotten him far, but with the help of social media, it could take him to the top.

"Then we'll hire someone for that."

"I can do it!" Lexi readily agreed, but both Rahlo and Terri looked at her like she was crazy. Rahlo would never give her that much access to him, and she knew it.

"Uh, I actually have someone in mind," Terri lied, shooting her down. "But right now, go celebrate," Terri encouraged. "Just don't go overboard."

"I got this, nigga." Rahlo waved him off. "We up!" he told Bruce. "I need two sections right by each other."

"We partying?" Esha raised her eyebrow.

"Like some fucking rockstars, sis." He draped his arm around her shoulder, leading her toward the exit. Lexi followed behind them, trying to stay separated from Esha's friends, who she thought looked like a bunch of thirsty groupies, but failed. Her feelings were hurt that Rahlo didn't seem to notice she wasn't at his side. Taking the L, Lexi dipped off to the side and called an Uber.

∞∞∞

As promised, Rahlo had the whole strip club jumping. Dressed in a pair of black jeans and limited edition Jordans, Rahlo stood on the couch shirtless with jewels sprawled across his bare chest. The ice on his wrist matched the diamonds in his grill, and a pair of cream, wood-frame buffs rested on his face. Lifting the bottle of Ace to his lips, Rahlo couldn't help but smile. He was giving off rap star and all eyes were on him. The moment would have been better with Duke there, but a break between them was much needed.

"This is wild." Esha's friend stood beside her rocking to the music. She had been to the strip club plenty of times, but it was nothing like this. The music ranged from new rap to old-school juke music. Drinks were endless and the flashing lights made her feel like she was on the set of *Paid In Full*.

"Girl, when Rahlo goes in...he goes hard," Esha told her, tossing a handful of ones in the air. "I mean, look at him," she continued. "My fucking brother is out here on some rich boy shit and I love that for him." Esha proudly smiled, watching Rahlo take another sip of his drink.

"I be fixin' the weave while she suckin' my dick. Pull it out then I titty fuck," Rahlo rapped along with Da Baby as flashes from cameras lit up his section. The dancer in front of him dropped down to the floor into the splits and made her ass cheeks bounce to the beat. With a sucker in her hand, she brought it to her lips and stuck her tongue out.

"I like when they pretty and ghetto," Rahlo smirked. The dancer wanted his attention and now she had it. Removing the sucker from her mouth, she slid it down her body until she reached the thin fabric that separated her thick pussy lips and

the floor. Sliding her panties to the side, the dancer inserted the sucker between her folds and twirled it around.

"I know you fucking lying!" Esha bucked, not believing what the woman was doing. "This bitch about to get a yeast infection."

Bringing it to her lips, the dancer popped the sucker into her mouth.

"Oh my damn." Bruce grabbed his dick. Nine times out of ten, the dancer wanted Rahlo, but from the freaky shit she was doing, he wouldn't mind spending a couple of dollars to fuck.

"Eww, y'all like that shit?" Esha frowned, disgusted.

Standing to her feet, the dancer made her way to Rahlo.

"What you trying to do, lil mama?" He licked his lips.

"I thought I made it clear," she cooed.

"Nah, I need you to be verbal."

"I. Wanna. Fuck." She boldly stated.

"Grab a couple of your friends and let's bounce." Rahlo grabbed his dick. Falling in some pussy would be the perfect ending to his night.

"You got it, daddy. Let me bank out and we'll meet you out front in an hour."

"Aye, pretty bitches. I don't do chipped polish and thinning laces," he warned her.

"Got it!" She laughed, mentally crossing a few dancers off the list.

"I guess I should call it a night." Esha rolled her eyes. "Yep, but I need you to show me something." Rahlo sat on the couch and scooted close to her. He pulled out his phone and started fumbling with the screen.

"What are you doing?" Esha asked.

"I need to look somebody up on Instagram," he slurred.

"Boy, what? Do you even have Instagram?"

"No, make me one."

"Oh god," she laughed, pulling out her phone. "Who is she?"

"This lil chick I met at that bar fight. I wanna find her."

"You like her?" Esha cheesed.

"I wanna get to know her, but she got a nigga."

"So then how are you going to get to know her?" Esha's face dropped. "Don't go breaking up happy homes."

"If it's so happy, then a little conversation shouldn't be able to break it up, right?" Rahlo rebutted.

"What's her name?"

"T-baby," he grinned.

"Her real name, boy, not some nickname you gave her."

"Taylor."

"Taylor what, boy. It's a million Taylor's on Instagram."

"I don't know her last name, but she work at that bar downtown. The one where Duke fought G. Top Notch."

"Speaking of Duke, did something happen? I noticed that he wasn't at the show and he's not here."

"Don't really wanna talk about it."

"Then just listen." Esha leaned in closer. "It's okay to outgrow people. Duke is still running around doing the same shit that got him locked up, but you're on a different path. You're destined to be great, and sometimes on the climb to the top, you have to clip all the extra baggage."

"Ain't tryna hear that shit, Esh." Rahlo waved her off, even though her words pierced his chest.

Knowing he got the message, Esha dropped the subject and went online to find the bar. When she located their website, she went right to the staff pictures. Without even having to ask, Esha knew which one was Taylor from the grin on Rahlo's face.

"She's pretty," Esha noted, digging Taylor's cute blonde cut.

"Pretty as fuck. That picture don't do her justice. Find her Instagram."

"Boy, we're sitting in the middle of a strip club and you want to stalk some girl's Instagram?"

"Yea." Rahlo bobbed his head. "Sounds about right."

It didn't take Esha any time to find Taylor's page. Passing the phone to Rahlo, he sat back and scrolled through her pictures. Her thick ass had his dick throbbing. There was no way God gave a woman that much ass, but there she was, flaunting that big muthafucka around like he wouldn't take her down. Like he wouldn't take her to Pound Town with a one-way ticket.

"Don't be hearting nothing," Esha told him. "That girl gone think I'm stalking her."

Ignoring her, Rahlo scrolled through Taylor's pictures loving what he saw. She was so confident that it radiated off the pictures. Her style was out of this world and he loved her hair. The short blonde pixie cut worked for her. The lashes and makeup were an added bonus, and he was digging the brown lip liner that outlined her full lips. He'd give his left lung to be able to smear it with his dick.

"Hm," Rahlo scoffed when he came across a picture of Taylor and a man. From the caption he knew it was her man, but he knew his future wife wasn't fucking with a nigga on social security.

"You ready, daddy?" The dancer returned, breaking his trance. Rahlo started to tell her to move around, but then he saw her friends. Handing Esha back her phone, Rahlo tossed Bruce a nod.

"I guess that's our cue," Esha mumbled to her friend.

"Bitch, I wanna go with them."

"Too bad," Esha sassed. "Brother, be safe and make sure you wrap it up. Check the condom before and after."

"No doubt, sis." He kissed her cheek. "I love you."

"I love you too, brother. Call me in the morning."

"Will do," Rahlo promised, tossing Bruce a head nod, who pushed off the wall and led the way through the crowd.

∞ ∞ ∞

"Love and happiness. Something that can make you do wrong, make you do right," Papa crooned, blowing smoke from his lips. "I used to get plenty of women to this song." He twirled his narrow hips. "Al Green had the ladies weak in the knees and they fell right in front of me."

"Don't nobody wanna hear that." Von turned his face up, waving around the smoke that floated through the living room.

"You should. You worried about that singing school teacher, shittt if I was you, I'd have all the honeys marching to my tune," he coughed. "Call me little drummer boy."

"Papa, you need to stop smoking," Taylor giggled.

"And you need to stop hiding." Von turned to his daughter. "Don't think I haven't noticed how you don't go out. What did he do?"

"Oh hell nah, get my shit," Papa yelled out. "Trooper, go get my gun and bulletproof vest."

"Papa, please," Taylor chuckled. "That vest is as old as you are."

"See," he pointed his index finger at her. "I almost forgot you were my granddaughter. Watch ya mouth. I might be old, but-"

"Please don't finish that sentence," Von cut him off.

Taylor listened to them bicker back and forth. They argued all day every day, but she knew it was all love. When her mother died, Papa jumped in the driver's seat and planned the funeral, helped Von move out of his house, and became a primary parent to Trooper. As much as Papa got on their nerves, he was a vital part of their tight knit family.

"Who wants some?" Trooper asked, strolling in the living room with Papa's army gear on. The bulletproof vest hung off his shoulders and the AR gun case was just as tall as him. With a helmet on his head, Trooper mugged them before he started coughing.

"It smells like a skunk in here." He covered his mouth and nose.

"More like purple dank, but you get the picture," Papa chuckled.

"Put that gun case down, and Dad put that joint out. You're not even supposed to be smoking," Von warned.

"Boy, I used to dabble in crack, coke, and shrooms. This lil weed barely put a dent in the shit I used to do. I would say ask ya mama, but she somewhere being a garden tool."

"Which garden tool?" Trooper wondered out loud.

"The one that sleeps with your best friend and blame it on menopause," Papa snorted.

"Dad!" Von hissed.

"Yall too sensitive." He waved them off. "And go put my shit back. Ya scary ass daddy not about that life."

Shaking her head, Taylor glanced down at her phone and ignored yet another call from Jasper. He was livid that she wasn't answering the phone or his follow-up texts. With Taylor taking a break from work, he had no other place to catch her. Whenever she posted a picture, it was from her bedroom, living room, or porch.

"You wanna talk about it?" Von asked, noticing the shift in her demeanor.

"Nope," Taylor sighed.

"Are yall still together?"

"I don't know."

"What does that mean, Tay? You're either with him or you're not. All of this new age mess gets people's feelings hurt."

"He's just been so clingy, Daddy. I love him, but I need space."

"It's nothing wrong with that. Jasper's already in family mode, and you're still trying to figure out your life. Space might be best." Von finished her sentence.

"And he's jealous as heck." She exhaled, palming her face.

"Usually, when a man is cheated on, it messes with their pride and manhood. Men, by nature, are protectors and providers. If a man is doing everything he can to provide for his family and he finds out his wife cheated, it's going to cause damage beyond repair. He'll become insecure and, in some cases, irrational, especially in his next relationship. You are still young, Taylor, and I never comment on your relationship, but Jasper is not it. You are out of his league, baby."

"He heard me talk about wanting to freak on another man," Taylor admitted.

"First of all, my daughter doesn't freak on anything." Von scowled. "And second, did you and the other man do anything?"

"No. I was on the phone with Kiki and he heard me talking about a rapper."

"How did he react?"

"He was tripping," she sugarcoated the truth.

"As he should have. If you're going to be talking about another man, make sure yours is out of earshot."

"I know for next time." Taylor rolled her eyes. Von kissed the top of her forehead and pulled her into his side. "I love you, baby girl."

"I love you, too. What's been going on with your music teacher?"

"Shit," Papa answered for him, limping back into the room. "They on some take it slow and get to know each mess."

"What's wrong with that?" Taylor quizzed.

"Everything. Why get to know someone and then they have bad snatch?" he inquired. "Then you in love and her insides feel like undercooked grits."

"Papa!" Taylor burst out laughing.

"I'm just saying. He should at least sample the product before he buys the whole damn store."

"I'm not buying anything. We're just getting to know each other," Von corrected his father.

"You do know it's okay to move on, right?" Taylor rubbed Von's arm. "Mommy wouldn't want you to be alone."

"I'm not alone. I have yall."

"Like hell you do. Lil missy right here is about to move in with her senior citizen boyfriend and Trooper is always on his game. You're quite lonely if you ask me."

"I got you then."

"No, you don't. I'm about to move to a nursing home. They

get more action than you."

"You wanna leave us, Papa?" Taylor playfully pouted.

"With the way them old biddies be cutting up in them nursing homes, hell yea."

"On that note, I'm going to sit on the porch for a while," Taylor said, standing up from the couch, but a wave of nausea made her sit right back down. Grabbing the empty chip bag off the end table, Taylor quickly opened it and threw up her breakfast. The chicken and waffles she scarfed down that morning hit the spot, but as her throat and stomach contracted, Taylor hated that she ever ate it.

"Arrrgghh," she gagged, pushing the chucks of meat up.

"Oh, hell no! I know you didn't get pregnant by that nutcase," Papa scowled.

"Get her some water," Von told his father.

"You get it. I need to hit my joint again."

Taylor held her stomach until the last of her breakfast emptied into the full chip bag. Bent over, her mind started to wander a million miles per hour. There was no way she could be pregnant. Most of the time, she swallowed his nut, and even then, she faithfully took her birth control. Taylor was so careful that even when she thought she missed a day, she doubled up or took a Plan B. Having a baby was not in her near future, and having one by Jasper wasn't even a thought.

"Taylor, are you pregnant?" Von asked, rubbing her back.

"No," she denied as she shook her head. "I'm not pregnant. I can't be pregnant."

"Girl, you sound like a damn fool," Papa stated from the doorway, blowing smoke out of his mouth. "Anytime you open your legs to a man with a working dick, there's a chance of you becoming pregnant."

"Dad, chill," Von warned.

"There you go with that gentle parenting shit again. Well, look on the bright side, ya kids already messed up. Maybe you can save the new addition."

"That's enough!"

"Don't fucking yell at me! You should be yelling at her ass. Sitting here throwing up and full of foots. I know one damn thing, she better not get that on my couch. Hell, moving to a nursing home might not be so bad after all," Papa ranted, walking back into the kitchen with a trial of smoke in his wake. "The hell I'ma do with one more kid?"

Chapter 9

"Whew, I'd hate to be in your shoes," Kiki expressed, holding her chest. "I mean, damn, you can't even get an abortion. Four months. How the hell are you four months pregnant and didn't know?"

Taylor shot Kiki a death glare and glanced back down at the papers in her hand. Four fucking months. A baby had been brewing in her stomach for four months and she had no idea. Taylor wanted to sue the FDA, her doctor, and anybody else that assured her that by popping dumb ass birth control, she wouldn't get pregnant. Was it 100%? No, but she was careful. Jasper even pulled out, so being pregnant wasn't on her mind.

"Oh god." Kiki threw her head back in laughter. "His old, hexagon shaped ex-wife is going to die," she rattled. Taylor's eyes filled with tears as she stuffed the papers in her purse.

"I can't have this baby. I don't even want it." She wiped her face. "Hell, after the way he locked me in the house, I don't want him either."

"Well, you heard the doctor. They can't do it because you are in the second trimester."

"Then trip me, drown me, bitch hit me with your car, anything, but I can't have this baby."

"First of all, I'm not about to hit you with my car. Mike just got me this one and he made me promise I wouldn't hit anybody else with it."

"You hit him!" Taylor bucked her eyes, recalling the moment when Kiki called her crying because Mike was in the hospital. Dropping everything, Taylor ran to her side only to find out it was Kiki who had put him there.

"Eww, the baby already making you mean. I bet it's a girl. I hope it's a girl because the world does not need another Jasper."

"KiKi."

"Ok, my bad. Let me be serious." She fixed her face. "I think you should tell him. If you don't want it, sign your rights over to him and go on about your life. Niggas do it all the time. Being a deadbeat mom is the real gem."

"This is just so fucked up." Taylor dropped her head behind the steering wheel.

"Awe, friend, don't cry. Jasper is a nut case, but at least we know he'll take care of his baby...and you, for that matter."

"Him taking care of us isn't the problem." She wiped her eyes. "I was really trying to be done with him."

"Then fuck it. We don't tell him."

"I just need time to think about it," Taylor exhaled, leaning back against the seat.

"Then think fast because ain't that his flat face sister?" Kiki nodded toward the clinic. Taylor glanced over and groaned. Sure as shit, Jada was walking out of the clinic with a little white aftercare bag in her hand. For a split second, Taylor thought about jumping out to stop her, but Jada looked like a deer caught in headlights.

"I doubt she'll say anything." Taylor looked away as Jada hopped in a car that Taylor had seen plenty of times. "Looks like she just had an abortion her damn self. I'm the least of her worries."

"Whew, we need to call this part of your life young and reckless. This some real life soap opera shit."

"Right. Small fucking world. Her lil hoe ass fucking Kool." Taylor shook her head watching them pull off. She knew for a fact her secret was safe. Telling on Taylor meant telling on herself and Jada wasn't stupid.

∞ ∞ ∞

Jasper called Taylor's phone once more, only to be sent directly to voicemail. He knew she still had him blocked, but it didn't stop him from calling. A week without hearing her voice, touching her, or simply being in her presence was literally driving him crazy. When Jasper wasn't sitting outside her job, he was riding by her house, but to no avail, he didn't run into her.

"Why are you sitting in the car like you lost your best friend?" Sherri asked, strutting over to his car.

Jasper had to do a double take. Never in the years that they were married had Sherri dressed so provocatively. The white mini skirt and crop top she sported hugged her body in all the right places. The red lipstick and fresh blowout had her skin glowing, and Jasper couldn't control his eyes. They wandered over her enticing cleavage and then lowered to her meaty thighs.

"Boy, stop looking at me like that," Sherri giggled, low-key loving the way his stares made her heart flutter. For once, he wasn't looking at her with disgust.

"Where Jalen?" Jasper cleared his throat. Bringing his eyes back up to her face.

"He's inside taking a nap. You can come get him up. You know that boy be acting like you when he's woken up out of his sleep," she suggested and then turned on her heels. Holding her head forward, Sherri switched away like Gloria from *Waiting to Exhale*. She prayed he was watching her ass bounce around under the short skirt, or she was going to kill Jada.

Rubbing his hands over his face, Jasper sighed deeply before exiting the car. Sherri was on bullshit and he didn't have time for it. His mind was boggled enough from dealing with Taylor and adding Sherri on top of it wasn't ideal.

"Man," he mumbled, getting out of the car.

Taking his time walking up the pathway, Jasper tucked his phone into his pocket and kicked a couple of rocks along the way. As soon as he opened his mouth to call out to Jalen, the cat caught his tongue. Literally. Sherri's hairy cat caught his tongue. Spread eagle, she laid on the couch serving pussy soufflé. Her small pink bud poked through her hairy lips and the sight caused Japer's stomach to turn. He wasn't used to all that hair anymore. Taylor kept her pussy waxed and smooth just the way he liked it.

"Aye, what the hell are you doing?" Jasper frowned at her.

"Showing you that young hoe ain't got shit on me. Come here," Sherri cooed, pulling her hood back to expose the rest of her pink bud. "Come taste me, you know you miss it."

"You tripping right now. Where's my son?"

"He's asleep, now come here. I know she left you, and I'm here to make you feel better."

Thanks to Jalen's close relationship with Taylor, Sherri learned that she hadn't been over to Jasper's house and didn't plan to return anytime soon. Taylor promised Jalen that she would get him next weekend and let him play with her brother. Sherri cringed at the excitement in her son's voice but decided to put her newfound information to use.

Jada told her to spice it up. Jasper was used to dealing with a younger girl, and if she wanted to compete, she needed to dress the part and show Jasper she could be a freak too. Sherri thought it was silly, but she allowed Jada to pick out her clothing and style her hair.

"No thanks." Jasper backed up.

"Wait," Sherri begged, closing her legs and rolling off the couch. On her knees, she crawled over to him and pulled at the waistband of his pants. "Let me make you feel better," she pleaded.

"Nah, I'm straight." Jasper swatted her hands away.

"Jasper, please," Sherri desperately pleaded, pitifully gazing up at him. When he didn't fight it, Sherri unbuckled his pants and pulled down his boxers. His dick sprung from the boxers and popped her in the chin.

"This don't mean shit," he told her as her lips wrapped around his dick. Allowing his head to fall back, Jasper closed his eyes and imagined it was Taylor on her knees pleasing him.

∞∞∞

Rahlo sat on the porch bobbing his head to the new beats his producer sent over. His new album was going a lot better than he thought it would be, and Terri was already putting together a small tour to promote it. The tour would go to Grand Rapids, Chicago, Cleveland, Brooklyn, Philly, and a few additional stops. Rahlo was geeked but low-key anxious. Different companies wanted to fly him out, other artists wanted features, and while it was exciting, Rahlo was still trying to process it. His rise to stardom was happening in the blink of an eye.

"Can I have a piece of paper?" A little voice requested.

Rahlo saw her, but he didn't hear what she said because he had headphones in.

"Helllloo," she sang, waving her tiny hand in his face.

"Hey, pretty girl." He smiled, removing the headphones to give her his undivided attention.

"Hi Rah." She shyly smiled. "Can I have a piece of paper?"

"Lily, I know you're not over here bothering people," Lexi scolded, walking up the sidewalk.

"She straight," Rahlo assured her, ripping a piece of paper from his notebook. Lily thanked him before taking the paper and running off down the steps.

"Whatttt," Lexi joked. "I remember when you used to bite my head off for touching your notebook."

"Because you used to ask for more than one piece."

"To write you love letters," she bashfully flirted.

"I remember." He winked at her, causing a lump to form in her throat. "What you doing over here?"

"Picking up Lily from my mama." Lexi sighed, leaning on the banister. "Thanks for the Venmo. I paid Lily's daycare up for two months and got my car fixed. I really don't know what I'd do without you." She leaned forward and kissed his cheek.

"No problem, I don't mind looking out for shorty," he replied. Lexi blushed and looked away.

"How was the after-party?" She changed the subject.

"Shit was lit." Rahlo grinned. "Why you dip like that?"

"Cause-" Lexi shifted on her feet. "I know them hoes were

all on your dick, and I can't handle all that. Plus, I didn't know if ole girl from the studio would be there," she probed, hoping he'd touch on the subject. "The label put yall together? I mean, do they do stuff like that?"

"Don't question me, Lex, you're not mine."

"But you know I wanna be." Lexi nibbled on her bottom lip. "I miss how we used to be."

"I'm straight," Rahlo shot her down for what felt like the millionth time.

"You're still not over that?"

"That?" He snorted, loving how she downplayed a situation that forever changed his opinion of her. "You left me Lex. You went to college and let a random nigga get you pregnant. All that shit was on you."

"Rah, I apologized so many times. I just wanted something different. I've been running away from Detroit my whole life, and what do I do?" Lexi scoffed. "My dumb ass got away and landed right back in the hood. I'm working at a job that I hate, I'm raising my daughter by myself, and sometimes I just wish I would've believed in you more. I wish I could've held you down." Lexi's shoulders slumped and Rahlo could tell she was on the verge of tears.

"Lex, I have plenty of love for you, but I can't focus on what we could've been. I'm about to start traveling, and right now, music is my bitch."

"What about later, like after you settle down? Could it be with me?" she desperately inquired.

"The fuck you want me to say? I don't know what the future holds."

"I'll take that." Lexi smiled at the glimpse of hope she thought he provided.

Rahlo returned his attention to his notebook, ignoring the

goofy grin on her face. He hated it when people refused to hear the truth so they picked up what they wanted out of a conversation to make themselves feel better. Fucking Lexi was one thing, but he'd never settle down with her. She was a sweet girl, just not the girl for him.

"Rah, you got a few dollars?" Emory asked, walking outside dressed like she was about to hit the club.

Her long weave was pulled back into a low ponytail, and like always, she was rocking nothing but labels. Emory didn't care that her shoes were Coach, her dress was Fendi, and her accessories were Fashion Nova. The point was she had it like that and dared anybody to question her bold accessories choices. Rahlo thought it was funny she was rocking a two thousand dollar dress she begged for and didn't even have half of that amount in her pockets.

"Aye, do I have the letters ATM stamped on my forehead or something?" Rahlo scrunched up his face. He kicked himself for even pulling up at her house, but oddly, that's where his writing flowed the easiest.

"No, but I have stretch marks on my stomach and droopy pussy lips from when they pulled your big head ass from my womb. Don't be like the rest of these stingy ass niggas around here. I raised you different, so act like it."

"Again, not my responsibility. Go find the nigga that you laid down with."

"Rahlo, gone with all that. I'm ya mama and ya daddy." She waved him off.

In elementary, Rahlo wondered why the kids in his class had a father and he didn't. They came to luncheons, basketball games, and parent-teacher conferences. Rahlo couldn't get Emory to attend anything, let alone a man he never met. At first, it didn't bother him, but the older he got, the more questions he had, and neither Emory nor Esha could provide answers. They couldn't teach him how to piss while standing up, to throw a ball, or even flirt with girls. Emory's idea of answering his questions was slamming the door in his face or telling him to go outside. Esha did the best she could, but she was still a fatherless child herself. Everything Rahlo learned about being a man came from the streets and men he saw on TV. It was truly the blind leading the blind.

"Hmph." Rahlo closed his notebook and shot Bruce a text. He was ready to dip. Emory and Lexi were fucking with his mojo.

"Hmph my ass. You mean to tell me that you're too bigtime to give ya mama a lil change."

"Here, man." Rahlo dug into his pocket and handed her five hundred dollar bills.

"See, that's why you my favorite." Emory leaned down and kissed his cheek. "Always taking care of yo mama. These other niggas could never." She went back into the house, stuffing the money in her pocket.

"Your mama is a mess," Lexi laughed.

"If that's what you wanna call it." Rahlo shook his head. He'd call her a lot of things and a mess was the nicest. Glancing toward the street, Rahlo saw Duke walking in his direction.

"Yall still not talking?" Lexi asked.

"Where you hear that at?" Rahlo glared at her.

"Around, but I understand. It's okay to outgrow people. You and Duke were best friends when we were growing up, but yall grown now. You have this budding rap career...what does he have?" she asked, watching Duke open the gate. Lily ran into his arms and Duke picked her up. Lexi's heart dropped. Rahlo heard her but wished she'd take her own advice. He outgrew her ass too, but she wasn't getting it.

"Boy, if you don't put my baby down," she snapped,

stomping off the porch.

"Shut up," Duke ignored her. Pulling a few dollars out of his pocket, he handed them to Lily and whispered something in her ear, making her giggle.

"Come on, Lily," Lexi snapped, damn near dragging her daughter out of the yard. From the porch, Rahlo watched the interaction and made a mental note to address it at a later date.

"Sup," Duke spoke, walking closer to the porch.

"Shit." Rahlo nonchalantly tossed him a head nod.

"Aye, about the other night. I was fucked up and I'm man enough to admit I was in my feelings."

"For what though?" Rahlo quizzed. "You acting like I don't look out for you."

"I never said that shit, but the same broke niggas you don't have nothing in common with, I do. I'm not out here making moves like you. I still nickel and dime, counting on fiends to get high for my next dollar. All you gotta do is wake up and your account is a little fatter."

"Nigga, what?" Rahlo furrowed his eyebrows. "I grinded for everything that I have. This shit didn't come overnight, the fuck!"

"I just need my own source of income. I can't keep letting you pay my way. I mean, shit, you gave Bruce a job, and I keep waiting for you to extend the same setup to me. It's cool bouncing around on stage while you perform, but I'm not some fucking hype man."

"First off, I didn't give Bruce shit. He's always been on some bodyguard shit. It only made sense for him to step into the role. The nigga not only drives me around, but he accompanies me to meetings, shows, and clubs. Everything that he gets, he earns."

"So why haven't I been offered a role?"

"Nigga, doing what?" Rahlo chortled. "You hot-headed as fuck and you don't like people. What are you able to bring to the table other than bullshit?"

"Damn, tell me how you really feel."

"When have I ever sugarcoated anything?" He cocked his head to the side. "I'm stating nothing but facts."

"Aight, I get it." Duke bobbed his head, clearly in his feelings.

Rahlo knew his words stung a little, but he was dead serious. Bruce was able to conduct himself in a room full of CEOs. He understood there was a time and place for everything, and he also knew how hard Rahlo worked to make his dreams come true. He was there to witness the blood, sweat, and tears, whereas Duke only heard about the struggle from behind bars. They were best friends and Rahlo would always have his back, but at the same time, he needed Duke to understand that there was more at stake and he had more to lose.

"Let me ask you this, what do you wanna do? Is there some kind of business idea you want to explore? I'll invest in your ideas."

"That's the thing. I don't know what the fuck to do. I've been in and out of jail all my life. The only thing I know how to do is hustle. Unless you trying to give me some money to flip, I don't know. I just want a role."

"Look, man, I'll see what Terri can put together for you," Rahlo gave in against his will. "But this shit is serious, and if you aren't going to take it seriously, then walk away."

"I'm down, nigga." Duke grinned. "I'll do whatever I need to do to stay on the straight and narrow."

"I hear you talking."

"About time you niggas made up," Bruce said from the

truck.

"Shut yo hog head cheese eating ass up," Duke jested.

"These hoes love a chubby nigga. Maybe if you eat a lil mo, yo pants wouldn't always hang off your narrow ass."

"Fuck outta here. Skinny nigga, big draws," Duke boasted.

"We know," Bruce chuckled. "That's why they always hanging off yo ass. Get yo cry baby ass in the car."

Chapter 10

Taylor posted one last picture on Instagram before pushing her iPad to the side. The pajama set she sported was comfortable, and she was thankful the company asked her to market the item. The cashmere felt smooth against her soft skin and the colors made her eyes pop. It had been a week since she found out she was pregnant, and for the first time, she didn't look half bad.

Throwing up and constipation had been a part of Taylor's daily routine, sometimes three or four times a day. When she wasn't sleeping, she was hovering over the toilet begging God to give her a redo. With only a small pudge, Taylor looked bloated to the naked eye, but to those close to her, it showed. The only reason she was up posting was because the company was offering double what she normally charged, and being that most of her followers were thick girls, Taylor had no doubt the company would sell out of the cute pajama sets.

"Tay, you want to eat? Papa made chicken," Trooper asked, tapping on her door.

"Yea. When he makes my plate, bring it up."

"You want juice or water?"

"Water," she replied. "Thanks, Troop."

"Welcome, and I wanna use your card," he sang, closing the door behind him.

Taylor snickered, knowing he wasn't doing anything for free. Trooper was one of the most hustling lil boys she knew. There were plenty of times Von or Papa had to pick Trooper up from school because he was selling Kool-Aid and sugar in the bathroom. Von was pissed off, but Papa appreciated his hustler instinct.

While she waited for her food, Taylor scrolled Instagram on her phone, hearting comments and laughing at the negative ones. She was used to the hecklers coming for her body and shaming her for the confidence she possessed. Some were men, mad that she wouldn't reply to their messages, and others were women who wished they had the confidence to live in their skin so freely. Just as she was about to log off, the new notification caught her attention. No one other than Rahlo was sliding in her DMs.

SouthwestRah: Let me get your number baby girl.

Staring at the screen, Taylor tried to control her thumping heart.

Taydoesitbest: Why?

SouthwestRah: To call yo fine ass, the fuck?

Taydoesitbest: I don't think that's a good idea. You already said you don't wanna be my friend, why would I give you my number?

SouthwestRah: If I say I'll take yo whack ass friendship can I have your number?

"Oh my god," Taylor laughed out loud.

Taydoesitbest: LMFAO! Why my friendship gotta be whack?

SouthwestRah: Cause a nigga tryna get to know you and you blocking yo blessing.

Taydoesitbest: Who says you're a blessing?

SouthwestRah: God did.

Taylor chewed on her bottom lip. She was pregnant as hell and knew she didn't need that type of drama in her life, but her fingers moved to send the number as if they had a mind of their own. Taylor didn't have time to think about what she'd done because a FaceTime from an unknown number popped up on her screen.

"Oh my goddd. Why would this man FaceTime me," Taylor squealed but still found herself answering the call.

"And here I was thinking you was scary," Rahlo's deep voice teased the second her face appeared on his screen. He was surprised she even picked up the call.

"Boy bye." She playfully rolled her eyes. "Who FaceTime's someone as soon as they get the number?"

"Me."

"You skipped a few steps."

"I ain't feel the need to text and do all that back-and-forth shit. I know what I want, it's you that needs to stop fighting fate."

"You can't flirt with me. We're friends, remember," Taylor reminded him.

"You're so fucking pretty T-baby. Like I could stare at yo fine ass all night." Rahlo ignored her comment. As far as he was concerned, she could keep that let's be friends shit to herself. There was nothing friendly about the things he wanted to do to her. "You got lip fillers or are those your real lips?"

"What the hell?" she snickered. "These are my real lips, fool."

"Aye, I gotta ask. You'd be surprised by some of the women I ran into. Like it's one thing to wake up next to a wig, but to wake up to deflated lips is a different story."

"You lying!" Taylor laughed even harder.

"Dead ass. Shorty whole top lip was gone," he grunted as if he was still pissed about it. "I'm a sucker for big lips and felt bamboozled as fuck."

"That's sick." Taylor twisted her lips. "But these are my natural lips."

"Hm." Rahlo's eyes lowered, studying her mouth. "Blow me a kiss."

"Friends, Rahlo, remember?"

"Nah," he sexily slid his tongue across his teeth. "I said that to get the digits. I'm still on that ass, pretty girl."

"I have a boyfriend," she uttered.

"Ask that nigga if he wanna fight."

"Oh my god," Taylor giggled. "Be serious."

"I am, but that nigga don't have shit to do with me, but you keep bringing him up."

"He has nothing to do with you but everything to do with me, and you can't just be calling me all times of the night," she warned, pulling her lip into her mouth.

"Why not?" Rahlo asked, popping a couple of Lemonheads in his mouth. "You don't live with the nigga."

"And how do you know that, Mr. Cleo?"

"Your Instagram."

"Are you stalking me?" Taylor sat up, adjusting the pillow between her legs.

"Not at all. You put the shit on the internet for people to see, and I'm one of those people who analyzes everything, and from what I see, you really don't like the nigga. Shit, you don't even live with him."

"I don't?" Taylor quizzed, intrigued by the bullshit spilling from his lips.

"Nah, you don't. See, you was waiting for a nigga to come and snatch you from granddad."

"Rahlo!" She laughed out loud. "Why would you call my boyfriend a granddad?"

"Why would you call his old ass a boyfriend?" he snorted. "That nigga hasn't been a boy since he walked in the million-man march."

"Oh you hating?"

"Like a muthafucka," Rahlo admitted, making them both laugh.

"Whatever, so how you know I don't live with him?"

"Because your bedframe is pink and lined with rhinestones," he started. "You have a neon light above your bed that spells out your name and a lot of fuzzy pillows, like the one you're holding now," he noted. "When you're over at granddad's house, the headboard looks old and boring as hell, just like him."

"Oh hell nah, let me start taking these pictures down. Wait, you have Instagram? I couldn't find you."

"I didn't. I had my sister follow you and I went through your pictures. I only made one today so I could talk to you."

"Stalking ass," Taylor goaded, low-key swooning at the thought of him going through her pictures and remembering details.

"Something like that. You have a son?"

"No," she shook her head. Technically, it wasn't a lie because she didn't know what she was having. Hell, if it weren't for her constantly throwing up or her growing belly, Taylor would have hidden it until the baby popped out her ass while she was at brunch. "That's my little brother Trooper on my page."

"Oh, ok." He sighed in relief. "I thought we was about to dealing with that old nigga until lil homie turned 18."

"I do have a stepson though."

"He don't count because when you leave granddad, he can take his snotty nose son with him."

"Op, don't talk about Jalen, he's my baby."

"For now," Rahlo said, looking down at his watch. "It was nice talking to you, beautiful, but I gotta go. These niggas in the studio waiting."

"You called me in the middle of your session?"

"Yea. You posted yourself in those little ass pajama shorts and I had to let you know what's up."

"It's work."

"That's how I know ya nigga weak. Ain't no way you about to be posting all that sexy shit online. I'd be in every picture wishing a nigga would."

"It's called trust."

"It's called being a damn fool," Rahlo grunted. "I want you to come to my listening party."

"Why?"

"Because I know you'll be honest."

"Can I bring my boyfriend?" Taylor asked.

"You know damn well Mr. Rogers old ass ain't about to sit in a studio. Old people don't like loud music."

"Rahlo," Taylor laughed out loud. "Can you please stop calling him old?"

"Then stop bringing his old ass up. Second thought, yea, bring pops. I want him to see me take his girl. Ain't no shame in my game."

"Anyway, have a good session, and I'll think about it."

"Aye, lock my number in your phone."

"What makes you think I want your number saved in my phone," Taylor sassed.

"Because you know that old nigga not making you smile like this."

"Whatever, Rahlo."

"Mm. My name even sounds different rolling off your tongue. I need to get you in the studio so I can record that. *Rahlo*," he mocked her.

"Let me find out that's how you game all the girls."

"Nah," Rahlo denied, gazing at her. "Only you." He winked. Unable to take anymore, Taylor hung up the phone and fell back in her bed. Closing her eyes, she smiled at the thought of standing beside him in the studio. She couldn't sing for shit, but that's what auto-tune was for.

"Trooper!" She suddenly called out. "Where is my plate?"

"I'm coming, lil hungry," he yelled back, using his foot to kick her door open. Taylor looked down at the plate and frowned.

"Where's the rest?" She gazed down at the food on her plate or lack of food.

"Papa said eat this and if you don't throw up, he'll give you more."

"PAPA!" Taylor whined, staring at the scoop of rice, half of a wing, and a few pieces of corn.

"I said what I said. Eat that and I'll give you a little more," Papa replied, walking past her room.

"Told you!" Trooper shrugged. "Your card please." He held out his hand.

"Y'all make me sick." She rolled her eyes but reached on her nightstand and handed him the card.

∞∞∞

Jasper clamped his eyes shut as he pounded into Sherri from behind. Once again, he went to pick up his son and got caught in her hairy fly trap. Even if he wanted to turn it down, he couldn't, Jasper was used to fucking two or three times a day, and with Taylor MIA, the palm of his hand was sore and his balls were full.

"Yes, Jasper," Sherri moaned, throwing her ass back to meet his rapid thrusts. She hated to admit it, but Jasper had learned some new moves since their divorce. Back when they were together, Jasper was big on missionary, but now he fucked her from the back, the side, and with her legs pinned to the wall. His dick was taking her to new heights, and Sherri prayed Taylor never came back into the picture because she was sure she couldn't give it up.

"Shut up," Jasper snapped, annoyed at her attempts to sound sexy. Sherri had never been vocal and she was fucking with the images behind his closed lids. He might've had his dick in Sherri, but in his mind, he was fucking Taylor. Just the thought of her glossy lips and thick round ass sent him over the edge.

"Ah shit," Jasper grunted, pulling out and releasing his load on the bed. Breathless, he fell back against the headboard and closed his eyes. This had been his routine. Right after the last drip of nut leaked from his dick, guilt hit his body and soul like the plague. Fucking Sherri made him feel dirty, yet every time she opened her legs, he slid between them.

While his eyes were closed, Sherri took the opportunity to grab her phone from the other side of the bed. Quickly opening it, she snapped a few pictures before Jasper opened his eyes. Staring at her with disgust, he stood from the bed and started snatching his clothes off the floor. Sherri rolled her eyes to the sky, knowing what type of time he was on.

"Go get Jalen ready," he demanded, refusing to look in her direction.

"If you gon' act like this every time we have sex, then maybe we should stop," Sherri snapped, tired of him playing the victim. "I mean, I didn't make you lay down with me, Jasper."

"Look, just get my son so we can go home."

"What about this home, Jasper? I think we need to talk about us and the home we made." She crossed her arms under her naked breasts.

"We ain't no fucking family. You cashed in that card to fuck a nigga from your gym."

"Because you wasn't fucking me like this!" Sherri yelled. "You wasn't loving me the way you love her! It's like I got the shitty version of you, and she gets the best pieces of you. Am I supposed to keep sitting back and just watch her take my life?"

"Yea, I'm about to head out because I'm not about to do this with you." Jasper shook his head.

"Why? Huh? Why didn't you fight for us?" Sherri cried. "Why would you just walk away so easy?"

"Sherri, lower your voice," he gritted through clenched teeth.

"No. I don't care! My son gets to watch you love another woma-"

"Because you cheated, Sherri," Jasper barked, making Sherri jump back. "Riddle me this," he walked up on her.

"Did you ever change anything for me? No. You didn't start changing until another nigga noticed you. You were tired of missionary, but when did I find out, huh? Marriage counseling! You wanted dates but also wanted this big ass house and private dance lessons and shit. So while you were busy telling another nigga how neglected you were, I was busy trying to give you everything you wanted, but it still wasn't good enough."

"Jasper-"

"This family was over the second you started changing to impress another nigga. Bring my son outside." Jasper snatched his keys off the dresser and bypassed her, not caring for the tears and soft whimpers coming from her mouth. As far as he was concerned, she could go find another nigga to dry her tears because he'd never dry them again.

Jasper stalked out of the house, pissed off that Sherri even thought she had a chance. Fucking her was one thing, but rekindling a marriage he didn't fuck up was another. Then there was Taylor. They were into it, but she was his baby, and although she was mad, he knew their separation was temporary.

"Hey brother," Jada greeted, walking up the sidewalk with a couple of bags in her hand. Lifting his head, Jasper cursed under his breath but played it cool. "What you doing over here?"

"Getting my son."

"Uh-huh. Taylor still must be mad at you," she smirked, sensing his sour mood.

"You and Sherri both need to find some business and stop discussing mine."

"Boy bye. You my brother, so your business is my business, and while we're talking, Sherri told me yall are trying to rekindle things."

"Sherri a bald face lie. I'm not trying to rekindle shit with her."

"Hm." Jada snorted. "Then why are you over here sleeping with her every chance you get? I think that's wrong."

"Mind your business, Jada."

"My nephew's well-being is my business. It can't be healthy seeing you go back and forth. You know he watches everything you do."

"And you're annoying as fuck," he rebutted just as Jalen bounced out of the house with his backpack strapped to his back and his iPad tucked under his arm. Sherri stood behind him wearing Jasper's t-shirt and leggings.

"There goes my big boy," Jada cooed. Jalen jumped off the porch and ran into her waiting arms.

"Hi TT."

"Be good for your daddy, Jalen," Sherri called after him.

"I will. I hope we see Taylor this weekend. I miss her," he rattled, running to the car. Sherri rolled her eyes behind his back and Jada laughed.

"We're going to go see her," Jasper promised. Jada stopped laughing as Sherri gave him the finger.

She felt slighted. There she was, standing with his dick on her breath and her insides stretched, and he was talking about visiting another woman as if he wasn't just taking her to Pound Town. As if her pussy juices weren't dripping from his sack.

"Girl, forget him." Jada held up the bags. "Let's go drink so I can tell you this tea."

"Ow, is it hot?"

"Blazin' hot," she exhaled. "Grab some glasses and meet me in the living room."

Chapter 11

"I honestly don't know why we're friends," Taylor grunted, walking alongside Kiki and Candi.

Somehow, she let them talk her into attending Rahlo's pre-listening party. According to Hot 107.5, it would be the party of the year. Not only would Rahlo do a live performance, but his manager got Kash Doll and a few other Detroit artists to drop by and do a song or two. What was supposed to be a low-key listening party had turned into a mini-concert, and everybody who was somebody wanted to be there.

"Stop with the dramatics." Kiki waved her off. Taylor might as well have been mute because Kiki didn't hear a thing she said. She was going to the party, if not to snatch a man, then to pass a few of her business cards out to some of the plus-size ladies. "He personally invited you to his listening party and you think I wasn't about to jump on the opportunity to go? You already stole my man, the least you could do is put me in the same room with other niggas on his level."

"Period," Candi agreed. "I wanted Rah too, but since he's all up your ass, I need to see what else is out there."

"Wait," Taylor paused. "Don't both of yall have a man?"

"A what?" Candi frowned. "Girl ain't no ring on this manicured finger. As long as I'm unwed, I'm free to hop in niggas' beds."

"Period!" Kiki clapped her hands.

"Kiki bye. Let Mike try that shit."

"And I'll slice his ass from head to toe and send his body parts to all the bitches he calls himself fucking with. Sharing is caring, right?"

"You're sick," Taylor replied, knowing that Kiki would do just that.

As soon as they turned the corner, Taylor wanted to slap Kiki and Candi. Not only was she battling morning sickness, but she allowed Kiki to dress her up and drag her out of the house to be surrounded by men she couldn't have, weed she couldn't smoke, and liquor she couldn't indulge in, and now she was expected to stand in line beside half-naked women who had on way too much perfume and pounds of makeup.

"Nope, I'm not about to stand here." Taylor shook her head. "Yall go ahead, I'll take an Uber back home." She turned around to walk away, but Kiki stepped in front of her.

"Girl, you were personally invited by Rahlo himself," Kiki said loud enough for everyone to hear her. "We are not about to stand in this line." She strutted right past the line with Candi on her heels. Once they made it to the door, Taylor listened to a woman promising to give the guard some pussy if he let her in.

"So what's up? Are you going to let me in or not?" the girl asked, twirling her braid around her finger.

While she flirted, Taylor took the time to take in her appearance and knew off-rip that she wasn't getting past the door no matter what she promised. Her weave was stiff, and from the back, you could see the tracks that were barely hanging on. Her outfit was a few sizes too small, which caused her stomach to look bigger than it actually was, and her ankles were ashy. She should've tried a little harder if she was trying to get into a party with celebrities and other top-name people.

"Not." The guard turned his nose up at her.

"Ah, excuse me. We're on the list," Kiki cut in.

"Ain't no list, big sexy." The guard eyed her, liking what he saw. "I'm the deciding factor and right now there are about thirty people ahead of you. You wanna do something to change my mind?"

"No sir. You are barking up the wrong tree. I'm not about to offer you some pussy or any type of sexual favors to get in this party. Lowering my standards for a free drink and finger foods could never be me."

"Excuse me?" The girl frowned.

"Didn't he just tell yo ashy ass that you weren't getting in?" Kiki snapped. "Why are you still standing here and breathing all in my ear at that?"

"Girl, fuck yo big ass."

"Sis, you big too. The only difference is I slay my shit and you look like a stuffed animal. Back the fuck up."

"Yall hoes can't be fighting in here," a deep voice said, stepping around the corner. Taylor scowled. She knew his loudmouth ass from anywhere.

Duke rounded the corner, looking as if he had just stepped off the cover of GQ. No longer was he wearing baggy clothes that hung off his ass or reeking of liquor and weed. With a fresh cut and rocking a custom blue suit, Duke was handsome and cleaned up well.

"Ah hell," he groaned, seeing Taylor and Kiki standing there. "I should have known yall manly asses was in the center of some bullshit."

"Boy, fuck you. I guess because somebody bought you a suit and paid for your nappy ass head to get cut, you think you all that," Taylor snapped, not in the mood for his bullshit.

"Are you the butler or something? If so, open up this door and get me a drink while you're at it," Kiki added.

"Fuck both of yall bald headed asses." He told Rahlo he looked like a Jeffrey reject, but Rahlo told him to suck it up. There was no way he was attending his party in black Air Force Ones.

"Can you just go get Rahlo?" Taylor snapped, tired of going back and forth with him. It was past her snack time, and she was ready to call it a night.

"You better be lucky he told me to come look for your funny shaped head ass," Duke snarled, opening the door for them.

"Awww, they gave the bum a job," Kiki taunted.

"Fuck yo fat ass."

"Nigga, you couldn't handle it if I gave you the instructions." She blew him a kiss. A few women in the hallway snapped and clapped their hands, causing Duke to stare in their direction.

"The fuck yall ugly asses cosigning for?" he glared. "Yall can't even get in," he laughed and shut the door in their faces.

Once inside, Taylor's eyes scanned the room in amazement. She had been invited to plenty of industry parties but always turned them down. Being an influencer who moonlighted as a waitress at one of the hottest bars in Detroit came with invites to almost everything. Kiki sometimes went to rub elbows with baller wives and boss bitches, but Taylor always declined. Now that she was in the beautifully decorated room, she kicked herself for missing out on so much.

"Bitch, this is tight!" Kiki loudly whispered.

"Swear," Candi agreed. "A bitch should have pulled out the

red bottoms for this."

"Nah, they fine right where they at." Kiki waved her hand in the air. "You wear them bitches so much that red done turned to purple," she said seriously, making Taylor laugh.

"Don't be a hater. I got those for prom." Candi tooted her lips.

"Bitch, you damn near thirty! Hang them muthafuckas up. Prom done came and gone and you still holding onto them bad boys," Kiki continued.

"You know what-" Candi stood tall and picked invisible lint from her all-black body suit. "I'm going to go find me a drink and a nigga with a lil money."

"Sounds like a plan. Maybe he can replace your prom shoes," Kiki teased, sticking her tongue out. Candi gave her the middle finger and walked off in the other direction.

"Why you play so much?" Taylor bumped Kiki with her hip.

"No, why she play so much? Bitch talking about prom shoes. Sis need to hang them up or store them shits in a box for memories."

"Her breath smells better."

"I told her she needed to do something about it if she wanted to hang with us, told her she needed to floss and use a lil mouthwash."

"You didn't!" Taylor laughed out loud.

"I did. She wanna be a part of the bad girls club so her breath needs to be up to par."

"You play way too much."

"Anyway, do you want a sho-" Kiki started but stopped, slapping her forehead. "Damn, my bad. I forgot you can't drink because you're about to have-"

"Will you shut up!" Taylor hissed, looking around to see

if anyone heard her. If Jasper found out she was pregnant because a gossip blog published the story, Taylor would die. She knew she'd have to tell him eventually, but right now wasn't the time, and that wasn't how she wanted him to hear it. "Go find you a drink and have a seat. You messing with Candi and about to air out all my lil business. Let me find you woke up and chose to be a hater."

"As if." Kiki rolled her neck. "I'm about to go get a shot. Text me if you need me." She danced her way across the floor, headed straight to the bar.

Taylor laughed a little before turning her head in the other direction. Small crowds of people filled the space. Some laughing, some engaged in serious conversations, and others simply vibing to the music. From the roughness of his voice, Taylor could tell it was Rahlo playing in the background. She guessed it was one of his new songs because a few people were buzzing about how dope it was.

"You looking for me?" A deep voice whispered against her ear. Fighting the grin that threatened to expose her excitement, Taylor slowly turned around.

"Lord," she moaned, gazing up at him. Rahlo was fine as fuck, and if anyone disagreed, she would happily chin check they ass.

Standing there, he was dressed in a pair of fitted black slacks and a white button-up with the first three buttons undone to expose a glimpse of his tatted chest and diamond chains. On his feet were a fresh pair of Yeezy's, and his wrists were lightly flooded with a few diamonds and a gold Rolex compliments of the label.

"Damn, tell me how I make you feel then." Rahlo took a step forward, wrapping her up in his Gucci cologne and minty breath.

"Like lord, can you give me a little space," she lied, stepping back to put a little more space between them.

"The lies you tell," Rahlo smirked. "A nigga looking like money, huh?"

Taylor snorted at his cockiness but never denied it. He was giving Morris Chestnut in the 90s. Fresh cut, perfect lineup, pretty white teeth, and that fucking dimple. She wanted to find something wrong with him, but there was nothing. From his exposed ankles to the top of his thick, silky waves, Rahlo was perfect.

He probably got a little dick, Taylor thought. She reasoned that no man was that perfect.

"You look aight," she downplayed the truth. Rahlo was more than aight and every woman watching them could vouch.

"Just aight?" The corner of his lip turned up and that damn dimple sunk into his cheek.

"Yep. Your head seems to be big enough. No need for me to sing your praises too."

"Yea ok." He chuckled. "Why didn't you tell me you were coming? I'm happy I sent Duke out there to check."

"Because I wasn't going to come, but Kiki and Candi dragged me out of the house."

"You didn't wanna see me?" Rahlo pouted, causing the dimple to cave into his cheek.

"Not really, but since you're all on my jock, I thought I'd show up." Taylor playfully fanned herself. Rahlo let out a low chuckle and rubbed his chin. The simple move caused Taylor's heart to leap from her chest.

"I'm on your jock, your bumper, and that ass if you let me.." His eyes slowly roamed her body. Even if Taylor wanted to answer, she couldn't. Between the thumping from between her thighs and his intense gaze, Taylor was at a loss for words.

"Rah," a feminine voice interrupted their connection. "Terri said it's time."

"Good looking, Esh," he acknowledged. "Aye, don't go nowhere," Rahlo told Taylor, who cocked her head to the side.

"You asking me or telling me?"

"Whichever one will help you sleep better at night." He winked, backing away with Esha at his side. "Just don't go nowhere, pretty girl."

From across the crowded room, Lexi snaked her neck trying to get a better look at Rahlo and the girl from the studio. She watched how he whispered in her ear and grinned at whatever she said. Lexi didn't know who the girl was, but her pop-up appearances had Lexi interested. Rahlo swore he wasn't focused on a relationship, but the stars in his eyes told a different story.

"Keep stretching that long muthafucka and you gone turn into a giraffe," Duke joked, walking up beside her, sipping from a champagne flute.

"Shut up, who is that girl he was talking to?"

"Some loudmouth bitch who keeps popping up everywhere."

"Sounds like you a little jealous," Lexi bantered, sipping her drink.

"Fuck outta here. I don't want her big ass," Duke denied, lifting the glass to his lips. He wasn't a champagne type of nigga, but the bubbly drink in his glass was hitting the spot. Mixed with the blunt he smoked, Duke was feeling nice, and his low eyes said it all.

"I'm not talking about her." Lexi shifted on her feet. "I'm talking about Rah."

"The fuck you just say to me?"

"Boy, calm down. I'm saying you know how protective you

are of Rah. Ole girl could be coming for your spot."

"Fuck outta here." Duke waved her off as Rahlo took the stage. "But fuck all that." He moved a little closer to her. "Where my daughter at?"

"Darius!" Lexi screeched, frantically looking around. When her eyes landed back on him, an evil smile pulled at his lips. He was enjoying seeing her squirm.

"Oh, now I'm Darius?" Duke chuckled at her nervousness. "See, you need to be worrying about what's going to happen when he finds out I'm the one who popped that pussy open first. While he was running around the house trying to find you back then, I had you bent over the dryer tearing that lil pussy up."

"Duke shut up!" Lexi hissed. "Are you drunk?"

"A lil bit." He backed up, lifting his glass in the air. "This fancy shit is potent."

"You need to get it together. We agreed-"

"Yea fuck all that shit. I only agreed to playing the background because I was locked up and we both needed his help, but now that I'm home, I want to be in my daughter's life and not as your fucking friend. The shit is getting harder to explain to her."

"Duke, now is not the time," Lexi warned, watching Rahlo rap one of his new songs. The crowd was feeling it, but she couldn't hear anything besides Duke publicly claiming her child.

"I know you don't think you have a chance with that nigga." Duke glanced at Rahlo then back at her. "You crazy as fuck," he laughed out loud. "My dick stayed in your mouth just as much as that nigga's and you think he's going to take you seriously?"

"He doesn't know that," Lexi replied. "We were a mistake."

"A mistake that kept happening." He licked his lips. "But this is your story and I'll let you keep telling it."

"Are you going to tell him?"

"I'm grown as fuck and don't need to tell that nigga shit."

"Good."

"I'm also not about to play the background anymore."

"Darius, you need to think about what you're saying. Rahlo helps with her tuition, he helps me around the house, and more. What do you think will happen when he finds out we've been keeping this from him? You're not in the position to step up and handle all the responsibilities that come with having a child. You don't even have a steady job."

"Bitch, fuck yo hoe ass," Duke gritted.

He didn't need her to remind him that he could barely support his child. If it wasn't for Rahlo looking out for him, he'd be back to robbing niggas. Being Bruce number 2 was only going to last for so long. Duke wasn't with the whole get the car, drive me around town type of shit. Working for Rahlo instead of with him made Duke feel useless, and that was something he couldn't get with.

"Don't talk to me like that." Lexi lowered her eyes. "And you're worried about him cutting me off, but guess what? I'm pretty sure he'll cut you off too."

"It's bros over hoes all day. Finish ya lil drink and then go pick up my daughter," Duke demanded. "And if you are lucky, I might let you suck me up for old time's sake."

"Fuck you."

"Drink some water too," he tossed back. "I heard through the grapevine that your mouth has been a lil on the dry side. You can't be out here with a sandpaper tongue," Duke taunted, leaving Lexi standing there mouth wide open.

Pissed off, Lexi stood there watching Duke move closer to

the stage as if he didn't just ruin her night. He bobbed his head to the music and rapped along with Rahlo, who was now on stage beside Kash Doll. Everyone in the room was lit and no one noticed that Lexi was standing there having a panic attack. The palms of her hands started to sweat and her eyes wildly darted around the room as she gathered her thoughts.

Lexi wished she could go back in time and redo all the mistakes she made. Letting Duke sweet talk his way into her panties would be number one. No one knew about her and Duke, and she wanted to keep it that way. No one needed to know that Duke took her virginity on her bedroom floor or that he regularly visited her when she moved to college. Not only was Duke fucking her like crazy, but he was breaking into the dorms. She tried to get away from trouble, but trouble followed her upstate, only this time when he departed, he left her a parting gift.

"Aye, I know you didn't sneak off to the bathroom and snort that shit," Bruce said, walking up beside her. Lexi snapped her head in his direction and frowned.

"Do I look like a crackhead to you?"

"Crackheads come in all different shapes and sizes."

"Shut up, Bruce." Lexi rolled her eyes and stormed off. She didn't have time to joke around with Bruce when Duke was threatening to blow up her life. There was no doubt in her mind that if Rahlo found out about their secret, he would probably hate her, and a future with him would be the least of her worries.

Across the room, Rahlo thanked everyone for coming out and passed the microphone to another Detroit artist who was featured on his album. Exiting the stage, he did a quick survey of the room to locate his sister and wasn't surprised to see her engaged with Taylor. Esha was protective of her brother, and since Rahlo expressed his interest in her, it was only right she checked her out.

"That's what I'm talking about, baby!" Terri commented, handing Rahlo a bottle of water and a towel. The label big wigs were feeling the album and wanted to add a few more cities to his tour. "You impressed them," he whispered, nodding toward the group of men standing in a circle.

"Oh yea," Rahlo cockily agreed, knowing he poured his heart out on the track.

"Yea," Terri nodded. "I have a few people I want you to kick it with."

"What kinda people?"

"Someone to manage your social media and another producer I want you to link with. He's new, but his work is fire."

"I'll meet the producer, but I have someone else in mind for the social media shit." He glanced in Taylor's direction. Terri followed his line of sight and frowned.

"Ok, ok. Give me her information and I'll check her credentials. If she's legit, I'll bring her in for an interview."

"Nah, bypass all that shit. She straight."

"Rah." Terri gave him a stern look.

"Nigga, stop whining and introduce me to the producer so I can kick it with my people."

"Come on, he's over here." Terri wanted to say more but chose not to. He was learning that Rahlo was going to do what he wanted to. Before they could make it across the room, Duke stumbled in their direction. Immediately, Rahlo could tell he'd had one too many. His white button-up was now untucked and his pants were sagging. It was evident the expensive champagne was catching up to him.

"Aye, these industry chicks some fucking freaks," Duke slurred, throwing his arm around Rahlo's shoulder. Terri groaned but again kept his thoughts to himself.

Duke was a different subject and one he didn't care to keep discussing. When Rahlo approached him to give Duke something to do, Terri looked at him like he had two heads. He couldn't think of anything Duke could efficiently do without fucking it up. It was Bruce who suggested making Duke security. He was already mean as fuck and he wouldn't have to talk to people. Terri laughed at the idea of Duke saving Rahlo before himself. If anything, he'd be the one to start the trouble, but Terri kept his mouth closed. Rahlo was going to have to learn the hard way that sometimes loyalty came with an expiration date.

"Hell yea. You should see my DMs." Rahlo chuckled. He had about twenty women promising to do twenty different things to him.

"Look," he whispered. "It's about five of them outside, and when this stiff shit is over, we're going to have a real party."

"Rah," Terri cleared his throat.

"Nigga, go drink some fucking water. I know you see us talking." Duke's deep voice captured the attention of other people in the room.

"Aye, chill," Rahlo lowly growled, not in the mood for either of their bullshit.

"I'm saying this nigga wanna be yo pops so bad." He snorted. "The streets raised us. The fuck a tight suit wearing ass nigga gon' teach you?"

"Let's walk." Bruce popped up out of thin air, grabbing Duke by the elbow. He didn't even give Duke a chance to refute because he started escorting him to the door.

"Here you go," he laughed. "Escorting me out like I'm your bitch or something."

"Just walk, bro," Bruce told him.

On his way out, Duke snatched a glass of champagne from

one of the waiters. Rahlo watched them walk away, fighting the urge to shake his head, but he was sure his displeasure was etched across his face. Duke had one job: work the room, make sure nobody got too drunk, keep the over-aggressive groupies at bay, and assist Bruce with any security needs. From the looks of it, Duke was the one who needed to be watched.

"He's going to be a problem," Terri uttered. "Let's go meet the producer I was telling you about."

Taylor, Esha, Kiki, and Candi were seated near the bar, talking and scoping out the men they deemed worthy of a second glance. Thus far, Candi had already collected two numbers and was working on number three. Whoever was the most generous would get the date and, if they spent enough, some booty too.

Kiki was on her business kick. Her skintight distressed jeans with gold chains and off-the-shoulder white crop top caught the eye of everyone she walked by. Kiki's walk was so fierce that she made you believe she was important even if you didn't know her. When asked what designer she was wearing, Kiki happily told them House of Ki and handed them a card. If they didn't remember anything, they'd remember the amount of confidence she had when she strolled away as if she owned the room.

"Wait, so Rahlo is your brother? Like same mama, same daddy?" Kiki asked, twisting her lips.

"Shakia!" Taylor bumped her.

"Girl bye, I can ask her that," Kiki hissed, turning her back to Taylor. "Women be quick to say that's the bro but be sucking the nigga balls on the low."

"Uh no." Esha scrunched up her nose. "I can assure you that he's my blood brother and his balls are nowhere near my mind."

"Oh my god!" Taylor slapped her forehead. "Why would

you even ask her that?"

"Bitch, for you, duh."

"Her?" Esha cocked her head to the side. "You like my brother?"

"No," Taylor denied and shook her head.

"Yes," Kiki countered. "She wanna suck his balls."

"Shakia!"

"Girl, stop calling my damn name all loud. You do wanna suck his balls, and if you don't, I do."

"I can't with this girl." Taylor and Esha both laughed out loud. "I'm going to slide to the bathroom. Kiki, please don't say anything crazy."

"Girl, gone and take your pissy ass to the bathroom." Kiki waved her off.

Taylor gave her best friend the finger and hopped off the bar stool. If she didn't have to use the bathroom for the 10th time, she would've told Kiki to kiss her ass, but her full bladder was pressed for time.

As she walked across the room, Taylor locked eyes with Rahlo, who was standing there talking to a group of guys. She could have sworn one was Big Sean but couldn't confirm because Rahlo's gaze had her attention. Lifting his eyebrow, he silently questioned where she was headed.

Bathroom, she mouthed and kept it pushing.

In the midst of relieving herself, Taylor closed her eyes to allow the wave of nausea to pass over her. Being pregnant was not for the weak, and she wasn't even pregnant *pregnant*. All the books said she was supposed to be laying on the couch, eating snacks, drinking Vernors, and watching her favorite shows while her second trimester coasted by. Instead, she was throwing up, hangry all the time, and the number of times she used the bathroom drove her crazy. Her first trimester was nothing like the smiling, jolly hoes on TV. She was more like the grouch that lived in the garbage can on *Sesame Street.*

"Ugh!" A voice groaned on the other side of the stall. "I pulled out my best fit for this damn party. I spent money on a pair of shoes that's killing me, and this man is pining after a bitch who looks like she ate two of me," the woman vented. Taylor guessed she was on the phone because she didn't hear a reply.

"Right! That's what I'm saying. I mean, she's pretty for a big girl, but she don't have shit on me. Then she has short blonde hair, looking like a fucking stuffed pineapple." She laughed into the phone.

"Girl, Rahlo probably just wants some pussy. I hope he gets that shit out of his system so we can work on us. I know these hoes in the industry are treacherous, and I need to stake my claim before one of these hoes sinks their claws in him."

"Oh, this bitch talking about me," Taylor laughed to herself, knowing she was the only plus-size woman with short blonde hair in the party.

Hearing enough, Taylor wiped herself and stood to pull up her jeans. After flushing the toilet, she stepped out of the stall, and the woman responsible for all the lil slick comments looked like she saw a ghost. Unbothered, Taylor stepped up to the sink and proceeded to lather her hands with soap while staring straight ahead, ignoring the woman who kept looking at her out the side of her eye. Drying her hands, Taylor removed her lip gloss and retouched her lips before blowing herself a kiss for being a bad bitch. A bitch that made hoes like the one standing next to her uncomfortable. A bitch that was feeling sick as fuck but wouldn't let the hating hoe standing there shifting on her feet know it.

"I don't want your nigga," Taylor spoke through the mirror, boosting her already perky breasts. "But you better believe if my *fat* ass wanted to feed him this fat ass *pussy*, that nigga will happily sit at the table and dive in headfirst."

"Excuse me?" Lexi's eyes bucked.

"I didn't stutter." Taylor turned to face her. "And if you gotta wait for him to fuck another bitch before he takes you seriously, then guess what, sis...my pineapple looking ass is the least of your worries. Good luck though," She winked and left Lexi there with her jaw on the floor.

Once on the other side of the door, Taylor let out a snicker while shaking her head. Being called fat wasn't new to her, but her response was. There was a time when Taylor would quickly pop someone in the mouth, but now she was calmer. It took her years to understand that it was jealousy, and every action didn't need a reaction.

"Damn, I thought you fell in the toilet," Kiki quipped when Taylor returned to the bar.

"Close," Taylor snorted. "My fist almost fell into a bitch face."

"Who?" Kiki hopped off the bar stool, ready for whatever.

"It's a nobody, but let's go. I need some real food. These lil fancy ass tea cup salads and tiny pieces of chicken ain't getting it."

"Yall leaving?" Esha questioned, searching the room for her brother. She wanted to warn him that his lil boo was about to dip out on his ass.

"Yes, we are," Taylor told her as Candi danced her way back to them.

"You right on time," Kiki told her. "It was nice meeting you, Esha."

"You too," she warmly smiled. "Hey, uh, Taylor, you're not going to wait for Rahlo?"

"Nah," she declined and shook her head. "Seems like he

has a waiting list," Taylor disclosed as Lexi walked in their direction. With her head held high, Lexi stepped right in between the women, neglecting personal boundaries.

"Hey sis," she greeted Esha with a fake smile plastered on her face.

"Uhhh, hey." Esha awkwardly hugged her back, not wanting to embarrass her any further. In all the years she'd known Lexi, she had never called her sis. Lexi was one of Rahlo's friends, not hers.

"Damn, lil buddy, you about to step on my feet," Kiki frowned, looking Lexi up and down. Off rip, she didn't like her or the territorial pheromones that surrounded her.

"Oh, my bad, girl. I didn't even see you standing there." She laughed lightly, holding her chest.

"Then you need to get your eyes checked," Candi warned.

"Uh, are yall like video girls or something?" Lexi ignored her smart comment.

"Are you like a groupie or something?" Kiki rebutted.

"Nah, she's part of Rahlo's waiting list," Taylor corrected her. "Esha have a nice night. It was so nice talking to you."

"You too! Be safe," Esha replied. With that, Taylor, Candi, and Kiki sauntered right out the door, not bothering to say goodbye to the man of the hour.

Chapter 12

"Tayyyyy," Jalen screamed, running into her arms.

"Hey baby," she cooed, lifting him from the ground.

"I missed you so much."

"You talk to me every day," Taylor giggled, kissing the top of his head.

"So you can answer the phone for him and not me?" Jasper sulked, poking his lip out.

Taylor glanced up at Jasper and rolled her eyes. She couldn't deny he looked good as hell in his white linen shorts and matching button-up with beige loafers. His hair was neatly cut and his facial hair was trimmed to perfection. His style mirrored Blair Underwood, and she was there for it. Well, everything except his jealous fits.

"Uh, can we get some tokens?" Trooper asked, not wanting to stand there while they talked.

"Sure thing." Jasper reached in his pocket and pulled out a fifty. He didn't get a chance to tell Trooper what to do with it because Jalen snatched the money and they ran off, leaving Taylor and Jasper standing there.

Earlier that day, Jalen called Taylor asking if she could take him to the arcade. Taylor started to say no, but since her dad was out on a date and Papa was hanging with his BINGO buddies, Taylor decided that taking Trooper to the arcade wasn't a bad idea. She was leery about being face to face with Jasper but figured she couldn't hide forever. With a baby growing in her womb, talking to him was inevitable.

"Can I get a hug?" Jasper asked, eyeing Taylor from head to toe. The black leggings she wore hugged her thick thighs, and he loved the Biggie T-shirt and Yeezy's she paired with it. Taylor's brown skin was glowing and he could smell the vanilla bodywash she loved so much. If she wasn't pissed with him, Jasper would've pulled her into a bathroom to show her how much he missed her.

"I don't think I'm ready for all that." Taylor twisted her lips.

"Baby-" he stepped forward, but Taylor stuck her hand out to stop him. "Look, I was wrong for how I reacted, but you were wrong too."

"I was," she admitted. "I had no business thinking about another man in that manner."

"And in my bed at that."

"It was wrong."

"So why am I the only one who's in the dog house?"

"Because look at how you flipped out, Jasper. You mushed me, pushed me, and then kept me locked up in the house for a week."

"Why you making me sound like one of them weird niggas off those Lifetime movies." He chortled.

"Because that's what you were acting like."

"And I'm sorry, but you make me fucking crazy." He

stepped forward, cupping her face. "I'm crazy about you, baby, literally gone in the head crazy about you, and I can't stomach the thought of another nigga on your mind. I'll do better though."

"Well, I'm not ready for us to pick back up where we left off, but I'm willing to try."

"That's all I can ask, baby." He nodded as if he understood, as if he wasn't going to bully his way back into her life.

"So that means no checking my phone, popping up acting all crazy, and trusting me." Taylor tilted her head to the side.

Jasper looked dead in her eyes and lied. He was never going to stop checking her phone or tracking her down, but for the sake of gaining her forgiveness, Jasper agreed.

"I got you, baby." He buried his head in her neck. "I fucking missed you."

"We missed you too," she whispered.

"We?" he pulled back, looking her up and down.

Taylor took a deep breath and reached out for his hand. Jasper's heart thumped against his chest as she placed his hand on her hard stomach.

"We," she repeated.

"Don't play with me." He stared into her eyes for reassurance.

"Nope, I'm pregnant. Four months, going on five," Taylor admitted, pulling the corner of her lip into her mouth. Speechless, Jasper pulled Taylor into his arms and planted kisses on her face.

"Stop, boy," she giggled. "We're in public."

"So," he uttered. "I'm so fucking happy, baby. We in this shit for life." Jasper hugged her, missing the uneasy expression on her face.

"You need anything? You hungry? Are you supposed to be on your feet?" Jasper questioned, pulling back to get a better look at her.

"I'm ok for now," Taylor promised. "The morning sickness comes and goes, but thankfully today I'm ok."

"Damn, baby, I'm happy as hell. I thought you were on birth control."

"I was, but apparently, that shit failed," she spat bitterly, causing the lines in Jasper's forehead to surface.

"You don't want to have my baby?"

"Honestly, no." Taylor exhaled. "I'm not ready to be somebody's mother right now. I'm still trying to figure out what I want to do with my life."

"And you can do that with my baby."

"No, I can't." She shook her head from side to side. "It takes years to find balance. Some people don't find it until their child goes off to college."

"You're just nervous, baby. You're so good with Jalen and Trooper, I know you'll be even better with our baby." Jasper stroked her cheek.

"I can drop them off anytime I want, can't do that with my own."

"So what are you saying?" He dropped his hand. "I know you don't think you're about to have an abortion."

"I thought about it," Taylor admitted, leaving out the part that it was a few weeks too late.

"Yea ok," Jasper chuckled, swiping his thumb across his nose. "Well, it's a good thing you got your mind together because, like I said," he touched her stomach. "This is for life."

Taylor cleared her throat, trying to swallow the eerie feeling looming in the pit of her stomach.

"And you know that club gig is a wrap. I'll start picking up more shifts," Jasper promised.

"I haven't been to the club, but I should be fine. I've been saving and I'm still working with a few advertising people."

"You can wrap that up, too. I don't need my pregnant woman on Instagram showing her ass."

"I'm not trying to be funny, but you can't afford to call those kinda shots."

"You heard what I said. I'll pick up overtime to make up the difference." Jasper kissed her forehead. "Let's go find the boys. Jalen is going to be so happy."

∞ ∞ ∞

A few hours later, Taylor was back at Jasper's place, but this time felt different. She felt like a prisoner returning to their cell after being out in the yard all day. Jasper, on the other hand, was stoked! He kept telling her how much he missed her, how he was going to make love to her, marry her, buy them a house, and pump her with more babies. Taylor only smiled, but deep down, she wasn't feeling it. She was hoping that after they made up things would return to how they were, but in all honesty, she felt trapped.

"Tay, I have so many videos!" Jalen said, running into the living room with his iPad in his hand.

"You do?" She turned to face him.

"Yep," he grinned.

"You can show her later. Tay needs to get some rest," Jasper told him. "Yall can go play in the back."

"You ok, Tay?" Trooper asked, ignoring Jasper's orders.

"I'm fine, Troop," she promised.

"K. Call if you need me." He backed out of the living room griming Jasper. Taylor snickered at his protective manner. In fact, all day he had been giving Jasper the side eye. Whenever Jalen went to show Jasper how many tickets he won, Trooper stood next to his sister.

"You must've been talking about me," Jasper snorted.

"Huh?"

"I'm saying Trooper was my lil homie and now he's not even looking at me."

"For one, I don't talk about my business in front of kids, and two, kids can read people. Maybe he's not feeling your energy." Taylor shrugged.

Jasper opened his mouth to address her comment, but his phone started vibrating on the table. Taylor thanked God for the distraction and slipped off to the back of the house while he answered.

"What's up, Sherri?" Jasper asked, sighing loudly into the phone.

"Dang, why you gotta say it like that?" She laughed playfully, not picking up on the irritation in his voice.

"Because you calling my phone. Jalen has his iPad, so if you wanna check up on him, call his number."

"Well, actually rude ass, I was calling to see if I could come over."

"What?" Jasper frowned, cutting the volume down on his phone.

"I could cook for yall, watch a movie, and when Jay goes to sleep..." she cooed.

"No. Look, I'm chilling with my girl, and if it's not about Jalen, don't call me."

"S-S-She's back?" Sherri stuttered.

"Yep."

"What about us? I though-"

Her sentence was cut short when Jasper ended the call. His girl was home and Sherri's hairy services were no longer needed.

∞∞∞

Rahlo pushed his brand-new Durango through Southwest with a grin on his face. The fully loaded SUV was black and chrome with tinted windows. There wasn't a payment plan attached, nor did he need a cosigner. Rahlo walked into the Dodge dealership and dropped stacks on the counter, making damn near every associate run in his direction. It was one of the best feelings in the world.

After picking out a truck off the showroom floor, Rahlo signed the necessary paperwork and drove out of the building with pride coursing through his veins.

"This muthafucka clean!" Duke admired from the passenger seat.

"Right. I wanna cop me one of these bitches," Bruce agreed from the backseat.

"Aye, swing by Dre crib," Duke said, looking up from his phone. "Boy owe me a band and I need to collect."

"Then do that shit on your own time." Bruce frowned, not in the mood to deal with any of the drama that followed Duke around.

"Nigga, you ain't driving so it ain't up to yo fat ass."

"Keep talking shit and I'm going to knock yo small ass head through the windshield."

"Chill yall." Rahlo cut the radio down. "I'll swing by

Southwest because I need to see my sister and then we'll head downtown to the studio. Terri set up something with the new producer."

"How do you feel about meeting all these different people?" Duke quizzed, blowing smoke through his nose.

"I love it. I've made connections with some dope ass people in this industry. In order to get to the heights I want to reach, I need to surround myself with people who have more than I do."

"More money?"

"Money, information, influence, connections, all that shit. I'm trying to grow and I can't do that shit by sitting at the same table. Having just enough is never enough."

"On God," Bruce agreed, but Duke didn't respond. He didn't have the same mindset as them. He wanted to call all the shots, and to him, being the biggest nigga in the room was power. All that making connections shit they could keep. He had a handful of friends and didn't need any new ones.

Twenty minutes later, Rahlo pulled up on McGraw Ave. with the music blasting. Women stretched their necks to get a glimpse at the driver while niggas clutched the guns in their waistbands, ready for whatever. It was nothing for them to have a shootout in the middle of the day, not caring about the bystanders. Women, kids, elders, and dogs were subjected to bullets when they started flying.

"Ole superstar ass nigga," Dre clowned when Rahlo rolled the window down.

"Something like that." He casually smirked. There was no need for him to brag. The watch on his wrist did that all by itself.

"Where my shit at bitch?" Duke hopped out of the passenger seat.

"Shut up, passenger princess ass nigga," Dre jested, patting his pockets. "Let me run in the crib real quick."

"Don't take all day either or I might fuck yo mama off GP," he hollered out.

"Wouldn't be the first time yo nasty tried it." Dre gave him the middle finger.

"You tried to sleep with Wanda?" Bruce asked in disbelief.

"You didn't?" Duke raised his eyebrow.

It wasn't a secret that Dre's mother sold lunch specials in the day and pussy at night. Dre hated it, but when his father left them high and dry, Wanda didn't have many options. Her kitchen and legs were a revolving door, but she was well paid and her son was well taken care of. It wasn't until Dre caught an attempted murder charge for beating a man to a pulp for beating her did she stop hoeing. The man claimed Wanda gave him an STD, and he in return gave it to his wife, and she left him. Wanda swore she was clean, but the man wasn't hearing it and knocked her around the living room until ten-year-old Dre came out of the room with a bat.

"Nigga, no! Ms. Wanda cool and all, but I'm not fucking her. I think my daddy and granddaddy hit her."

"Sounds like a right of passage to me."

"You a nasty ass nigga." Rahlo laughed, turning to face the loud commotion. Removing his buffs, he squinted to make sure his eyes weren't playing tricks on him.

Everyone in Southwest treated Chef with respect because of who he used to be. Although drugs claimed his soul, Chef didn't fuck with anybody, so Rahlo was confused as to why a few young niggas were surrounding him like they were about to do something. Being the type of man Chef was, Rahlo knew he wouldn't back down. Crackhead and all, he was still a man.

"Rah," Bruce called out, seeing his jaw clench but it was too late. Rahlo was out of the car heading over toward the crowd.

"Crackhead ass nigga," someone taunted. "This ain't your streets no more."

"Crackhead and all, I bet I can still tap dance my way into your mama stale ass draws while yo bitch pack my pipe," Chef popped his shit. "And if I'm feeling frisky, I might fuck yo manly looking grandma. Whole family can get this crackhead dick."

Whap!

The young boy swung, knocking Chef's frail body to the ground. On impact, his body bounced across the broken pavement like a basketball.

"Bitch ass nigga," the young hustler jeered, lifting his foot to kick Chef, but didn't get a chance to release it before Rahlo's fist rammed into his jaw, twisting his head to the side.

Whap!

"Who the bitch now?" Rahlo chastised, punching the boy in the face again as if he was trying to detach his head from his shoulders.

Whap!

"Fight back, bitch," Rahlo urged, knowing that he couldn't. The first hit had him dazed, the rest were pure torture.

"Rah, chill the fuck out!" Bruce pushed his way through the crowd as Duke stood to the side cheering him on. This was his type of excitement.

"Get the fuck off me!" Rahlo snatched away from Bruce, wiping sweat from his forehead. "Just because I'm not in the streets don't mean my word ain't valid. Chef is off limits, and behind him, I'm coming guns blazing. I suggest you niggas spread the word." He grilled the young squad as they peeled their friend off the ground. His mouth was bloody and the force behind Rahlo's fist had his eye swollen.

"Southwest bitch!" Duke threw up his set. "Yall niggas ain't down for real. The same nigga yall hustle beside just got his ass handed to him and yall standing there with hands in ya pockets. Couldn't be me," he taunted the wannabes. "Get the fuck from around here before I run ya pockets."

"Nigga, help him up," Bruce gritted, tossing his head toward Chef.

Duke sucked his teeth but did as he was told. Once on his feet, Chef snatched away from Duke and pointed his shaking finger at Rahlo.

"I don't need you to do that."

"Do what?" Rahlo spun around. "Stop that nigga from jumping on yo ass like a muddy puddle."

"These lil niggas don't scare me!" Chef bellowed, slapping his frail chest. "They call me a crackhead, but pop pills and drink lean all damn day. The way I see it we all crackheads. The only difference is I smoke mine and they swallow theirs."

"He got a point," Duke agreed but pressed his finger to his lip when Rahlo and Bruce glared in his direction. "My fault."

"I'm not worried about that little crumb snatcher or his friends," Chef continued. "He thinks he's hot shit now, but even the mighty fall," he preached, picking up his top hat. "Now, if you wanna help, grease my palms so I can go smoke the pain away."

"Nigga, you need a doctor," Duke bucked. "I think dude knocked your hip loose. You leaning to the side and shit."

"A rock a day keep the pain away." Chef hunched his shoulders and bopped away with the twenty dollars Bruce handed him.

"Come on, killer man." Dre bopped back toward them. "Yall making the block hot. First, this superstar nigga flaunting his truck, and now he knocking niggas out like Tyson."

"Give this nigga his bread so we can go," Rahlo said, headed back to his truck. It hadn't even been ten minutes and his phone was already vibrating off the hook. Someone posted the video of him knocking out the dealer, and now they were calling him #theknockoutking.

"Bread?" Dre frowned but straightened his face when Duke shot him a look. "Aye, you think you can take me on Michigan Ave?" Dre asked, following Rahlo. "My baby mama ain't answering the phone but posted on Facebook with some nigga. I need to check that shit because she got me fucked up."

"Nigga, no," Bruce answered. "How the fuck you out here hustling and don't have a car or nothing to show for it?"

"I'm investing," Dre replied with a sly grin on his face. He was an investing ass lie. Dre did just enough to stay afloat. It was nothing for him to lose all his money in a dice game or at the strip club. As long as his mother wasn't selling pussy, he was going to live his best life one day and eat noodles and tuna sandwiches the next.

Dre knew he was going to die in the streets. For him, a young black man hustling, moving fast without any regard for the next person, it was inevitable. The same streets that raised him would eventually turn on him and take his life. There was no loyalty in the concrete jungle and everyone had an expiration date.

"Then invest in a bus pass, nigga," Bruce grumbled.

"We going that way," Duke reasoned.

"Rah, come on. Look out for your boy one time," Dre pleaded.

"You clean?" Rahlo glared at him.

"Yea." He nodded, getting in the back seat. "Aye! I'll be right back. Yall hold it down," Dre hollered out the window.

"Sit yo *can-I-get-a-ride* -ass down." Bruce frowned.

"You still a mean ass nigga," Dre chortled. "He always this uptight?"

"Just sit back and ride before I put yo ass out," Rahlo demanded, cutting up the radio to drown out his thoughts.

They weren't even a good ten minutes into the ride when Bruce noticed they were being followed by an unmarked police truck. Just to be sure, Bruce had Rahlo make four rights, and sure as shit, the officer did the same thing. Once they stopped at a light, three more unmarked cars blocked them in.

Bloop bloop

The flashing blue and white lights normally would have sent Rahlo into panic mode, but not this time. He had insurance and his license, and there wasn't anything illegal in his possession.

"Yall be cool," he told the men in the car.

Looking through the mirror, Bruce noticed the panic in Dre's eyes. He started shifting in his seat and broke out in a light sweat. Dre was a two-time felon. If he got caught with anything else, he was going to prison for a long time. Without a second thought, he removed the sandwich bag full of weed from his pants and quickly stuffed it under Rahlo's seat.

"The fuck is you doing?" Duke gritted. "Get that shit, nigga."

"I can't go back to jail," he mumbled as two officers approached the truck.

"Good afternoon, fellas," the black officer greeted while his partner stood beside him with his hand on his waistband and a grim look on his face.

"Afternoon," Rahlo replied. "Did I do something wrong?"

"You tell me," the partner snottily interjected. "Your truck fits the description of one that just fled from a crime scene."

"Nah, not me," Rahlo denied as two more officers joined

them.

"I'm going to need you gentlemen to step out of the car."

"For what?" Bruce spoke up. "I know my rights, and unless we've done something to prompt a search or you see drugs or guns, we don't have to get out."

"A wise ass, huh," the black officer smirked. "Well, I'll tell you this." He bent down in the window. "A car fitting this description was just reported leaving a crime scene. That is reason enough for us to execute the search. We can do this the easy way or the hard way."

"Man," Rahlo exhaled, pissed off but still obliged. At this point, he'd be okay with a ticket and going on his way, but from the look on the officer's face, that wasn't going to happen.

"Rah," Duke said in a hushed tone, but Rahlo didn't hear him as they exited the car. One by one, the four men were cuffed and led to the curb while the truck was searched. Rahlo was irritated but kept his composure. Bruce was ready to knock Dre's head off, and Duke was praying that they missed the illegal contents, but when the officer turned around with a sly grin on his face, Duke knew it was a wrap.

"Well, well, well," he taunted them, tossing the zip lock bag in the air while his partner shook a pill bottle he found stuffed between the seats.

"Ain't this about a bitch," Rahlo vexed, dropping his head.

Chapter 13

"Is this how it's going to be?" Sherri asked, watching Jasper pull up his pants. She was still in her post-coital haze and was hoping they'd get lunch or something before he ran back home to Taylor. With the cover thrown across the lower half of her body, Sherri tried to wrap her arms around Jasper, but he pushed her back.

"This ain't that." He removed her hands from his body and continued to get dressed.

As much as Jasper couldn't stand Sherri, he loved slutting her out. Since she was trying to win him back, Sherri let Jasper fuck her in every hole on her body and graciously accepted it when he nutted in her mouth, on her face, and up her back. Sherri thought he enjoyed all the freaky shit, but Jasper got a kick out of making her look like the hoe she was.

"My god, Jasper, would it kill you to act like you still love me even a little bit?"

"Let's not get this situation twisted. I have zero feelings for you, nor does me being here mean I want to rekindle things," he clarified.

"I am your wife and you're treating me like some side bitch."

"You're my ex-wife and I'm treating you how you're acting," Jasper coldly told her. "Like a fucking slut."

"Whatever, Jasper." She waved him off. "If I'm so much of a slut, then why do you keep fucking me?"

"Because Taylor is pregnant and I can't hit it how I'm used to," Jasper said matter of factly.

"What?" Sherri bucked. Jada had already filled her in about seeing Taylor at the abortion clinic, so she thought the situation was taken care of. The last thing she expected was for Jasper to broadcast it as if he was happy, but the grin on his face said exactly that. "Y-y-you got her pregnant?" She stuttered as her heart broke into a million pieces.

"Yep!" Jasper smiled proudly. "She's having my baby, and I think I'm going to ask her to marry me."

"Marry you?" Sherri belted as her head began to spin. Marriage? A baby? It was all too much for her to process. "The scent of my pussy is all on your dick, and you're going to stand here and say you want to marry that bitch."

"Don't call her out of her name."

"Fuck her!" she yelled, jumping into his face. "You're a weak ass nigga!"

"Back up," he warned, feeling his eye twitch.

"Make me! You are a weak ass nigga, and that's why I cheated because you too fucking soft. It's easy to walk all over you."

"Fuck you, Sherri," Jasper gritted, feeling heat creep up the back of his neck.

"No, fuck yo weak stroke ass and that young bitch. I hope

she cheats on yo ass too."

Whap!

Sherri didn't know when it happened, but her body flew against the wall. The stinging on her cheek was evidence that a hit occurred, but her mind couldn't process that her childhood sweetheart had knocked the lights out of her ass. With wide eyes, Sherri peered up at Jasper, not recognizing the person standing there grinning down at her.

"Oh my god." She grabbed her face in shock.

"You brought that shit upon yourself." Jasper lowered to the ground, where she was leaning against the wall. "I'm going to marry Taylor, and I'm going to move Jalen in with us. I'm tired of this back-and-forth shit, and I'm tired of paying child support when he's with me most of the time anyway."

"You're not taking my son," Sherri mumbled.

"*You're not taking my son,*" he mocked, followed by a sinister laugh. "Shut the fuck up before I smother your ass and they find your corpse."

"Jasper," she gasped.

"Don't get scared now." He nicked her chin. "This what you wanted, right? You walked all over the good guy, and now that the bad guy is knocking your head between the bed and nightstand, you wanna look all shocked."

"Can you just get out of my house?"

"The house that I paid for," he reminded her, pinching the brim of his nose. "You better hope I don't put you out and move my girl and our baby in this bitch."

"You wouldn't," Sherri choked out, caught off guard by this version of him.

"Keep talking hot shit and you'll see." He winked, backing out of the room. Seconds later, Sherri heard the front door slam, and only then did she get up.

Timidly, she tip-toed to the front door and watched Jasper pull off. For the first time since their marriage ended, Sherri was 100% sure she didn't want him back. Fucking her rough was one thing but slapping her upside the head was something she couldn't tolerate, and she was telling his mama.

∞∞∞

"How has he been acting?" Kiki quizzed, with the phone pressed to her ear.

"Alright, I guess, but honestly, I miss my space," Taylor sighed, glancing around the living room. She didn't know if she was overreacting or traumatized, but being back in Jasper's house had her paranoid. She rarely talked on the phone and found herself jumping when he reached out to her. Whenever she was laying in his arms, Taylor felt nauseous and the baby started moving like crazy. Every time Jasper tried to initiate sex, Taylor told him her stomach was cramping. It was bad enough he tried to kiss her.

"Then leave, ugh. I don't know why you even gave him a second chance. I would've told his unstable ass to kick rocks."

"I don't know what I was thinking," Taylor sighed.

"Me either, but it's not too late to dip on his ass. You don't have to be there. Say the word and Mike and I will be right there," Kiki let her know.

"Mike tired of being put in my bullshit."

"So. He knew what it was. You've been my best bitch since forever, and he knows how I'm coming behind you."

"Tay, can I have some candy?" Jalen asked, bouncing into the kitchen.

"I don't think it's any here, baby. Call your dad and have him stop and get you some," Taylor answered, looking up from her phone. "Tell him to bring me some hot chips and almond M&M's too."

"Where Loony Tunes at anyway?" Kiki asked.

"He went to do something for his mama."

"Or is he hiding in the bushes waiting to see if the mailman flirts with you?"

"What about this?" Jalen asked, holding a pack up. "I found it under Daddy bed. Can I have some?"

"Let me see that," she squinted. "Ki, let me call you back." She ended the call without waiting for her to respond.

Jalen handed Taylor the pack of what he thought was candy and ran back into the room to get his phone. Taylor examined the box and almost screamed. As far as she knew, she had been taking her birth control pills like clockwork, but the one month supply she held in her hand said something different. Getting up, Taylor practically ran to the back of the house and into Jasper's room.

"Where did you get this?" she asked Jalen, trying not to startle him.

"Am I in trouble?' He looked up at her. Taking a deep breath, Taylor tried to calm herself down.

"No, just show me where you got this from."

Getting out of the bed, Jalen crawled all the way under his dad's bed and returned with a Jordan shoe box. Taylor took the box from him and poured the contents on the bed.

"Oh my god!" She covered her mouth.

Everything she thought she had lost while visiting him over the years fell from the box. Her spare car keys-that he helped look for but pretended he hadn't seen them. Her old phone that she thought she had lost, but clearly she hadn't since it was in the box perfectly fine. Her work badge- that he swore wasn't at his house, a few pairs of her favorite panties and tons of lip gloss. As if that wasn't bad enough, she spotted boxes of the fake birth control that replaced hers. Even if he tried to deny it, the receipts from Esty were stuffed to the side. Fucking placebo pills. For months, she had been swallowing placebo pills while Jasper purposely tried to get her pregnant.

"Tay, you ok?" Jalen whispered, touching her shoulder.

Taylor heard him but was focused on the expired driver's license stuck to the side of the box. Picking it up, she examined it and was about to put it down when the birthdate caught her eye.

"The fuck?" She squinted. Taylor was outdone. Jasper lied about his age and she felt sick to her stomach. For years, she had been sleeping with a man who could have been her father, uncle, or something other than her boyfriend.

"I'm fine." She wiped the tears from her eyes and quickly stuffed everything back in the box. Her mind was running a mile per second trying to piece together everything she stumbled upon. Taylor knew Jasper was controlling, but this took things to the next level. His ass was flat out crazy, and she knew that if she confronted Jasper, he would try to lock her in the house. The last time caught her off guard, but she wouldn't make the same mistake this time.

"Jay, don't tell your dad," Taylor told Jalen. "Put this back under the bed."

"Ok, cause I'm a spy and I can keep secrets," he promised, doing as he was asked.

"Uh-huh," she mumbled, texting Kiki.

"Yep, I see everything. Wanna see?" Jalen continued but didn't wait for her to answer. Running over to his backpack, he picked up his tablet and went to the videos.

"You better not be spying on me," Taylor fussed, turning to face him. It wouldn't be hard to believe since his Daddy belonged on SVU with his creepy ass. Her blood boiled just thinking about his nasty ass. The nigga really trapped her and stole her car keys, forcing her to pay almost two hundred dollars for another copy.

"Only bad people who do bad stuff," he swore. "See," he pushed the tablet in her face.

The first video was a random man throwing a cup on the ground at the park. Taylor giggled because Jalen was in the background calling the man a disgrace. The next video was of his mother letting the water in the kitchen sink run. She was washing dishes with the phone pressed against her ear. Taylor was about to swipe past it, but Sherri's conversation caused her ears to perk.

"Bitch please, he'll always be my husband," she said and then laughed at whatever the caller said.

"Like be for real. What the fuck that fat, young ass girl gone do that I can't?"

"Don't call Tay fat, Mommy!" Jalen screamed.

"Boy, hush, and you better not be recording me."

"Girl, yea. Jalen be so far up her ass you'd think she pushed him out."

Taylor didn't say anything. She simply swiped to the next video. This time the tablet slipped from her hands. Her stomach twisted, and without warning, she ran to the bathroom sink and allowed the vomit to expel from her mouth.

"Tay," Jalen whispered, standing on the side of her.

"Give me a minute, Jalen." She closed the door in his face.

Taylor didn't know what was more disturbing. The fact that she just saw Jasper and Sherri fucking on the living room couch like old people or that Jalen had it on his tablet. She could tell he was hiding from the angle of the camera. His parents were so into what was happening between them that they didn't notice they were being caught red-handed. Jasper couldn't even argue that the video was old because Jalen's tablet was only a few months old.

"Ow," Taylor groaned, leaning on the sink as her stomach contracted. The pain ripped through the bottom of her stomach and up her back. "Mmmm," she moaned, trying to catch her breath.

After a few minutes, the pain passed and Taylor dried her eyes. Gathering her composure, she rinsed the sink and then her mouth.

"Jalen, did you text your dad?" Taylor asked, opening the bathroom door.

"No."

"Ok, don't. I'll tell Kiki to bring you something when she comes over." Taylor gave him a half smile.

"Are you mad at me?" he whispered, looking at the ground.

"At you?" She rubbed the top of his head. "Never. Hand me your tablet and go watch TV."

"Ok, are you going to tell my daddy?"

"Nope. It's our secret," she promised, taking the cracked tablet from his hands.

Going to the video, Taylor checked the time stamp and noticed that it was only a week ago. Shaking her head, she went through all the pictures and videos on his tablet, deleting any traces of herself. Once that was completed, she sent the video of Jasper and Sherri fucking to Kiki and cut the tablet off.

Jasper had her fucked up. A week ago his mouth was attached to her anus as he promised to take care of her and their baby. A baby that he trapped her with. Jasper was full of shit, and Taylor wished she would have farted in his fucking face.

The house was unusually quiet when Jasper returned home. He was surprised because Taylor always allowed Jalen to run through the house like a madman. They usually built forts with the couch cushions or did some kind of challenge Jalen saw on TikTok. Jasper chalked it up as the pregnancy getting to Taylor. He made a mental note to tell Jalen to be more mindful now that she was pregnant. All the crawling around on the floor and jumping on the bed would have to pause until after she gave birth. Before exploring a little further, Jasper dipped his head into the refrigerator. Just as he was about to move, the freezer door was slammed on his head.

"Ah fuck," he ducked. Jasper thought he was in the clear until the bottom door was slammed on his head again.

"Nasty, cheating ass nigga," Taylor hissed, kicking him when his body hit the ground. "You are sick!

"Taylor, what the fuck?" he barked, holding his head trying to stop the ringing in his ears. "What is your problem?"

"You!" she screamed, kicking him again. "You are my problem, you sick fuck!"

"Baby, what are you talking about?" Jasper staggered to his feet while holding his head.

"Don't baby me!" Taylor screamed, holding the bottom of her stomach as the pain surged through her core once again. "Ah," she cried, gripping the counter.

"Baby, what's wrong?" He stepped toward her, but Taylor backed away from him. His touch only made the situation worse.

"Don't touch me, Jasper! How old are you?"

"What? Baby, you know how old I am."

"No, I thought I did, but your expired license says something different," she said, holding the bottom of her tight stomach.

"You went through my stuff?" He narrowed his eyes at her. In a split second, his face transformed from confusion to anger.

"Tay-" he started but was cut off when the front door flew open.

Like it was her house, Kiki walked in with Mike on her heels. With a trash bag in her hand, she started picking up everything that belonged to her friend. Bewildered, Jasper scrunched up his face and glared in their direction. He thought maybe he had a concussion because there was no way this was happening.

"Best friend, this yours?" Kiki asked, holding a lamp that was on the end table. Taylor gave her a knowing look. She knew damn well the lamp wasn't hers.

"No."

Crash!

"Oops." Kiki dropped the lamp, breaking it.

"Aye, what the fuck is this?" Jasper squinted. "Why are yall in my shit?"

"Because yo clingy, mothball smelling ass trapped the wrong bitch. It will be a cold day in hell before you ever see my god baby," Kiki sniped. "Are you ready, best friend?"

"Yep." Taylor wiped her face and stood up as best as she could. The pain in her stomach traveled to her back and it was making it hard for her to move.

Whipping his head in Taylor's direction, Jasper noticed she was holding her overnight bag along with his Nike duffle bag.

"Where do you think you're going with my baby?"

"Jasper, bye. This might not even be your baby," she lied.

"What?" He bucked, glaring at her, knowing he heard her wrong.

"Yea. See, while you were out fucking Humpty Dumpty, I was getting my rocks off too."

"Bitch!" He leaped forward to grab her but was stilled by the cold metal pressed into the back of his neck.

"Watch ya mouth, old man," Mike warned. "Kiki, help her to the car, and I'll grab her bags."

"Taylor!" Jasper called out from where he stood. "I could shoot them you know. This is my house and this man has a gun on me. I could shoot them and get away with it."

"Boy, fuck you, and if you haven't figured out why I'm leaving, check your son's iPad," she tossed over her shoulder before wobbling out the door.

Once they made it outside, Mike backed away from Jasper with Taylor's bag in his hand. He didn't trust Jasper at all, so he kept his gun trained on him until he was out of the door. When the door closed, Jasper ran to the door trying to get Taylor's attention, but they were already gone.

"Fuck!" he cursed, but then Taylor's words struck him like lightning. Running back to the kitchen, he picked up the cracked tablet and opened it.

"Fuckkkk," he dragged. He didn't have to push play to see it was his naked ass on Sherri's couch. He was literally caught ass out.

Taylor rode in the passenger seat, wiping the falling tears from her eyes. She didn't know if she was more upset about

Jasper cheating or the fact that he trapped her.

Eighteen fucking years, she thought.

"Mmmm," Taylor moaned, rubbing her stomach.

"You probably need to go home and take a warm bath," Kiki said, glancing over at her. Taylor felt like she was peeing on herself and the feeling caused her to reach between her legs.

"No," she swallowed, holding up her bloody hand. "I think I need to go to the hospital."

Chapter 14

Two months later

"He grew up in a crack infested neighborhood. Did we think he was going to be clean?" The host laughed into the microphone.

"Now, hold on, there are success stories. I believe Rahlo was just dealt a bad hand," the co-host stated.

"Yea, artists like Big Sean, Kash Doll, and Dough Boy Cashout are from Detroit too and they have been successful. I understand being dealt a bad hand, but you have to know when to limit yourself from the wrong type of crowd. Rah is just getting his feet wet in this industry, and already he's in fights, becoming hashtags, and now he's in hot water involving drugs. Sounds like he's hanging with the wrong type of people."

"Well, I just hope he realizes that everyone is not your friend."

"Fuck outta here," Rahlo scoffed, turning off the podcast.

He was over it all. Everyone had an opinion about his life, about the people he hung around, the places he frequently visited, they thought they knew it all. What they saw was only a glimpse of what his life was really like. Rahlo never imagined being in the limelight would have him hating the very talent that he once loved. Since signing the deal, he felt like his whole life was under a microscope, and he detested it.

It was one thing for his fans to bombard him, asking for pictures and autographs, those moments he loved. It was the online heckling, the podcasters, and the TV hosts that blew him. The amount of fake news they reported had him wanting to track them down on some revenge shit. Different outlets reported he was a drug addict, that he'd always popped pills, and that the drugs in the car were his. Some said he was a Big Meech wannabe, which was the furthest thing from the truth.

Rahlo didn't know what kind of connections Terri had, but he was grateful for him. The judge wasn't moved by his act of loyalty and told him he'd be a fool to throw his life away for a friend. Still, Rahlo refused to snitch, and there wasn't a chance in hell that Dre was going to say the drugs were his. Even if he wanted to, he couldn't. Thanks to Bruce, his mouth was wired shut and he was eating through a straw.

Rahlo's lawyer painted him as a pillar of his community and called several witnesses to testify on his behalf. None of that mattered though. The judge was tired of drug addicts and dealers and wanted to make an example out of him. Since it was Rahlo's first offense, the D.A. offered him a reasonable plea deal. There would be no jail time, but he'd have to attend NA meetings for one year and complete 100 hours of community service at the recreation center. Rahlo took the deal, but his perfect record was stained.

"You want something to eat?" Esha asked, breaking his thoughts. Rahlo looked over at her and shook his head.

Food was the last thing on his mind. He was more worried about the public's opinion.

"You know you can't hide forever," she sighed, dropping

across from him.

"I'm not hiding." He frowned at her.

"You sure?" Esha cocked her head to the side. "They done started a hashtag on Twitter, #WhereisRah?"

"Straight up?" Rahlo cracked a smile. There were still some people who loved him.

"Yes, and Terri is blowing my phone up. You're missing studio sessions, you pushed the tour back, and your album is scheduled to drop in two months. You need to climb out of this funk and get on your shit."

"It ain't that easy, Esh."

"And nobody said it would be, Rah." She tossed her hands in the air. "But that doesn't mean run when things get tight."

"Ain't nobody running," Rahlo said with a frown.

"I can't tell. It's been two months and all you do is go to meetings, the rec, and back home. Have you even talked to Bruce? Duke?"

"No," he sneered. "I don't feel like dealing with people." Rahlo shifted on the couch. He wasn't mad at his boys per se, but it never failed that every time Duke was around, some bullshit kicked off.

"Look, I'm just going to lay it out flat. This is your fault. I keep telling you that you don't owe nobody shit. You hustled day in and out to get yourself out there. You got that deal and the checks have your name on them. You aren't Superman and you don't need to save everybody. That includes mama, Duke, Chef, and anybody else. You need to save yourself before you can help other people. You're straddling the fence right now. You can't have one foot in the hood and the other one trying to make music. They're a pair for a reason, you need to pick a side," Esha preached.

"As far as people's opinion, this is what you signed up for.

Being a public figure, opinions come with the territory. You either let someone else's opinion of you mess with your head, or you stand on what you believe and tell them to suck your-"

"Esha."

"You get the point," she snickered, rising from the couch. "Either way, you have to make a move."

Rahlo exhaled and allowed his head to fall back on the couch. Esha was right and he agreed with everything she said. It was time for him to make a choice and being broke wasn't an option. Picking up his phone, he texted Terri.

Book me a session.

"Aye, call Bruce for me," Rahlo called out to Esha.

"I already did," she sang.

"How do you know your lil pep talk was going to work?" he smirked.

"Because I didn't raise a quitter." Esha winked, taking a sip of her tea. Rahlo nodded in agreement while looking down at his phone.

Terri: Already done and this time I booked the studio in Southwest. Bruce said it's safe. The new producer will meet you there. I'll have a couple of bottles and girls waiting. Let me know if you need anything.

Rahlo couldn't contain the smile that pulled at the corner of his lips. His team was solid. They respected his space and welcomed him back with open arms. Everyone was ready to jump back into their position, and Rahlo loved them for that.

"Oh, and please call Lexi. She's been calling my phone for a week, and I'm trying not to cuss her out," Esha yelled out from the kitchen.

"Cuss her out." Rahlo shrugged. "I told her I'd call when I wanted to talk."

"I bet if Taylor was calling, you'd answer," she threw out.

"I would, but I'm off baby girl. I reached out to her a couple of times and it's radio silence."

"I don't think it's personal. She hasn't posted anything in about a month."

"Maybe her nigga got her on lock," he guessed.

"Nah, she doesn't strike me as the type to sit down because a man said so."

"You got all that from one conversation?"

"One conversation is all it takes."

"Yo big head ass think you know everything."

"I do, that's why you always coming to me for advice."

"Yea aight, Oprah."

"Boy bye," Esha laughed. "Oprah wish she had the sauce like me."

∞∞∞

Taylor stared blankly out of the window. Summer was turning into fall, which was her favorite season. She loved the soft arrays of light brown, pink, and burgundy colors the leaves turned to before they fell. She was obsessed with Ugg boots, tight jeans, and cropped sweaters. And then there was the tan on her skin that still lingered from the summer. Yet this time, she felt nothing. Since losing her baby- his baby- Taylor had fallen into a dark place that she couldn't climb out of. The sad part was Taylor couldn't tell if the feeling came from losing the baby she never wanted or all the changes her body was going through with no baby to show for it.

At twenty-two weeks, she gave birth to a tiny baby girl. Her experience wasn't anything like she could've imagined.

Taylor's hospital room wasn't busy like the ones in the movies. There wasn't a loud fuss over who'd hold the baby first, and the cold silence that loomed over the room made her bones ache.

Taylor hated the whole ordeal and wished they could have put her to sleep, but they needed her help to deliver the baby. They placed her legs in stirrups, they draped a blue cloth over her waist, and finally they asked her to push. The nurses looked at her with empathetic eyes, the doctor coached her through the delivery, and Von held her tight when the baby didn't cry. She knew it was a stillborn, but Taylor was praying for something different. She hoped to hear a whine or any sign of life, but there was nothing. Taylor knew she'd never be the same.

"Tay, you want something to eat?" Von asked, popping his head in the living room.

"I don't have an appetite," she answered dryly, adjusting the warm towel on her breast.

Gorging. Another reminder that her body went through labor with no baby to show for it.

"You haven't eaten in a couple of days."

"I can't make myself eat. I'm just not hungry."

"The doctor said-"

"I know what they said!" Taylor snapped. "And I said I'm not hungry."

"Tay."

"I don't want to eat, Dad," she choked out, unable to stop the tears from falling. "I can barely breathe and you want me to eat. My chest is on fire, I keep feeling kicks that aren't there, I hear the cries of a baby that never existed, and I just want to sleep."

"Baby, I know it's hard-"

"And that's what I don't understand." Taylor laughed

cynically, wiping the tears from her face. "I didn't even want her. Hell, I tried to get an abortion, so I shouldn't feel like this. I asked Kiki to hit me with her car. I asked for this." Her shoulders shook as she cried a little harder. "I should be happy, but I feel like I just lost a piece of me. I feel like something is missingggg," she cried, breaking Von's heart.

"Because you did, Tay, and she'll always be a part of you, but baby, you can't let the grief consume you. We are fighters and I need you to fight for me."

"But I don't want toooo," she whimpered, falling into his side. "I've been fighting to live since Mommy died and I'm tired. I don't wanna be strong anymore."

Von wrapped his arms around Taylor as she cried into his chest. It wasn't a soft cry. The sounds that erupted from her chest were filled with pain and agony. Snot dripped from her nose as she clung to her father's shirt for dear life.

"I lost herrrrrr," Taylor cried. "I lost my baby, and I can't even tell Mommy because we lost her too."

"I know it's not fair, but death is a part of life. It hurts us because the person is no longer here in the physical form but in spirit," Von paused and smiled. "In spirit, they are here. They're in the first glimpse of sunlight in the morning, the breeze that causes the hairs on your arm to stand, and the shadow in the night that gives you comfort when you need it. Your mother is here, baby girl, and your daughter is here too." He kissed her forehead.

"I feel so guilty."

"It's normal, Tay. After your mother passed, I felt guilty because I sent her to the store," Von confessed. "We had food in the house, but I wanted something different." He paused, feeling himself tearing up. "I had to have her famous spaghetti and fish."

"That wasn't your fault." Taylor rubbed his back.

"My heart knows it, but my mind disagrees. Our subconscious is a muthafucka sweetheart, and while I know it wasn't my fault, I can't help but think what if. It's the unknown that makes us overthink. I know losing the baby is heartbreaking, and I know it hurts, but you have to push through because that guilt will consume you. Go get a little sunlight and I'll make you something light to eat."

"Ok," Taylor gave in as Von helped her stand to her feet. Wrapping his arms around her, Von placed a kiss on her forehead. When he felt something wet on his chest, he let her go. Von looked down and quickly looked away.

"Uh, baby girl."

"Hm?"

"You might need to change your shirt. Your uh-your shirt is wet." He motioned for her to look down.

Confused, Taylor glanced down and looked at her shirt. Embarrassed, her hands flew to her breasts to cover the huge wet spots. The doctor told her it would clear up in a month or so and even offered to give her medicine to stop lactation, but she turned them down. The side effects were worse than the actual pain and irritation.

∞∞∞

Pulling an oversized hoodie over her head, Taylor sat on the porch and inhaled the earthy aroma. A few neighbors were cutting their grass, and others were raking up the leaves constantly falling from the trees. Closing her eyes, Taylor took a deep breath and exhaled. Her dad was right. The fresh air was just what she needed.

"Damn girl, I was wondering where you were." Kool interrupted her peaceful moment with his loud voice. "That nigga be keeping yo ass on lockdown for real."

"Hey Kool."

"You good?" he asked, sitting on the porch next to her.

"Eh, I've been better."

"You wanna smoke?" Kool raised his eyebrow. "It always helps me with my problems. I take one hit of this shit and poof."

"You know what," Taylor smirked. "Smoking doesn't sound too bad right now."

"Oh shit, it must be my lucky day. My annoying ass baby mama finally left me, and the woman of my dreams wants to smoke with a nigga."

"Kool, please."

"I'm just saying. I've been trying to get you on my team for years."

"Nigga, please. I'm smoking with you, not joining your roster of women with low self-esteem and daddy issues."

"Why they gotta be all that?" Kool laughed, sparking the blunt between his lips.

"Cause that's what they are." Taylor shrugged. "You wouldn't know what to do with a real woman."

"You probably right. I like my women a lil on the slow side."

"Kool," Taylor laughed.

"I'm dead ass. The fuck I'm gon' do with a smart bitch? She start cussing me out using big ass words and I might have to pop her in the mouth. Nope. Give me the slow hoes that don't know the difference between their, there, and they're." He exhaled the smoke and stretched his arm out to pass her the blunt.

"When's the last time you ate coochie?" Taylor asked, staring at the blunt.

"About a week ago," Kool answered seriously. "I'll stick a bitch all day, but I don't put my mouth on everybody. My mouth is my temple, ya dig?"

"Where do you come up with this mess?"

"Fuck if I know." He hunched his shoulders. "I kinda just go with the flow. Life is too short to be serious. Smoke a little more, laugh a little harder, and fuck all that extra shit. Somebody said that shit, I just don't remember who."

"Hmm, I like it." Taylor pulled from the blunt. Inhaling the thick smoke, she closed her eyes as the weed coursed through her body, closing the door on all her overspilling emotions.

"Damn girl, you even sexy when you look like you want to jump off a bridge."

"Boy," she scoffed, opening her eyes to see him lustfully staring at her. "Thanks, Kool, I needed this."

"No problem, T-baby. You know I fucks with you the long way."

For hours, Taylor and Kool sat on the porch talking about the most random shit ever. One minute they were in a heated debate about football teams, and the next they were on his Instagram Live making girls twerk for twenty-dollar cash apps. Kool was a plumb fool, but she was thankful for him. Not only did he provide a much-needed distraction, but the weed caused her appetite to return.

With a bag full of goodies, Taylor and Kool walked down the street high as hell, sharing a bag of sour patches. Every so often, he tried to put his arm over her shoulder, and in return, Taylor pushed him, almost making him trip on the cracked sidewalk. Kool didn't take it personal. He simply wanted to try his luck. Taylor was high, but not high enough to succumb to community dick.

"Aw, hell nah." Papa frowned when the duo walked up the street falling over each other in laughter. "Don't tell me you let

Kool get the rebound."

"Damn, Papa," Kool laughed, not in the least offended. "I'm not good enough for your granddaughter?"

"Hell no!" He bucked his eyes.

"But I'm good enough to sell you weed?"

"Yep." Papa nodded. "I'll give you that. The best weed man in town."

"Period, Papa," Taylor agreed. "I think you might be my new smoking buddy."

"And you got her high, Lord." He shook his head but was happy to see her laughing and moving around. "Well, don't be stingy." Papa snapped his fingers. "Let me hit it."

"Ah shit, it's a family affair in this bitch." Kool bopped over to the porch and pulled out another blunt for Papa.

"I'm about to go inside and eat my snacks. Thanks, Kool." Taylor smiled at him.

"Can I get a hug for all my feel-good services?" He opened his arms.

"No, nigga." Taylor tossed him a bag of chips. "We're even."

"Good night, Tay." Kool winked at her.

"Good night, Kool. Papa, I'll see you inside."

That night Taylor slept like a baby.

Chapter 15

"Yo Yo Yo. This is Nesha Re and I'm in the studio with Detroit's very own Southwest Rah!" The radio host announced, followed by a round of applause prompted by the switchboard.

"What up doe, Re?" Rahlo spoke into the mic.

"You," she flirted. "You are what's up. I'm digging this look on you." Nesha Re checked out his outfit. The brunt orange puffy vest and wheat Timbs screamed New York, but the fitted D hat and wood-frame buffs said Detroit. "It's giving fall in the city."

"You better stop looking at me like that, you know I been feeling you for a while."

"Rah, stop." She blushed. "But speaking of your relationship status-"

"Oh, that's what we're talking about?" He chuckled, causing the dimple to sink into his cheek.

"Now we are. The girls wanna know if you're single."

"I am," he admitted. "There is a shorty that caught my eye,

but right now, my focus is music."

"I dig that," she nodded. "Then tell us what's your type."

"Honestly, I like thick girls."

"Thick? Like the fake booties, big breasts, and small waist?" She twisted her lips.

"Nothing against my ladies that went under the knife, but I like my women a little more juicy, if you will. I want the legs, thighs, and fupa to match all that ass." Rahlo licked his lips. "I want the real deal."

"Say that shit then!" Nesha Re clapped her hands. "See, you got me cursing on air."

"I'm just being honest. I want my woman black and homegrown."

"Whew." She fanned herself. "Ladies, if you are listening, Rah just said he's a part of the BBW club. Jump in his inbox and may the best woman win."

"You silly," he chortled, taking a sip of water. Nesha Re melted at the way his lips wrapped around the bottle.

"So this upcoming album...give me some tea." She fanned herself.

"It's almost done. Shoutout to my manager Terri and all the producers that's been holding me down."

"Now look, you already established a fanbase before signing with Eastwood Entertainment. Has anything changed?"

"My fanbase is growing." He leaned forward and rubbed his chin. "My day ones know I'm bringing the heat, and everyone is just catching on."

"People compare you to J. Cole, Kendrick, and sometimes Da Baby. How do you feel about that?"

"I love the big homies and respect what I've learned from

studying their music, but I'm in my own lane."

"Meaning?"

"Comparing myself to others only increases the pressure on my shoulders. From where I'm standing, there's only one me, just like there's only one of them. Personally, I think that's why it's always so much competition amongst artists. We all bring something different to the table, there's no need to compete. It's enough for everybody."

"That was well said." Nesha Re nodded her head. "I hope yall new artists are listening. This man is wise beyond his years. The late great Hussle said it best. There is no traffic in your own lane."

"Shout out to Nipsey," Rahlo agreed.

"So you know I have to be nosey." She gave him a knowing look.

"Do ya thang."

"Recently you were in the hot seat over an arrest involving drugs."

"Yea." He shifted uncomfortably.

Terri warned him that the conversation would come up. It was actually part of the reason he agreed to do the interview. With an album dropping, he wanted to clear up a few things. There were so many narratives in the streets about who he was, and Rahlo didn't like it. He was called a crackhead, a druggie, a fraud, and accused of supporting teen drug use. None of those things applied to Rahlo and he needed to make that clear.

"So I know you in real life. You grew up the block from me, we went to the same school and even tried to date in ninth grade," she laughed, recalling them breaking up over a diss song he made about her brother.

"True."

"But I also know that you are private and choose not to speak on your personal life, but with everything circulating about you right now, what can you tell your fans about that situation?"

"I-uh," he paused to collect his thoughts. "I was put in a situation that I had no business being in. All responsibility falls on me for not following my first mind and that's that."

"People are also questioning your street credibility. How do you feel about that?"

"Hm." Rahlo picked up the bottle of water and took a sip. "I'm self-made." He cleared his throat. "Before I signed, I was in the streets every day pushing my shit like dope. I made those mixtapes and performed the songs in strip clubs, I booked my own shows and sold tickets. My street cred is legit, and nobody can take that shit from me. Social media is a façade. People hide behind filters and keyboards because they feel safe, but I'll say this." Rahlo leaned forward with his mouth inches away from the mic. "Ain't no bitch in my blood and don't take the smile on my face for a weakness."

"And there you have it folks. Play with ya mama and not my boy." Nesha Re clapped her hands. "I wanna thank you for clearing that up. We're about to get into this new song, but first, enjoy this commercial from our friends at Shoes for Less." She tapped the switchboard, turning off the microphone.

Backing away from the desk, Nesha Re stood to her feet with a smile on her face. It had been years since she last saw Rahlo and she was honored to be the first radio host to officially interview him after signing.

"Boy," she cheesed, rounding the table. Rahlo met her in the center of the room and pulled her into a hug. "And you smell good." She held him tight. "It's so nice to see you, and I can't thank you enough for coming on my show."

"Thanks for having me. I don't like all this public speaking bullshit, but you made it easy."

"I mean, I might get a red flag later for all the cursing on air, but I'll live."

"My fault."

"Nah, I get it. How are you really feeling though?"

"I'm feeling good," Rahlo admitted. "I was in a dark place for a second, but I'm over that shit and my head is clear."

"Good. Mental health is everything. Take care of you and everything else will fall into place."

"Thanks, Nesha, I appreciate that."

"And I appreciate your fine ass coming in here looking like a snack, talking about you want a thick girl. Boy, you about to make me break up with my man."

"Nah, don't do that."

"Hm. Maybe I won't for now, but let's jump back into your interview. From here, it'll be light."

"And I'll try to keep the bad language at bay." He grinned.

"You don't have to. This my show and I want you to be yourself."

"You asked for it." Rahlo reclaimed his seat, ready for whatever else she was about to throw at him.

∞∞∞

Taylor and Kiki maneuvered through the crowded restaurant trying to keep up with the hostess. *Breakfast for Dinner* was a new restaurant that only opened in the evening and sold every kind of breakfast food you could think of. Their waiting list was ridiculously long, but Kiki was able to get them a table after she made a custom tutu for the owner's daughter.

"Can we get the food to go?" Taylor asked once they were seated.

"No, we cannot. This isn't a to-go dress." Kiki stuck her leg out, showcasing her thick thigh courtesy of the high split. The silk red dress took her weeks to make, and she wanted to ensure it got the exposure it deserved. The back dipped low and stopped right above her crack, showing off the trail of hearts that started at the nape of her neck and went down her spine.

"It's too many people in here." Taylor turned her nose up. She wanted the food, but they could keep the experience.

"Girl, fuck all these people. I'm just trying to cheer you up, so stop all the complaining and figure out what kind of mimosa you want. Matter of fact, they can just bring us a bottle of champagne and a shot of orange juice."

"I'm not about to get drunk in here messing with you."

"You're right. We are not about to get drunk," Kiki agreed. "We're about to get toe up from the flo' up. I already told Mike to expect a call from me because I don't plan on driving back."

While Kiki checked out the menu, Taylor scoped out the restaurant. She noticed everyone was in some kind of silk or satin material. The low lighting was very sensual and she was feeling the smooth music that hummed in the background. A sweet vanilla scent filled the air from the single oversized candle in the middle of the restaurant. Alongside the walls were twin beds and the sign above them read breakfast in bed. The whole setup was cute, and Taylor loved the out-of-the-box thinking.

"Hello, ladies. My name is Black and I'll be your waiter tonight," the deep voice said, snapping her out of the daze.

"Do you come with the food?" Kiki flirted. She loved a fine, toned, black man and wasn't afraid to let it show.

"Sorry, sweetheart, I'm not on the menu," he chortled, licking his pretty dark lips.

"Leave this man alone," Taylor hissed.

"Anybody ever told you that you look like Kofi Siriboe?" Kiki asked, touching his arm.

"Bitch, they gon' kick us out."

"Nah, I've never heard that," the waiter told her.

"Well, let me be the first to tell you that if you ever wanna quit the waiter gig, you should try acting. You don't even have to talk. All you need to do is stand there and smile with your fine ass."

"I'll keep that in mind," he replied with a chuckle. "Can I start you ladies off with a glass of water?"

"Uh, no. Do we look like a couple of amateurs to you? Bring us a bottle of Yellow Label Brute and a small orange juice," Kiki ordered.

"And bring me a water. I don't know what she's talking about," Taylor told him.

"Coming right up, ladies," the waiter said, backing away from the table.

"Girllll, if I was single, I'd fuck his fine ass in the bathroom." Kiki fanned herself, watching him walk away.

"Mike gon' knock your head off, keep playing."

"Girl bye. Mike and I have been together since high school. He knows I'm not going anywhere. I'll flirt my ass off, but I'm a one-man woman...unless I meet Kevin Gates. Him and them yoga poses get me every time."

"Nah, It's 50 Cent for me. He had my good sis Vivica Fox out here sprung."

"Oh, that's a good one," Kiki agreed. "So, how are you feeling?"

"Better. Believe it or not, I've been chilling with Kool crazy ass."

"Oh god, no. Please don't rebound with him."

"You sound like Papa," Taylor giggled. "It's nothing like that. He's just funny as hell and keeps good weed."

"Whew! I was about to say." Kiki wiped the pretend sweat from her forehead. "Has Jasper reached out?"

"I'm pretty sure he has, but I blocked him on everything. I even blocked Jalen."

"Not you blocking the son too," Kiki exclaimed.

"I had to," Taylor sighed. "I love Jalen, but I can't stay connected to him and expect Jasper to respect my boundaries."

"Does Jasper know about-"

"No, I haven't told him and don't feel the need to. He can make another baby with his triflin' ass ex-wife. I hope she burns that nigga this time around."

"Girl, I wanna post their ass on Pornhub so bad. We can get paid. People love watching those cheesy ass sex scenes."

"Ugh, don't remind me. I can't believe he was fucking her nasty ass."

"Here you go, ladies." The waiter returned, setting the drinks on the table. "Are you ready to order?"

"Yes," Kiki spoke up. "I'll take the T-Bone steak, medium well with scrambled eggs and home fries."

"Got it, beautiful." He turned to Taylor. "And you?"

"The salmon and cheese grits. I also want a side of cheese eggs and a buttery biscuit."

"You got it. I'll go put this in."

"Thanks, lil daddy," Kiki winked.

Taylor shook her head and turned her attention to the

commotion at the front of the restaurant. She couldn't see anything from where she was sitting, but she could hear people making a fuss over something. Taylor hoped like hell there wasn't about to be a fight because she left her .22 at home.

"Oh shit." Kiki turned in her seat with a big grin on her face. "Looks like we came out on the right night."

"Why you say that?" Taylor furrowed her eyebrows.

"Oh, you about to see in a few seconds," she grinned, pouring some champagne into her glass.

Taylor opened her mouth to question her further, but the sight before her caused the words to jam in her throat. It had been a couple of months since she last saw him, and there he was, looking better than she remembered. The bronze-colored shirt looked good against his dark skin, and the print in his silk pajamas caused her upper lip to twitch. A medium-sized gold chain rested on his chest, and a gold Rolex shined on his wrist. It was way too soon for her to be thinking about sex, but Rahlo had her ready to fall to her knees in the middle of the restaurant. When their eyes connected, he stopped mid-stride and turned to walk in her direction.

Taylor's heart loudly thumped in her chest as the dimple in his cheek deepened from the grin that graced his face. The man was too fine for words, and Rahlo knew it. His stroll was one of confidence, and Taylor knew deep down he could back it up.

"And here I was thinking you were on your Cinderella shit," he teased, approaching her table smelling better than anything the restaurant had to offer.

"Cinderella?"

"Yea, you dipped out on a nigga and didn't even say goodbye. I looked for your glass slipper and everything," he joked.

"Boy bye." Taylor playfully rolled her eyes and stood to her feet. She stuck her hand out for him to shake it, but he left her hanging.

"We're past that." He slapped her hand away and pulled her in for a hug. His hands caressed her back as he buried his face in her neck. Taylor quivered at the feeling of his lips pressed against her neck. "Damn, why you always so soft, man?"

"Nigga, I go to the bathroom and you out here caked up with her mean ass." Duke frowned, seeing Rahlo and Taylor embraced like long-lost lovers.

"Did it ever occur to you that I'm not mean? I just don't like you," Taylor shot as Rahlo released her.

"We don't like you," Kiki added.

"I'm about to go to my table, but if I call you tonight, are you going to answer?" Rahlo asked, reaching out for her hand.

"Nigga, are you begging right now? I done counted about ten bitches drooling over you and you over here begging her to answer the phone," Duke quizzed. For him, the math wasn't mathing. Ten trumped one any day.

"Bro, go sit down and I'll be over there in a minute," Rahlo hissed.

"Right. Go sit down, lil bus boy," Kiki taunted.

"Aye, fuck yo acorn shaped ass."

"Right back at yo lil dirty ass. I don't know if they told you, but you have to take a shower before you put on new clothes."

"We'll be over here," Bruce chuckled, tapping Duke on the shoulder, signaling for him to keep it pushing.

"Back to you." Rahlo turned Taylor's face with his finger. "Are you going to answer the phone?"

"I might."

"You look different." He examined her face.

"Life tends to change a person's appearance, what can I

say?" She lowered her eyes to the ground.

"I hope that old ass nigga isn't the cause."

"Is." Kiki rolled her eyes. Taylor shot her a look and she clamped her mouth shut.

"Don't you need to be getting to your table?"

"You rushing me off, Tay baby?" He cocked his head to the side.

"Yea. People are staring at us."

"So, fuck these people. I'm trying to see what that nigga did to upset my baby." Rahlo stroked her cheek.

"Aww, yall so cute," Kiki cooed.

"I'm fine," Taylor promised.

"Yea aight. We'll see. Make sure you answer the phone tonight. I'd hate to get my people to track you down and show up unannounced."

"I'll answer."

"You better," he smirked, backing away from her. "Bye best friend." He nodded at Kiki.

"Wow, so you can be her best friend and not mine?" Taylor pouted.

"You know what's up," Rahlo told her.

Kiki sat back and twisted her lips.

"What?" Taylor rolled her eyes. "What do you have to say?"

"Nothing."

"Hmm."

"Well, I will say look at God. You and Jasper are over, and Rahlo seems like the perfect distraction to get you back on track."

"Uhhh, no. I'm not about to jump out of one relationship

into another."

"Why the hell not?" Kiki squinted, lifting her glass to her lips. "Rah is feeling you, and from the way you blush when he's around, you're feeling him too. No need for the playing hard to get game, that nigga is a star. You better snatch him before one of these thirsty hoes beats you to the punch."

Taylor pulled her bottom lip in her mouth and glanced back at Rahlo. He was seated on one of the twin beds with a few women surrounding him. Taylor was sure one of them was going to get the dick.

"Hmph," she turned around. "Like I said, I'm not looking for anybody right now, and I don't think that will change any time soon."

∞∞∞

Jasper turned the liquor bottle up to his lips and took a swallow of the warm liquid. His divorce from Sherri was lightweight compared to how he was feeling now. Taylor's absence had him drinking in the daytime, drinking on the job, and neglecting his son and personal hygiene. His world was literally upside down without her, and he blamed Sherri. With his phone in his hand, Jasper scrolled through the pictures on Taylor's Instagram, hoping that she posted something new, but to no avail, there was no update.

"Miss my baby," he mumbled, staring at her older pictures. Jasper watched old videos of her playing with Jalen and doing a quick vlog of her day. Taking another sip, he backed off her page and went to Kiki's.

"The fuck?" He pulled the phone closer to his face to examine the picture she'd just posted.

Here he was, dying, barely able to breathe, and Taylor was

sitting in a restaurant looking stunning. He hated her outfit, but that wasn't his concern. She should've been seven months by now, and he didn't see the stomach to match. She actually looked smaller than he remembered and that didn't sit right with him.

"I'm over here damn near dying without her and she living her best life with this hoe," he spat. "And where the fuck is my baby? I know she didn't have my baby and didn't say shit," Jasper scowled, clicking the drop down to read the comments.

@KiKitheBody-Hook me up with your girl.

@KiKitheBody-Tell her to turn around, let me see the back of them shorts.

@KikitheBody-Tell @Taydoesitbest to post, I miss her.

Seeing enough, Jasper dropped a few negative comments of his own. It was a burner page, so he wasn't worried about her followers coming for him in real life.

*@KiKitheBody-*Yall big hoes need to put on some clothes.

*@KikitheBody-*This picture reeks of bad decisions and daddy issues.

@KikitheBody- Ain't the other girl pregnant?

Taking another drink, Jasper laughed to himself and started to log off, but Kiki posted another picture that caught his attention. She captioned it, **Finally Fuck Nigga Free**. In the picture, Taylor was sitting on what looked like a swing with her legs crossed. Her head was tilted back, and she was laughing. Again, he zoomed in on her stomach, and there was no evidence of a pregnancy. Jasper's blood boiled thinking about her going into labor and not telling him. He didn't care that she called herself breaking up with him, their baby would keep them bonded for life.

"Got me fucked up," he mumbled, taking another sip and tossing the bottle out the window. Jasper had questions and

Taylor was the only one who could answer them. Thanks to Kiki, he knew exactly where to go.

∞ ∞ ∞

True to her word, Kiki got Taylor tipsy off the champagne and barely there orange juice mimosas. They ate good, laughed harder, and the party really turned up when Rahlo, Duke, and Bruce joined them. At first, Taylor was a little hesitant, but Rahlo made it clear that he didn't have any personal boundaries around her. If he wasn't rubbing her lower back, he was whispering something in her ear. Taylor got tired of playing hardball, so when he draped his arm around her shoulder, she leaned into his embrace.

"Where to next?" Kiki asked once they were outside.

Besides security, there were only a few other people in the parking lot. The restaurant was heavy on no loitering. Once you ate, they wanted you in your car and away from their establishment.

"Where you trying to go, big sexy?" Bruce asked, pulling her under his arm. Leaning down, he whispered in her ear, making a giggle slip from her lips.

"She needs to take her ass home, don't she got a nigga?" Duke scoffed, ready to move around. This was not the night he had in mind. He knew Rahlo was on some laying low shit, but this was not it, plus there weren't enough women to go around. "Matter fact, don't both of yall got a nigga?"

Duke couldn't understand why Rahlo's head was up Taylor's ass when he had his pick of damn near any woman in the industry. Literally, his inbox was flooded with requests from women. Some were bold enough to ask him for one-night stands, and others wanted him to escort them to events or industry parties.

"How about you go sit in the car," Taylor slurred. "Cause you talk way too much."

"Where yo nigga at?" Duke quizzed. "He know you out here dressed like a groupie trying to get fucked."

"Chill," Rahlo warned Duke.

"Oh, I gotta chill 'cause Thelma and Louise tryna get dicked down in the middle of the parking lot?"

"Maybe if you had somebody to dick you down, you'd be a little happier," Taylor slurred.

"He gay?" Kiki asked.

"I'll body both of you tack head hoes," Duke growled.

"Are you going home with me?" Rahlo questioned, slipping his hands around Taylor's waist.

"What are you going to do to me if I say yes?" She pressed her body into him. It was obvious she was drunk, and Rahlo didn't want her like that. He had been around enough women to know that the drunken smile on her face was a mask for something deeper.

"Tuck yo fine ass in the bed," he told her, stroking the side of her face. "Or we can talk about what's bothering you."

"Talk? I thought you wanted to do it," she whispered, thrusting her midsection into him.

"Nah, I don't want to *do it*." Rahlo chortled.

"Can I at least have a kiss?" Taylor pouted.

"What happened to *I'm not looking for anybody right now?*" Kiki teased, recalling her exact words from a couple of hours ago.

"Is that Mike?"

"Where?" Kiki stepped out of Bruce's embrace and nervously looked around the parking lot. "You play too much."

"Now, my kiss." Taylor poked her lips out, but before Rahlo could react, they were blinded by a vehicle wildly pulling into the parking lot. The driver didn't stop until the truck was inches away from them. Protectively, Rahlo pulled Taylor behind his back, and Bruce did the same with Kiki while pulling the gun out of his pocket. Duke followed suit and pulled the strap from behind his back, ready for whatever. This was the action he had been waiting for all day. They could keep that lovey dovey shit, popping a gun made his dick hard.

"This why you left me?" Jasper slurred, stumbling around the car and stepping in front of the lights.

"Jasper," Taylor whispered.

"*Jasper*," he mocked. "Yea, it's me. What the fuck is this? I can't get in touch with you about my baby and you out here being a hoe."

"For one, she left you because yo nasty ass was still fucking your ex-wife. Don't play with my best friend," Kiki corrected him.

"Shut yo fat ass up," he sneered.

"Jasper, you need to leave," Taylor told him. Her buzz was completely blown and she was embarrassed.

"Why I gotta leave because you out here fucking with this rapping nigga?"

"Can I shoot this drunk fool?" Duke asked, feeling his trigger finger twitch.

"That's about the most sensible thing you've said all day," Kiki agreed. "Pop him dead in the mouth."

Rahlo glanced around at the people in the parking lot now staring in their direction. This was not what he needed after the arrest, but he couldn't walk away leaving Taylor there, so he did the next best thing.

"You leaving with this nigga?" he asked, looking down at

her. He already knew the answer, but Rahlo wanted to hear her say it.

"No," Taylor slowly shook her head. "I'm leaving with you." She tugged at the hem of his shirt.

"Then let's ride my baby." Rahlo led her away by the small of her back.

In disbelief, Jasper watched Taylor walk away like he didn't mean shit to her. Like the last three years didn't mean shit to her. He was aware of his actions and knew fucking Sherri would have repercussions, but this was all too much and he didn't know how to handle it, so he lashed out.

"This what you on? Keeping my baby away from me?" Jasper belted. "Taylor!" he shouted her name. "You can't just block me out!"

"Can I at least blow the nigga shit out?" Duke asked, irritated that they wouldn't let him get any action. "I mean, he did just call you a rapping nigga."

"No, bring yo ass on," Bruce told him, helping Kiki climb in the truck.

"This shit ain't over!" Jasper promised.

"*This shit ain't over*," Duke taunted. "Get yo drunk ass on somewhere."

Chapter 16

Taylor woke up the next morning in a bed that wasn't her own. The night's events were a blur, but she did remember leaving the restaurant with Rahlo and coming back to his place. She remembered taking shots with Kiki and twerking to one of Rahlo's songs. After Bruce and Kiki disappeared, Taylor and Rahlo ordered snacks from Door Dash, but she passed out before they arrived. She didn't remember changing into a big shirt or walking to a bedroom.

Sitting up, Taylor wracked her brain trying to remember if they had sex, but from the print she saw last night, she would be aching with a mixture of pain and pleasure.

"Bout time yo snoring ass woke up," Rahlo greeted, walking into the room with a towel wrapped around his waist. Taylor snapped her head in his direction, ready to talk shit, but her mouth went dry. Standing in the doorway like some kind of pornstar, Rahlo ran a brush across his waves. Each stroke caused the muscles in his abdomen to flex. Taylor's eyes lowered, catching the beads of water sliding down his toned abs and tatted chest.

"Keep looking at me like that and I'm going to give you all the dick you were begging for last night."

"I-I wasn't." Taylor closed her mouth.

"You were." Rahlo stopped brushing his hair and advanced toward her. "In here begging me to taste you, suck you, fuck you…all that freaky shit."

"Oh my god, and what did you do?"

"Took about five cold showers." He stood in front of her. "Six, if you count the one I just took. I ain't never in my life had blue balls."

"Let me see," Taylor snickered. "Do they really get blue?"

"The only way I'm pulling my dick out is if you're going to wrap those soup coolers around it."

"You're horrible."

"I'm horrible, but you're asking to see my dick."

"Oh lord, I'm never drinking again." She covered her face.

"As long as you're around me, you straight. I don't want anyone else to meet the drunk you."

"You sound a little possessive."

"Something like that." He winked, backing away from her.

"So about last night." Taylor cleared her throat, feeling the need to explain Jasper's behavior.

"We can talk about it over breakfast. I made some chicken and waffles. There are extra towels in the bathroom and I'll leave a pair of my shorts and a shirt on the bed for you."

"You cooked?"

"Yea," Rahlo nodded. "I needed another way to relieve all this tension, so I cooked. Chop, chop." He clapped his hands. "Third door on the left."

"Don't rush me," Taylor said, but still slid out of the bed to do as she was told.

Rahlo stopped combing in his dresser long enough to watch her switch out of the room. Reaching down, he adjusted the towel that held his throbbing dick hostage. The way her ass swallowed up the panties she wore should have been a crime. All he needed was five minutes to slide them bad boys to the side.

"Shit," he grunted, rocking up at the thought of hitting her from the back. "Now I need to take another fucking shower."

∞∞∞

Twenty minutes later, Taylor ambled into the kitchen wearing Rahlo's t-shirt, basketball shorts, and socks. A plate of chicken tenders, waffles, cheese eggs, and sliced strawberries sat on the counter waiting for her. Taylor didn't know what looked better, the food or the cook, who was currently on the phone while trying to pour juice into a cup. Making her way around the counter, Taylor took the juice from him and filled the two cups he had sitting on the counter.

"Aight, let me eat and I'll give her a call," Rahlo spoke into the phone but kept his eyes on Taylor, who was moving around the kitchen like it belonged to her. At this point, he didn't hear anything Terri was saying. Taylor's booty eating his basketball shorts had his full attention.

"Aight aight, bye," he ended the call.

"You cooked all this?" Taylor asked, popping a piece of chicken in her mouth.

"Yea, is that hard to believe?"

"Yea."

"Why?"

"Because you fine as hell, you're sweet as pie, you rap, and you cook. I mean, you're like the total package. What are your red flags?" She cocked her head to the side.

"My red flags?" he chortled. "What kinda question is that? You act like I'm about to give you a list of reasons for you not to fuck with me."

"I'll tell you mine," she snickered. "This chicken is good by the way."

"I'm happy you like it." He licked his lips. "I'll tell you mine if you tell me yours."

"I can be moody, stubborn, and I don't follow directions well."

"Sounds like a typical woman to me." Rahlo shrugged and dodged the napkin she threw at him. "And violent," he added.

"I'm just saying. All women aren't moody. We just get tired of the world. We gotta be everything to everybody with a big smile on our faces. The moment we express how we feel, we're complaining, we're ungrateful, we're angry."

"Calm down, baby girl, I'm just fucking with you. I appreciate women. I was raised by a black woman and she's everything to me. I value everything you as women bring to the table."

"That's more like it." Taylor popped a strawberry in her mouth. "Your turn. Tell me your red flags. You beat women, you're into ropes and chains, you like snowballs?"

"The fuck is a snowball?" He scrunched his eyebrows together.

"When the chick catches your nut and feeds it to you."

"I'll put your pretty ass out if you say something else like that." Rahlo dropped his fork. "The fuck I look like swallowing my own nut?"

"I'm just playing. Go ahead, tell me." She zipped her lips.

"I've been called rude a time or two, I can be jealous as fuck over what's mine, and I don't mind cracking a nigga shit."

"Jealous?" She tooted her lips, traumatized by that word. "That's enough for me right there. I'll take my food to go, please."

"Is that why you left granddad? He was too jealous?"

"That and he cheated and lied to me."

"What his old ass lie about?"

"His age for starters."

"Fuck outta here, niggas don't do that shit." He laughed, chewing his food.

"I'm serious. I found out he was thirteen years older than me."

"Thirteen?! Damn you couldn't tell?"

"Nope. Black don't crack, right?"

"Well, his loss." Rahlo shrugged. "I'm not going to pretend that I'm sad about it because I'm not." He wiped his mouth. "Are you over him?"

"I'm getting there." Taylor tucked her lip into her mouth.

"What do you need?"

"Time. I uh-" She stopped to gather her words. Talking about the baby she lost was still hard.

"No pressure, baby girl. Let's just eat and we can talk a lil later."

"Sounds good." Taylor smiled, cutting into her waffle.

"Rahlo Darnell!" A woman's voice screeched, followed by the front door slamming.

"Crazy women, that's a red flag," Taylor said, picking up her juice. She was unbothered by whoever was stomping through his house. She was going to finish her food and possibly get seconds, so whoever the angry chick was would have to wait until she finished eating.

"The fuck!" Rahlo jumped up.

"You told Terri to cut me off?" Emory asked, turning the corner. She stopped at the sight of Taylor sitting at the bar. "Oh, this why you acting funny? Got a lil money and hoes and you think you can treat ya mama any kind of way."

Mama? Taylor thought, checking the woman out. She looked every bit of 30-something, but her style was lacking. Emory was dressed in a tan bodysuit with a big purple bonnet on her head. Her nails were long and over the top with jewels and stones. The dramatic lashes on her face looked like they were about to walk away if she blinked too many times. It was hard to believe that she was the woman he was just praising. Taylor didn't get loving or motherly vibes from her.

"Who gave you my key?" He reached for her keys, but Emory quickly backed up.

"I took it off your sister's ring, but that's beside the point. Why would you tell Terri to cut me off? I have a hair appointment and I need to go get an outfit for my auditions."

"Do you hear how crazy you sound? It's not my job to get your hair done. You spending money like the shit grow on trees and stop applying for shit using my name. Terri told me about the credit card bullshit."

Rahlo wasn't surprised when he found out Emory had been applying for credit cards and loans and trying to get a car in his name. It took him years to fix his credit- credit that she fucked up, and now she was at it again, but Rahlo expected nothing less.

"Wowww!" Emory rolled her neck. "You really about to show off for this lil hoe who probably stored your used condom in her purse."

"Trust me, I don't want his baby, sis. I'm only here for the food," Taylor corrected her. "You seem a little hangry. Did you eat? It's more in-"

"Who is this?" Emory rolled her neck.

"None of your business. You need to bounce." Rahlo grabbed her by the elbow, but Emory yanked away from him.

"So what about my audition?"

"What audition, Emory?"

"Mothers of the D."

"The fuck is that?"

"A reality show that focuses on the mothers of rap stars. They called me and asked if I wanted to audition."

"You bullshittin'," Rahlo chuckled, pinching the bridge of his nose.

"No. You getting your coins and I need to get mine." She rolled her neck. "Plus, they have Tokyo, Blac Chyna's mama, hosting the show."

"Tokyo?" Taylor chuckled. "That sounds like drama on top of drama."

"Ain't nobody ask you." Emory shot her a look.

"Nah, you can cancel that. You need some money, then get a job, not exploit me."

"A job?" She bucked her eyes as if he called her out of her name.

"J-O-B," Rahlo gawked, knowing it was something she never had.

"Can I have your eggs?" Taylor asked, interrupting them. For a second, they forgot she was sitting there, witnessing their outlandish discussion.

"Haven't you had enough?" Emory scowled, glancing down at her almost bare plate.

"No more than you, sis. You a lil thick around the hips and the camera adds ten pounds."

"Are you calling me fat?"

"I mean, you're not skinny, but ain't nothing wrong with a lil meat." Taylor popped her lips.

"Where did you find this ghetto ass girl?" Emory asked Rahlo, who was trying not to laugh. Taylor was a real clown. "I mean, you can at least get a girl who respects your mother, but what am I saying, you don't even respect me half of the time."

"Em, chill," Rahlo glared. "You're reaching."

"So, can I have the money?" She dismissed his warning, getting back to the reason she was there in the first place.

"No. I'm not about to keep getting your wigs changed every week. You better get some box braids."

"So you really gon' act funny with your lil money?"

"Lil?" he chuckled. "It's not little when your hand is out. In fact, I'm the best son in the world when I'm giving you what you want."

"Whatever, Rahlo. I'll find another way to get the money. Just remember even the mighty fall."

"Not you wishing for this man's downfall." Taylor shook her head. "The hate is real."

"Girl, fuck you. You must be down on your luck or something. My son has a fetish for helpless ass women."

"Hmph," Taylor grunted. "I wonder where that stems from?"

"Bi-"

"Emory, chill. Go buy one of them wigs from Dollar Tree and throw on a hat."

"You know what, I'm about to leave and let you finish whatever this is because you're acting mighty brand new.

Don't call me crying when she steals your jewelry or burns you." Emory pushed the Gucci purse on her shoulder and stormed out of the kitchen and then the front door.

"Fuck I'ma call you for? You can't fight or replace shit," Rahlo yelled after her.

"Whew." Taylor rubbed her now full stomach. "Mamas that think their sons are their man, double red flag."

"So you gon' eat all my food and keep talking shit?" He turned to face her.

"I'm just saying...mama bear came in here demanding money and shit. I thought sis was a loan shark.

"You got jokes," Rahlo laughed, shooting his sister a quick text. She needed to be more careful where she laid her keys. Emory was on some bullshit and he didn't trust her at all.

"So, is she the strong black woman you were referring to?"

"Nah, smart ass, I was talking about my sister. Esha is my backbone."

"Oh. Whew, I wasn't going to judge you, but I was looking at you sideways."

"Emory- my mama is a different story. She wasn't exactly the nurturing type. Esha took care of me. She was a kid herself, but she had my back, and I'll always appreciate her for that."

"Aww, see, I love that. Sibling love at its finest."

"What about you? Is it just you and your little brother, or do you have more siblings?"

"Nope, just me and Troop. My parents had me young. They were seventeen, so we kinda grew up together, but Trooper, he's their redo. They had him when I was damn near out of the house."

"Redo?"

"Yea, by the time he came along, they were both

established, and he didn't have to bear witness to the struggle."

"That bothered you?"

"No, I love my little brother. He's a little me with boy parts."

"So, you and your parents are tight?"

"Yep. My daddy is my ace boon coon. He's such a gentleman and always gives me room to grow and still catches me when I fall. He doesn't always agree with my decisions, but he understands that his place in life is to steer me in the right direction and trust that I'll make the right choices for me, not him."

"That's dope," Rahlo nodded. "And your mom?"

Taylor smiled, thinking about her mom.

"My mom was everything. She was my best friend."

"Was?"

"Yea, she passed away a few months before my twenty-first birthday."

"Aw fuck, I'm sorry for your loss." He reached out and rubbed her thigh.

"Thanks." Taylor smiled warmly. "I love talking about her. My mom was everything and I'm grateful to have known her."

"That's a good way to look at it."

"What about your people?" She changed the subject. "Is your dad like your mom?"

"Wouldn't know, I never met the nigga. Emory was fucking about three different niggas, and she pinned me on all three until they found out about each other. Three different DNA tests and three different no's."

"Aw shit." Taylor covered her mouth. "That's some real Jerry Springer shit."

"Right. She was out there."

"You ever feel like you were missing anything?"

"I used to when I was growing up, but I wasn't the only nigga without a daddy. Shit, I wasn't the only one with a hoe for a mama. I'm sure her ass is on every *Freak Nik* video ever made."

"Oh my god!" Taylor laughed out loud.

"Bitch, we gotta go now!" Kiki ran from the back of the house. Both Rahlo and Taylor peered in her direction. She had one shoe on, the other in her hand. Her wig was twisted and she was struggling to pull her dress over her ass. "Mike just tracked me here and this nigga is acting a fool."

"I thought you turned your location off?" Taylor hopped off the chair without hesitation.

"I did! He tracked the car and wants to know who lives out here. I told him this was your cousin's house, but he's not buying it. We're all over the Shaderoom, and he screenshotted me pictures of Bruce in my face."

"Correction-" Bruce walked up behind her, pulling the dress over her exposed ass. "You were all in my face."

"You liked it though." Kiki wagged her tongue out at him.

"Yall foolin'." Rahlo shook his head at them flirting as if her nigga wasn't on his way to cause a scene.

"Oh bitch, we about to die." Taylor ran to Rahlo's room, snatching her purse and phone. "I told your hot ass to sit down somewhere."

"Actually, you didn't. Last night you told me to jump on his big fine ass."

"You think this nigga fine?" Rahlo twisted his neck. "Regurgitate all my food and have this nigga cook for you."

"Not you being jealous over some pussy you didn't get," Bruce teased.

"How you know what I got?"

"You didn't, nigga." Taylor hit him with her shoe as she passed by.

"Oh lord, he's calling again. We gotta go." Kiki ran to the door.

"Aye!" Rahlo caught Taylor by the wrist before she could get too far. Gently pulling her into his embrace, he tucked her hair behind her ear.

"Yes?" She gazed up at him.

"I got a lot of shit coming up, but I wanna kick it with you."

"I think I can make that happen. I go back to work this week, but call me and I'll take a break."

"Let me find out you sweet on the kid." He grinned, causing the dimple to sink into his face.

"I might be," Taylor flirted.

"Alright nigga, she'll call you." Kiki grabbed Taylor's other hand, yanking her to the door. "We gotta go. Mike about to kill us and you talking about cakin'."

"Us?"

"Yes, hoe, *us*! We in this shit together."

Rahlo waited until they climbed in the car before closing the front door. When he turned around, Bruce was leaning against the wall, smacking on a piece of chicken.

"The fuck you looking like that for?"

"You like homegirl?"

"Do you like her crazy ass friend?" Rahlo countered.

"A lil bit, but shorty got a man, and I don't do all that underhand shit."

"So you didn't fuck?"

"Nah." Bruce shook his head, pushing off the wall. "I ate her pussy though."

"You a simp," Rahlo taunted, strolling back into the kitchen to clean up his mess.

"Never that, but I'm not gon' lie. Shorty is kinda fire. If she wasn't in a relationship, I'd definitely be trying to see what's up with her."

"Since when that stop you?"

"Since niggas started killing over their bitches. If she was my shorty, I'd murk the shit out of a nigga. I didn't even hit the pussy, but the way her shit was gripping my fingers, I know the pussy is fire." Bruce snatched another piece of chicken off the plate before Rahlo put it away. "What's up with you though? I know yall wasn't talking all night."

"Don't worry about it, fat boy." Rahlo poked his stomach as he walked by. "I'll be ready in two hours. Terri sent over the schedule. I have a photo shoot at 1 and a meeting with the label at 5."

"This the meeting about the album?"

"Hell yea. This shit is high-key stressful as fuck. When I was doing my own shit, it was simple. I rapped and put the shit out. Now it has to go through a few different channels and be approved before being released to the public."

"And you got this, nigga. They just a bunch of niggas in suits. You're the talent."

"Let me find out you a motivational speaker on the side." Rahlo cracked a smile.

"I am," Bruce boasted. "You need to be paying me for all the knowledge I just dropped on your ass."

"Fuck outta here." Rahlo waved him off, walking out of the kitchen. "Two hours, my nigga, be ready."

"Stay ready and you ain't gotta get ready."

Chapter 17

"You better come out here and talk to me!" A female voice screeched, followed by the slamming of a car door.

Taylor's eyes popped open at the commotion. For a second, she thought she was dreaming. Being back at work was kicking her ass, and Taylor didn't know if she was going or coming. Instead of her normal three nights per week, Taylor was working six days, sometimes doubles. It was only the second week, and she was tired as hell, but working so much helped keep her mind off Jasper and their situation.

Since he saw her with Rahlo, Jasper had been calling her off weird numbers and threatening her through text messages. Taylor screenshotted the messages and sent them to Kiki. Jasper was acting deranged, and if anything happened to her, she wanted someone to know. He was doing way too much, and she couldn't escape the weary feeling that crept into her heart with every call and text. To say he felt played was an understatement. It didn't matter what he'd done, Jasper's only concern was Taylor trying to move on, and with his child at that.

"Jada, get the fuck from around here with that bullshit." Kool laughed, too high to deal with her bullshit.

Knowing she heard him wrong, Taylor jumped out of the bed and slipped on her Crocs. There was no way Jada was outside acting a fool. The good Lord wouldn't bless her with such tea so early in the morning. Opening her bedroom door, Taylor bypassed Papa, who was making his way down the hallway with his coffee in one hand and his morning joint in the other.

"Save me a seat," he told her.

"Ok," Taylor giggled, knowing his nosey ass wanted in on the action.

Pushing the front door open, Taylor was surprised to see Jada standing in front of Kool's house next to Sherri. Jada's hair was all over her head and her clothes were disheveled. Sherri was rubbing her back, trying to calm her down as if she wasn't the one to hype her up to get her feelings hurt.

"You dirty ass nigga! I had to abort my baby, but this ghetto bitch gets to keep hers!" Jada yelled, stepping forward.

"Girl gone, it's too early for this shit. I know you see me out here meditating and getting in touch with my inner self." He blew smoke in her direction. "You waking up my neighbors and shit."

"Boy, fuck yo inner peace, your neighbors, and your fat ass mama."

"That's bold," Kool chuckled. "What my mama do?"

"She gave birth to your triflin' ass," Jada spat.

"What I miss?" Papa asked, joining Taylor on the porch. His question fell on deaf ears because his granddaughter had completely checked out. Taylor's eyes were locked on Sherri and her right leg started bouncing.

Taylor thought she was over the betrayal, but she wasn't.

Sherri's hoe ass didn't owe her any loyalty, but she had given her so many passes that she deserved an ass whooping. Before her mind and body could get on the same page, Taylor was off the porch and headed in Sherri's direction. Blinded by rage, she stormed across the street, rolling up her sleeves in the process.

"Tay!" Papa called out, causing everyone to look in his direction. "Don't do it, Miss Sophia," he groaned, spilling his coffee. "Done wet my damn joint."

"Taylor, lis-"

Whap!

Sherri's head snapped to the left from the blow that was delivered to her face.

"Aw hell," Papa grimaced. "Kool, get this girl."

"Talk that shit now," Taylor taunted, knocking Sherri to the ground as Jada backed up.

Whap!

"He's your husband, right?"

Whap!

"You should've kept that nigga." Taylor popped Sherri again, not giving her a chance to fight back. With every ounce of pain and anger in her body, Taylor manhandled Sherri the way she'd been wanting to since they met. Scratching her face, pulling her hair, and pounding her head into the ground, Taylor took all her frustrations out on Sherri as if she were a punching bag. Seeing enough, Jada tried to intervene. Pulling Taylor by her hair, Jada tried to free Sherri from the ass whooping she rightfully deserved, but it proved to be a big mistake. Spinning around like she was possessed, Taylor turned her rage toward Jada, and from the look in her eyes, Jada knew she had fucked up.

Jada wasn't as big as Taylor, but she tried to tussle. Keeping the hold on her hair, Jada clocked Taylor in the face, only pissing her off more than she already was.

"This wasn't your fight, but your fake ass can get it too." Taylor stood up and wiped the blood from her nose. With fury coursing through her veins, Taylor cocked back and punched Jada so hard that her front tooth loosened on impact.

"Damn...fuck her up, Tay!" Kool cheered her on until Papa's cane went across his back. "Ah fuck," he cried out.

"Break them up before my grandbaby end up in jail," he demanded, popping Kool again.

"Aight aight, damn!" Kool bent down to pick up Taylor but was clocked in the eye.

"Shit," he cried out.

"I swear your useless ass is only good for selling weed," Papa cursed.

"What the hell is going on?" Von bellowed, darting across the street.

When he pulled onto his street, he knew his eyes were playing tricks on him. There was no way his baby girl was in the middle of the street fighting like a hoodrat, but sure as shit, there she was.

"Tay, enough!" he ordered, bending down to pick her up.

"Fuck these bitter hoes," Taylor spat, standing to her feet. "Now run and tell your ex-husband that."

"I swear I think I'm in love." Kool smiled, still holding his eye. "A shit talker and she can back it up."

"Shut yo weak ass up and go get me a dime bag," Papa hissed, walking back across the street. "And help these girls to they car."

"Fuck them!" Taylor yelled as Von dragged her across the street.

"Stay yo ass right here while I go help them, and you better pray they don't press charges on your ass," Von scolded, forcing her to sit on the couch.

"You don't even know what happened."

"You're right, I don't. What I do know is that my child, who has previous anger management issues, just beat the hell out of two women in broad daylight. If they press charges, you're going to do time, and there is nothing that I can do about it," Von barked before backing out of the door.

Outside, Papa was leaning on the passenger side of the car, talking to Ms. Riley. With all the commotion, Von forgot she was there. They were on their way to lunch when he discovered he left his wallet at home. The last thing he thought he'd see was his grown ass daughter in the middle of the street fighting.

"So you happy with him?" Papa asked, leaning into the car.

"Dad, go in the house," Von demanded.

"How about you tend to Laila Ali and let me tend to this pretty little honey," he flirted.

"Give me two seconds, baby," Von pleaded, heading across the street where Kool had his phone out recording a video.

"And this is what happens when you try to be big and bad. These hoes rolled up on some boss shit and got their asses handed to them by @Taydoesitbest. If you're not following her, do it. Me and shorty about to settle down real soon," Kool said into the camera.

"Cut that damn camera off," Von hissed. "Ma'am, are you ok?" he asked, helping Sherri stand to her feet.

"No! I'm not ok. I'm pressing charges on that lil hoe," she cried out.

"Calm down with the name-calling."

"Like I said, that hoe is going to jail, and I'm-"

"You ain't gone do shit but take your Peppa Pig looking ass home before I post that video of you sucking dick on the internet. Try explaining that to the world. Not only did you go from wife to side bitch, but you fuck like a sloth and your nipples look like chewed up candy," Taylor said, walking up behind Von, ready for part two.

"Show me," Kool laughed.

"Tay," Von warned. "Go back in the house."

"After Humpty Dumpty and Peppa Pig get in their lil hooptie and leave."

"You're on a roll," Kool clapped.

"Please, just leave," Von begged, helping Jada stand up.

"What an amazing mother you are." Sherri dusted off her pants.

"Excuse me?" Taylor squinted.

"Tread lightly," Von warned, glaring at Sherri.

"You heard me? For a woman that just gave birth to a baby, you're out here fighting, looking dumb as hell. You need to be in the house breastfeeding, or do you not breastfeed because you're too busy drinking and being a hoodrat?"

"Right, where is the baby? You know my brother has the right to see his child!"

"The baby," Taylor chuckled. "There is no baby," she spat coldly, turning on her heels.

"Now get gone hoes!" Kool clapped his hands, shooing them away.

Von didn't wait to see them leave. Instead, he made his way back across the street, where Papa was asking Ms. Riley how well she could play the flute. Taylor wanted to laugh, but she was too pissed off to pay them any attention. Sherri and Jada had her fucked up, and Taylor was ready for part two. She didn't think fighting could feel so good, but she was pumped and ready for whatever.

"I'll tell you what," Papa chortled, limping in the house. "There is never a dull moment around here."

"Tay, what the hell was that?" Von asked, ignoring his father.

"It was her out there acting like she was raised in the Wild Wild West," Papa snorted. "See how far this gentle parenting shit is getting you."

"Dad, please."

"Whatever, I'm going to go find Kool. Ms. Pretty lady, welcome to the family." Papa grabbed his lighter off the table and stumbled to the front door, calling Kool, who was in the middle of the street waving a lace front in the air.

"What the hell was that Tay?" Von questioned, staring at his daughter, who was tapping away on her phone. When she didn't answer, he called her name a little louder. "Taylor!"

"She deserved it! The entire time I was with Jasper she tried to talk to me out of the side of her neck and used the fact that she pushed a baby out of her dried-up womb as an excuse to keep calling and popping up in the middle of the night. That ass whooping was payback."

"And if she press charges?"

"I'm going to make sure her bare ass is posted on every website, posterboard, highway sign and more." Taylor rolled her neck.

"Girl, you are hell," Ms. Riley snickered under her breath.

"Oh my god!" Taylor glanced at the door and covered her mouth. "I am so sorry. I didn't even notice you standing there."

"It's ok, I understand. In the heat of the moment, tempers flare and we block out everything around us."

"Tay, we're going to talk about this later," Von told her. "I came home to get my wallet. I didn't want yall to meet like this, but Ariel, this is my daughter Taylor. Tay, this is Ariel."

"It's so nice to meet you, sweetheart." Ariel stuck her hand out.

"Nice to meet you, too." Taylor shook her hand. "I'm so sorry about all of this. I'm normally not like this."

"She's a lie," Papa yelled in the house. "Aye, music teacher... Do you smoke?"

"Papa!" Taylor giggled. "You can't ask this woman that."

"Oh, I can't ask if she wanna smoke, but you can give her a front row of WWW Smackdown."

"Are yall always this funny?" Ariel giggled.

"Yep, we'll laugh you right out of-"

"Papa!" Both Taylor and Von hollered.

"I'm going down the street." He waved them off. "Everybody can have some fun, but let me make a lil comment and it's *Papa*," he muttered, limping out of the house.

"I'm going to go clean myself up." Taylor backed out of the living room.

"You do that and meet me at the car. I know your fighting behind done worked up an appetite."

"I did," she giggled. "Give me twenty minutes." Taylor put a pep in her step.

"I'm sorry about all of this." Von pulled Ariel into his arms.

"It's ok. I like how feisty she is. Reminds me of myself back in the day." Ariel wrapped her arms around his neck.

"Let me find out my sweet music teacher used to be a hell raiser."

"Hmm, something like that," she smirked. "If you're a good

boy, I'll show you something," she flirted, pecking his lips.

"Please-" Papa held his hands together in the praying position. "Show his ass something that will change his life."

Von released Ariel, shaking his head.

"Yep, just a normal day in the Williams household."

Jasper sat on the toilet at work, checking Taylor's social media pages for the third time within the last twenty minutes. When he didn't see anything new, he switched gears and stalked Kiki's page. There were new pictures of her clothing line and a few gym pictures, but none of Taylor or their baby. Jasper thought it was weird but wrote it off as them trying to keep his baby away from him.

Boom boom boom

"Yo, I need you to come out of the bathroom, big dog." Jasper's manager, Charles, beat on the door, causing Jasper to drop the phone on the floor.

"Gimme a minute," he snapped.

"You can take longer than that because you are fired."

"Fired?!" Jasper roared, jumping off the toilet. He wiped his ass, praying that he didn't get another hemorrhoid. Sitting on the toilet for hours at a time had him walking in discomfort for days.

"Yes, fired. You've been coming to work drunk, hungover, and now you're sitting on the toilet for hours at a time. It seems like you need a little more free time, and I'm going to give it to you," Charles said matter of factly.

Jasper pulled up his pants, picked up his phone, and snatched the door open. Charles, along with security, was there waiting to escort him off the property. There was no need for small talk. Jasper had been warned one too many times.

"I want a union rep," he said as he pushed past them.

"And you're entitled to that, but right now you are reeking of liquor and you're useless. Please leave."

"Useless," he slurred. "Fuck this crusty ass job."

"Yea yea, talk your shit on the other side of the door. You're no longer welcome here, so get to stepping." Charles ignored his rant.

Jasper didn't bother going back to his line. He stopped by his locker, grabbed his jacket and keys, and dropped his work badge and Hilo keys on the bench. With a couple of *fuck you's*, Jasper stumbled to his car, not caring that he'd just lost his livelihood.

Getting in his car, Jasper pulled out his phone and went right back to social media. Stalking Taylor from afar had been his daily routine since she left. Seeing that nothing had changed, Jasper dropped the phone in the cup holder. As soon as he started the car, his phone went off. With Eagerness, he picked it up thinking it was Taylor, but he was sadly mistaken.

"Yea, Ma," he huffed into the phone.

For weeks, Etta had been on his case about being a deadbeat. If he wasn't at work, Jasper was somewhere on his phone, ignoring life around him. Jalen didn't fit into the equation and he didn't feel bad. Jasper claimed he'd make it up to him once he got his favorite girl back.

"Where are you? That wild ass girl done jumped my baby and Sherri," Etta yelled into the phone. "My child is missing a patch of her hair."

"What wild girl?" Jasper quizzed, cranking up his car.

"Taylor!"

"They fought my girl?" he yelled into the phone.

"Are you out of your mind?" Etta gasped in disbelief. "That girl just assaulted your sister and your wife-"

"She's not my wife! Sherri is not my fucking wife."

"Hmph. I beg to differ. I know about you two playing with fire. It's no wonder Taylor left you. I told you that yall should've worked things out. I told you it was too soon for you to just move on without trying to fix your marriage, and now look at this mess you created," Etta preached.

"Ma-"

"No!" she cut him off. "We're not even going to talk about the baby you know nothing about. According to your sister, she didn't look pregnant."

"Because she had the baby."

"Wow, so she had the baby and didn't call you? Are you even the father?"

"Of course, I'm the father. Did they hurt her?"

"Boy, I swear that girl put blood in your spaghetti. There is no way you're almost forty and acting like this."

"Like what? A man in love?"

"No! Like a damn henpecked fool."

"Oh, like daddy?" he laughed.

"Don't you dare bring him up."

"Why? You didn't want me to be like him, so you raised me to be a doormat. To overlook things I knew were happening right under my nose."

"I raised you to fight for family!" Etta yelled. "Your father was weak and gave up. He left at the first sign of hardship and never looked back. I taught you to be a standup man. To take care of your responsibility. Now, I'm sorry for what Sherri did to you, but I'm not to blame."

"You taught me to be a fucking sucker, and instead of

you having my back and cutting her off, you allowed continue to come around as if she didn't do anything wro You made her feel entitled, and I hope Taylor knocked both of their heads loose." Jasper ended the call.

Chapter 18

"When are they going to announce the dates for your tour?" Lexi asked, pulling her shirt over her head.

It was Sunday night and Rahlo found himself with an opening in his busy schedule. He would have rather spent it with Taylor, but she was at work, and Lexi was blowing up his phone. She told him she had a room and wanted him to join her. Since Duke had plans, Rahlo gave Bruce the night off and chilled with her.

Upon entering the room, he was taken aback by the balloons, rose petals, and candles. Lexi was standing in the middle of the room wearing a cute pink teddy, standing next to a massage table. Going with the flow, he allowed her to lead him to the bubble bath she had waiting for him. Lexi scrubbed him good and then sucked his toes. From there she massaged him and sucked him until he nutted in her mouth. Lexi was hoping they would lay up, but Rahlo had other plans, and she wanted to scream.

"Next week," Rahlo replied, wrapping the condom up before taking it to the bathroom. Lexi rolled her eyes. She was hoping that in the heat of the moment, Rahlo would slide in her raw, but she was sadly mistaken. Lexi tried to jump on his dick right after she sucked him up, but Rahlo bent her over the couch and strapped up. The dick was A1, and Lexi would never deny it, but she wanted more.

"What do you think about me coming on tour with you to a few cities?"

"Nah."

"Dang, you don't even wanna think about it? I mean, you could have on-the-road pussy?"

"I could get that anyway," Rahlo shot over his shoulder.

"Excuse me?" Lexi's face fell flat.

"I'm just saying."

"Is that all I am to you...pussy?" She loudly smacked her lips.

"Don't start this shit," Rahlo sighed.

"No, I wanna know. Is that what I am to you?"

"Yea," he answered bluntly. "I fuck you because it's convenient and I don't have to work for it."

"Wow."

"Is it a lie?" Rahlo questioned. "You come to me, I don't come to you. Sex isn't on my mind right now, but when you're constantly spreading your legs in my face, I'm going to take that shit. I'm a man."

"A man," Lexi snorted. "I just don't get it. We have history and I'll be good for you. I'll be good to you. I'm loyal, trustworthy, and-"

"Trustworthy?"

"What?" she gawked. "You don't think I am?"

"You left when I needed you."

"I was young," Lexi reasoned.

"And ain't nobody blaming you for being young but stop acting like I'm the worst nigga in the world because I don't want to be with you."

"Rah, I'm sor-"

"Nah, I don't need an apology. I just need for you to accept shit for what it is."

"So even after all this?" She stretched her arm out to the lit candles and half-eaten fruit tray."

"This is on you. I never asked you to do this shit. Nobody asked you to go the extra mile. Pussy is pussy, I could have fucked you in the back of my whip and been good."

"You're such an asshole, Rahlo." Lexi stormed away.

Rahlo chuckled to himself and picked his phone up off the nightstand. He didn't sign up to deal with her emotional roller coaster, and he wasn't about to sit there while she cried about a situation that wasn't going to change. Tapping the screen, Rahlo noticed that it wasn't his phone. He started to put it back down, but a text from a familiar number caught his eye. The number wasn't saved, but he knew it just like he knew his own. Glancing at the bathroom door, then back at the phone, he shrugged and proceeded to unlock it. Lexi was forgetful, so all of her passwords were the same. Her birthday. Clicking on the notification, Rahlo read it.

313-898-0834: Aye, where that little pink thing she sleep with?

Scrolling up, Rahlo continued to read the text thread. He thought maybe he was missing something. Duke wasn't a friendly nigga, and Lexi wouldn't just leave her child with anyone.

313-898-0834: Get my daughter ready, I'll be on my way in a minute.

313-898-0834: Aye, I'm on my way.

313-898-0834: You gone give some pussy when I get there?

313-898-0834: Aye, stop calling this nigga. We in the studio laughing at your desperate ass.

313-898-0834: Ima need a few more days to get that money for Li shoes. See if Rah can give it to you.

"And another thin-" Lexi snatched the bathroom door open to continue her rant but stopped short when she saw her phone in Rahlo's hand. Frozen in place, she tried to read him, but it was pointless. The vacant look in his eyes told her everything she needed to know.

"I can explain," Lexi panicked, taking a step forward. Rahlo thumbed his nose and tossed her phone on the bed. He wasn't even mad that she was fucking Duke. Lexi could've been fucking half of the niggas on the Eastside and it wouldn't move him. It was the fake love for him. She stayed on his line trying to rekindle shit but failed to mention that she had a baby with his best friend and then was asking him for money.

"No need to, shorty. You not my bitch," he spat disrespectfully. "I wouldn't give a fuck if King Kong stuck his dick in you."

"Rah, it wasn't like that. It happened once."

"You a once ass lie," Rahlo called her out. "You got pregnant in college, which means that nigga was coming out there to see you." He put two and two together. "You really on some hoodrat shit."

"I know this is bad, but we can work it out," Lexi pleaded.

"Work it out?" Rahlo said in disbelief, stepping into his Jordans. "Ain't shit to work out. You been loving the crew."

"It was a mistake," she swore, watching him slip on the black peacoat and Detroit fitted hat.

"Nah, your dry mouth ass knew what the fuck you were

doing. Fake ass hoe. Don't call my fucking phone no more."

"You seriously disrespecting me right now?"

Rahlo stared dead in her face and laughed. It wasn't a chuckle or forced laughter. It was a laugh that made his shoulders shake and tears form in his eyes. Lexi's eyes quickly swept the room in case she missed something because she didn't see a damn thing funny. As long as she'd known him, Rahlo had never disrespected her, but there he was, talking to her like she was a bitch off the street.

"Aye, go drink some Pedialyte to hydrate and stay the fuck out of my face." He bypassed her, knocking over the massage table in the process. "The next time you short on your rent or need some extra money, call Duke." Rahlo slammed the door in her face.

"Shit!" Lexi fell back on the bed, kicking her legs like she was having a seizure. Giving Duke the heads up crossed her mind, but then again, she wanted him to be caught off guard like she was. **

"Girl, I wish I was there!" Kiki stressed, walking in a circle. "I would have been blowing Sherri's shit out." She punched the air. "What Saucy Santana say... *Step off in the spot, bop-bop-bop.*" Kiki swung her arms. "Hoe would've needed dentures fucking with me."

"I'm pretty sure a few of her fronts are loose." Taylor tooted her lips, stuffing her tips in her apron.

The thought of Sherri walking around toothless made her heart smile. For a person with so much mouth, she couldn't fight worth shit. Then there was her sidekick. Taylor wasn't even going to fight Jada, but she just had to jump in on some *I got my girl back shit.* Kool was calling her Chun Li and asked if he could add his baby mama to the list of beatdowns.

"You think she gone press charges?" Kiki questioned. "If she do, I'm really going to tag her motor scooter riding ass."

"I want the bitch to press charges. All I have to do is hit the button and upload her ass to Pornhub. I have the category and everything."

"What's the category?" Kiki snicked.

"Granny gone wild." Taylor giggled.

"You stupid."

"I'm dead ass."

"Tay, you have someone in section three asking for you," Candi said, popping her head in the employee lounge.

"Is it Jasper?" she asked, not in the mood to deal with his bullshit.

Von told her she needed to tell him about the baby, but Taylor's stubbornness wouldn't allow her to. It wasn't proven, but she blamed him for everything she went through, so therefore she'd tell him when she was ready and not a minute sooner.

"Nope, it's Southwest Rah," Candi grinned.

"Nope, I'm not about to deal with his smart mouth ass friend. I'll fuck around and chop his ass in the throat." Taylor shook her head.

"Is Bruce with him?" Kiki asked as if Mike's threats to beat her ass didn't mean anything.

"He's alone," Candi revealed.

"Ugh, I guess," Kiki pouted. "Go out there and talk to your man and then we can talk about your Fuck Boy Free party."

"You throwing me a party?" Taylor grinned.

"Yep! Swinging dicks, some of those sensual massages, and drinks galore."

"I like the sound of that."

"Shit, me too," Kiki agreed. "Now gone and talk to our man.

I'll cover your tables for you."

"Thanks," Taylor said, removing her apron.

Standing in front of the mirror, she fingered her hair and took a couple of deep breaths to control her breathing. Taylor didn't know why she was nervous, but every part of her body tingled with excitement. Applying a thin coat of lip gloss to her full lips, Taylor checked her appearance once more before going out to the floor.

Big Energy by Latto blared through the club speakers, vibrating the walls and shaking the dance floor. It was ladies' night at Top Notch and they were showing out. Tight dresses, long weaves, braids, and made-up faces covered the dance floor and bar. Men stood around watching, too cool to dance, while others bumped private parts with any woman that gave them the time of day.

Bypassing crowds, Taylor hugged a few people and took a couple of pictures with others. She wasn't famous or anything, but people knew who she was from social media. Feeling a pair of eyes on her, Taylor gazed up, and there he was, leaning over the balcony, patiently watching her walk in his direction.

"Bad bitch I can be your fantasy. I can tell you got big dick energy," she sang, climbing the stairs. The black biker shorts she wore disappeared between her thighs, cuffing her fat pussy print. By the time she made it to the top of the stairs, the shorts looked like panties.

"Tay, what's going on, baby girl?" The burly guard greeted her, allowing his eyes to roam her meaty thighs.

"Another day, another dollar," she smiled, bypassing him.

"Bring your friendly ass in here." Rahlo met her at the landing.

Taylor wanted to melt. There was no way God created such a fine specimen and dangled him in her face while she was emotionally unavailable. Rah was giving Patrick St. James in his Givenchy jacket, black jeans, and Jordans. His fade was fresh and his skin was nice and moisturized, which she appreciated.

"Let me find out you jealous," Taylor giggled, walking into his awaiting arms.

Instead of replying to what she already knew, Rahlo hugged her tight, bending a little causing her back to arch and her ass to poke out a little more. Burying his head in her neck, Rahlo's lips brushing across her skin caused her to quiver and her nipples to harden.

"T-muthafuckin baby." Rahlo held her close to him. "Why do you always feel so fucking soft?" he murmured against her neck.

"Because I have a little extra cushion?" she teased, inhaling his cologne. "You smell good."

"I'll make sure I spray some on your pillow. I know you tired of smelling Old Spice," Rahlo jested, releasing her.

"Old Spice?"

"Yea, that's what old niggas wear, right?" he quizzed, picking up his glass off the table.

"You play all day," Taylor laughed, playfully rolling her eyes. "What are you doing here? Alone at that."

"What do you mean?" He took her hand, guiding her to the couch.

"For one, you're famous as hell. Shouldn't you be with security or something? What if some crazed groupie tries to kidnap you."

"I'm not that famous," Rahlo downplayed.

"Stop it. You just joined Instagram and have over five million followers. I'd say you're up there."

"Let me find out you be checking for me."

"Never that," Taylor blushed, looking away.

"Not you being shy after you ate all my food and called my mama a red flag." Rahlo tilted the glass to his lips. "You want something to drink?"

"No, thank you. I can't drink on the clock, and oh my god, that chicken was so good. Can you cook for me again?"

"Yep, I'll cook you breakfast, lunch, and dinner. Come stay the night with me again."

"Or you could just bring me some food since you are requesting my presence."

"Nope, if you not coming over, you can eat the dry ass chicken they serve here."

"You did not just hoe our chef. He does a good job."

"You a good job lie. I had feathers all in my chicken strips."

"I'm not about to play with you." Taylor laughed out loud. "What are you even doing here? Shouldn't you be performing or surrounded by a bunch of half-naked floozies?"

"Honestly, I had some shit on my mind and just needed time to think without all the extra pressure."

"And you came here?"

"Yea, you're here." He peered over at her.

"You wanna talk about it?" Taylor asked, trying to ignore the spark between her thighs.

"Not really, just being in your presence is good enough for me." Rahlo reached out and stroked her chin. "When do you get off?"

"At three."

"You wanna hit the stu' with me afterwards?"

"At three in the morning?"

"Yea, I do my best work before the sun rises."

"Fine, but no funny stuff."

"Why? You still not over that nigga?"

"I'm over him, it's the situation that still has a hold on me."

"You ready to talk about it?"

"Nope, but you can tell me about the lil stick figure that was at your listening party."

"Who?" Rahlo frowned.

"I don't know. I never seen her before, but she knows your sister."

"Oh, that was probably Lexi."

"Hm," Taylor grunted. "Is that like your little boo or something?"

"No," he answered quickly, twisting his face as if her name burned his ears.

"Don't be looking like that. Sis is on your bumper. Shit, I don't know if I should even be here talking to your right now." Taylor glanced around the section as if she was nervous. "Sis said it was her time and I'm not trying to step on her toes."

"Stop it. I'm single as fuck unless you're trying to change that..."

"Nope. I'm not interested in another relationship." Taylor shook her head. "I'm trying to be a city girl and I can't do that tied down."

"Don't tell me you let grandpa spoil it for everybody else."

"If that's what you wanna call it, then yep. He spoiled it and I'm not in a place to give anyone my energy."

"You were just dealing with the wrong kinda nigga, but I'ma fix all that. Don't worry." Rahlo ran his tongue across his bottom lip. Taylor's eyes dropped to his lips, wishing it was her he was licking. When he noticed the shimmer in her eyes, the dimple in his cheek deepened as a grin stretched across his face. "All you gotta do is ask and I'll fix that too."

"I'm not interested in being fixed." She shook her head, inches away from his lips. "Now, if you're offering a little comfort dick, then I'll take it."

"The fuck is comfort dick?" He frowned.

"A little pick me up when I'm sad, straight dick, no attachments. Some warm arms to keep me warm, dick to keep my insides toasty. Just come through and fuck my bad mood away and bounce."

"You wild," Rahlo laughed out. "But check this, I'm not trying to be your rebound dick, so I'm not fucking you until you're healed from all that other shit."

"What makes you think I even wanna mess with you like that? He broke my heart, how am I supposed to believe that you're not going to do the same thing?"

"That's what you worried about?" He scooted closer to her. "The only thing I wanna break is beds, T-baby. I wouldn't purposely hurt you. I don't know what Bill Cosby did to you, but I'm not him."

"Hmph, you sound so sure."

"I am, and in due time, I'm going to expose you to real."

"Excuse me," a voice yelled over the music. Both Taylor and Rahlo looked up. For a second, they forgot they were sitting in a club. They were so close together that if either of them leaned forward, they'd kiss.

"Can we get a picture and autograph?" One of the girls asked. There were about seven of them and they were looking at Rahlo with stars in their eyes.

"Actually-" he started, not wanting what was happening between him and Taylor to end.

"Sure, and I'll take it," Taylor jumped up. The group of girls didn't wait for a response from Rahlo. They quickly ran to his side, climbing all over each other to be close to him. Rahlo shot Taylor a knowing look before straightening up for the picture.

"Say Rahhhhhhh," Taylor requested as she held her phone up.

"Rahhhhhhh," the girls sang.

After taking a few more pictures, she Air-dropped them to the girls with iPhones and quickly left the section before Rahlo could protest. Just to ease his mind, Taylor shot him a text and let him know she'd meet him outside when the club let out.

∞∞∞

"How do you deal with people's negative opinions of your music?" Taylor asked, dipping her pizza in ranch before taking a bite. Rahlo bit into his pizza while mulling over his thoughts. They were on her Live, and he wanted to be careful about what he said, but he also wanted to be as honest as possible.

As promised, Taylor joined Rahlo in the studio. While he wrote lyrics to a song he was being featured on, Taylor shopped on Pretty Little Things and other cute boutiques. When she was done with that, she ordered a pizza and got on Instagram Live. To her surprise, Rahlo grabbed a slice of pizza and joined her. Together, they read the comments and answered questions from different people.

"I won't sit here and say it doesn't bother me when someone says some off-the-wall shit, but people are entitled to feel how they want. We live in a world where people take shit way too serious. It's one thing to voice your opinion, but I'm still going to do and say what the fuck I want to."

"I like that answer." Taylor nodded and wiped the sauce from her lip. Leaning forward, she read a few comments off the screen and laughed. "Yall nosy as hell," she snickered.

"What they say?" Rahlo asked, leaning over and invading her personal space. Taylor closed her eyes as she inhaled his cologne but quickly regained her composure because the world was watching.

"Am I smashing Taylor?" He read the comment and snorted. "Yall are nosey ass shit, but nah. She being stingy."

"Shut up." Taylor pushed him out of the camera's view. "I keep telling yall that Rah and I are just friends."

"That's it?" Rahlo gazed in her direction.

Taylor tried to break their stare, but she couldn't. Rahlo's alluring gaze had her completely captured, so when he used his thumb to wipe the sauce from her lip, she allowed him to. A smile spread across his face when her jaw dropped. Taylor pushed him back and returned her focus to the screen.

"Alright, somebody said Nikki or Cardi," Taylor read the screen and glanced over at Rahlo.

"I like both," he answered. "They both bring something different to the table. Two different types of rappers. That's the problem, people are always comparing them like it can't be two great female rappers."

"True, but that's the world we live in. There can only be number one." Taylor hunched her shoulders, reading another question. "Someone asked, are your lips as soft as they look?"

"You wanna test them out?" Rahlo's eyes lowered to her mouth.

They fuckin' fuckin, someone commented, making her laugh and end the Live.

"You play too much." Taylor bumped his shoulder.

"I'm just saying. You want me to get on here talk about braiding hair and shit, nah." Rahlo shook his head. "Nah, I'm feeling you, and I'm never not going to let it show."

"Yea yea, I hear you."

"If you play your cards right, you can feel me."

"You swear you all that."

"I am, but you are too. Match made in heaven if you ask me." Rahlo winked at her.

"Yea ok, Cupid. I'm about to go."

"See, there you go eating and leaving me again."

"Hush, it's five in the morning and my eyes are heavy."

"Aight, I'm almost done."

"Good because if I stay any longer, you're going to be carrying me outta here."

"That don't sound too bad." Rahlo licked his lips. "I'd happily carry your thick ass."

"I bet you would, freak. Just get done so we can go."

"Aight, you got it, T-baby." He started cleaning up their mess and returned to the booth while she wrapped up in his jacket and waited for him to finish. Taylor didn't know when it happened, but somewhere between listening to Rahlo rap and the softness of the couch, she closed her eyes and was out like a light.

Rahlo didn't bother waking her up, instead he laid on the couch and pulled her on top of him. With Taylor's head resting on his chest and her soft body pressed against his, Rahlo closed his eyes and went to sleep.

Chapter 19

"Do you care to explain yourself?" Taylor asked, glancing over at Trooper, who was sitting in the passenger seat looking out the window.

"No," he mumbled, not bothering to face her.

"Well, too bad. Anytime I have to stop doing what I'm doing to come pick you up, you're going to explain yourself to me."

Taylor was sitting at the nail shop with Kiki when Trooper's school called her to come pick him up. Not only was he being dismissed early, but he was suspended for three days. Trooper's school was twenty minutes away, but Taylor got there in ten with her nails half done. Her first thought was that he got caught selling Kool-Aid again, and then she thought maybe he got into a fight.

"I didn't ask you to get me."

"Trooper, please don't make me pull this car over," Taylor scolded.

"Fine! I did it," he nearly yelled.

"Did what?"

"Whatever they said."

"Trooper."

"Finneeeee," he dragged, turning in his seat. "Last night Daddy and Ms. Riley went to the movies to see *Transformers*, and he promised that he was taking me."

"How do you know they went to the movies?"

"Cause I heard Ms. Riley tell Ms. Jackson -the ugly math teacher I don't like."

"Trooper," Taylor snickered.

"She is ugly though," he swore. "Ms. Riley said Daddy asked her to move in."

"He what?"

"Yea, so I waited til lunchtime and glued her classroom hamsters together."

"You what?" Taylor burst out laughing.

"I used the glue in her desk and glued the hamsters together."

"Trooper, no."

"I don't want her to be my mommy, Tay," His eyes filled with tears. "I want my real mommy to be my mommy."

Taylor's heart broke at the crocodile sized tears rolling down his cheeks. Trooper rarely talked about their mother because he hardly remembered her. He was so little when she died that his only memories came from pictures and home videos. On rare occasions, he'd ask Taylor for a story about her, but other than that, he didn't bring her up.

Pulling into a gas station, Taylor cut off the car and turned to face him.

"Trooper, no one will ever be able to replace Mommy." She

wiped his tears. "Mommy will always be in our hearts."

"But she's going to move in. I don't want the music teacher living with me," he snarled.

"That doesn't mean you have to call her mommy, Troop."

"Will I get A's in her class?"

"I'm sure it doesn't work like that."

"Then can you ask her can I play a different instrument? I don't like the flute," he compromised.

"I'll see," Taylor tittered.

"Are you going to move?" Trooper quizzed.

"One day, but you don't have to worry because when I do move, you'll have a room at my house."

"So I'll have two rooms?" His eyes lit up.

"Yep. Two of everything," Taylor promised. "Come on, let's go in here and get a snack." She removed the keys and grabbed her purse. Going to the other side of the car, she opened the door for Trooper and helped him out.

"Tay, I love you. You the best big sister in the world." He hugged her waist.

"I love you too, Troop, more than you'll ever know."

"Are you going to tell?"

"Sure is, buddy. They had to skin that woman hamsters and now they look like rats."

"Ewwww," Trooper covered his mouth.

Taylor grabbed his hand and walked toward the gas station. It was a warm fall day with temperatures in the high 70s, the block was lively. Everyone was out trying to catch a little sun before the bipolar Michigan weather made a quick switch. Not too familiar with the neighborhood, Taylor clutched Trooper's hand, keeping him close in case anything popped off.

"Let me get a dollar, pretty lady," a man begged, holding his top hat out to her.

"Uh, sorry, I only carry cards," Taylor replied and kept walking.

"You sure? Gimme a buck and I'll give you a nu-"

"Chef!" Esha hollered his name before he could finish the sentence.

"Damn, girl. Calling my name like you yo mama, about to mess up my sell."

"I wasn't about to buy anything from you." Taylor's eyes widened.

"Girl, ignore him." Esha waved Chef off. "What are you doing on this side of town?"

"Picking up my brother from school."

"How you doing, handsome?" Esha looked down at the mini version of Taylor.

"Hi." He waved shyly.

"Boy bye, don't be acting all shy when you just got suspended."

"Tay." He bumped her, not appreciating that she was putting her business all out.

"Better stay in school, or you'll be on the corner selling d-" Chef started to preach, but again he was cut off.

"Chef!" Esha belted. "Here," she handed him a twenty-dollar bill. "Please go do something that doesn't involve you giving out motivational speeches."

"I'll be here every day, 9-5." Chef winked, replacing his top hat and bopping down the street to score his next hit.

"Oh my god," Taylor laughed. "He is a mess."

"Girl, you don't know the half of it." Esha shook her head. "How have you been?"

"Good, I can't complain. I mean, I could, but I'll keep it to a minimum."

"I hear that, but let me get going. I have a client in thirty minutes, and I can't be charging late fees if I'm going to be late."

"That's a good business slogan." Taylor laughed. "These stylists be on some other shit."

"Tay, my snack please." Trooper pulled her arm.

"Ok, boy." She glared down at him.

"Uh, I hope this isn't weird, but do you wanna go have a drink sometime?" Esha questioned. She genuinely enjoyed Taylor and Kiki's company the last time they were together.

"It's not weird at all. I think women should normalize making new friends and going out on friend dates." Taylor whipped out her phone. Esha read her number off.

"And please bring your designer friend."

"Trust me, her crazy ass wasn't letting me come without her anyway."

"Good, I'll see you soon."

"You too," Taylor smiled, holding the door open as Trooper drug her inside.

Trooper tried to prolong their ride home as much as possible. He begged Taylor to stop at the Nike store to get him some new cleats for football tryouts. After that, he claimed he was hungry and knew his sister was a sucker for seafood. Without much convincing, they ended up at Crazy Crab. By the time they made it home, the sun had gone down, and Von was sitting on the porch waiting for them.

"Do I really have to go in?" Trooper asked, poking his lip out.

"Yes, you did something wrong. Stand on it and apologize for your actions."

"You think he gone whoop me for real this time?"

"He might."

"Can you go in first and hide all the belts?" Trooper begged, slurping his drink.

"No." Taylor snatched the cup. "At least act like you're sorry. You can't walk up there sipping your drink like you're unbothered."

"Can you hit me so I can cry?"

"No, fool."

"Aw man, ok," he pouted and exited the car. Slowly walking up the sidewalk, he counted his steps, stomping on every crack, hoping the universe would work in his favor. Since his mama was gone, he was praying that if he stepped on a crack, it would break his daddy back.

"Don't come walking up here like you're sad. I have three different ass whooping tools," Papa spoke first. "You want the switch, house shoe, or belt?"

"I got this, Dad," Von assured him.

"Well have it then. He standing there trying to force tears down his pie face."

"Do you have anything to say?" Von questioned, glaring at his son.

"Yes," Trooper nodded his head. "I glued Ms. Riley hamsters together," he mumbled.

"Why Trooper? What would possess you to do something like that?"

"You."

"Me?" Von squinted.

"Switch, house shoe, or belt?" Papa whispered.

"You asked her to move in," Trooper pouted.

"Oh hell nah!" Papa jumped up, nearly falling off the porch. "Move in where?" He peered at Von for answers.

"She told you that?" Von asked, ignoring Papa's advances.

"No, she was talking to the math teacher and I heard her. I don't want her to move here. I don't want her to be my mommy." Trooper's eyes filled with tears.

"Come here, son." Von stretched his arms out. Walking up the steps, Trooper slipped into his father's arms and rested his head on his shoulder. "It was just a conversation," he explained. "We've been getting to know each other these last few months and I like her. I actually have feelings for her."

"But what about Mommy?"

"Your mommy will always be the love of my life. She'll always be my number one girl, but Mommy moved on to another universe."

"Like Ironman?" Trooper cocked his head to the side.

"Yes, just like Ironman." Von gave him a warm smile.

"I don't want my teacher to live here."

"I respect that and I'll slow it down. You are my number one priority, and until you're comfortable, I'll pump the breaks on the whole moving in situation."

"Ok." Trooper cheesed.

"Now, go write her a letter and apologize for what you did to her hamsters." Von swatted him on the butt. "And you better spell everything right."

"A letter?" Papa gawked. "The woman hamsters were glued

together by the ass and you want him to write a letter."

"He's sorry," Taylor added her input, walking up the steps.

"And he'd have a sorry ass whooping." Papa clapped his hands. "Yall killing me with this gentle parenting shit. This is why kids shoot up shit, don't have enough structure."

"Whoopings don't solve everything," Von retorted.

"Did you get good grades?" Papa asked.

"Yea, I liked school."

"Did you get a degree in engineering?"

"Yea," Von answered.

"Do you have a savings account, 401K, and a couple of stocks?"

"Yea, Dad, where you going with this?"

"Do you wanna know why you turned out so good?"

"Because I studied hard and applied myself."

"Wrong." Papa shook his head. "It's because I tore that ass up. You couldn't even take a deep breath around me. I stayed on yo ass like white on rice, and now look at you, successful."

"So you saying that beating your kids is the answer," Taylor inquired.

"It's the only answer." Papa pursed his lips.

∞∞∞

Later that night, Rahlo was laid across the couch with his eyes closed. He had been running around nonstop for three days, and his schedule was finally starting to catch up to him. If he wasn't in the studio, he was meeting with choreographers for the tour, picking out dancers, rummaging through looks with his stylists, and more. By the fourth day, Rahlo told them he needed a break.

Now that he was alone, he couldn't go to sleep. His mind was all over the place, trying to map out how the next couple of months would go. The tour would start in Detroit, and from there, it was up. The album release party was closing in, and the album would drop right after that. Thanks to Terri, he was performing in Las Vegas before the Javonte Davis fight. The publicity from that alone boosted his ticket sales.

Then there was the fact that Terri kept trying to stick him with Kori, a singer on the label. She was new and they wanted to sell the young love image, but Rahlo wasn't having it and told them if they put them in the same room on some funny shit, he was going to hoe her life and then theirs. Terri took heed to his warning and simply asked him to do a feature on her hit song, *Stuck on It.*

"Yo," Rahlo answered, half asleep. His phone had been going off for over an hour, but all he needed was a minute of quiet time.

"Somebody broke into my house!" Emory screamed into the phone. "Everything is gone."

"What?" He jumped up, snatching the covers off him.

"Are you sleep? My whole life is in shambles and you're somewhere laid up with a bitch!"

"Kill the noise, Em. I'll be there in a minute."

"Hurry up! My Gucci, Prada, and Chanel is goneeee."

"Where Esha?"

"Hell if I know, I called you first!" Emory yelled. "Lord, they took a bitch good wigs."

"I'll be there in a minute." Rahlo ended the call and sent Bruce a text.

Meet me at Emory crib.

Slipping on his shoes, Rahlo grabbed his keys and left. He knew a little alone time was too good to be true.

∞ ∞ ∞

As soon as he pulled up on the block, Rahlo wanted to hit reverse. In true Emory form, she was standing in the middle of the street looking like the very drug addicts she talked about. Her straight back braids were in dire need of a touch-up. Her edges were nonexistent due to the excessive amount of glue she applied to her laces. Dressed in a housecoat and slippers, Emory dramatically held onto AJ for support while the police took her statement.

Parking, Rahlo pulled his hood over his head and exited the car. The house was surrounded by police cars, a fire truck, and plenty of bystanders who were getting a kick out of the show. When her eyes landed on her son, Emory took her performance to the next level.

"Yall niggas in trouble now!" She clapped her hands. Instantly she went from robbery victim to gangsta boo. The officer shifted on his feet, clearly tired of Emory's bullshit. They had only been on the scene for ten minutes and she had been through about five different emotions.

According to Emory, she wasn't home when it happened. The back door was kicked in and everything of value was stolen. The TVs had been ripped off the walls, her room was ransacked, and the stash she kept hidden in a shoe box was gone. The money was her rainy-day fund, and now here it was pouring and she didn't have an umbrella, let alone a box full of money she didn't earn.

"You want me to handle it?" Bruce asked, walking up beside Rahlo. He was tickled as fuck at the scene before them but decided to save his jokes for a different day.

"Nah, but back these thirsty muthafuckas up." He nodded his head toward Emory's audience.

Doing as he was asked, Bruce started moving the small crowd back while Rahlo dealt with Emory, who was now snapping on the officer who was taking her statement.

"I told you I was out! My whereabouts ain't important," she barked. "Worry about where my shit at!"

"Ma'am, you need to calm down," the officer warned, ready to toss her in the back of his car for disorderly conduct. Not only did she reek of liquor, but she was loud and belligerent."

"Wowww, I gotta calm down because you're too incompetent to do your job. A job that my hard-earned taxes pay for. What's that slogan? Defund the police, defund the police," she chanted, thrusting her fist in the air.

"Em, chill the fuck out. You doing too much," Rahlo growled, grabbing her by the forearm pulling her out of the officer's face.

"I'm hurt." Emory turned on the waterworks again.

"Sir, do you live here?" the officer asked Rahlo.

"Nah, this my mama."

"Ok, well my guys are wrapping it up. The back door is kicked in, and unless you plan on getting it fixed, then I believe your mother should stay elsewhere tonight."

"Aight." Rahlo nodded, walking Emory away from the officer.

"My lord, what am I going to doooo," Emory cried, holding onto his arm.

"It's ok, Auntie. As soon as we sign a deal, I'm going to buy you a house. Ain't no way you should be living in the hood." AJ walked up, rubbing her back. Although he was comforting his aunt, his eyes were locked on Rahlo's.

"You got something to say, my nigga?"

"Yea." AJ thumbed his nose. "You living in a big ass loft, driving this lil truck and trickin' at the club, but ya mama house getting robbed because she still live in the middle of the hood."

Instead of defusing the situation, Emory rubbed AJ's arm as if she was trying to calm him down as if he had a reason to be upset. Rahlo glanced down at her hand and then back up at AJ and Emory.

"Nigga, you couldn't get signed even if somebody wrote the raps for your pinch eyed ass," Rahlo spat, making Bruce laugh in AJ's face, further embarrassing him. "You talking about buying her a house, how about you pay ya mama bills and mortgage first."

"Don't worry about my mama. We straight."

"Yall straight with my help, nigga. I pay her fucking bills and been doing it because your non-talented, slow talking, tight pants wearing ass trying to chase a dream that ain't yours. Yall straight because I make sure it's food on the fucking table, so instead of talking shit, yo crusty ass need to be thanking me."

"Rahlo, that's enough." Emory held her hand out.

"Oh, it's enough because this lil wannabe ass thug is about to cry?" Rahlo taunted. "I'll tell you what, pack the remainder of your shit and go stay with this nigga in his mama basement."

"Now you know I'm not trying to stay with anyone. I booked a room at the Marriott," she said like she had it like that.

"Yea, that's what I thought. Get whatever them niggas didn't steal and let's go," he demanded. Emory tightened her robe and walked toward her house with urgency in her step. She was no fool and knew that Rahlo would leave her in a heartbeat.

"And while you're allowing Emory to drag you around, embarrassing the fuck out of you in the streets, I suggest you do your homework. Her money-hungry ass will spend every dime you have before it hits your pockets," Rahlo snarled at AJ. "And you keep commenting on shit that I have, but check this out, I hustled for it. The loft, the *little* ass truck, the amount of money I trick in the club, I earned it. You wanna be me so bad, but you're not willing to grind for it. Next time you comment on anything about my life, you'll be picking your face up from the ground."

AJ didn't respond. He boldly glared at Rahlo, wishing he could beat his ass. Little cousin and all, his smart mouth ass could get it, but AJ knew better. If Rahlo didn't knock his head off, Bruce would happily do it. Sucking his teeth, AJ stormed off and hopped in his mother's car.

"The fuck I miss?" Duke asked, walking down the street.

"Where you been?" Rahlo countered, eyeing him from head to toe.

"With my bitch."

"Since when do you have a bitch?"

"Since now, nigga." Duke lifted his eyebrow in confusion. "Is it a problem?"

"Nah." Rahlo shook his head. "No problem at all."

"I'm ready, son." Emory trotted out of the house with an arm full of her things. "Take me away from this shitty neighborhood." She tossed her things in the back seat and slammed the car door.

"Aye-" Rahlo turned to Bruce. "Put your ear to the street and let me know if you hear anything. I'm going to send someone to pack up what's left."

"Will do," he replied. "You need me tonight?"

"Nah, I'm in the crib tonight. Tomorrow, I have to be downtown at nine in the morning. After that, I have a couple of meetings and they want me to select the final dancers for the tour."

"Nigga, you need a secretary." Bruce's eyebrows met in the middle of his forehead.

"I'm already on it. Terri has been interviewing people for me, so we'll see how that goes."

"It's a party on the Eastside, yall trying to slide?" Duke asked, making his presence known. For some reason, he felt like they were talking over him.

"I'm straight." Rahlo peered over at him, uninterested.

"Uh, aight, then I'm rolling with you," Duke suggested but was stopped in his tracks.

"Nah." Rahlo shook his head. "I'm straight. I'll get up with you later. I have a lot of shit going on and don't have time to bullshit."

Duke rubbed his chin and slowly backed up. He couldn't put his finger on it, but something was different. Rahlo wasn't responding to his texts and he rarely answered his calls. They hadn't really hung out, so he knew it wasn't something he did. Duke was truly puzzled.

"You got something you need to get off your chest?" He cocked his head to the side.

"Nah, I'm straight." Rahlo's jaw flexed. "Do you have something you wanna get off yours?"

"You the one standing here like you have a chip on your shoulder."

"A chip? Nah," he chortled, shaking his head. "Just finding out muthafuckas ain't as real as they claim."

"You taking shots?" Duke asked.

"Did you get hit?" Rahlo rebutted, stepping forward.

"Yea aight. I can see you're tight about all this shit that's happening with your moms, so I'm going to give you space. When you feel like talking, let me know." He backed away with a perplexed expression on his face.

Chapter 20

"Where you at?" Rahlo lowly questioned, pressing the phone to his ear. It was a little past midnight, and he could tell from her background that she wasn't at home.

"Downtown with Kiki and a couple of other people. What's popping with you?" Taylor asked, walking away from the noise.

It was Friday night, and since they both had the day off, Kiki wanted to pop out and get a little taste of the city in the fall. Their first stop was a local taco bar, and from there they hit Eastwood Bar and ended up at the casino.

"You on your city girl shit, huh?"

"A little, you know how I do," she teased.

"I see you trying to get fucked up," Rahlo grunted.

"Why would you say such a thing?" Taylor giggled, pulling her lip into her mouth. Getting fucked didn't sound like a bad idea.

"Because you know them other niggas can't compete."

"I don't know." She twisted her lips. "These niggas out here on ya girl bad."

"Keep playing like I won't pull up and show out."

"What about the press?"

"Fuck the press," he snorted, making her laugh a little louder.

"Anyway, I know you didn't call me to threaten my life. What's popping?"

"Shit," he sighed. "The album is ready."

"Ohhhh shit! You ready?"

Rahlo sighed. He thought he was ready weeks ago, but now he wasn't so sure. It was going to be hard to put a smile on his face like his personal life wasn't getting the best of him. Emory was getting on his nerves about buying her a condo, he and Duke were in a gray area, and there simply wasn't enough time in the day to get everything done.

"Somewhat," he said after some thought.

"Somewhat? Boy, you're about to be famous *famous* now. Everybody and their mama is going to know your name. Your first concert is at Little Caesars and it's almost sold out. That's a big deal," she praised him, unknowingly warming his soul.

"You geeking me up, T-baby?"

"Yep."

"I appreciate that."

"Get yo caking ass off the phone," Kiki yelled out. "Homeboy over here is about to take us to an after-hour spot."

"Rah, let me go. I'm single and I swear this girl is vicariously living through me."

"Fuck all that. Let me come pick you up."

"Why?" She cocked her head to the side as if he could see

her.

"So we can chill."

"It's two in the morning, Rahlo. I'm not some booty call."

"I never said you were, so what's up? Can I come pick you up?"

"Yea," she responded, wanting to see him just as much as he wanted to see her.

"Drop me a pin and I'll be on my way."

"Ok." Taylor ended the call and did as she was told.

Stuffing the phone in her pocket, Taylor sauntered back toward Kiki with a wide grin on her face. Right off, Kiki knew who was on the phone and who was responsible for their night ending early.

"Noooo, we supposed to be out hereeeee," Kiki whined, stomping her feet. "You're supposed to be a hoe, and I'm supposed to be your wing girl."

"And you can, just not tonight. Rah is about to pick me up." Taylor cheesed, unable to hide the way she felt if she wanted to.

"What about them?" Kiki tilted her head toward the two men standing a few feet away from them. Both men were easy on the eyes, and if the circumstances were different, Taylor would have loved to chill with them, but Rahlo had her full attention.

"They would've been fun, but..."

"Rahlo trumps them."

"And do," Taylor agreed.

"Ugh, I guess I'll go home. I'm still in the dog house and I was hoping that one of them would rub my feet."

"Bitch, you do everything but cheat. You might as well fuck a nigga and get it over with."

"Nope. My coochie belongs to one man." Kiki patted her pussy through her pants, making Taylor laugh out loud.

"Seriously though, I want to see him. We've been talking on the phone and-"

"Ugh, don't even explain. I know you like him and I'm happy for you. I mean, at least now you can put me in the same room with Usher, Rick Ross, and Kevin Gates. Rahlo's superstar status can take us places because all Jasper could offer was work picnics and Metro park passes."

"You stupid," Taylor laughed. "So you don't think this is a mistake?"

"What?" Kiki gawked. "Chilling with a superstar and possibly on the brink of a new relationship? Not at all, and if it is a mistake, we're going to have fun while it lasts."

"We?"

"Yes, bitch. Me, you, and Rah. Let that nigga know we share everythinggggg."

"What's the deal, ladies? Are we sliding or nah?" One of the men asked, becoming impatient with their whispers and loud laughter.

"Nah," Rahlo answered, popping up out of thin air.

Rocking an all-black Polo jogging fit with the hood pulled extremely low, Rahlo looked like he was on his bad boy shit. Taylor's middle instantly twitched when their eyes met. The drinks in her system already had her on tip, but seeing him pushed her over the edge.

"Oh shit, Southwest Rah, can I get a picture?" The same man asked in the manliest way possible.

"Nah, but thanks for looking out for them." He dismissed the men. "You ready?" Rahlo's eyes focused on Taylor.

"Damn, I thought you was coming with us, shorty," one of the men questioned, raising his hands.

"Fuck outta here with them toddler ass hands. Them shits ain't big enough to handle one cheek, the fuck you gon' do with two?" Rahlo glared at him. "Let these niggas know what's up before I get outta character around this bitch."

"What he said." Taylor snaked her arms in his. Both men wanted to call her out of her name, but by the way Rahlo stared them down, they knew it would've been a big mistake.

"Ki, you need us to walk you to your car?" Rahlo asked.

"Nope, yall go ahead. I'm about to call Mike and have him meet me at Legends. I'm tired of being in the doghouse." Kiki whipped out her phone.

"Yall go ahead." Bruce turned the corner. "I'll make sure she gets home safe."

Kiki hung up her phone with the quickness. She wasn't expecting to see him since he claimed he didn't mess with women in relationships.

"So much for getting out the doghouse, huh?" Rahlo taunted.

"What doghouse?" Kiki wagged her tongue out at him, walking right into Bruce's arms. Taylor didn't know what he said to her, but she nodded her head and cleared her throat.

"Uh, Tay, my mama fell down the stairs, and I'm about to go sit in the hospital with her," Kiki said aloud.

"Oh my god, when?" Taylor's hand flew to her mouth. They had been hanging all day and she hadn't once mentioned anything about her mama falling down the stairs.

"If Mike calls you," Kiki slowly repeated. "My mama fell down the stairs and I'm at the hospital." Her eyes darted to Bruce then back to Taylor.

"Ohhh, I get it." She slapped her forehead.

"Bout time, we'll catch up with yall later." Kiki waved as Bruce led her in the opposite direction.

"You ready?" Taylor asked Rahlo, who was now looking at her sideways. "What?"

"That's what y'all do?" he questioned.

"That's my best friend. If she said her mama fell down the stairs, then guess what? I'm going to cry my ass off and relay the message."

"So she'd do the same thing for you?"

"In a heartbeat," Taylor confessed without blinking. She didn't need to break down the schematics of their friendship. What was understood didn't need to be explained.

"Yea aight, come on, city girl." He pulled her under his arm.

"Where's your car? I didn't hear you pull up."

"I didn't drive," Rahlo told her. "I only live a few blocks away from here. You mind walking?"

"Nope, it's your world."

"Don't tell me that." He took her hand into his.

"You right," Taylor nodded. "You might get big headed."

"I finally got your fine ass in my grasp, T-baby. My head already big as fuck."

"You swear you pressed," she simpered, feeling her cheeks warm up.

"I am, and the sooner you realize that, the better off we'll be."

Taylor didn't reply. Instead, she held onto his arm as they walked down the almost empty street. A few people whispered as they walked by trying to figure out if Rahlo was Southwest Rah. His hood was so low that it was hard to tell, but they snapped a few pictures anyway. Taylor couldn't get over how laid back he was. The man was worth some serious money, and there he was, holding her hand while walking in downtown Detroit like he didn't have a worry in the world.

"Aye, my man, let me draw you and the pretty lady," the street artist said as they bypassed him.

"I'm straight, big homie," Rahlo replied.

"I'm fast, only takes about five minutes. All you have to do is sit there and talk to this pretty lady and I'll be done in no time," he suggested, needing the sale. "No posing, I draw what I see."

"Aight, five minutes," Rahlo told him, removing his hood.

"Cool, cool, just stand over here under the light for me." He pointed to the selfie light he had set up in the corner.

Rahlo moved under the light and pulled Taylor close to him. Inches away from her face, his eyes fixated on her plump lips. Without warning, he leaned forward and kissed her. Taken by surprise, Taylor's eyes widened, but she quickly fell in line. Rahlo sucked her lips, her tongue, and then her lips again. Just as he imagined, they were soft and tasted like mint. When Taylor started moaning in his mouth, Rahlo pulled away.

"Why you got me out here on some sucker shit?"

"You kissed me!" Taylor's eyes bucked.

"Because you all in my face with these damn soup coolers."

"Op, did you just call my lips big?"

"Big as fuck, but I been wanting to do that shit."

"Before or after you made me your getaway driver?" She twisted her lips.

"Girl, gone with all that," he laughed.

"I didn't take you for the mushy type." Taylor wiped her lip gloss from his lips.

"Mushy?"

"Yea. How many men you know that's going to stop in the middle of the street for a cartoon drawing?"

"I don't know what other niggas would do. I simply wanted to support the cause. I appreciate people who hustle versus standing around with their hands out. This man probably got a family to feed."

"You just trying to make me fall for you, huh?" Taylor wrapped her arms around his neck.

"That's the plan." Rahlo winked.

"Here you go, boss man." The street artist stretched his arm out to hand them the picture.

Taylor removed her arms from around Rahlo's neck and took the drawing.

"Aw, this is so cute," she laughed. His take on cartoon drawing was different. Instead of drawing them like a standard portrait, he captured them in their natural state. Taylor's head was down with her hand on Rahlo's chest. It appeared as if she was laughing, and Rahlo was staring at her with stars in his eyes. The artist captured the dimple in his cheek and everything.

"I fucks with this," Rahlo acknowledged, digging into his pocket. "How much I owe you?"

"Nothing," the man shook his head. "Can you just share it on your page and tag me? My handles are on the back.

"I got you," Rahlo said, still pulling out a hundred-dollar bill and handing it to him. "Time is money, remember that."

"This is beautiful," Taylor cooed. "Thank you."

"You made it easy." The artist winked.

"Yea ok." Rahlo glared at him. "Let me go before you be drawing muthafuckas with ya toes."

"Op," Taylor laughed out loud.

∞ ∞ ∞

Two hours later, Taylor was showered and dressed in a pair of Rahlo's Nike briefs that fit her like bike shorts and a T-shirt. Lying in the middle of his bed, she giggled at the Kevin Hart comedy special that played on the TV while Rahlo sat next to her with his notebook between his legs and a blunt hanging from his lips. His free hand rested on her exposed thigh, and whenever she laughed, he caught a glimpse of her booty jiggling.

"That nigga ain't that funny." Rahlo frowned, squeezing her thigh.

"Don't be a hater, he's hilarious." Taylor whipped her head in his direction. "And ain't you supposed to be writing?"

"I am, but then you start laughing, then ya ass start moving, distracting a nigga and shit."

"I tried to cover it up, but you keep moving the cover."

"Because the cover fucking with my view."

"Then stop complaining." Taylor smacked her lips.

Moving his notebook to the nightstand, Rahlo climbed out of the bed and put out his blunt. Taylor watched him disappear in the bathroom before turning her attention back to the TV. Somewhere between laughing at Kevin Hart and yawning, her eyes started to flutter.

"Wake yo ass up." Her eyes jolted open at the sound of his deep voice.

"No, you're like a Vampire. I'm sleepy," Taylor whined, pulling her leg up toward her chest.

"I got the munchies though."

"Then go find something to eat."

"Ok." He grinned sneakily. Removing the beater from over his head, Rahlo crawled onto the bed, burying his face between her cheeks.

"W-what are you doing?" she asked in complete shock. The only thing separating his nose from her bare ass was the thin fabric of the briefs.

"About to eat something." He bit her butt cheek. "That's what you said, right?"

"I did but-"

"But what?" Rahlo muttered, gripping the waistband of her briefs. "Can I eat?"

"Um, I-"

"Don't think too much into it. Just let me eat your pussy and I'll let you go to sleep." He gently rolled the underwear off her ass. Instead of replying, Taylor lifted a little so he could pull them from between her thighs.

"Good girl." He bit her cheek again. "Do me a favor."

"What?"

"Put a pillow under your stomach."

Doing as she was told, Taylor removed the pillow from under her head and put it under her stomach. Smiling to himself, Rahlo licked his lips at the sight of her ass in front of him as if it was Sunday dinner. He could hear her shallow breathing and smell the sweetness of her essence. "God is good," he blessed his food before diving in.

Using both hands, Rahlo parted her cheeks, nearly nutting at the sight of her glistening pussy lips from the back. Taking his time, he licked each cheek while using his thumb to massage her clit. Taylor's body froze when she felt his tongue meet her asshole. As if he was trying to get the last drop of a slushie, Rahlo stretched his tongue and lightly fucked her hole while his finger toyed with the inside of her pussy.

"Oh my god," Taylor cried out, gripping the sheets.

"Taste so fucking good." Rahlo slapped her ass.

Pulling her closer to him, Rahlo lowered his head and wrapped his lips around her clitoris. Pressing his finger to her asshole, he massaged it while simultaneously sucking on her pussy. Taylor's stomach clenched and her moans became a little louder.

Whap!

"Don't be shy, throw this fat ass pussy back." Rahlo slapped her ass.

Doing as she was told, Taylor wobbled her booty in his face, smashing his nose and forehead in the process, just the way he liked.

"That's right, make that muthafucka dance." He grinned.

"Shit," Taylor moaned out loud, feeling herself letting loose. Each time she popped her pussy, his finger dug a little deeper, hitting her G-spot. A heatwave swept over her body and Taylor swore she started seeing stars.

"Hmmm." Rahlo's lips smacked against her pussy, enjoying the sweet juices that leaked from her body. "I'm hooked, T-baby." He kissed the inside of her thigh. "I'm fucking hooked."

"I'm sleepy." Taylor yawned again.

"Let me clean you up and you can sleep all you want."

"But I don't wanna get upppp," she whined.

With ease, Rahlo picked Taylor up bridal style. Bewildered, she held onto him for dear life. No man had ever picked her up. Hell, no man had ever tried, and he was lifting her off the ground like she was light as a feather.

"What, you thought I couldn't handle all this ass?" He kissed her neck. "Put me down," she demanded.

Doing as he was asked, Rahlo placed Taylor on her feet.

She pecked his lips once more before squatting in front of him. Gazing up in his eyes, Taylor watched his jaw clench. The dimple in his cheek deepened as his hard gaze fell upon her.

"You sure all that can fit in that pretty little mouth?" He questioned, watching her wrap her hand around his shaft.

"I don't know," Taylor licked her lips. "Let's see."

Starting with slow sensual kisses, Taylor's lips covered the head of his dick and then moved down his shaft. He was slightly bigger than Jasper, but she was up for the challenge. Cupping his balls, Taylor opened her mouth and allowed saliva to drip down his sack before she started to massage it. With her eyes still trained on him, she took him into her mouth and didn't stop until her lips grazed the base of his shaft. Her eyes watered and her throat contracted as she slightly gagged, yet she never took her eyes off him.

"Play with your pussy," Rahlo demanded, pumping in and out of her mouth.

Reaching down, Taylor toyed with her wet pussy. When she slipped her fingers inside, only then did she close her eyes.

"Nah, look at me," he grunted. Taylor's eyes slowly opened. "Tay-baby, I hope you over that nigga because there is no going back." Rahlo thrusted his dick between her thick lips. "This ain't no rebound fuck, I'm about to nut in your mouth, and then I'm going to stretch that pussy out beyond repair."

"Uh huh," she agreed with a mouth full of dick.

"I'm about to fuck your world up, girl," Rahlo promised, grabbing the back of her head. Taylor popped his dick out of her mouth.

"Not if I fuck yours up first." She winked and then slapped his dick against her tongue.

Chapter 21

"So.... I'm waiting." Kiki's hand rested on her hip. "I want to hear every nasty little detail."

"Me too!" Candi insisted. "I'm mad y'all didn't call me to come out."

"It was last minute," Taylor assured her. "But it's nothing to tell," she said modestly.

"Bitch, you lying!" Kiki accused. "You been walking around all night like you spent the evening riding a horse."

"Because I did." She tooted her lips and twisted out of the employee lounge before either of them could respond.

It was a few days after her hook-up with Rah, and she was still feeling the side effects of being with him. Love bites decorated the inside and outside of her thighs, butt, and stomach. Since she bruised easily, they were purple, and if anyone saw them, they would have sworn she got beat. Taylor swore that was his plan because she couldn't wear her normal outfits. Thanks to Rahlo sucking on her skin like a vampire, her leggings were pulled up high and her tops covered her stomach.

"Don't play, bitch." Kiki hurried behind her, pulling her into the hallway behind the bar.

"Fineeeee, since you're all in my business." Taylor playfully rolled her eyes. "It was everything! Like I've had good dick before, and I've had my ass ate like a warm peach cobbler on a cool fall day, but this nigga, Ki-" she paused, closing her eyes. "He ate my pussy so good I started to flip his ass over."

"You fucking lyingggg!" Kiki burst out laughing.

"If I'm lying, I'm dying. I've never did that nasty shit before, but I'm telling you, I almost channeled my inner Suki."

"Eatin' a nigga ass," Kiki rapped.

"Eatin' a nigga ass," Taylor repeated. "But I'm not about that life, so I swallowed his babies and bounced on his dick like a pogo stick."

"You should have recorded that shit 'cause, whew, I would love to see that."

"Freak ass."

"Have you talked to him?"

"I have, multiple times, actually." Taylor cheesed. "He's busy but definitely makes time to call or shoot me a quick text."

"Friend, I'm so happy for you. You bagged some superstar dick and I couldn't be prouder."

"Shut up, fool."

"I'm for real. He's nothing like Jasper's old, desperate, senior citizen ass. Wait, have you talked to him since the restaurant pop up?"

"Nope, and I don't want to. Don't get me wrong, I loved Jasper. He helped me get through a critical period in my life, but his underlying intentions weren't pure. I was so blinded by the honeymoon stage of our relationship I missed all the red flags. He slowly but surely introduced me to the real him. Even if he wasn't fucking Sherri the entire time, he was still on some psycho type shit. Like how you steal my keys then help me look for them, knowing you got them?"

"Right!" Kiki exclaimed.

"Then you steal my birth control, get me pregnant, and act surprised." Taylor shook her head in disgust. Even saying it out loud rubbed her the wrong way.

"That part! Like nigga, I'd rather you cheat on me then to get me pregnant. The fuck. I don't wanna have kids until I'm in my forties and the doctor says my clock is ticking. Even then, I might push it to fifty." Kiki smacked her lips. "I have an empire to build."

"Right! He took that option away from me, and I'll never forgive him."

"Me either. He almost took us out of the game. How am I supposed to dangle in these streets and my partner in crime knocked up?"

"Speaking of game, what do you call yourself doing with Bruce?" Taylor perched her hand on her hip. "While you all in my tea, spill yours."

"He's fun." Kiki shrugged.

"Don't play."

"No, for real. I love Mike. Like wholeheartedly love that man from the top of his head to the bottom of his feet."

"But?" Taylor cocked her head to the side.

Kiki's head fell back, and she let out a deep sigh. "But we're all each other know. We've become comfortable with each other."

"And that's a bad thing?"

"Yea, sometimes. There's no thrill. Literally the same shit, minus the time I hit him with my car. That shit was exhilarating."

"You crazy," Taylor laughed.

"I know this sounds selfish, but I want to date other people. I want to live my life and not worry about someone else's feelings. Mike and I have been together since high school, and we'll always be best friends, but I think us separating is for the best. If it's meant to be, we'll find our way back."

"Well, you know I love you, but don't end your relationship because you think Bruce has something better to offer."

"It has nothing to do with Bruce. Don't get me wrong, he's fun, but I'm not about to commit to anything but another fad diet. I'm determined to lose this gut in ten days."

"Period, and if that one doesn't work… try another," Taylor encouraged.

Removing her vibrating phone from the apron tied around her waist, Taylor clicked on the screen and grinned at the text from Rahlo. Kiki leaned over and frowned.

"Who the heck is that?" Taylor giggled at her pettiness. She saved his number under Bloodsucker with a vampire emoji.

"Rahlo."

"*Rahlo*," Kiki mocked. "You good as gone. I'm trying to be a hot girl and you're falling in love."

Bloodsucker: *Come see me.*

"What our famous boo say?" Kiki asked, looking over Taylor's shoulder.

"Nope, not this one, sis," Taylor warned before replying.

I'm on the afternoon shift at work. I can come after though. Are you in the studio?

"Oh, it's like that?" Kiki teased. "You ain't never wanna

tussle over Thurgood Marshall."

Bloodsucker: Why you picking up shifts? You need something?

"Yep, tread lightly, sis," Taylor threatened, looking down at her phone. She admired his willingness to help her, but his money was the last thing she wanted. From where Taylor was standing, it seemed like he had enough people in his pockets, but that was a conversation for another day and time.

No, I don't need anything. It's easy money so why not? she replied.

Bloodsucker: I get it T-baby. I love the hustle. Maybe you can take me on a date when you get paid. I can eat too, so bring ya tips.

Laughing out loud, Taylor pulled her lip into her mouth and replied.

I can do that without my check. I have a few dollars in the bank.

Bloodsucker: Oh shit. Let me find out I'm fucking with a baller.

"What yall talking about?" Kiki asked, trying to peek at the screen. "Oh my god, yall cute. Aww, I wanna flirt with somebody."

Bloodsucker: I'm in the hood today. Bruce mama is having a rib cookoff and I'm posted. Come through.

"He wants me to come chill with him." Taylor blushed, showing her the text.

"Then let's go. We can meet at my house after you go home and change. I'll drive my own car because you're always leaving me when he comes around."

"You mad?" Taylor wagged her tongue at her.

"Never that, but tell him we're coming."

"Where yall hoes going now?" Candi asked, walking up behind them.

"To the dentist," Kiki lied. "Wanna come?"

"Bitch," Taylor snickered.

"For your information, I made another appointment to get the situation resolved."

"Good. After you handle that, you're more than welcome to hang."

"Girl, fuck you." Candi stormed away.

"You wrong." Taylor shook her head.

"Yea, and they have a special place in hell for me. Are we going to chill with Rah or nah?"

"Yes, fool. I'll go home and change. Pick me up from there."

"Sounds like a plan." Kiki danced away. "Let me go make my final rounds. I'll see you about five."

"See you then," Taylor guaranteed.

Bloodsucker: Talk to me T-baby. Are you fucking wit ya boy or nah?

Taylor's heart thumped at his eagerness for a response.

Damn, you pressed, she replied.

Bloodsucker: Like a panini sandwich T-baby.

Snickering, Taylor sent one last text and dropped her phone in the apron pocket.

Fine, send me the address.

On the other side of the city, Rahlo sat on the porch watching the scene in front of him. Bruce's mother, Dena, was one of the best cooks in the city, and her rib cookoff was simply a reminder that she was the best to ever do it. It was cold as hell, but the mention of her cooking brought out everybody like a Beyonce concert. Although there were several other tables, hers was packed, and the food was usually gone within an hour. This year was bigger and better than ever. Bruce bought her a new grill and more ribs than she knew what to do with. He also put a tip jar on the end of her table and made sure everybody dropped something in her bucket. The ribs were free, but her time was not.

"You talk to Duke?" Bruce asked, biting into what seemed like his tenth bone.

"Nah," Rahlo answered, turning his cup up.

"You wanna let me in on what's going on?"

"Not really."

"Aight, no pressure, but when you ready to talk, let me know."

"Aight, Dr. Phil," Rahlo jested, glancing down at his phone.

Emory was texting him yet again, talking about the Marriott wasn't up to her standards and she wanted to move to MGM. According to her, they had a suite on hold but needed a card to put on file. If she was waiting on him, she was going to be waiting because Rahlo wasn't moving her nowhere but to Motel 6 if she kept complaining.

"Oh my god," a voice screeched. "You're Southwest Rah, right?" the high-pitched voice screamed.

"I am." Rahlo peered up from his phone, taking the dark skin beauty in.

"Can I get a selfie, please?"

"Only if I can get your number?" Bruce flirted, checking her out.

"Gina! Don't get fucked up," a man hollered, limping toward her with a cane in his hand.

"Daivion, stop playing with me. My name is Rina, asshole." The girl frowned.

"Your name gone be homeless if you don't stop acting like a groupie. I'm the biggest nigga in your life. You need to be asking for my picture."

"Dai? The fuck is up nigga?" Rahlo pushed up from the porch to greet one of his childhood friends.

"You know him?" Rina's eyes widened at her boyfriend hugging one of her favorite rappers.

"Know him? I'm the one that taught this nigga how to rap!" Dai gawked. "And get yo ass over here. The fuck you standing next to him like he your nigga for?"

"Dai, please." Rina rolled her eyes. "Do you think I can get a picture?" she asked Rahlo.

"Sure thing, sweetheart." Rahlo pulled her under his arm.

"Nah." Dai put his cane between them. He poked Rina in the side, making her move over so he could stand next to Rahlo. Sucking her teeth, Rina stood next to Dai as Bruce snapped a couple of pictures of them.

"Ugh, you get on my nerves." She rolled her eyes. It was all good though, she planned on cropping him out anyway.

"Ask me do I give a fuck? Get a couple of them wipes out of my fanny pack and go find a bitch to take home. Check her teeth, toes, and fingers."

"This nigga," Rahlo laughed.

"You ain't said nothing but a word." Rina popped her lips. She was always down for a good time, and with Dai, every night was a good time.

"You still wild as fuck," Bruce chortled. "Where twin?"

"Nite a family man nowadays. His girl dragged his ass to Disney World a week ago."

"Straight up?"

"You got kids too?" Rahlo asked.

"Fuck nah, unless you wanna count the ones on Rina's tongue. A couple hundred on that muthafucka," Dai said, making Bruce and Rahlo double over in laughter. "Oh shit! Lina! I found our girl," he called out, watching the thick beauty walk toward them.

"What is that girl's name because you done called her about ten different names?" Rahlo asked.

"Something with a -ina, but fuck all that. I want her."

Rahlo followed his eyes and grinned. Dai could try, but he was barking up the wrong tree. Shorty approaching them was strictly for him. He spent hours carving his name inside her pussy and mouth. Rahlo dicked her down so good that Taylor might as well walk around with a taken sign wrapped around her neck.

"I hope you have some hot chocolate since you got me in the cold," she complained, walking up to them. "I mean, who grills when it's freezing outside?"

"I got whatever you need, baby. Tell me what your fine ass desire and I'll make it happen," Dai flirted. "I'll warm your thick ass up. Matter fact," he glanced down at her thighs. "You can warm me up."

"Watch out." Rahlo pushed him to the side, reaching out for Taylor, who walked right into his arms. "You look good, T-baby." He licked his lips.

"As fuck!" Dai added. "This nigga treating you right?"

"Move around," Rahlo warned.

"It's hot as hell out here." Kiki fanned herself, strolling up.

"Lord girl, you thick ass fuck." Dai licked his lips. "Pina! I found another one."

"Nah, you straight." Bruce pulled Kiki into him. "Why you ain't tell me you was coming?"

"Cause I'm trying to see what you be on," she replied

smartly.

"Damn, where yall find them at? Is there any more?" Dai inquired.

Rahlo ignored Dai and checked Taylor out. She was dressed in a skintight body suit that hugged her body as if the fibers were infused to her skin. The front dipped right below her breasts, and he could tell she wasn't wearing a bra. The bubble jacket she sported wrapped around her waist, placing her ass on display for the world to see.

"You look good, T-baby." He pulled her in for a hug.

"Thanks." She smiled, burying her face in his chest. Taylor wasn't surprised by his public display of affection. Rahlo wanted the world to know he was feeling her.

"You want something to eat?"

"No, but a drink would be good."

"What do you want? Bruce's mama got a few things in there, and if it's not something you want, I'll have someone go get it," Rahlo told her.

"Oh, hell yea! I'm definitely trying to see what's up now." Dai nodded. "Anytime a nigga start offering shit that's not here, it's something to write home about, and baby, I got the letter."

"This nigga," Bruce laughed.

"Ignore this man," Rahlo chuckled. "What do you want?"

"I'll do vodka and cranberry."

"You sure you don't want something to eat?"

"Not right now."

"Aight." Rahlo stepped around her. "Sit tight."

"What about me, rude ass?" Kiki smacked her lips.

"What you want, Ki?"

"I'll take the same thing, bestie," she cheesed.

Rahlo went inside the house to see if Dena had what they needed for drinks. Dena loved Rahlo, so she went in her room and pulled out a new bottle of Titos, and sent her nephew to the store for a few bottles of cranberry juice. While they waited for the juice, Rahlo gave them Titos and orange juice, which did the trick of knocking the edge off.

In no time, Taylor was vibing with his people like she'd known them all her life. They laughed, joked, and danced until the sunset. The cookoff turned into a party when everyone cut their headlights on and turned up the music.

"What yall know 'bout this hit right here?" Chef bopped in the middle of the circle, bouncing in his dress shoes as Tamia poured from the speakers. "Come here thick and lovely, I know you know this dance." He stretched his hand out to Taylor.

"I do." She smiled, handing Rahlo her cup, and joined Chef in the middle.

"See, back in my day, we danced with the ladies. It was none of that standing there shit," Chef preached, taking Taylor's hand and twirling her around.

"*When I think about us, I think about the way that we make love. The way that you make me sweat, make me want a cigarette,*" Taylor sang as she and Chef fell into sync. She danced with him but sang to Rahlo, who was recording them.

"That's right, baby girl." Chef danced with ease. "Step, step, step, cross, ayeeee," he coached while moving around her.

"*I can't get enough of you.*" Taylor winked, moving her hips, making Rahlo's dick twitch.

"Sing that shit, girl," Chef encouraged even though her high pitch tone was hurting his ears. It was the thought that counted.

Chef had always been a ladies' man. Even now, a few of the

older women watched him, almost forgetting that he was a crackhead. The drugs took a lot of things away from him, but that bop...that sexy ass bop was still there, and it was evident his hips were still lethal by the way he danced with Taylor in his arms.

"Bop, bop, bop, now cross," he coached Taylor. "I like this girl," Chef called out as people cheered them on. Taylor unknowingly won a special place in Rahlo's heart. Chef wasn't the most put-together nigga, but she didn't care. She danced with him like he was the best looking thing around.

Near the end of the crowd, Lexi watched the scene with a bitter taste in her mouth. If she didn't like Taylor before, she really didn't like her now. She watched the way Rahlo gazed at her and it made her stomach turn. Lexi couldn't even get a call back to explain herself, but he had time to marvel over a fat bitch dancing with the neighborhood crackhead.

"The fuck is this?" Duke asked, creeping up behind her with red eyes.

"What are you on?" Lexi squinted. She had seen high Duke plenty of times, but this was different. His eyes were bloodshot red and wide open. She noticed the way his pupils were dilated and a light sweat danced around his hairline.

"Weed, the fuck?" he frowned. "He brought that bitch out here?" Duke nodded to the circle where Talyor was now standing between Rahlo's legs. His arms rested over her shoulders with a cup in his right hand.

"I guess. What's going on with yall?" Lexi asked, already knowing. She just hadn't told him and didn't plan on it. In her mind, they wouldn't have gotten caught if Duke hadn't texted her.

"Don't know. That nigga on some funny shit. I guess that fame shit going to his head."

"Did you ask Bruce?" she fished.

"Bruce is that nigga yes man. He was never really my friend. Fuck them though." Duke shrugged his shoulders, trying to hide the fact that he was butt hurt. His friendship with Rahlo was about the only consistent thing in his life.

"Whoa!" Lexi bucked her eyes. "Where is this coming from?"

"People been switching up on me since I was born. I don't expect a couple of niggas I grew up with to remain loyal to me."

"Now, if it were anybody else you were talking about, I'd agree, but this is Rahlo. He's been holding you down since grade school. This is the same person that used to steal food so you could eat. He used to give you his clothes when Esha bought them for him. He held you down through all of your bids."

"Even with all that shit, he still switching up on me."

"Is he switching up, or are you threatened by this version of him, and you're switching up?" Lexi asked, confusing him. "Rahlo is still the same loving, giving person he always was. It's you who's acting different. You said it yourself, you don't fuck with the new people in his life, but those new people are giving him the credit he deserves. His elevation is happening because he's been a blessing to so many people."

"You stay riding that nigga dick, but riddle me this, if he's so fucking loyal, why is he tonguing that bitch down and you standing over here looking dumb?"

"Because I chose the wrong person to be loyal to," Lexi countered and walked away.

Duke waved off her. He didn't give a fuck what she was talking about. Lexi could keep all that self-righteous shit to herself. Duke wasn't trying to hear it. His mind was extremely clouded and the little blue pill on his shoulder wasn't helping. Blinking a few times, Duke focused on clearing his vision.

Popping pills had become a habit he formed on his last

stint in jail. Weed was cool, but in prison, he needed something a little stronger. He needed something to block out the cries, moans, and arguments around him. He craved for something to help him keep his head down, and the pills did just that. It made the time go by a little faster. The more he popped, the more disconnected he felt from the world. Pills had been his dirty little secret and scapegoat.

"Why these niggas been in they feelings? Always talkin' bout some money, but ain't never got no chicken, ay!" Rahlo rapped, bobbing his head to Sada Baby. In the zone, Taylor raised her hands, hitting the Blade Ice Wood underneath him. She was fucked up. Her eyes were low, and Rahlo kept feeding her drinks while whispering all the nasty shit he wanted to do to her when they got back to his place.

"That's the type of shit that got them jealous," Taylor rapped, dropping her shoulders.

"Sup Rah." Duke walked up, posting next to him. Instead of speaking, Rahlo tossed him a head nod.

"That's how you feel?"

"The fuck you want? A hug?." Rahlo cut his eyes at him.

"Where the fuck you been?" Bruce asked, lifting his head from Kiki's neck.

"Minding my business, fat boy. I see yall love fucking with bitches that are unavailable."

"Who are you talking to though?" Kiki squinted. Drunk and all, Duke could catch a quick fade.

"I'd advise you to chill, you in my hood and I'll pay one of these bitches to blow yo shit out."

"You don't have to pay, my nigga. We give out ass whoopings for free," Taylor spoke up.

"See, I really like this girl," Chef laughed loudly. "You sure you don't wanna move over to the dark side?"

"Back up." Rahlo pulled Taylor into him as if she could fit inside his skin. "Duke, you can move around with all that rah-rah shit. Ain't nobody gone touch her."

"You know she got a nigga, right? Never took you for a side nigga."

"And I didn't take you for a jealous nigga. The fuck you worried about who I stick my dick in for?"

"I ain't worried." Duke scrunched up his face.

"Good, then we on the same page." Rahlo glared. Duke nodded his head with a crazed look in his eyes. Chef knew the look all too well.

"With that being said, unleash my dance partner so we can do the turbo hustle." He snapped his fingers, trying to ease the tension.

"Nah, she straight." Rahlo moved Taylor to his side. "Matter fact, we about to dip. Ms. Dena, can I get them to-go plates?"

"You sure can, sweetheart. Thanks for coming."

"I always come through for family." He winked at her.

Duke stood back and watched Rahlo move around dapping people up, promising tickets to shows, but not once addressing him. In Duke's eyes, it was a big fuck you.

Chapter 22

Two weeks later

Rahlo viciously threw jabs at the punching bag in the corner of his living room. It was the day before his party and his anxiety was at an all-time high. It didn't help that Emory kept sending him pictures of condos, and Lexi was blowing up his phone trying to explain a situation he gave zero fucks about. Terri was on his ass about dropping a verse on his label mate's album and preparing for the tour. It was a lot going on. Sweat poured down his face and his knuckles were sore, but he swung through the pain.

"You still a lil nigga," Bruce taunted, strolling in the living room, plopping down on the couch.

"Fuck outta here." Rahlo flexed, wiping the sweat from his forehead. "I'll forever be Big Rah to these lil niggas."

"Aye, what's up with you and Duke?"

"Nothing," Rahlo snorted, picking up his water off the table. Bruce stared at him dully, not buying his nonchalant response.

"Something is up. That nigga usually at your side like a shadow, but lately yall been on some silent fighting type shit."

Rahlo sat the water down and locked his hands behind his head. Duke was his best friend, but shit didn't feel the same between them. Even when they were cool, it felt like some kind of weird energy brewing amongst them. Rahlo tried to shake it off, but it was getting harder and harder to ignore.

"Did you know he was Lily's daddy?"

"Lily?" Bruce frowned. "As in Lexi's daughter?"

"Yea."

"Get the fuck outta here!" Bruce waved him off.

"Dead ass," Rahlo said seriously. "The last time I was with her, I made a mistake and picked up her phone thinking it was mine. I started to put it down until I saw his number on the screen. I read a few of the text messages on some lame shit, but it was all there. While she was swallowing my dick, this nigga was watching their kid."

Speechless, Bruce wiped the corners of his mouth, wondering how he missed the signs. There were plenty of times when Duke would disappear, but he chalked it up to him doing some shit he had no business doing.

"That's some slime shit." Bruce was really shocked. "How long they been fucking?"

"I don't know, and honestly, I don't care. It's the disloyal shit for me. We're boys, fuck that, we're brothers, and that shit came out of left field. I feel like if he was hiding this, what else is he doing behind my back? I done held this nigga down through countless bids, bailed his people out plenty of bullshit, yet he smiling in my face while I give Lexi money for their kid. Picture that, me supporting the whole family."

"You gon' address it?"

"I'm not about to confront this nigga over Lexi's desert

storm ass pussy." Rahlo frowned.

"Like you said, it's not about her. It's about them hiding the shit and smiling in your face."

"Nah, I'm straight. I have a lot of shit going on, and I don't have time to be in my feelings about him or nobody. He knows what's up. Duke not as stupid as he portrays to be."

"So what's the move?"

"Right now, I'm focused on making this money," he said, watching Taylor walk out of his bedroom wearing his boxers and a t-shirt. "And her."

"Oh, I'm sorry, I didn't know you had company." Taylor stopped in her tracks and went back in the room.

"It's cool, T-baby, this nigga is about to leave."

"Where the fuck I'm going?"

"I don't know, but you gotta get the fuck out of here," Rahlo told him, nodding to the door. "I need to kick it with shorty about a few things."

"Yea aight, if you about to get some booty, just say that," Bruce teased.

"Don't worry about it, nigga. Aye, you heard anything about my mama's house?"

"Nah, not yet, but we'll hear something soon. You know niggas can't hold water."

"Aight, let me know." Rahlo gave him pound before walking him to the door. After locking it, he ventured off to the back of the house to find Taylor.

Entering his bedroom, he found her repacking her overnight bag. Since she worked the night before, Rahlo was surprised she was up so early. He was hoping to release his frustrations on the punching bag, shower, and then release a little more on her. Since she was packing, he could tell that probably wasn't going to happen.

"You just gone stretch out all my draws, huh?" Rahlo teased, walking up behind her.

"Something about my pussy resting where your dick belongs makes my heart warm."

"Man, what?" he chortled.

"I'm kidding, but I like this brand."

"I'll get you some," Rahlo promised, sitting on the bed and pulling her down onto his lap. "What are you about to get into?"

"Go home and see my guys. Trooper sent me a text this morning asking if I could come home."

"So I'm picking you up from home tomorrow?"

"Picking me up for what?" Taylor quizzed, mentally running through her mind to see if she missed something.

"The party."

"Oh, I-I uh didn't know I was invited."

"What?" He frowned. "My face been buried in your ass all week. What other invitation do you need?"

"I didn't want to assume anything, so if you want me to go, you need to ask me."

"Seriously?"

"Dead ass," she replied with folded arms.

"I got you." He nodded, prepared to give her the confirmation she needed.

Gripping her by the waist, Rahlo pulled Taylor onto his lap so that her feet were planted on each side of him. Reaching back, he grabbed a condom from the nightstand and lifted his hips slightly to lower his shorts. Taylor's eyes danced with excitement at the pleasure that was sure to come. Ripping the condom open, he rolled it down his hard dick and tossed the wrapper to the side.

"Sit on it," he demanded.

Pushing the boxers to the side, Taylor slid down on his dick without hesitation. Closing her eyes, she savored the moment, enjoying the feeling of him stretching her open. Patiently, Rahlo stroked her nipples through the t-shirt while she adjusted to his width. He, too, was enjoying being submerged in her warm, wet walls.

Placing her hands in the center of his chest, Taylor lifted up on the balls of her feet and started to rock her hips in a back-and-forth motion. As if a song played in her head, she rode his dick to a beat only she could hear. The smacking sounds her juices created echoed off the wall, along with the soft moans that escaped her lips.

"Do that shit, T-baby," Rahlo encouraged, giving her ass a swift slap. He was learning that Taylor liked to ride dick. With her, the shit was a whole experience. If it wasn't the way she gyrated her hips, it was the way her insides continued to squeeze his dick even after he nutted.

Whap!

"Ask me," Taylor moaned, wobbling her booty in his lap.

In one swift motion, Rahlo did some kind of wrestler move and rolled over so that he was on top. Pushing her legs toward the headboard, he slipped back inside of her.

"Damn, this pussy feels like home." He kissed her lips. "Can I have it?"

"Uh huh," Taylor moaned.

"Say it," he demanded, fucking every ounce of sense out of her. "Say it!"

"It's yours, I'm yours!" she cried.

"Good girl, now what do you want me to do?"

"Make me cum," Taylor begged.

"My pleasure, T-Baby." Rahlo kissed her once more before he started roughly thrusting into her.

"Fuck yessss!" she cried loudly as he pounded into her. With each stroke, Taylor felt her insides quiver, and before long her toes were curling, and Rahlo was emptying his nut in the condom.

Breathlessly, she raised up on her elbows and stared at him.

"What?" Rahlo asked, confused.

"You still didn't ask."

"What the fuck was that?"

"That was you using your dick instead of your words....so ask me."

"You love having me do sucker shit, huh?"

"I'm waiting."

"T-muthafuckin-baby, can you come shake that ass for a real nigga at my party?" Rahlo gave her an award-winning smile that caused her heart to skip a beat. The dimple in his cheek caved in, adding to the intense throbbing between her thighs.

"You swear you pressed."

"Like some church pants with extra starch," Rahlo joked, leaning over to kiss her lips. His fingers found her slippery middle and he started to massage her clitoris. Taylor moaned in his mouth and slowly twirled her hips on his fingers.

"Fat muthafucka wet, gripping, and taste sweet as fuck."

"Well, I guess now I know why you aren't answering the phone," Emory spat, disgusted by the sight of Rahlo finger fucking Taylor.

"The fuck?" Rahlo snapped, removing his fingers from between Taylor's thighs. Grabbing the cover, he threw it over her body. A normal person would have left after catching the duo in such a compromising position, but Emory stood there with her arms folded across her chest as if she'd just caught her man fucking another woman.

"You wasn't answering, so I thought something was wrong, but I see that's not the case." She glared at Taylor. "You in here with a bitch that smell like Long John Silver."

"Excuse me," Taylor furrowed her eyebrows, knowing she heard the woman wrong.

"Yea, you're excused right to the bathroom to wash your funky ass. I mean, damn son, you are famous now and I know you can pick a better, healthier looking bitch."

"Lady you got me f-"

"Emory, get out," Rahlo snapped.

"Hurry up, we have shit to do and you're laid up with this-"

"Em!" he barked.

"Fine." Emory stormed out of the bedroom, slamming the door in the process.

Taylor quickly jumped out the bed and started gathering her clothing. The last thing she wanted to do was deal with another bitch who thought she was taking their place. As much as she liked Rahlo, Taylor was over all the drama. Life wasn't supposed to be so hard, and this time, she was going to be smarter than the last.

"Gimme a minute, T-baby." Rahlo climbed out of the bed, pulling up his shorts.

"Uh, no, it's fine. I'll leave," she insisted, jumping up and down to get into her leggings.

"She don't run shit."

"Yet this is the second time she barged in your place being disrespectful like I won't knock her ass out of them last season shoes. To save her the embarrassment and me the jail charge, I'm going to leave."

"Tay."

"Rahlo, I like you, but I'm not about to play with your jealous ass mama. I hope you have a great party, and if our paths cross in the future, I hope we can do this again." Taylor placed her hand on his chest.

"Yea, fuck all that. I'm about to set her straight and then I'll call you," he sternly stated.

"Rahlo."

"T- baby, you should have gave me that speech before you started hypnotizing me with this sweet ass pussy. I waited for you and that old nigga to end, and I waited for you to get over him. I'm not about to let you run from me. You are about to consistently get all this dick, straight gas, no brakes. Now give me a kiss and tell me you'll see me later."

"Rahlo."

Silencing her with his hand around her neck, Rahlo gave it a light squeeze and sucked her lips, making her knees buckle a bit. His mouth found her chin, then her neck and collarbone. Soft moans escaped her lips as his hand slipped inside the front of her pants. Like a feen, he feverishly stroked her clit, wanting to send her off with the proper goodbye. When her pants became a little heavier, her knees weakened, and his hand became drenched, Rahlo knew his job was done. Delivering one final kiss to her lips, Rahlo removed his fingers and stuck them in his mouth.

"Now, what did I just say?" He asked with his lips inches away from her.

"Y-you'll see me later," she stuttered.

"Good girl." He kissed her once more and slapped her on the ass.

"But you better get your mama because I'm not above knocking her wig loose," Taylor promised, going into the bathroom to clean herself up.

Once she was finished, Rahlo walked Taylor to the front door. Leaning in, he kissed her lips and gripped her booty, wishing they had a chance for a round two. Emory was leaning against the counter watching their every move. She didn't like how intimate Rahlo was being with Taylor and the salty look on her face it all. Clearing her throat, Emory bucked her eyes in their direction so they could hurry up.

"Don't go ghost on me," Rahlo warned, ignoring Emory's petty antics. "I'll call you later, and if you need anything for the party, let me know."

"Ok." Taylor nodded, knowing she was about to block him. The dick was damn good, but she didn't have time for all the extra shit. Pecking her once more, Rahlo let her go, and Taylor slipped out of the door.

"Ugh. I didn't take you for a chubby chaser," Emory snorted. "It's so many pretty girls out here and you want her sloppy ass."

"Aye, give me my key." Rahlo held his hand out. "You're too comfortable walking in my shit like you pay bills in this bitch."

"You not gone wash your hands first?" She turned her nose up.

"You can kill all that shit. Her pussy smells like warm apple pie."

"Wow, and this is how you talk to your mama." Emory dropped the keys in his hands.

"Why are you here?"

"Because I've been sending you houses, and you haven't replied. I'm ready to move out of that hotel. I think the housekeepers are going through my stuff."

"Emory, I'm not about to buy you a house."

"Why not?"

"Because I'm not. I don't even own a house yet," he told her. "If you want me to update your security system and get you new locks, I'll do that."

"Wow, so AJ was right. You are switching up on us."

"First of all, fuck AJ, and if he feels so strongly about you getting a house, then tell his long face ass to get you one. Matter fact, tell that nigga to pay your hotel bill too."

"Ugh. I don't understand why you are being so difficult. You have the money, just call Terri and tell him to look at the listing I sent," Emory exhaled.

"That's what I am to you? A fucking meal ticket?" Rahlo bellowed.

"That's what I was to you," she snapped back.

"Are you insane? Esha took care of me! She fed me, bathed me, walked me to school. She gave me her lunch money so I could go on field trips. You didn't do shit!"

"Rahlo, change the station."

"Let me ask you a question. Do you listen to my music? Can you even name one song?"

"Not really," she admitted.

"Right, but you want me to fund this glamorous ass lifestyle and you can't name one fucking song," Rahlo scoffed.

"I gave birth to your disrespectful ass. You owe me!"

"You pushed me out and then gave me to my seven-year-old sister. I don't owe you shit."

"I should have aborted you!" Emory pushed him, mad that he wasn't bending to her will. "I should have aborted you because all you do is talk about what I didn't do for you."

"I wish you would have because maybe I would have been blessed with a mother who actually gave a fuck about me. I've been trying to buy your love for years and now I see shit for what it really is."

"Finally!" Emory wiped the tears from her eyes. "I'm happy your slow ass finally got it. I never wanted you, Rahlo, and the only reason I kept you was because they gave me more state assistance."

"Get the fuck out of my crib, Emory."

"Happy to." She snatched her purse off the couch and stormed out of the loft just as quickly as she came.

Sherri waited until Jasper went to sleep before she tiptoed past him. Since getting fired, Jasper lost his apartment and had been posted up at her house like he paid the bills. It would've been okay if Jasper did something around the house to compensate for his lack of financial help, but all he did was drink, lay on the couch, and stalk Taylor.

At first, Sherri tried to be understanding since she played a part in his breakup, but as of lately, Jasper had been on some other shit. He'd get drunk and rant about killing Rahlo and kidnapping Taylor. There were plenty of times she walked in on him punching the wall while pretending he was doing bodily harm to someone. Sherri knew he had a few screws loose when she went through his phone. The numerous calls and texts he sent Taylor was sick, and she was disgusted by the way he talked about her on Instagram. Whenever Taylor posted a picture, he was the first to call her a fat bitch, sloppy hoe, and every other name that degraded her body.

Jalen was terrified, and Jamie didn't want to come home. All Sherri wanted was for Jasper to get out of her house, but because his name was still on the deed, it was easier said than done. It got to the point where she started praying to God for all the things she'd done wrong in life. She wished she could go back and leave well enough alone because this Jasper was not the same Jasper she married.

"I love you too, Tay," he mumbled in his sleep before turning over.

"Crazy ass fool." Sherri shook her head and slipped out of the door. She didn't know what was about to happen, but the feeling in her bones told her that trouble was on the horizon.

With a little free time on her hands, Sherri headed downtown to get her nails done. She was kid-free and had a little money in her pocket, thanks to her other baby daddy coming through. She told him she was short on cash but left out that Jasper wasn't paying her child support and had been staying at her house. Sherri reasoned he didn't need to know all the details and hoped Jamie didn't tell him either.

∞∞∞

"So what are you going to do?" Jada asked before biting into her salad. Sherri glanced at her before sticking a fry in her mouth. It amazed her that Jada had all the remedies to help her get Jasper back but none to get rid of his stalking ass.

"I don't know, but I wished I would have left him alone. Once again, I'm stuck with the shitty parts of him while he mourns his relationship with Taylor." Sherri rolled her eyes.

"Well, she is holding their baby hostage. How is he supposed to get over her when she won't even let him see the baby?"

"I think she lost the baby."

"Why you say that?" Jada bucked her eyes. "Did she post

something?"

"No, but she hasn't reached out to him at all. She doesn't post pictures of the baby and her stomach is flat as hell. She looks a lot skinnier, too."

"Have you told Jasper?"

"No, the last time I said something about her, he nearly stapled my head to the wall."

"Girl," Jada shook her head, "I can't believe he hit you like that. Your eye was black for almost two weeks." Sherri didn't need the reminder because every time Jasper raised his voice, she flinched.

"I think you should tell him. Maybe it will be different coming from his sister."

"Hell no. I'm not trying to be all in his business."

"Since when?" Sherri's eyes doubled in size. "I could have sworn it was you who advocated for me to press him. You had no problem being in his business when you kept inviting me over while he was there."

"I admit that it was wrong. Jasper was happy, and we should have left well enough alone."

"Fine time for you to come to that conclusion," Sherri scoffed, picking up her wine.

"Are you blaming me?" Jada sat up in her seat, seeing the conversation taking a left turn. "I didn't take your hand and make you cheat on your husband."

"But you set it up," Sherri argued. "You introduced me to Jay, and you let us use your apartment-"

"I didn't make you do anything you didn't want to do. You are grown as fuck and old enough to make your own decisions. You chose to cheat on your husband."

"And you helped me."

"But I didn't tell you to get pregnant by the nigga and try to pass the baby off on my brother."

"You know what, I'm going to go before I slide your young ass across this restaurant." Sherri cleared her throat, standing to her feet. "And while you're so quick to talk shit about me, how about you go get that baby sucked out your ass? What's this, number 4?"

"Fuck you, Sherri," Jada spat.

Sherri pushed her purse on her shoulder and opened her mouth to respond, but Kiki beat her to the punch.

"Not yall in this nice ass restaurant arguing," she giggled. "I thought yall thot boppers had a little more class, but I see I was wrong."

"Excuse me." Jada wiped her mouth and stood up. She didn't want to be caught off guard again.

"Your rotten womb ass is excused. Grandma, what number abortion is this?" Kiki asked Sherri, whose gaze was focused on Taylor.

"Girl, come on. I wore my good heels and don't want to get blood on them from stomping these hoes." Taylor ushered Kiki away by the small of her back.

"Not you choosing you be chill today. Let's turn up for old time's sake," Kiki pleaded.

"No, fool. You see people are already looking at us."

"So," she shrugged, stepping outside of the restaurant.

Taylor thought her eyes were playing tricks on her when she spotted Jada and Sherri sitting in the back of the restaurant in a heated argument. Kiki wanted to go over and toss a couple of drinks around, shake a few tables, but Taylor was over the entire situation. Coincidently as they were leaving, so was Sherri, and Kiki couldn't resist the chance to say something.

"Uh, Taylor, do you have a second?" Sherri asked, pulling

her coat a little tighter. She didn't know if the chill came from the shifty Michigan wind or the icy stare that Taylor delivered.

"What the fuck do your saggy pussy lips ass have to say to my best friend?" Kiki quizzed.

"Uh, I'm talking to her."

"And I'm talking to your trout mouth ass. Bitch, we are outside the restaurant and I'll beat your ass up and down this sidewalk. Fucking with me, you'll be permanently riding on those scooters you love so much."

"Shakia," Taylor snickered.

"I'm just saying. You don't need an apology from her. Her old ass knew what she was doing."

"Look, I'm not trying to apologize." Sherri shifted on her feet. "Jasper is being weird."

"What's new?" Kiki chuckled.

"No, like he's been stalking you on Instagram. He has fake accounts and literally sits around and waits for you to post. He follows the guy you've been seeing, and he's been saying some off-the-wall stuff that I think you should take seriously. I've never seen him like this, and I just wanted to give you the heads up."

"Noted." Taylor turned on her heels to walk away, but Sherri did the very thing she said she wasn't going to do.

"I'm sorry," she blurted.

"What?"

"I'm sorry. You were good to Jalen, and I was jealous of what you and Jasper had. I came onto him while you guys were broken up, and I'm really sorry. It took me some time to see the role I played in this, and I'm legit sorry for any hardship I caused."

Taylor slowly turned around and stared at her before

speaking.

"Girl, fuck you and this thought-out apology. You can take that weak ass shit and shove it up your loose ass pussy," Taylor hissed. "Matter of fact, I have an apology of my own."

"Best friend, what do you have to be sorry for?" Kiki frowned.

"I'm sorry that I was blessed with good pussy that drove the love of her life insane."

"Oh shit!" Kiki covered her mouth.

"I'm sorry that your son loves me more than your tired ass, and I'm sorry you couldn't let go. Whatever Jasper is going through, it's because of you. I'm pretty sure he was a good man before you ruined him, reducing him to a stalking, overbearing, insecure ass man. Payback is a bitch, and I can't wait for karma to come around and knock your ass down. Have a shitty fucking life."

"Hoe," Kiki added before Taylor yanked her toward the car.

Chapter 23

Rahlo sat in front of his iPad and listened to his virtual assistant, Chyna, go over his schedule for the day. The first time he met her, he felt silly as fuck. Chyna lived in New York but applied for a job to handle his day-to-day scheduling. He was leery about dealing with someone he'd never met, but Terri assured him she was legit. Thus far, Chyna has done an excellent job. She stayed on top of his bookings and whatever else he needed. She proved that she didn't need to be in his face to do her job, and Rahlo appreciated her.

While Chyna talked, Terri sat across from him on the phone with the party planner, ensuring everything was all set for the night. Not only was this Rahlo's big night, but it was also his. Tonight, they'd sip champagne with millionaires and make connections with other artists and producers while showing them that Rahlo was the hottest thing coming out of Detroit.

"Oh, and another thing. Your date didn't confirm, nor did she reply to my messages about the hairdresser, MUA, or-"

"The fuck is a MUA?" Rahlo glowered, annoyed that Taylor

decided to test his gangster.

"Makeup artist." She snickered at his frustration. "I have the team on standby, so if you get in touch with her, we can send them right over."

"Aight, keep the MU whatever, but cancel the hairdresser."

"Ok."

"Send Esha a text and tell her to meet me at my place at 4."

"Got it. Oh, and the invite for Darius hasn't been opened."

"Cancel it," Rahlo demanded, causing Terri to peer in his direction.

"Got it, anything else?"

"Nah, that's it for right now." Rahlo thanked her and ended the call.

Closing the iPad, Rahlo glanced over at Terri, who was also ending a call. Taking a seat at the table, he cleared his throat.

"Wanna talk about what's going on between you and Duke?"

"Not really," Rahlo replied.

"Alright, but it's not going to be a problem, right?"

"Nah, it's nothing."

"I just want to remind you of what's at stake. The things we have lined up... we've come too far to slip."

"The fuck is you talking about? Ain't nobody slipping."

"Well, I want to make sure we keep it that way." Terri pulled at his tie. "Who is this young lady you're taking to the party?"

"My young lady," Rahlo smirked.

"Do I need to run a background check?"

"Nah, she's straight."

"Ok, I'll take your word for it."

"Aight, let me get out of here. I need to make a couple of things shake. I'll see you tonight."

"Don't be late."

"Yea yea." Rahlo waved him off as he exited the office.

"One more thing," Terri called out. "I got a call from Zeus asking about a contract for your mother. She's signing onto a show called *Mothers of the Stars*."

"She what?" He was pissed off, the bullshit surrounding Emory didn't end.

"Yea, it's not a good look, so if you can, talk to her."

"I'm on my way over there now." Rahlo shook his head.

"Always some fucking bullshit," he muttered, headed toward the elevator.

In the car, Rahlo tried to call Taylor again, and just like the previous times he called, it went right to voicemail. His irritation was at an all-time high and he was going to make her pussy pay the price.

The ride to Southwest was quick. Since Rahlo wasn't footing the bill, Emory had to move out of the hotel and return home. She called him every name in the book, but Rahlo didn't budge. If she wanted to stay in the room, she needed to provide a method of payment. With all her shit packed in trash bags, Emory went home pissed off at the world.

Double parking in front of the house, Rahlo hopped out, ready to strangle the woman who gave birth to him. He wasn't even surprised that she went behind his back and still auditioned for the show. Emory was messy and would fit right in. Stepping into the house, Rahlo stopped at the front door when he heard a voice that didn't belong to his mother.

"Look, just let me take a bath and I'll be out of your hair," Chef pleaded.

"No!" Emory spat. "You're not about to track up my house with your muddy ass shoes and musty clothes."

"It's mighty funny how you talk down on me when you're the one who did this shit to me."

"Excuse me?"

"You heard me. You think that I don't know it was you who gave me that laced blunt?" Chef squinted at her. "I always knew it was your sneaky ass."

"I-I-"

"You about to lie, so save it. You're the reason I'm walking around looking like *The Walking Dead*." He stepped forward. "And while I might be living hell on earth, the place you're going to is much worse. You're a conniving, money-hungry bitch, and when the floors open up and you fall into the pits of hell, I'm going to spray lighter fluid on your gold-digging ass."

"Fuck you!" Emory spewed. "Yea, I did it, and I'd do it again. You thought you were so smart, I showed you! Flaunting all those bitches in my face, giving me chump change while you promised those hoes bright futures. That wasn't the first time I laced your blunt, you got hooked and couldn't deny the craving." She laughed wickedly.

"You laughing now, but how would Rahlo feel if he knew the truth? You think he'd be so quick to provide you with this fake ass glamorous life if he knew you kept him away from his father?"

Rahlo stumbled a bit, knocking the bottle off the table by the front door. His eyes started to burn and his ears rang with sirens that only he could hear. It wasn't until Chef shook his shoulder did he snap out of his trance.

"What the fuck did you just say?" Rahlo knocked Chef's hand from his shoulder.

"He's your father," Emory tautly repeated, unmoved by the hurt in her son's eyes. "You wanted to know who your father was, right? Well, here you go. Chef, meet your son. Son, meet your pipe smoking daddy."

"You're so fucking evil," Chef spat, wishing he could beat her ass, but he knew without a doubt that Emory would mop the floor with him.

"Yea, well maybe I should have laced his blunt too. Maybe then he'd have a little more respect for me," she sniped, crushing Rahlo's heart even more.

"Bit-"

"I wish you would disrespect me. How about you aim some of that displaced anger toward him? He knew he was your father, yet he let you feed his habit, satisfied with being treated like the neighborhood stray dog."

"Both of y'all stay the fuck away from me." Rahlo backed out of the door.

"Rah." Chef tried to stop him, but Rahlo glared at him with a gaze that muted him. "Don't call my fucking name, bro."

"Not bro- Dad," Emory corrected him with a light chuckle.

"Remember this day, Em," Rahlo warned her. "It's going to haunt you for the rest of your life," he promised. "And if you do that show, I'm going to make sure the world knows what kind of piss poor mother you are." With that, Rahlo turned to leave, feeling sick to his stomach. As bad as he wanted to go home and block the world out, he couldn't, so Rahlo hopped in his truck and went to his next destination.

Taylor lay on her stomach, flipping through her Kindle, trying to find something good to read. She was bored out of her mind, and since she was dodging Rahlo, she couldn't call him, and Kiki was out of touch. Taylor knew that was code for laid up with Bruce, so that left her all alone.

"Tay." Trooper tapped on her bedroom door.

"Yes?"

"Did you see it?"

"See what?" She sat up, giving him her full attention.

"Ms. Ariel had a toothbrush in the bathroom, but don't worry, I buried it in the backyard. Won't be using our toothpaste." He grinned proudly.

"Troop!" Taylor laughed out loud. "Why would you do that?"

"Papa said that's the first step. A toothbrush and then next thing you know she decorating the living room."

"He told you that?" She squinted.

"No, he was on the couch with that stuff that smells like a skunk and I heard him talking to his self again."

"Troop, you can't keep destroying her stuff."

"Fine, I'll go get it and put it back." Trooper bounced out of the room before she could stop him.

Laughing to herself, Taylor rolled out of the bed and followed him downstairs. When her foot hit the bottom step, Taylor stopped in her tracks. She could smell his cologne before she even turned the corner. Comfortably sitting on her living room couch, Rahlo and Papa were sharing a blunt as if they were long-lost friends.

"What are your intentions with my granddaughter?" Papa coughed, passing the blunt.

"Tonight, I just want to enjoy her company if that's ok,"

Rahlo replied, inhaling the smoke. "She be playing me to the left though. You have any tips?"

"Simple. Don't be a pushover. My granddaughter is headstrong and she'll walk all over you if you let her. The last nig-"

"Papa!" Taylor shouted, interrupting him mid-sentence.

"And she do that shit a lot. *Papa, Papa, Papa,*" he mumbled. "Good luck with this one." Papa grabbed his cane. "What's your net worth again?" he asked, limping away.

"I'm well off," Rahlo modestly answered. Taylor shook her head in embarrassment.

"That's a good man right there," Papa whispered, bypassing her. "Don't mess this up for us," he hissed.

Taylor didn't reply. Instead, she focused on the man sitting on her couch with slumped shoulders. He casually blew smoke out of his mouth while keeping his gaze on the bay window in front of him.

"What are you doing here, and why are you smoking with my granddad?"

"I told you not to go ghost on me."

"And I told you all my red flags. I don't have time for bullshit. You're just getting started in your rap career, and to save myself the heartbreak, I'm going to stay to myself."

"Come sit with me." He patted the seat next to him.

"Ra-"

"Taylor." He glared at her.

Doing as she was told, Taylor moved to his side and sat down. Clearing her throat, she shifted on the couch, waiting for him to speak.

"A lot of shit is changing around me, and I'm conflicted on who to trust. Muthafuckas are showing their true colors, and with every secret revealed, I lose a lil bit of myself."

"Did something happen?" Taylor asked, scooting closer. His eyes were a lot sadder than she was used to, and the pain in his eyes broke her heart.

"Are you fucking with me?" Rahlo's deep voice came out just above a whisper.

"Huh?" She swallowed the lump in her throat.

"You know that I'm feeling you, so me applying pressure isn't a surprise, but I can't keep chasing you. I'm in a fucked up headspace, and I need to know that you're with me." He intensely stared at her. "If you fucking with me like I'm fucking with you, then I need you to go pack that lil bag you be so quick to fill, and let's bounce. My sister is at my crib ready to start your hair; a stylist and a MWA are there too."

"A MW what?" She squinted in confusion.

"The chicks that do the makeup." He inhaled the smoke.

"Oh, a MUA."

"Yea that. So what's up? Are you rolling with me, or does our adventure stop here?"

Taylor chewed on the corner of her lips before responding. It didn't take much thought; she liked him and was enjoying the time they spent together, but the thought of his mama turned her off.

"Your mama-"

"Is a non-factor," he said coldly, puffing the blunt again. Taylor lowered her mouth and pressed her lips to his mouth, prompting him to blow the smoke in her mouth.

"I'll go pack my bag," she smiled.

"That's the shit I'm talking about. They don't make 'em like you no mo'," Papa cheered from the kitchen. "Big dick energy."

"Papa!" Taylor screeched.

"Girl, shut up and go pack that damn bag like he said."

Trooper tiptoed past his sister and walked into the living room, where Rahlo was now standing at the front door. He was so into his phone that he didn't see Trooper standing there sizing him up. It wasn't until Trooper cleared his throat did he look down.

"Who you here for?" he asked.

"Taylor."

"Why?"

"I want to take her to a party," Rahlo answered, getting a kick out of being questioned by a miniature version of Taylor.

"You bringing her back?"

"Yea, but not tonight."

"Hmph," Trooper snorted. "You trying to leave yo toothbrush here?"

"Not at all, lil man."

"Carry on," he dismissed Rahlo and slipped out the front door to get Ms. Riley's shoes out of the garbage before anyone found out they were missing.

∞∞∞

"*Being broke did somethin' to my spirit, asked niggas to plug me, they act like they didn't hear me. Look at me now, driving German engineering.*" Tee Grizzley played in the background while Rahlo twisted a blunt. He was standing in the middle of the VIP section, high out of his mind, yet his fingers had a mind of their own.

It was hours after his album release party and everything went off without a hitch. Rahlo performed, worked the room with a bedazzling Taylor at his side, and rubbed elbows with big-name artists, actors, and producers. Rahlo gave out plenty of empty smiles and tense handshakes to keep up appearances. No one but Esha and Taylor noticed the distant look in his eyes. His laughs were forced, and he kept a glass glued to his hand all night.

At midnight, the album was released and the real party began. Rahlo had Bruce gather his people and had them transported to a section at Eastwood. He ordered bottle after bottle, rolled blunts galore, and allowed Taylor to dance on him. In fact, he kept her at his side for comfort. If his face wasn't buried in her neck, his hands were planted on her ass and his tongue was down her throat.

"Joy road bitch, but the money long as six mile. Brick mile, knock your bitch down. Pick her up, knock her back down, pull her tracks out," Taylor and Kiki animatedly acted out while rapping to one another.

Rahlo lit his blunt and blew out the smoke. All eyes were on their section, and he couldn't blame them. His pockets were full, he was in the works of buying his sister a shop, and his album was about to take over every chart. It was truly a time to be alive, yet deep down, he felt sick to his stomach. Emory's voice and Chef's face kept popping up in his head. The betrayal, the hurt, it was all too much, and to avoid blacking out, Rahlo smoked. It was the only way to keep the crazy thoughts at bay.

"What's poppin'?" Duke's voice boomed over the music. Rahlo slowly turned his head in Duke's direction and smirked. He was wondering when he was going to come around.

Rahlo hadn't seen Duke or heard from him since the cookoff. Through Bruce, he learned that Duke was back to his old ways, and this time it didn't bother him as much. Rahlo was learning that people were going to do what they wanted. As much as Duke claimed he hated prison, Rahlo felt like it was his safe space. Behind bars, there was no pressure to survive and he was free of responsibility. Rahlo's only hope was that he was prepared to do the bid alone this time.

"Sup." Rahlo gave him a half nod.

"About the party," Duke started, but Rahlo stopped him. There was no need for him to go into detail because he didn't care to hear any excuses.

"Don't explain yourself to me."

"Baby, come dance with me." Taylor popped up, slipping her arm around Rahlo's waist.

"Don't you see us talking?" Duke barked at her.

"Nigga-"

"I got it, T-baby," Rahlo lazily said, placing a kiss on her forehead. "Go dance and I'll be over in a minute."

"The fuck is this?" Duke frowned. "This your bitch now?"

"Watch your mouth," Rahlo warned through clenched teeth.

"So this what it is? You bucking over a bitch that ain't even yours?"

"Watch your mouth nigga and this is my last warning."

"I'm saying, since when is this your girl?"

"Since when is Lexi yours?"

Caught off guard by the question, Duke's eyes doubled in size before returning to normal. He had literally just started back fucking Lexi that morning, and that was only because his dick was hard when he woke up. Rahlo couldn't have known that quickly, so he was confused.

"Lily is your daughter, right?"

"Bro, let's talk about this outside."

"Nah," Rahlo refused. "We can talk about it now. How long?"

"I hit it first," Duke admitted. "I been fucking her off and on for years. I stopped when yall was in a *relationship*, but when she left, I went out there."

"So why the fuck you ain't say shit?"

"Because I was in jail and she begged me not to. She needed your help, and honestly, so did I. It was wrong, but bro, you gotta understand where I'm coming from."

"Bro?" Rahlo snorted. "I'm not your shit. I don't understand it because I wouldn't do no shit like that behind your back."

"Don't tell me we falling out over pussy."

"It's not about the pussy, nigga. It's the fucking principal and I can't fuck with a nigga with no morals."

"Baby, come on, it's your party," Taylor slurred, reappearing, further annoying Duke.

"Bitch, don't you see us talking?" He screamed, stepping forward as if he was about to hit her.

Whap!

Rahlo swung, connecting his fist to Duke's jaw. Taylor stumbled back in shock as she watched the best friends go head-to-head. The women in the section started screaming as tables and drinks started flying. Snapping out of his high state, Bruce snatched Duke back while Esha did her best to hold Rahlo. The world stood still when Duke removed a gun from his back and pointed it at Rahlo.

Their childhood flashed before both of their eyes as it crumbled right in front of them. Breathing heavily, Duke pointed the gun at Rahlo, who stared into the barrel.

"Over pussy?" Duke scoffed. "You been knowing this bitch five minutes and you fighting me over this hoe?"

"She ain't gone be another bitch. I'm not these weak ass niggas and this gun don't scare me." Rahlo took a step forward.

"Fuck you, nigga! You think you better than me because

you got a little money now?"

"You funny as fuck. This lil money was feeding you, your baby mama, and child."

"Oh shit, this the real Rah. I know you been feeling like that."

"You shootin' or nah?"

"Fuck you, Rah," Duke spewed, sticking the gun in his pants.

"Fuck yo broke ass too."

Chapter 24

The next morning, Rahlo woke up sick to his stomach. His head was pounding and his knuckles were sore. He heard voices but couldn't pinpoint where they were coming from. They seemed close, but he didn't see anyone in the room with him. Sitting on the edge of the bed, Rahlo grabbed his head in hopes of getting it to stop spinning.

"Fuck," he groaned.

The night's events were a blur. He didn't remember much after fighting Duke.

Duke

Rahlo shook his head, not believing he'd fought his best friend, and he, in return, pulled a gun out on him. In a split second, they went from brothers to enemies. In Rahlo's eyes, there was no coming back.

"You up?" Esha asked, tapping on the bedroom door. She didn't wait for an answer before opening the door. "Whew, you look like shit."

"I feel like it, too," Rahlo admitted. "What time is it?"

"A little after five."

"In the evening?"

"Yep. We tried to wake you up, but you didn't budge. I guess you finally crashed."

"Shit." He rubbed his eyes.

"Taylor took your phone and had Chyna reschedule your day." She handed the device back to him.

"Where she at?"

"In the kitchen. That girl can cook."

"I'll have to check it out." He rubbed his temples.

"Rah, I- uh, I talked to Chef. I went by Emory's house to grab a few things from the basement and he told me what happened. Why didn't you tell me last night?"

"Tell you what?" Rahlo stood up, becoming pissed all over again. "That I have a fucking crackhead for a daddy? That I gave him money to put the shit in his body?"

"You didn't know, Rahlo," she reasoned. "Emory is dead wrong for what she did to the both of yall."

"Fuck her," he roared. "I'm done with her, and I put that on everything I love."

Dropping his head, Rahlo took a second to breathe. His emotions were getting the best of him, and he couldn't control the intense burning in his eyes.

"Rah." Esha tried to touch him, but he jumped back out of her reach.

"Don't comfort me, Esh. I'm not a little ass boy. I'm just pissed the fuck off," he told her. "How the fuck could one person be so fucking evil? I hate that bitch! She didn't even flinch. My mother looked me in my eyes and told me she wished she aborted me because I wouldn't buy her money-hungry ass a house. What kind of mother would do some shit like that?"

"I know, and it's ok."

"It's not ok, Esha. The shit was never ok. You were a fucking kid raising me because her dusty ass was running the streets being a hoe and a bad one at that. People wanna know why half the adults are walking around this bitch with anxiety and depression, it's because of people like her. Muthafuckas are passing their trauma on to their kids and expecting them to be normal. I have a fucking hoe for a mama and a crackhead for a dad."

"And you still made it out!" Esha grabbed the sides of his face. "Put all that shit behind you because it's the past. Focus on what's in front of you. Emory doesn't get to take your future too. You get a pass for last night, but from here on out, focus! You didn't come this far to lose it."

"Tell him, sis!" Kiki yelled from the living room."

"Bitch, hush," Taylor warned.

"They talking all loud and the nigga live in a loft. It's like five walls in here, so I can't help but listen."

"And listen, your friendship with Duke is over." Esha pointed her finger at him in a motherly manner. "He was never your friend. You felt bad and wanted to save him, but I'm telling you now, Duke is not your friend. He is a gaslighting user, and you don't need people like that in your circle. Let that man go live his life, and you live yours."

"I hear you," Rahlo exhaled.

"Period!" Kiki snapped. "I like her. She gives them long-winded motivational speeches. Fuck around and change your life after hearing her talk."

"I can't take you nowhere." Taylor shook her head.

"You been knowing that for years. Don't cry now."

"Get cleaned up. Chyna was able to cancel everything

except the studio session. They need your verse today and the session is set for eight.

"Fuck, I forgot about that."

"I figured, but you'll be ok after you put something on your stomach. Fuck all this bullshit and get to the bag."

Rahlo waited until she left the room to cut on his phone. Instantly, it was flooded with tags from social media, text messages, missed calls, and voicemails. Just the mere thought of replying to anything caused his head to spin, so he tossed the phone on the bed. Laying back, he closed his eyes and let out a deep sigh.

"Hey." Taylor's soft voice flowed through the room.

"Whattt, you didn't run for the hills yet?" He joked through closed eyes.

"Not you cracking jokes and you in here hung over." She climbed on the bed and straddled him.

"You didn't leave?"

"Nope, I want this." Taylor leaned down and kissed his lips. "I'm in it for the long haul."

"That's what the fuck I like to hear." Rahlo's hands found her waist.

"Do you wanna talk?"

"Not really, but I think we need to clear the air. I can't do any more secrets."

"Yea, I have a few things I need to tell you."

"Aight." Rahlo sat up with Taylor still sitting in his lap. "I got a minute before I need to be at the studio, so let's lay all this shit out, and we'll go from there."

"Ok." Taylor took a deep breath and let it all out. "I was pregnant by Jasper, but I lost the baby, and I still haven't told him. He calls me from different numbers all day, and his ex-hoe of a wife said that he talks about hurting me," she blurted in one breath.

"Why you ain't say shit?" Rahlo frowned.

"Because I don't need you to fix it. Jasper is going to talk until he's blue in the face."

"And a scorned nigga is worse than a woman. You need to tell him about the baby and move on. If he thinks there is still a baby, then he thinks there is a chance."

"Ugh, ok. I guess I'll call him," Taylor gave in, knowing it was the right thing to do.

"Do that because if I have to beat his old ass, I will."

"Your turn."

"My daddy a crackhead, my mama is a disgrace, and a nigga I thought was my best friend is on some funny shit and pulled a gun out on me yesterday."

"I-uh, what?" Taylor's mouth dropped open, not knowing what to address first.

"We can talk about this later." He kissed her lips. "Right now, let me get my shit together. You coming to the studio with me?"

"Yep, I'll go make you a plate." She slid off his lap and switched out of the room.

$$\infty\infty\infty$$

Bruce sat on the couch, waiting for the guest of the hour to arrive. Sitting in the damp basement was messing with his allergies, but the ass whooping he was about to deliver would be worth all the Benadryl he'd have to consume. Thanks to a Ring camera across the street from Emory's house, Bruce was able to see the robbery clear as day, only it wasn't a robbery, it was a fucking comedy show.

As clear as day, Bruce watched AJ pull up to the house in his mother's car. Emory ran to the front door and could be seen yelling at him from the doorway. Not even two minutes later, Emory ran out of the house with two hands full of her purses, shoes, and clothes. Seconds later, AJ pulled off, and she returned to the house.

"Alright ma, damn, I'll do it in a minute," AJ gritted, bopping down the wooden stairs that threatened to cave in with every step. When he flicked on the light and saw Bruce sitting there, he nearly jumped out of his skin. "What the fuck you doing in my room?"

"What the fuck your grown ass doing with Avenger sheets? Nigga, how old are you?"

"Those are collectibles."

"They're only collectibles if they stay in the original packaging, dummy. You old and dumb as fuck." Bruce shook his head. "I'm going to ask you one time, and if you lie, I'm going to break one of your fingers."

"You ain't gone ask me shit because I didn't do shit," AJ snarled, trying to walk past Bruce, but was stopped when Bruce grabbed him by the back of the shirt and slung him against the molded wall. "Calm your little scrawny ass down, nigga. I didn't even ask my question yet," he barked. "Damn, I had a whole performance planned and you wanna run like a little bitch."

"Look, it was her idea," AJ blurted.

"Who is her, and what was her idea?" Bruce asked, holding AJ in the air like a fly by its wings.

"Emory, she wanted me to drop the diss track on Rah, so I did it. She mad about him cutting her off and wanted to get even."

"Wait," Bruce laughed, dropping AJ to the ground. "Yall made a diss track about him?"

"Yea," AJ mumbled.

"Let me hear it."

"Mannn."

"Let me hear the fucking track," Bruce demanded.

Sucking his teeth, AJ pulled out his cracked iPhone and pulled up his email account. The producer he worked with was withholding the track until Emory paid for it, but he did send them a sample.

This nigga wanna be me, just call him my mini-me.

Don't know who his daddy is , I bet the dope dealer on the corner know who his daddy is.

"Seriously?" Bruce peered over at him. "You really about to release this off-beat ass song to gain five minutes of clout?"

"It was Emory's idea," he confessed.

"And it's your dumb ass voice," Bruce hollered, making AJ jump. "I'm going to give you a chance to fix it because you're a puppet in all of this. Call the whack ass producer and tell them to kill this shit."

"Come on, man. I put my own money on this shit."

"And you think I give a fuck? You have five seconds to get this shit handled, or I'm going to staple your muthafuckin' ears together."

"How?"

Whap!

Bruce popped AJ in the face so fast he swallowed one of his wisdom teeth and started choking.

"Nigga, you better die because I'm not about to give yo ass CPR," Bruce warned him, watching his eyes water.

"That's fucked up, man," AJ cried.

"Kill the fucking track or choking on your rotten ass teeth is going to be the least of your problems."

"Aight, man," he whined, holding his jaw.

Bruce stood to the side while AJ made the necessary call. When he was finished, AJ sighed in relief. He knew writing a diss track about Rahlo was a bad idea, but Emory hyped him up to do it, claiming that it would climb the charts. She even gave him a couple of insiders to help. AJ knew Emory was on bullshit when she took his money but didn't pay the producer.

"It's done. He's going to bury the track. Can you get out of my room now?" AJ asked, scared to make a move with Bruce standing over him.

"Nigga, you need to get out of your room. I feel a spot on my lungs just from being in this muthafucka and to think you sleep down here. That's why you slow, you been inhaling black mold," Bruce ranted, walking past him.

Feeling brave now that there was a space between them, AJ stuck out his chest and popped his shit.

"And tell Rah the next time he got a problem with me, he can tell me himself."

Doubling back, Bruce cocked back and punched AJ, knocking him into the hot water tank.

"Aw shit," he groaned, hitting his head on the pipes.

"He didn't send me, nigga. You're light work, and the next time I have to visit you, I'm going to make sure your mouth gets wired shut, then maybe you'll learn to keep your mouth shut," Bruce warned, knocking over all the DVDs as he walked by.

Once he was outside, Bruce shot Rahlo a text and sent him the clip from the Ring camera. For the time being, he'd keep the mixtape to himself. Bruce didn't want to add fuel to the fire. It was bad enough that Emory robbed herself, the mixtape was pushing it.

Bruce thought about heading back to Rahlo's crib, but he needed to check on a few things. His second stop was to see Dre. The wires were out of his mouth, and he was talking shit, claiming everything wasn't as it seemed. Word on the street was that everything wasn't his. He took full responsibility for the weed, but the pills didn't belong to him.

As luck would have it, Bruce didn't have to look far. Dre was standing on the corner kicking it with a couple of his boys when Bruce pulled up. He reached for the gun in his back, but Bruce stared him down, daring him to make the grave mistake of pulling a gun out on him. His mouth being wired shut would be the least of his worries.

"Man, Bruce gone with all that extra shit," Dre told him with his hand tucked behind his back.

"Nigga, move your hand from behind your back before I pull that muthafucka off and have you walking around this bitch with a nub," Bruce growled. "Yall lil niggas move around," he ordered, and like roaches, they scattered.

"For real, big dog, I'm not about to mess with yall niggas no more. My mouth was wired shut, I lost over fifty pounds, and people swear I'm on that shit."

"Would you please shut up whining, damn!"

"Look, bro, the weed was mine. I know I wasn't supposed to have it, but I don't even trust my mama with my stash. Rah is legit, I thought maybe he would've used his stardom to get out of the situation."

"So what the fuck are you saying?"

"The pills were Duke's. When I ran back in the house, I grabbed them for him. I don't even sell pills, but that nigga don't want nobody else to know he been fucking with fentanyl, so I go get them for him. I didn't owe him any money, the nigga wanted his pills."

"Fuck outta here. Duke don't do pills."

"You just don't see him doing them, and to be honest, when he's high, he talks about you and Rah. He-"

"Nah, I'm straight, no need to go into detail. I'm not big on hearsay. I'll go straight to the source."

"I feel you, big dog, and we still cool. That lil misunderstanding was my fault." Dre stuck his hand out for a pound, handshake, some kind of verification to let him know everything was smooth. "I mean, I would have done the same thing."

"You wouldn't have done the same thing because you're a lil bitch. The right thing to do would have been to take the charge because it was your shit, but just like a fucking snake, you put the shit under Rah's seat. I should beat your ass off GP." Bruce jumped, making Dre flinch.

"Bitch ass nigga," Bruce chuckled. "Got a gun and still scared."

Without a word, Bruce bopped away. He planned to pay Duke a visit, but this one was personal, and he felt like Rahlo should handle that himself.

Across town, Rahlo listened to Kori's verse with his eyes closed. Her part was done, and they needed Rahlo's verse to finalize the song. It was a love song, and while the label would have preferred them to record together, their busy schedules wouldn't allow it.

"Again," Rahlo demanded, frustrated that his mind was so clouded.

They had been in the studio for over two hours, and nothing was sticking. He kept stuttering and tripping over his words. Terri was growing frustrated because they were on a time clock and Rahlo was taking his sweet time.

"Is there anything we can do?" Terri asked. "You need the normal? Liquor, weed, women?" He whispered the last part, not sure how Taylor would react.

"Rah, just focus." Esha gave him a reassuring smile.

"I got it." He shot her a look. "Again," Rahlo requested, and the producer restarted the beat.

"Can't go to sleep without you by my side, I-I-fuck!" he kicked the barstool. "Everybody get the fuck out!"

"Aht-aht, You ain't gotta do all that." Kiki snapped her fingers as they piled out of the door. Well, everybody except Taylor. She walked them to the door and locked it.

"T-Baby." Rahlo peered at her.

"Shut up." Taylor walked over to him. "Let me help you." She dropped to her knees.

Rahlo watched her unbuckle his pants with her bottom lip slightly tucked inside of her mouth. Releasing his dick, Taylor admired that thick, brown masterpiece before swiping it across her wet lips.

"I know you're frustrated, baby, but you need to let all of that shit go right now," Taylor whispered, wrapping her lips around his head. "Focus on what's in front of you."

"Fuck." Rahlo's head fell back as she swallowed him whole without gagging. His hands softly caressed the back of her head, lovingly praising her. It was cute and all, but Taylor had something else in mind. They were on a time clock, and he could be gentle later.

"Stop that soft shit and fuck this throat." Taylor grabbed his ass, pulling him further into her wet mouth.

"What?" Rahlo's eyes popped open. Gazing down at her, he watched as she skillfully massaged his dick with her lips.

"You need some inspiration, right?" Taylor cooed, batting her lashes at him.

"Yea, but-"

"Show me." She kissed the tip of his dick. "Fuck my mouth until a melody forms." She kissed the shaft. "Choke me with this big ass dick until the muscles in my throat pull the rap from your soul."

"You fucking nasty," Rahlo grunted, turned on by her words.

"Only for you, baby. Ride my face like you ride the beat." She opened her mouth and lowered her head until her lips met the base.

Like a pro, Taylor sucked and stroked his dick like she was on a mission. She cupped his balls, making sure to massage them so they wouldn't feel left out. Rahlo felt his soul leave his body when she locked her jaws and sucked him hard. His knees buckled and the arches of his feet tingled. A moan escaped his mouth that he didn't recognize, and Rahlo contemplated bopping her on top of the head so she could release him from her trance. There was no way he should have been thinking about wedding rings, but he was.

Princess cut or square?

Platinum or rose gold band?

Fall or summer wedding?

With the way she was sucking his dick, she could have it all. As promised, Taylor pulled the stress right out of his balls, and he shot it down her throat. Without gagging, she wiped her mouth and stood to her feet like she didn't just change his life.

"Fuck," Rah groaned, spinning. He felt drunk all over again.

"Yo, why the fuck would you suck my dick like that?" he frowned at her.

"What?" Taylor giggled, confused by the frown on his face.

"That was some deadly ass shit, baby. I thought your pretty ass had me gone before, but now I'm really fucked up."

"Oh yea?"

"Yea." He kissed her lips. "I'm ready to record," he told her.

"I'll let Terri know," Taylor grinned.

After wiping her lips, she happily walked out of the booth and did as she was told. The producer and Terri returned, but Kiki and Esha went to go get a drink. Taylor stood by the door and watched Rahlo make magic.

Can't go to sleep without you by my side

I'm infatuated with you baby, you make me come alive

My heart racing shorty, I hope it's not a dream

You got me hooked on that sweet shit like a dope fiend.

"What did you do?" Terri asked Taylor, watching the words slip from Rahlo's mouth so effortlessly.

"I did my job." She shrugged as Rahlo rapped about his new drug of choice.

Chapter 25

Three weeks later

Not Easily Influenced took over the charts as predicted. It was number one on several platforms, and because of that, Terri added more stops to the tour. *Feeling You* was the hottest song on TikTok, and because of Taylor, there was a cute dance that went with the chorus. Then there was the song he did with Kori. Even though they didn't record in the studio at the same time, they sounded amazing together. Kori agreed to let Taylor be the lead girl in the video, and with the chemistry between her with Rahlo, they took the video to another level.

"I miss you," Taylor moaned into the phone.

"I'll be back tomorrow, and you can show me how much you miss me." Rahlo yawned.

He gravely underestimated performing every other night. Between driving from state to state, rehearsing, and performing, Rahlo didn't know if he was coming or going. The fans were a little more aggressive, and Bruce had to hire several more guards to travel with them. If they weren't trying to run on stage, they would be waiting by his hotel door. It didn't matter that he posted Taylor on his page, it seemed like that made it worse.

"Aw, you sound tired," she cooed into the phone.

"Shit, I am. That show last night was crazy."

"I know. Terri posted it on YouTube."

"That nigga be doing his thing. YouTube sent me a fat ass check."

"As they should. Now you can take me shopping," she joked.

"I was going to do that anyway," Rahlo told her. "When we go to Vegas, I have a couple of things up my sleeve."

"You don't have to spend your money on me."

"Shut up, don't tell me what to do with my money."

"Let me find out you fallin' in love."

"I already fell, baby, and I don't wanna get up," he admitted.

"You are so corny," Taylor snickered. "But I love you, too," she said with a soft smile.

"Aw shit. Save the date," he teased. "My girl said she loves me."

"Boy, hush. Anyway, I'm about to meet Kiki for tea. Call me when you wake up from your nap."

"Where at?"

"Tela's Breakfast Spot."

"Oh aight, love you, T-baby."

"I love you too, Rah." She ended the call, turning in her seat to face Kiki. "Ready?"

"Yep, I have my pepper spray, stun gun, and brass knuckles." She patted her purse. "I want him to get stupid."

"Ugh, let's get this over with."

"And if Rahlo finds out, you're on your own."

"Excuse me?"

"He's my famous best friend and I'm not about to mess up our friendship because you scared to tell him the truth." Kiki bucked her eyes.

"You switchin' up on me?"

"Yep. He got me front row tickets to see Drake. Bitch, I'm on his side, right or wrong."

"Get out of my car." Taylor snatched her purse from the back and exited the car with Kiki not too far behind.

"Girl, don't yell at me, and I don't know who you think you're fooling with that dumb ass hat."

"It's Fendi, thank you very much," Taylor sassed.

"It's ugly as fuck, thank you very much," Kiki shot right back in a mocking tone.

Entering the breakfast shop, Taylor pulled her hat down, hoping no one noticed her. She had no business meeting Jasper, but Von told her to tell him about the baby so he could move on just as she had. Taylor waited until Rahlo's tour started because she didn't want him to accompany her. The last thing she wanted to do was get him in more trouble.

With Kiki on her heels, Taylor searched the small café for Jasper. When their eyes met, he damn near jumped out of his seat to greet her. It had been months since he last saw her, and she was just as pretty as the day they met. She was a little slimmer, her hair was longer, but that ass...he saw the muthafucka from the front.

"Baby-" He cleared his throat.

"Nope, don't start with that baby shit. She's not anything to you," Kiki cut him off. "I'm going to the tea bar, and she has five minutes to chop it up with you, and then we're leaving."

"Who the fuck are you supposed to be?" Jasper sneered at her.

"The bitch that's going to pepper spray you, pop you in the face with brass knuckles, and shock the shit out of your crazy ass if you act up in here."

"I got it," Taylor giggled. Kiki shot Jasper one more hard glare before turning on her heels, hitting him with her purse.

Tucking her hair behind her ear, Taylor followed him to a table near the window. He already had two cups of tea on the table, but she didn't trust him enough to drink it. While he nervously stole peeks of her, Taylor boldly took in his appearance. His clothes were baggy, his hair was uncut, and he reeked of liquor. None of that bothered her more than the tattoo on the side of his face that read *Taylor*. She stared at the tattoo and then back at his eyes, which held a smile.

"I just got it. I knew you'd come back to me, and I wanted to show you how much I missed you."

"For one, that's crazy as hell, Jasper. Like, why would you do some shit like that?"

"Because I love you. Even after all we've been through over these last few months, I want us to work it out. You, me, and the baby. I'm so sorry about the shit with Sherri, and I'm over that. I'm over her."

"Jasper, it was more than Sherri. You were starting to suffocate me, and I needed space. Then you purposely got me pregnant."

"I fucked up."

"You stole my keys, my underwear, and whatever else. That was not love. You didn't love me, Jasper."

"I did and still do. Just let me prove it."

"Jasper," Taylor exhaled. "The day I left, I lost the baby."

"Then go find it," he demanded, raising his voice a little.

"Warning," Kiki said, holding the pepper spray in the air.

"Jasper, I gave birth to a little girl, and she was stillborn. There is no baby." She sadly shook her head. "I can give you the information to visit her, but she's gone."

"I-but-you-" he stuttered, feeling his chest tighten up. Taylor and their baby was the only thing he could think about. The baby gave him hope, and his brain couldn't register what she was saying. "Don't do this," he cried. "Don't keep my baby from me."

"Jasper."

"Don't Jasper me! You're keeping my baby away from me to be with that nigga," he accused, pointing his finger in her face. A few people peered in their direction at the outburst. Kiki hopped up from her stool, but Taylor held her hand up to stop her.

"I don't have a reason to lie to you, and I don't owe you shit," Taylor hissed. "You lied to me. You cheated on me. You did this, not me."

"The fuck is this?" Rahlo asked, stepping behind Taylor, possessively placing his hand on her shoulder.

"Wh-what are you doing here?" Taylor jumped, genuinely surprised that he was there. As far as she knew, he was still in Atlanta on tour.

"We can get into all that later, what's this?" He nodded toward Jasper.

"None of your business." Jasper wiped his face. "This is between me and my child's mother. She's still my girl, ya know. You can't just take something that's not yours."

"Don't do that Jasper." Taylor turned to face him.

"That's where you're wrong at, my nigga." Rahlo glared at Jasper, not caring that people were recording them. "She was mine before either of yall knew it."

"Baby, I just met him for closure," Taylor swore, standing to her feet. Jasper snapped his head in her direction, not believing she was calling him baby, and in his face.

"Closure for who?" Rahlo frowned. "You need an explanation from this nigga? You need him to coddle your feelings because I could've sworn I did that. I've been coddling your feelings and this pussy, so tell me what the fuck you need from him."

"Nothing," she exclaimed. "He called me asking for closure, and I'm tired of him calling, so I said yes. Plus, you told me to tell him about the baby."

"Oh, why you ain't lead with that shit. I was about to beat his ass and take you home and punish the pussy."

"Rahlo!" Taylor gasped.

"Can you move around so we can finish talking?" Jasper cleared his throat.

"Nah, let me sum the shit up for you though." Rahlo stepped forward. "You fumbled, like I knew you would. I allowed her to get over you for like five minutes, then threw a party in that pussy," he chuckled. "I'm sorry for your loss, but that's it, my nigga. There are no connections to her, so I'm going to need you to erase her from your membrane before I do it for you."

"Wow." Jasper cleared his throat and pulled at his wrinkled shirt. "This is the type of man you want? One who broadcasts to the world that he's fucking you?"

"The glow on her face says that all by itself," Rahlo smirked. "You done?" He turned to Taylor.

"Yes." She nodded, picking up her purse.

"Then let's go. We're about to fly to Vegas for the fight." He popped her on the ass.

"Bye, Jasper." She waved as Rahlo led her out of the café.

"Kiki, bring yo ass on," Rahlo called out. Dropping the menu she'd been hiding behind, Kiki did as she was told and ran behind them.

Jasper sat there fuming. He balled his fists up so tight that his nails pierced the palms of his hands. Even when it started to bleed, he dug deeper as his eyes filled with tears. From the window, Jasper watched Rahlo help Taylor into a truck, then lean in to kiss her. Right there in the parking lot, she allowed him to tongue her down. Clutching the gun on his waist, Jasper rocked back and forth.

"Sir, are you ok?" The waitress asked, seeing the tears falling from his eyes.

"I'm not, but I will be soon," he promised.

∞∞∞

Lexi glared at Duke, who was stretched out across her bed. Their daughter was at the foot of the bed watching TV, and the sight would have been cute if she didn't detest Duke. Instead of helping her like he promised, she found herself supporting him. Duke hung out until the wee hours of the morning and then strolled in the house high out of his mind.

"Duke." Lexi kicked the bed.

"I'm not sleep and don't come in here with all that loud shit. I know you see me and my shorty chillin'," he said through closed eyes.

"Did you make any money last night?"

"Nah," Duke chortled. "They tore my ass up in that dice game last night."

"And you think the shit funny? You need to find something

to do because I can't keep doing this by myself."

"The fuck you want me to do?" He opened his heavy eyes and stared at her. "I'm not about to work at a fucking fast-food chain, and I'm not about to sweat all day in a funky ass factory."

"So how are you supposed to help me with our child? You think she cares where the money comes from? As long as there's food in the house and a roof over her head-"

"Look, I'm not trying to hear all that shit. I had a bad night and that's what it is."

"You're pitiful," Lexi snarled. "Rah wasn't even her daddy and he provided for her."

Duke sat up and rubbed his thumb across his nose.

"I advise you to chill. You cheerleading for a nigga that don't give two fucks about you."

"He did before you came home fucking it all up for me. I'm patiently waiting for you to do something stupid so you can take your stupid ass right back to jail."

"Fuck you, Lexi, straight up."

"What, you mad because it's the truth? Instead of him becoming a product of his environment like your sad ass, he went out and made a name for himself. You're just the same sad ass, broke ass nigga you've always been." She rolled her neck.

In a flash, Duke was out of the bed with his hand wrapped around her throat. This wasn't the first time Lexi brought up Rahlo in a teasing manner. She knew exactly what she was doing, and normally it didn't bother him, but this time it did. It pissed him the fuck off that Lexi thought Rahlo was a better man than him, and the sad part was she always did. He took her virginity, but she wished it was Rahlo. Duke got her pregnant, but she wished it was his best friend. Rahlo held the keys to her heart, and he didn't want them. But Duke did, and it ate him up inside, knowing that she'd never love him and he'd never be good enough in her eyes.

"Bitch, fuck your funky ass!" Duke choked her.

"Daddy, nooo," Lily cried, pulling his leg.

"That nigga don't even want your dry pussy ass, and he never did."

"Du-"

"Don't cry now, bitch. This what the fuck you want, right? You wanna keep throwing that nigga up in my face like I won't body his ass. Like I won't body you in this bitch and raise my daughter on my own." Duke applied pressure to her neck, not caring that her eyes were popping out of her head.

"Daddy," Lily sobbed.

"He'll never be better than me, hoe." He released her, dropping her body to the ground.

Lexi gasped for air as tears rolled down her face. Lily tried to run to her side, but Duke scooped her into his arms. He stepped over Lexi, who tried to grab his leg, but he stepped on her, causing pain to shoot through her body.

"Duke, nooo!" Lexi cried, but her pleas were ignored. Duke snatched her keys off the floor and left out of the house, leaving her crying at the top of her lungs.

Crawling to her phone, Lexi picked it up and went to her contacts. To her surprise, when she dialed Rahlo's number, it wasn't blocked. In fact, a woman picked it up.

∞∞∞

"Helllloo," Taylor sang into the phone.

"C-can I talk to Rah?" Lexi sniffled into the phone. If it

were any other day, she would have went off about a woman answering Rahlo's phone.

Pulling the phone from her ear, Taylor tapped the screen to see the name. *Lexi.*

"Uh, hold on." She covered the phone and tapped a sleeping Rahlo.

Their flight to Vegas was in three hours and Rahlo wanted to take a nap before they boarded the flight. He was full as fuck thanks to the lunch Taylor made him and his balls were empty from her riding him until his dick went limp inside of her. The rest was much needed because as soon as they landed, it was go time. Rahlo was performing at the fight, then he got them tickets to see Usher, and the next morning he was heading to New York, and Taylor was returning home.

"Bae." She lightly tapped his leg. "Someone is on the phone."

"Is it Esha?" He groaned.

"No."

"Then hang up."

"I think something might be wrong."

"Then tell them to call 9-1-1." Rahlo turned his head. "The fuck I'ma do?"

"It's Lexi," Taylor read the name on the screen. "And it sounds like she's crying."

"Then tell her ass to call Duke. Matter fact, block her ass again. T-Mobile fucked up all my settings."

Lexi sat on the other end of the phone crushed. She couldn't believe how easily Rahlo was dismissing her as if they didn't share a friendship at one point.

"Rah." Taylor shook him.

"Put the shit on speaker," he snarled.

"Don't be yelling at me, and if you don't want me to answer the phone, then don't sit it next to me." Taylor pushed him and tried to climb out of the bed, but Rahlo sat up and snatched her by the waist. Pulling her back onto the bed, he pressed his body against hers.

"My fault, T-baby. I'm just tired as fuck." He kissed her lips.

"Then take the call and I'll put your phone on DND."

"Aight." Rahlo picked up the phone. "Yo."

"Really, Rah?" Lexi scoffed, pissed that she had to listen to him cater to another woman. "I never thought we'd be reduced to something so small. We-we're-"

"Aye, I know damn well you didn't just wake me up out of my sleep to talk about a friendship your conniving ass fucked up."

"Duke took my daughter," she blurted, followed by tears.

"So, that's her daddy, right? The fuck you calling me for?" Rahlo frowned, adjusting his arms around Taylor's waist.

"Because he's high and he took my car."

"Then call your local police department."

"Rah, I know I messed up, but Duke isn't acting like himself and he choked me," she cried. Rahlo waited for a second to see if her pleas would pull at his heartstrings, but nothing happened. In all honesty, he was annoyed that she called him, thinking he was about to save her.

"And he isn't helping me. I barely have enough money to pay rent, and Lily-"

"Aye, I'm not trying to hear all that shit. I don't have anything for you, Lex. Had you come to me on some grown up shit, I would have looked out for you because Duke was my nigga and I understand the situation. You and that nigga played me like a simp, so no, I can't call him, and I don't want to hear about your financial issues." Rahlo ended the call and tossed his phone on the bed.

"Whew," Taylor fanned herself. "I'd hate to be on your bad side."

"What, you think I'm wrong?"

"No, but I do think the situation with Duke is wearing on you. Friendship breakups are just as bad as romantic ones, if not worse. As much as I dislike him, he's been your friend since grade school. Even if yall don't fix the situation, it's always good to clear the air. You'll feel better."

"I'll see." Rahlo heard her but wasn't in a hurry to talk to Duke. Their fight was still fresh on his mind. "And you are on my bad side. I'm just too tired to punish that pretty pussy," he yawned.

"Let me find out being famous is wearing you out."

"Is that what I am?" He gripped her meaty butt cheek, pulling her closer to him. "Famous?"

"Yep, and I'm about to start snapping on these hoes too. Every day somebody tagging me in something. You and groupies, you and Kori, you and the stage manager. Whew, I don't see how the girlfriends of rappers do it."

The first time Rahlo posted a picture of Taylor, the internet went crazy. Some fans thought the new couple was cute, and then there was an alliance of haters who lived up to their name. They called Taylor names, hating her for being with such a fine man, and some even wished death on her. It didn't bother Taylor initially, but they started doing the most. One person in particular started tagging her in pictures that were taken from a distance. In some, Taylor was having lunch with Kiki. Others, she was at the Trampoline Park with Trooper and caked up at various places with Rahlo. Taking it a step further, the person released her phone number and address. When Rahlo found out, he made Taylor change her number and switch up her schedule.

"You jealous, T-baby?"

"No, not at all. I know what I am and I know what we have. Them sideline hoes could never."

"Say that shit then, T-baby. All that confidence makes my dick hard." He took her hand and placed it inside his shorts.

"I thought you were tired." Taylor stroked his dick.

"I was, but then you started talking that black woman empowerment shit."

"Say it loud." She climbed on top of him. Leaning up a little, Taylor slowly slid down on him. A low moan escaped her lips.

"Fuck!" Rahlo's hands went behind his head. "I'm black and I'm proud."

∞∞∞

Duke was high out of his mind and didn't have a worry in the world. Lexi was blowing up his phone to return her daughter, but he kept sending her right to voicemail. He didn't have shit to say to her ungrateful ass. Instead of her being happy that he was trying to be a father, she was comparing him to another nigga, as if his presence wasn't good enough.

"Sup, young blood," Chef greeted, bopping down the street.

Dressed in a pair of knee-high shiny black boots and a waist-length pea coat, Chef was killing the game. He found a black and white mink hat with the matching scarf, and you couldn't tell him nothing. The fresh snow on the ground made his outfit that much better. With his cane in his hand, Chef bopped down the street singing *Santa Don't Come to the Ghetto*.

"Sup," Duke nodded, not in the mood for company. He wanted to enjoy his high all by himself.

"You know me. Trying to come up on a buck, and if I'm

lucky, bust a few nuts," he rapped.

"Why the fuck you always rhyming? That shit is annoying. Get your cat in the hat ass the fuck away from me."

"Whoa, who pissed in your crack pipe?" Chef questioned.

"What you just say to me?" Duke pushed up from the car. "I'm not a fucking crackhead."

"The streets speak, my boy. If you're not on crack, you're not far from it. Pills, right? I call it the gateway to hell drug. Once you're on this side, ain't no going back."

"Fuck you," Duke spewed, punching Chef to the ground. "You worried about me, but you need to worry about your bitch ass son."

"Ah, there he is," Chef taunted, rolling onto his back to make a snow angel.

"You a weird ass nigga, you know that?"

"And you're a crackhead in the making," Chef rebutted. "I always knew he was gon' be something, and I knew you'd be exactly what you are."

"What's that?"

"A hating ass lowlife," Chef chuckled. "I never understood why he kept you around and you're nothing but trouble."

Duke wiped the corners of his lips and delivered a swift kick to Chef's side. It didn't stop there. That kick felt so good that Duke kicked Chef over and over until he was spitting up blood.

"The fuck is you out here doing?" Dre jogged over toward him.

"Fuck this nigga. I hope he get frostbite on his nuts. Hoe ass nigga calling me a lowlife, but what the fuck is he?" Duke spat with spit flying from his mouth.

"I get it, but your shorty is in the back seat crying."

"I'm tripping up," Duke laughed, rubbing the top of his head. He looked back at his daughter and then back at Chef, who was limping away, leaving a blood trail in the fresh snow.

"Yea, shoot me to Radcliff. I'll give you gas money," Dre asked, getting back to the real reason he came outside.

"Come on."

"Aight, let me run back in the house real quick."

Duke didn't say anything; instead, he hopped back in the car, where Lily was in the back seat dosing off. It was getting late and he could tell she was worn out and probably ready to go home. Removing the phone from his pocket, he clicked on Rahlo's number and wasn't surprised that the voicemail picked up. Taking a deep breath, he spoke.

"Yo Rah…"

By the time Dre came out of the house, Duke ended the voicemail and was ready to call it a night. The pills he had been popping all day was catching up to him and he was tired of Lexi calling him. After strapping his baby girl in, Duke kissed her head and pulled off.

Rod's Wave *Tombstone* played in the background as he drove in silence. Duke wracked his brain trying to figure out when did his best friend's success become a threat to him. He had never been the jealous type, which is why he couldn't recognize the signs. Hell, he couldn't even recognize the self-sabotage that loomed over his head like a dark cloud. Even though Rahlo was hitting him off, Duke convinced himself that Rahlo was doing it out of pity. So much bad had happened in his life that the gesture made him feel less than.

"Yo." Dre tapped him. Duke didn't even notice he had zoned out.

Bloop bloop

The sirens behind them sent Dre's heart to his ass. Dirty

wasn't even the word to describe the amount of drugs he had in his backpack.

"You just ran a fucking light, bro!" Dre hollered, ready to jump out of the car. "You gotta lose them nigga, or we're both going to prison."

"The fuck you got in there?" Duke questioned.

"Fed time," Dre admitted.

"Fuck!" Duke pounded the steering wheel. "Aight, I got it." He slowed down, allowing the officer to catch up to him. When the officer was out of the car and heading in his direction, Duke smashed on the gas. The car swerved a little before he pulled into traffic.

"Oh shit!" Dre screeched. "Go nigga go!" He smacked the dashboard in excitement.

"Daddy," Lily whined, wiping her eyes. "I wanna go home."

"We're going home now, baby," Duke assured her, turning the block as hard as he could. The car did three full spins before he was able to gain control again.

"Go, nigga, they coming," Dre pleaded, looking in the review mirror. They were now being chased by three cars.

Duke skillfully turned down side streets, drove across lawns, and hopped curbs. Like a professional race car driver, he maneuvered through alleys and all. A smile spread across his face when he noticed that he lost them.

"I do this shit, nigga," he bragged.

"Daddy," Lily cried.

"We're almost home." Duke turned to look at her tear-stained face. He felt all types of fucked up.

"Yo, watch out, watch out!" Dre screamed in a high-pitched tone that would be his last.

In slow motion, Duke turned to face the front. He stepped

on the brakes, but because of the slick ground, he slid right into oncoming traffic. Dre's body catapulted out of the windshield, and Duke swerved to avoid hitting him and ended up hitting a pickup truck instead. The sudden maneuver threw his body to the dashboard and then to the passenger side where Dre once sat. Duke heard the officers running toward him, yelling at him to get out of the car, and if he could speak, he would have told them to suck his dick. He heard Lily groaning in the back seat and prayed that she made it through.

"Get the fuck out of the car!" The officer hollered, snatching his door open. "There's a child back here!"

"Where's the driver?" They questioned, pulling Duke from the car. Unbeknownst to them, he was the driver. When they tossed him to the ground, his broken rib punctured his lung. With blood dripping from his lip, Duke closed his eyes. His whole life had been nothing but chaos, and he finally felt free at that moment.

∞∞∞

"Why you so fucking sexy, man?" Rahlo tucked his bottom lip as he watched Taylor strut around the room in her black bandage dress and open-toe pumps. Her hair was trimmed into a cute pixy cut that only she could rock and her makeup was beat. "My blonde bombshell." He licked his lips.

"Stop it before we're late." Taylor giggled, feeling her nipples harden at his stare.

"Please stop." Kiki gagged from the other side of the room. "All yall do is have sex and sleep. I'm surprised her ass ain't pregnant yet."

"Oh, a baby! Rah, you should have a babyyyyy," Esha cooed.

"Bruce, they drinks cut off," Taylor said, picking up her own glass.

"You don't want my babies?" Rahlo asked, grabbing her by the waist.

"I do eventually, but you just dropped an album, you're on tour, and I know you don't think I'm about to take care of a baby by myself," she fussed.

"Rah and Taylor sitting in the tree," Esha and Kiki sang. *"F-u-c-k-i-n-g."*

"Yall need to grow up," Bruce laughed. Kiki moved to his side and pulled at his beard.

"You jealous, big baby?"

"Where yo nigga at?" he snorted. "Worry about if that nigga jealous."

"We're on a break for your information." Kiki rolled her eyes.

Their break was mutual, but Kiki was missing her man. She was a notorious flirt and had even crossed a few lines, but Mike was the love of her life. He was the man she was going to settle down with, but they were still young, and to avoid causing irreparable damage, Mike moved out and was doing his own thing, and Kiki was feeling the burn.

"Come here, let me talk to you for a minute." Bruce took the glass from her hand and pulled her toward the door.

"Aye nigga, don't be all day. We need to be out of here in twenty minutes. I'm not trying to hear Terri's mouth," Rahlo called after him.

"Let me find out you scared of that nigga," Bruce yelled over his shoulder before disappearing through the double doors.

"Fuck outta here."

"Ugh," Esha groaned, flopping down on the couch. "I'm jealous. Everybody got a man but me."

"Good." Rahlo glared in her direction. "You don't need a man. Focus on opening your shop."

"Boy, shut up. I could have sworn I was the older sister."

"I feel you though, Esha. If you want, we can make you a dating profile," Taylor suggested.

"Don't play with me," Rahlo warned, shooting her a hard glare.

"Anyway," Esha waved him off. "I can't wait to meet Usher."

"Girl, you?!" Taylor held her chest. "If that man starts singing to me, I'm-"

"Going to sit yo ass down before I throw rocks on the stage and trip his skating ass."

"Let me find out you a hater," Esha snickered. "If Usher wanna sing to my friend, who are you to throw salt on his game?"

"I'm not worried." Rahlo shrugged. "My dick stay on her breath like mints.

"RAHLO!" Taylor screeched, pushing him.

"I'm just saying, if that nigga get in your face with all that singing shit, he's going to get a double dose of my nuts."

In true Rahlo fashion, he stood in the middle of the ring, putting on a show that would be talked about for months to come. His energy could be felt in the arena as he bopped around on stage, weaving between dancers. In his own world, Rahlo performed his hit songs with his chest. Nothing brought him more pride than hearing the audience fill in the words when he held the mic out. It was risky because the songs were rather new, but the crowd held him down. They knew the words and rapped them without missing a beat.

Off to the side, Taylor rapped her heart out, encouraging her man to do his thing. When the lyrics resonated with his feelings about her, Rahlo winked, and Taylor blushed and blew him a kiss in return. The crowd went wild when he leaned over the ropes and had Taylor wipe the sweat from his forehead. To thank her, Rahlo grabbed her by the nape of her neck and sucked her lips.

"This my muthafuckin baby yall," Rahlo said into the mic, making her blush. "Yall be hating on thick girls, but that's the shit I like."

"Yeaaaaaaa," the ladies in the building shouted.

"Fellas, if you're in here with a thick chick, I want you to make some noise," Rahlo demanded in the mic, and the fellas started to bark.

"Slap her on the ass because that aggressive shit gets their pussy wet," he spoke. "Ain't that right, baby?" Rahlo licked his lips. Taylor turned around and popped her booty for him, sending the crowd into a frenzy. "Make sure you back that shit up. I don't wanna hear none of that sleeping shit when we get home." Taylor gave Rahlo the finger as he bopped to the other side of the ring.

An hour later, Rahlo was thanking the crowd and exiting the ring. Per usual, Terri was recording his every move as they walked to the back of the arena. Rahlo stopped along the way and took a few pictures and signed autographs. By the time he made it to the dressing room, Taylor was horny and wanted some dick. Not just any dick though, she wanted some rap star dick.

"Oh my god, baby, you did that!" Taylor kissed his lips, pushing him down onto the couch.

"That shit got this pussy hot?" Rahlo sucked her neck, pulling the tight dress over her hips.

Feverishly, he fumbled with her pussy while she blindly undid his buckle. Once he was free, Taylor lifted up, and Rahlo pulled her down on his dick, making them both exhale.

"Mmmm," Taylor moaned lowly. Reaching up, Rahlo gripped her neck as she started to bounce on him.

"Fuck. I swear I love fucking you," he expressed, bringing her mouth to his.

"I-I-love you toooo," Taylor nearly yelled, grinding into him. "I love you, Southwest Rah," she belted, cumming in his lap. Rahlo stirred his dick in her juices but lost the battle when she started squeezing his dick, milking him for every last drop.

"Did I back it up?" she asked breathlessly.

"Hell yea, now you gotta go see this Usher nigga with my nut leaking down your legs."

"Hush," Taylor laughed, climbing off his lap.

Rahlo grabbed his phone out of his pocket and noticed he had over fifty missed calls and text messages. The only thing that caught his eye was the voicemail from Duke. While Taylor continued to clean herself up, he sat back and listened to the message.

"Yo Rah. I'm fucked up, bro. Shit ain't been the same since I've been home and I don't know what the fuck is going on with me. I could blame it on my fucked up childhood or the wack ass judicial system that actually do more harm to your mental when you go in versus fixing what was actually broken. I don't know why I be expecting shit to change when this is the hand that I was dealt though, this is the life I'm supposed to live. I know the shit with Lexi was wrong. I should have told you, but I'm telling you now. Lily is my lil girl, and I won't say I'm sorry for creating her, I'm just sorry for the way this shit played out. You my muthafuckin brother and I was wrong as fuck to pull that gun out on you. I'm going to get some help, my boy. Anyway, I'm proud of you nigga. Call me when you get this. Oh, and I beat up Chef on some high shit. His

dumb ass laid there and made a snow angel."

Rahlo chuckled and exited the voicemail. He was still pissed with Duke, but the thought of Chef laying in the snow tickled him. Rahlo tried to call Duke's phone, but it kept going to voicemail. Thinking his phone was probably dead, Rahlo ended the call and sent him a text. Grabbing his shirt, he slipped it on over his head and stepped out of the dressing room with a bubbly Taylor on his heels. Right off, he knew something was wrong. Nobody had to say it because the sadness in their eyes said it all. Kiki was rubbing Bruce's back as he stood there without a lick of emotion on his face. Terri couldn't look at him, but it was Esha. She did it for him. Tears streamed down her face, sending his heart plummeting to the ground.

"Who?" he asked, knowing it wasn't a matter of what happened but who.

"There was an accident," Esha choked out.

"Who?" Rahlo repeated, this time a little louder. His hands started to sweat, and his heart throbbed a little louder.

"Rah, there was an accident, and Duke was in a high-speed chase with the police. He's uh- he died on the scene," Kiki revealed, knocking the wind out of him.

Rahlo stumbled back at her revelation. He assumed he must've heard her wrong, or he was in some kind of twilight bullshit. Not his nigga. Not his best friend.

"Fuck is you saying? He just left me a message." Rahlo held up his phone. "Esha!" he hollered, "What the fuck is she saying?"

"Oh my god!" Taylor's hands flew to her mouth, witnessing him fall apart before her eyes. Rahlo probably didn't even know he had tears streaming down his face or that his hands were shaking.

"He was running from the police and crashed into

oncoming traffic, Rah. Dre and Lily were in the car with him. Dre is dead, and Lily is at the hospital in critical condition."

"And Duke?" Rahlo asked, unable to process the vile words spilling from her lips.

"Rahlo, listen to me." Esha reached for his hands, clutching them in hers. "Duke is dead."

Chapter 26

The weeks following Duke's funeral were a blur. Rahlo couldn't believe he was forced to sit through such an animated service. Duke would have hated it. In fact, he would have started shooting at the shady muthafuckas in attendance. His mother wore a green and white prom dress she found at Good Will. As if her loud dress wasn't enough, her obnoxious cries matched it. Rahlo sat toward the back, unaffected by her mournful cries. He couldn't remember the last time the woman saw her son, yet she was sitting in the front row acting a fool.

Duke's grandmother sat off to the side with her lips tooted in an I told you so manner. She always said there were two places he would end up, in jail or in the grave. Not knowing how powerful words were, she unintentionally damned her grandson. Instead of being the voice of reason he needed or the guidance his young mind craved, she gave up just like her daughter.

The whole funeral was a circus, and as quickly as it came, it went. Half the people who attended the funeral didn't appear at the burial but doubled back for the repast, which turned into a party. Rahlo spared no expense. Everything was catered, the endless bottles were free. In memory of Duke, they rolled dice, smoked, and drank liquor until the wee hours of the morning. Well, everyone except Rahlo. He sat back watching them celebrate a life they didn't give two fucks about.

"Bae," Taylor called out, pulling him from his thoughts.

"Mm?" Rahlo answered without turning to face her.

"You need anything before I leave?" She rounded the couch and sat in his lap. With her hand, she lifted his face so she could look into his eyes. The sadness in his eyes caused her stomach to churn. Rahlo wouldn't talk about the funeral. He wouldn't talk about Duke. Hell, most days he wouldn't talk.

"Nah, I'm straight, T-baby. Go check on your people," he reassured her.

"Are you getting out of the house today?" Taylor asked, stroking his chin hair.

"Probably not."

"Did you accept the invite for the Christmas party they're having at The Yacht Club?"

"I told Chyna to decline it. I'm not in the mental space to be around a bunch of jolly muthafuckas."

"It might help."

"Nah."

"Ok, I understand." Taylor kissed his forehead, not wanting to push. "Call me if you need me."

"Will do," he lied. Rahlo was silently thanking God that she was leaving. It wasn't because she was overbearing or anything, Rahlo just preferred to sulk alone. It was the holiday season, and he wasn't trying to bring her down with his sour mood.

Once he heard the door close, Rahlo sparked his blunt and pressed play on his phone.

"Yo Rah. I'm fucked up, bro...

∞∞∞

"I'm beginning to think you scared of that boy," Papa grunted. "If you think he's going to beat your ass, just say that."

"Dad, now is not the time," Von warned.

"Oh yea, well when is the time? When little Michael Myers is standing over your bed with that lady head in his hands?"

Von glared at his father and then back down at the shoes in front of him. He was at his wits end with Trooper and his mischievous ways. His latest stunt had Von ready to whoop his ass and cancel Christmas. He tried to be understanding, but Trooper was pushing him to the edge.

"Why, son?" he stressed, holding up the YSL heels Ms. Riley wanted for Christmas.

"Cause why she got a gift under *our* tree?" Trooper pouted.

"Good question." Papa clapped, causing Von to glare in his direction. "Boy, I taught you that look. Glare at his bad ass like that. Matter fact, whoop him."

"He better not whoop my baby," Taylor sassed, walking into the living room, ready to go to war behind her little brother.

"Then take his bad ass with you," Papa snapped. "He over here cutting this woman's shoes, getting in trouble in school. Nope couldn't be me. He'd have a hole the size of Texas in his chest."

"Trooper, go to your room and think about what you've done." Von pointed his finger in his direction.

"Aw hell, where is Kool? I need a joint. Why would you tell

this boy to go think about what he done did so he can go back there and think about burning this damn house down?"

"My brother would never." Taylor sat on the couch beside her granddad. "How is my favorite old man?" She kissed his forehead.

"Oh, now I'm your favorite since you dropped Frederick Douglass?" Papa snorted.

"Not Frederick Douglass," Taylor laughed.

"You know that man was old as shit. Tell me, what's going on with our superstar?"

"Excuse me?" She dipped her eyebrows.

"Girl, stop all that and give me the skinny. Are you keeping our main man happy? He promised me season tickets to the Lions games."

"Wow, that's all I'm worth? Season passes to see the whack Lions? I mean, they haven't won a game since you lost your hairline."

"See, now you're trying to get put out." He mushed her.

"Daddy, what's going on with Trooper?" Taylor asked, turning her attention to him.

"He's acting out, and I don't know why."

"You don't?" She frowned.

"I know he's upset about me dating his teacher, but he doesn't even have music this semester, so he don't see her at school," Von expressed as if it made a difference.

"Daddy, just like this is new for you, Trooper has to adjust to it."

"It's been months. My relationship with Ariel isn't that new."

"But it is. I grew up with you and Mommy, but Trooper doesn't remember much about her, and in his eyes, you're trying to replace her."

"Then what do I do, Ms. Know it all?"

"Talk to him," she suggested.

"Here go that gentle parenting shit," Papa huffed.

"Hear me out." Taylor held up her hand. "Trooper is a good kid, and if he's acting out, there could be something else wrong."

"Trooper!" Von hollered, startling them. Seconds later, Trooper walked into the living room with head down. His tear-stained face pulled at Taylor's heartstrings.

"Huh?" he whispered.

"What's going on, Troop? Why are you so angry?" Von asked.

"Cause," he mumbled.

"Cause what? And we don't have all day to play this guessing game," Papa warned.

"I don't wanna talk about it," Trooper whispered.

"Troop, you are in a lot of trouble right now, and if something is going on, then you need to speak up." Taylor rubbed his shoulder.

"Fine!" he sniffled. "The boys in my class asked if Ms. Riley wears granny panties. I don't even see her panties," he vexed. "They said I got a B in her classes because Daddy is delivering the D."

"Ahhhhh," Papa doubled over in laughter. "Say the thing about the D again, I gotta use that."

"Papa," Taylor warned, bumping his shoulder.

"It's not funny. They always teasing me, asking if she tucks me in at night, and I don't like it. You said she don't live here, but she's always here."

"Good point." Papa clapped. "She is always here."

"Dad, you're not helping." Von peered at him.

"I'm not trying to. I'm a neutral party in this conversation."

"Son, she doesn't live here, but eventually she will-"

"Now, why would you tell his unhinged ass that?"

"But you said she's not," Trooper pouted.

"Right now, she's not, but that's where the relationship is headed. You don't think we need a woman's touch around here?" Von rubbed the top of his head.

"We have Tay."

"Your sister has her own life, Troop. Tell me what will make this easier?"

Trooper leaned his head to the side and thought about his father's request. There wasn't really much he could do to stop what was happening, but there were a few things that could help.

"Only me and you go to the movies to see Marvel," he started.

"Easy," Von agreed.

"I don't want her to fix my uniform at school."

"Ok, I'll talk to her…. anything else?"

"Can I take some of her underwear to school?" he asked seriously. Taylor's eyes widened before she burst out in laughter.

"Gimme a pair too," Papa whispered.

"No, you cannot, and if I find out you did, that'll be the day I whoop your ass. Matter fact, stay out of my room. Do not touch her belongings."

"Fine," Trooper gave in. "What about she gives me a A+ in the next class?"

"Then they gone say you only got a A in the class because your daddy tapping that a-"

"Papa!" Taylor screeched, knowing where he was headed. "Troop, put on your boots and come help me get these gifts from my car."

"Christmas is in three weeks, why you bring them so early?" Von asked.

"Different companies sent me stuff and I have to post it. I have something for everybody, and I need yall to open them while I record."

"Oh nice! I love how you're more invested in the influencer world now. It's a lot better than the bar."

"I do miss the bar, but people were being creepy. I honestly been thinking about going back to school."

"Oh yeah? For what?"

"Public relations. I've been managing Rahlo's social media accounts, and I started his sister's business account, which boosted her clientele."

"I'm happy to hear that, baby. Seriously."

"Thanks, Daddy. I appreciate you not pushing me into a field I didn't want."

"Like I told you, Tay, this is your life. I'm just here in case you need a push. With that being said, I'll have my accountant reach out to you. I still have your college fund. It should be enough for you to start school and more," Von told her.

"Really?" Taylor's eyes lit up. Rahlo offered to pay for her classes, but this was much better.

"Really." He pulled her into a hug and kissed her forehead.

"I'm ready!" Trooper called out from the front door.

"Here I come." Taylor pushed up from the couch. "I love you, Daddy, like for real. Through everything, you've been solid and consistent. I'll never forget that."

"It's my job to set the bar high. Jasper was a mistake and played on the fact that you were in pain from losing your mother. It was only a matter of time before his true colors showed."

"Taylorrr," Trooper impatiently hollered.

"Boy, take a damn chill pill. Matter fact, take a melatonin and take a nap," Papa grunted.

"Is that them sleepy gummy bears you give me when daddy go out with Ms. Riley?" Trooper quizzed.

"Boy, shut up, you talk too much."

Outside, Taylor popped the trunk to her Jeep and shuffled around with the packages she had stacked in the back. Some were for her guys, and the others were for Rahlo. She hoped the Fendi robe and slippers would lighten his mood just a bit. Lifting a couple of gift bags, she turned to hand them to Trooper and jumped at the person standing behind him.

"What's up, baby mama?" Jasper greeted.

"What the heck are you doing here?" Taylor squinted. "Trooper, take these and go in the house." She handed him the bags.

"You ok?" he asked, sizing Jasper up.

"I'm fine, Troop. Go inside," Taylor promised. Trooper lingered for a few seconds before walking backwards inside the house, never taking his eyes off Jasper. "Boy, turn around and go inside," Taylor snickered.

She waited until he walked into the house before turning to face Jasper. He was now leaning against her truck, peeking inside the bags she had stored in the back.

"Jasper, what are you doing here?" Taylor asked, shifting on her feet.

"To get my girl back. I was in a bad place a few months ago, but I'm back. I've been seeking help, I got my job back, and I'm not drinking," he proudly listed.

"And all of that is good for you, but there is no getting me back, Jasper."

"Why though, baby? We were good together. I know I messed up, but I need you, and I'm willing to do the work. I realize what I did was wrong."

"Which part?" Taylor bucked her eyes.

"All of it, and if I could go back and change it, I would. I fucked up, and I missed you so much."

"Jasper, I'll always have love for you-"

"But?"

"But I'm in a relationship with Rahlo. I do think it's good that you're getting back on track, but you also need to move forward. There will never be another you and I." Taylor spoke softly, trying not to trigger him, but from how his eyes shifted, she knew it was too late.

Jasper clenched his jaw and glared at her with so much intensity that it made her stomach churn. Stepping forward, he leaned in so close that he could smell the strawberry lip gloss on her lips.

"I can't stand bitches like you," he gritted.

"Excuse me?"

"Your fat ass ain't excused. I bent over backwards to make you happy, and you still tried to walk over me. I wouldn't have tried to trap you if you would've allowed me to be a man. I asked you to move in, and you fucking laughed in my face and talked about me to your ugly ass friend. I tried to be the man you needed, and all you did was walk over me. I should have been went upside your head."

"Ok, Jasper, clearly you are in your feelings, and I'm going to let you get a pass, but I don't owe you shit. You cheated, you lied, and you schemed; therefore, you need to blame your damn self for everything that happened."

"You just like the rest of these bitches." He grabbed her wrist.

"Aye, old man, let her go before I spread your organs all over this beautiful white snow," Kool threatened, walking up behind them with a chopper the length of his arm on his shoulder.

"Let me guess, you fucking him too?" Jasper snorted, but he released Taylor's wrist.

"Nah, but I'm fucking your loose pussy sister. Tell her loudmouth ass to do some Kegels because the other day I felt like I was fucking a hula hoop."

"I'll fuck you up," Jasper swore but didn't move a muscle.

"You ain't gone do shit but get in your car and scoot the fuck on." Kool stepped forward, cocking the gun. "If not, I'll have your ass laying here like Swiss cheese."

"I'm gone." Jasper backed away and walked to his car as Von stormed out of the house with Papa on his heels.

"Get the fuck from around here!" Von yelled.

"Aww, look at *her guys* coming to the rescue," Jasper taunted. "Make sure yall stay around too."

Pow!

Kool let off a warning shot, making everybody jump.

"The next one is going through your temple, and if you come around here again, they're going to find your organs online for sale."

"Say that shit, Kool!" Papa clapped.

"I'm gone." Jasper hopped in his car and sped away.

"Thanks, Kool." Taylor released the breath she had been

unknowingly holding.

"No worries, shorty. You know I'm holding you down like gravity, but you do need to watch homeboy. He looks like he lost all his marbles and is scrambling to find them muthafuckas."

"Go get a restraining order on him!" Von told her.

"Nah, he needs a bullet," Papa said going back in the house. "A man like that won't learn his lesson until it's too late."

∞ ∞ ∞

Rahlo pulled onto Emory's block and cut off his truck. For weeks, he had been searching for clarity, and somehow, he always ended up where it all started. His love for music, his toxic relationship with his mother, and his friendship with Duke and Bruce. There was something nostalgic about the block, and he couldn't let it go.

With music playing over the speaker, Rahlo closed his eyes and bobbed his head. Visions of his friendship with Duke invaded his mind as his eyes burned from the tears he held back. Their fight seemed so petty now. All he wanted to do was call his best friend and work through their differences. They had been through the trenches together and were supposed to reach the top, but bruised egos and growth had been their downfall.

"Aye, you think I can stay the night at yall crib tonight?" Twelve-year-old Duke asked, scratching the top of his uncut hair.

"You gotta wait til' Esha go to sleep," Rahlo told him. *"Last time I got in trouble."*

"Man, that's yo big sister, how you get in trouble with her?"

"Nigga, she hit hard, and plus, she always buying me stuff, so I have to listen to her."

"Yall mama been around?"

"Nope, she met some man and been gone for like two weeks."

"At least she be coming back. My mama been gone for like five months. Her crackhead ass stole my grandma ring and ain't been back since. I hope her ugly ass get hit by a bus," Duke snarled, rounding the corner of the grocery store. *"How much money you get from Esha?"*

"Five dollars. I was supposed to get my hair cut, but you need it?" Rahlo asked, fishing around in his pocket. *"I'll tell Esh I lost it."*

"I need more than five dollars," Duke stressed. *"We don't have no food and I can't eat another syrup sandwich. Can you just put some stuff in your hoodie for me?"*

"Nah, man, last time Esha pinched the shit out of me."

"Then don't get caught." Duke bumped his shoulder. Rahlo took a deep breath and pulled his hood over his head.

"When I get rich you not gone have to steal no more. I'ma look out for you," Rahlo promised.

"Say word."

"Word."

"Fuck." Rahlo opened his eyes as the tears slipped down his face. "My fucking nigga," he wept.

The tears that fell on his shirt were for all the young black boys who were lost. The ones who weren't encouraged to make it out of the hood. The ones who didn't have a father figure and aimlessly walked around without guidance. His cries were for the black boys who never stood a chance. Sadly, Duke's story wasn't uncommon. There were millions of lives lost, and Duke was just another lost black soul.

Tap tap tap

Rahlo looked up and locked eyes with the last person he wanted to see. Outside his window, Chef was wearing a brown fur coat with the matching hat. Wiping his eyes, Rahlo rolled the windows and mugged him.

"You wanna talk, or you wanna tussle?" Chef asked, holding his hands up. "You might whoop my ass, but I'm not going down without a fight."

"Get in." Rahlo popped the locks.

"Don't mind if I do. It's cold as hell out here." He slid in the front seat. "What's up? Why you out here looking like you lost-" Chef paused. "Oh shit, my fault, youngblood."

Rahlo examined Chef as if it was his first time seeing him. He didn't know how he missed it. Chef had two dimples, he had one. They shared the same silky eyebrows and bedroom eyes. Minus the damage time had done to Chef's appearance, they looked alike. The whole time he had been searching for his father, he was right there in his face.

"This crazy as fuck. I've been looking for you my whole life, and you've been tap dancing up and down this street like a broke ass Prince," Rahlo said, breaking the silence. "Why you ain't say shit?"

"What was I going to say?" Chef mumbled, ashamed for the first time in years. All of a sudden, he felt dirty. He didn't feel worthy enough to sit next to the seed that was produced from his sack.

"I'm your father, for starters," Rahlo barked.

"But why? What did I have to offer you? I'm a fucking crackhead." Chef slapped his chest.

"I could've helped you."

"That's the thing. I don't need no fucking help. I love who I am. I accept me for who I am. I don't need anyone's stamp of approval. I don't go around making broken promises. What you see is what you get."

"That's so fucking selfish, bro."

"I'm selfish, Rah. I don't want to go to rehab and fix shit. This is my life and I love it."

"Then why the fuck you sitting in my car looking like an oversize squirrel?"

"Because I've been where you are. On top of my game, willing to help the world, but you can only help those who want to help themselves. The quickest way to fall from grace is to consistently be loyal to the wrong people. Everyone isn't meant to be saved. Your boy was on drugs," Chef revealed. "I'm sure it started some time ago, but he was a lost cause. There was no saving him. Your mother, she's a lost cause. I watched her rob her own house and then call you for help. Me," he touched his chest. "I'm a lost cause. I'm high 90% of the time and that's not something I want to change."

"So what are you saying?"

"I'm saying that you should move on. Allow your music career to take you to heights you never imagined. You don't owe nobody shit. Get the fuck out of the city and don't look back. Ain't shit here but heartache and disappointment," Chef preached, looking out the window.

"And what about you?" Rahlo questioned.

"I'm nobody. Don't think finding out who I am changes anything. I'm crackhead Chef," he touched his chest. "But you, you are muthafuckin' Southwest Rah." Chef reached for the doorknob. "You be easy and I don't want to see you around here no more. You don't have no more ties to the streets. No one needs to be saved."

With those final words, Chef exited the truck and bopped down the street without a worry in the world.

When Taylor made it back to Rahlo's place, he was sitting on the kitchen island with a blunt hanging from his lips and a bottle of Hennessey loosely dangling from his hand. She was happy to see he wasn't in the same spot but worried about his current state. His eyes were low and his body was slumped.

"Hey." Taylor slowly walked toward him.

"Sup, T-baby?" He gave her a lazy smile. The dimple in his cheek sunk in, making her smile back.

"You." She took the bottle from his hands.

"That's how you feel?" Rahlo raised his eyebrow.

"I'm feeling however you feel."

"You don't wanna feel like this, baby." He dropped his head, pulling from the blunt. "I'm fucked up."

"Talk to me." Taylor sat the bottle down and walked between his legs. "Tell me what's on your mind, baby."

"Life," he chortled. "You want me to tell you what's crazy?"

"What?"

"I used to see the glitz and glamour of this rap star lifestyle, and I wanted it. I wanted the endless bitches, money, the cars, and all that shit. I idolized how the stars lived, and I wanted parts. I wanted what they had, not knowing what was behind that shit." He paused and pulled from the blunt. "I didn't even think about the shit that happened behind closed doors."

"No one ever does. That part isn't meant for us to see."

"The shit I've been dealing with is wild as fuck, and you're the only thing that's keeping me sane. My nigga gone." Rahlo tried to swallow the tears that nearly choked him. "I should have been there. I should have fucking called him," he cried. "Fuck!"

"It wasn't your fault." Taylor took the blunt from him and dropped it in the sink. She moved the liquor bottle to the side and wrapped her arms around his neck. "Look at me." Taylor kissed his forehead.

"Hmm."

"I'm so sorry about what happened to Duke, and I'm sorry you lost him, but you can't beat yourself up over this. Do you honestly think he would have listened to you?"

"Probably not," Rahlo snorted, wiping his nose.

"And what would he say to you right now?"

"Tell me to stop being a bitch," he chortled.

"Sounds about right." Taylor laughed, wiping his tears. "I'm not going to tell you that, but I will say it gets better, and whatever I can do to help, let me know."

"Whatever?" He leaned in and kissed her neck.

"Whatever, baby." She poked her lips out. "You just have to keep pushing until you reach the top."

"Thanks, T-baby."

"I got you, boo. Through whatever."

"I'ma hold you to that." Rahlo winked, picking up the bottle off the counter. "Hey Google, play *Pussy Monster*."

Chapter 27

"Merry Christmas, Mr. 500K," Taylor cooed, pushing the bedroom door open with her foot.

"Damn, that's how you feel?" Rahlo's hand went to his rising dick.

Taylor never failed to amaze him. She was standing at the foot of the bed wearing a cute gold two-piece bikini set. The six-inch gold pumps wrapped up her thick thighs and connected to a garter belt. In her right hand was a bottle of champagne, and in the other was a framed picture of his album.

"I don't know if you know this, but I'm so fucking proud of you." She slowly walked over to his side of the bed. Rahlo's eyes bounced around, not knowing what to focus on. Her breasts spilled over the top, her booty swallowed the string of the bikini, and her thighs were so nicely presented that he wanted to spread them.

"Terri called," she continued. "The album went gold and they are throwing you a party on New Year's Day. You did it, baby! You blew the charts up! All of your social media accounts are doing numbers, XXL wants you to do an interview, and Chyna said you've been receiving all kinds of emails for collaborations."

"Oh yea?"

"Yea! You're a freaking superstar, baby. The whole world wants a piece of you. Your sister is on her way to start making Christmas dinner, but I wanted to give you your present first."

"What's my present?" Rahlo licked his lips.

"Pussy and mimosas. Come on." She dropped the picture on the bed and stretched her arm out.

Rahlo almost broke his neck jumping out of the bed. With his dick leading the way, he followed her into the bathroom, where she had a bath drawn and a tray of fruit sitting on the counter.

"T-baby." He marveled at the decorated bathroom. She had a large set of gold 5-0-0 balloons taped to the wall, gold streamers on the ceiling, and Drake rapped in the background about being proud. "You did this for me?"

"I sure did." Taylor squatted in front of him. "Hold this." She handed him the champagne and proceeded to remove his basketball shorts and boxer briefs. Leaning in, she kissed the tip of his dick and massaged his balls.

"Good morning, my loves." She swiped her tongue across them.

"You trying to get a ring?" Rahlo asked seriously. "If that's what you want, you got it," he promised, enjoying the tip of her tongue fumbling with his nuts.

"Not yet." She winked, standing to her feet. "Get in." Taylor motioned toward the warm candle-lit bath.

While he relaxed, she removed her heels and gold bikini. Joining him, Taylor slid into the water and sat directly on his stiff dick. Rahlo's mouth fell open and Taylor covered it with hers.

"Aye, I fucking love you," he confessed, moving his hips in the water.

"I love you, too," Taylor swore. "Lay your head back," she told him.

Doing as he was told, Rahlo laid his head back on the warm towel.

"Close your eyes," she instructed, "And don't drop the bottle."

"Aight," he obliged.

Taking her time, Taylor slowly rocked her hips while squirting a little face moisturizer in her hands. Rahlo nearly lost his mind as she rode his dick and caressed his face. Speaking love and greatness into him, Taylor made love to her man, making him fall deeper in love with her. When he was nice and lathered, she took the champagne and popped the cork. The bubbly liquid spilled down her breasts, and that was his cue to clean it up. Like a freak, he sucked her lips, her neck, shoulders and nipples. Lifting to the tip of her toes, Taylor bounced on his dick as the water slapped her on the ass.

"Fuck yea." Rahlo's arms locked around her waist, pulling her down further every time their thighs met.

"Fuck me, Mr. 500K," she moaned, and Rahlo lost his shit. His nut entered her as his head fell back. "You get a pass this time, but you better make me cum back-to-back later."

"Just call me Drake."

"You are so corny," Taylor giggled.

"Players fuck up." He kissed her. "Damn girl, that shit felt good."

"Let's wash up so I can give you your present."

"I like the sound of that."

Twenty minutes later they were both dressed in matching PJs. Rahlo thought it was funny that she liked corny shit like that, but he wore them and allowed her to take pictures. Taylor tried to give him her gift first, but Rahlo stopped her. When she was on the couch, he handed her box after box. Purses, shoes, a new camera, a key to his house, and a diamond necklace with an iced-out charm that said T-baby. Taylor was in awe and loved everything. When it was her turn, she ran to his room and returned with a small gift bag.

"You got me something off Shein? I won't be mad, but damn you cheap, T-baby," Rahlo said, shaking the bag. "You couldn't break the bank for your nigga?"

"Boy, open the damn gift!" Taylor rolled her eyes.

Anxiously, Rahlo removed the contents of the bag and frowned.

"Read the shirt," Taylor snickered.

"I knew this was some Shein shit," he joked. Opening the shirt, Rahlo's face fell flat. It wasn't a T-shirt. It was a onesie that read, 'My daddy is a superstar.'

"T-baby," he whispered.

"There's more," she urged him to read the papers from her doctor.

Rahlo's eyes scanned the paper and looked back up at her.

"You pregnant?"

"Yes, only two months, but nonetheless, pregnant."

This go around, Taylor knew something was different. Besides missing her period, her breasts were sore, she was always sleeping, and just the thought of Rahlo made her pussy wet. She had him leaving in the middle of studio sessions to fuck her. What took the cake was the morning sickness. She rolled out of the bed for three days straight, barely making it to the bathroom.

"Come here, man." He stretched his hand out and pulled her down into his lap. "When you find out?"

"Last week. I went to the doctor while you were meeting with Terri."

It was actually Kiki who dragged her to the doctor. Taylor was apprehensive since her first pregnancy ended in such a tragic way. She didn't want to grow attached to a baby she probably wouldn't get to keep. The thought alone scared her to death.

"And you want to keep it?" Rahlo asked. He was well aware of her previous pregnancy with Jasper, and although he'd hate it, Rahlo respected her decision either way.

"Yea, I mean, if that's okay with you." Taylor nibbled on her bottom lip.

"Hell fucking yea that's ok with me," he exclaimed. " I would have gotten you pregnant the first time you stepped your sassy ass in my section. This was God's plan, baby."

"So we're having a baby?" She chewed her lip.

"We're having a fucking baby." Rahlo kissed her, which led to him crawling back between her legs. "So you know what this means, right?"

"What?" She wrapped her arms around his neck.

"You're moving in with me."

"Are you telling me or asking me?"

"Whatever makes you feel better," Rahlo shrugged. "You can do your content in the guest room, and in the meantime, I'm going to find us something bigger."

"You know you don't have to do all that, right?"

"Hush, girl. I got this. How about you tell me why that old

nigga was all in your face?"

"Who told you?"

"I'm trying to figure out why you didn't tell me."

Taylor sighed and dropped her head. "I don't want you to get in trouble because of me. I can handle Jasper."

"Am I your nigga?"

"Yes, but-"

"No buts, I'm going to pay granddad a visit."

"Rahlo, think about your future," she pleaded.

"I am. I want all that nigga's information."

∞∞∞∞

Hours later, Rahlo's loft was filled with Taylor's guys, Ariel, his sister, Kiki, and Bruce. Esha threw down in the kitchen and cooked everything from ham to fried chicken, baked beans, Mac and cheese, yams, greens, a couple of cakes, and more. Rahlo offered to have it catered, but Esha wouldn't take no for an answer. It was the least she could do. Because of him, her shop was doing numbers. Esha hired other stylists, but clients wanted her. Taylor kept her social media pages trending, and that alone filled her books up.

After eating they exchanged gifts. As always, Rahlo was generous, handing out gift bags, a new game system for Trooper, roundtrip plane tickets for Von to any place he picked, and season basketball tickets for Papa. His gift for Bruce brought tears to all of their eyes. Bruce had been talking about opening up a carwash for a while now, something he felt was self-sufficient and low maintenance. When Bruce opened the deed to the carwash, he nearly cried. Rahlo told him they'd sit down and go over the paperwork, but the carwash was his.

Overwhelmed, Bruce hugged his day one and thanked him for everything he had done for him. For Esha, Rahlo bought her a utility van she had been looking into. It was fully equipped with a salon chair, hair supplies, and outlets.

Taylor sat back with tears in her eyes. She was happy, like genuinely happy. Their first Christmas together was perfect. Rahlo fed her soul, and she couldn't wait to bring their little person into the world. It scared her because they hadn't known each other that long, but she was ready for whatever the universe wanted to give her.

Every so often, Rahlo looked at the door as if Duke was going to walk in, but he never did. The pain in his heart would never go away. He just prayed with due time, he would find a way to live with it. Against his better judgment, Rahlo reached out to Lexi to check on Lily. She cursed him out and blamed him for what happened. Lexi claimed fame had tarnished his loyalty and she'd never forgive him.

"I think we should toast," Kiki said aloud, capturing everyone's attention. "I've learned through the years that family doesn't always mean blood. It can be your co-workers, your pets, or a famous ass superstar your best friend snagged," she joked, causing them to all laugh. "But for real, I love yall, and Taylor and Rahlo, I wish yall nothing but the best on your adventure in parenting."

"Bitch." Taylor dropped her head.

"Fertile Myrtle, you pregnant?" Papa asked.

"Oh shit, it's not my fault. Rah, why would you buy this good champagne and have me spilling the beans like this." Kiki took a sip of her drink.

"Oh my god, I'm going to be a TT?" Esha screeched, running to her brother.

"Hell yea, I beat the walls down," Rahlo smirked. "Oh shit, my fault Big V," he apologized to Von, who had his arm wrapped around Ariel.

"Tread lightly, young man."

"You got it."

"Tayyyy, why didn't you tell me?" Esha pouted. "We just had brunch."

"I needed to tell Rahlo first, but I got you this. I was going to give it to you later, but big mouth ruined it." Taylor handed her a small gift bag.

Eagerly, she pulled the onesie out and cooed.

"Oh my goddddd," Esha cried. *"My TT let me do it,"* she read the shirt and hugged it to her chest.

"Yo, Rah." Bruce cleared his throat and nodded to the door where Emory was standing.

Rahlo hadn't seen his mother since he learned about Chef being his father. She had reached out to Terri about her contract for the show she wanted to do, but after telling her they pulled the offer, he blocked her. Angrily, Emory took to social media and dragged Rahlo through the mud. She aired out all his business and even leaked his phone number. Esha wanted to beat her ass, but Rahlo told her not to. Karma was going to handle her. Now that she was standing there wearing too little clothes, a nappy wig, and missing lashes, he knew karma was in full effect.

"Uh, ma'am, this is not a soup kitchen," Papa told her.

"Who the fuck are you?" she questioned.

"Nope, wrong one," Taylor warned her.

"Emory, what are you doing here?" Rahlo calmly asked, unbothered by her appearance.

"I see you're doing just fine for a man that just lost his best friend," she taunted.

"Emory, you need to leave," Esha warned.

"And go where? I was evicted! My rent hasn't been paid in two months and they evicted me."

"Oh damn, that's fucked up. You should make a GoFundMe." Rahlo nonchalantly hunched his shoulders.

"A GoFundMe, are you serious? Write a fucking check or have Terri do something!" she screamed. "I am not about to go stay in a shelter."

"Troop, come to the back with me," Taylor told Trooper.

"Are they about to fight?" he whispered.

"I'll fill you in," Papa assured him.

"Wow, so this is what we've come to. You made a lil name for yourself, got a lil money, and it's fuck the people that's been here since day one," Emory scoffed.

"Again, I don't know what the fuck you talking about. Esha-" he pointed to his sister, "Is my day one. She's been the one holding me down. All you did was lie and use me, but that well has run dry."

"I'm your-"

"Shit!" Rahlo barked. "You're not my shit. Just because I don't address certain situations don't mean I don't see it. I see it. You robbed your own house, you made a diss track about me, you fucking lied to me my whole life about my father. You fucking embarrassed me and yourself. Those men you had tested, you knew they weren't my father, but you went through with that fake ass sob story thinking one of them would stick around. Jokes on you though, Emory. You are damaged goods, and I don't have shit for you."

Whap!

Her hand went across his face. "I deserve respect! I am your mother! You owe me your life."

"You gave birth to me, but that's it. I don't owe you shit. Get out of my crib and don't ever bring your begging ass back this way."

"Fuck you, Rah! I hope everything you touch crumbles and you end up like your crackhead ass daddy." She stormed out of the loft with her head held high.

"Whew," Papa whispered to Von. "And I thought we had some shit."

"Cut the music back up. It's Christmas," Rahlo said aloud.

"You good, baby?" Taylor touched his back. Placing his hand on her stomach, Rahlo kissed her forehead.

"I'm gravy, baby. I'm about to be a daddy. From this moment on, yall are my family."

∞∞∞

Jasper focused on the Instagram Live instead of watching Jalen open up his gifts. Seeing Taylor derailed him, and Jasper was back at square one. When he left her house, he stopped at the liquor store and got a drink. Instead of returning to Sherri's house, he sat on the corner and took the bottle straight to the head. Taylor had him fucked up! She had some nerve moving on after he apologized to her. His word should have been good enough, but it wasn't, and Jasper was livid.

"My best friend out here doing the damn thing! Tay, show them your bling!" Kiki said to the camera. Jasper watched Taylor lean into the camera and show her diamond-studded chain.

"Cheap shit," he snarled.

"Jasper," Sherri called his name. "He's trying to show you his VR set."

"I know what it looks like, I paid for the shit," Jasper snapped, not taking his eyes off the screen.

"She fucking with a boss!" Rahlo bragged, wrapping his arm

around Taylor. Jasper's eyes went to Rahlo's hand, which was on her stomach. People started going up in the comments asking Taylor if she was pregnant.

"Daddy, do you wanna play?" Jalen asked, but his question was ignored. Jasper commented on the video, calling Taylor a fat gold digger.

"Who the fuck is this creep?" Rahlo frowned at the screen, seeing the comment. "Whoever you are, get a fucking clue. She ain't gotta dig for shit when I place it at her feet."

"Perioddddd," Kiki screamed in the camera and blocked Jasper from their Live.

"Give me your phone." He wildly spun around.

"No," Sherri shook her head. "You're not about to stalk that girl on my phone. How about you pay attention to your son or, better yet, get your drunk ass off my couch and get a freaking clue."

"Just give me the damn phone so I can finish watching this Live. I think Taylor pregnant," he slurred. "How is she going to have this nigga baby and aborted mine?"

"Look, we're not about to discuss your failed relationship on Christmas," Sherri stopped him. If she had to hear about Taylor again, she was going to shoot herself. "How about you spend time with your son for once," Sherri fussed.

"Get the fuck off my back!" he roared, jumping to his feet. "It's your fault she left me!"

"Jasper, I think you should leave."

"Give me your phone and I'll go in the bathroom."

"No, leave." Sherri pointed to the door.

Jasper looked down at his son and then over at Jamie, who was sitting on the couch with tears streaming down her face. He wanted to feel bad, but something kept him from feeling any other emotion besides rage. Without warning, he snatched Sherri's phone off the table and stormed past her. He stumbled a bit and fell right into the tree, knocking it over. More than a few lights and bulbs broke on impact, sending shards of plastic and pine needles all over the living room carpet. Both Jalen and Jamie started crying, seeing their tree tumble to the ground. It took them days to create the masterpiece and seconds for it to get ruined. Jasper didn't even look back. He locked himself in the bathroom and logged back onto Instagram from Sherri's page.

"I'm going to kill this bitch," Jasper murmured, watching Taylor pop her ass on Rahlo. "I'm going to fucking kill her disloyal ass."

Chapter 28

The next morning, Rahlo woke up on a mission. He made sure Taylor was straight before he slipped out of the house. She was worn out after partying into the wee hours of the morning with their families. Although she couldn't drink, Taylor got turnt up by watching them. Rahlo, Bruce, and Papa smoked so much that they had to carry Papa to the car. The man was toasted and begging Esha to tuck him in.

Rahlo's first stop was to pick up Bruce. They had a meeting with Terri and the label. After Duke's accident, Rahlo paused the tour. He needed a minute to get his mind right, and Terri respected it. After the New Year, it was go time. There were still eight cities left, and after that, he wanted to jump right into the second album.

"You do know you don't need to do this, right?" Bruce reiterated. "I can go by myself." He glanced at Rahlo and them back at the house.

"Nah, this nigga getting on my nerves and I'm not feeling him popping up on my girl."

"Aight, fuck it. Let's go shake some shit up."

Together, Bruce and Rahlo walked up the snow-covered sidewalk. They had been hunting for Jasper all morning, and thanks to his son, they knew exactly where he was. As promised, the front door was unlocked.

"Ugh, it smells like ass in this bitch." Bruce covered his nose.

"The lil nigga said his daddy fell asleep after he shitted. I'm guessing he didn't make it to the bathroom," Rahlo said, pulling the gun from his back. Pointing it outward, he walked through the living room, wondering what the hell had happened. The table was upside down, the tree was knocked over, food was everywhere, and Jasper was lying in a pile of throw-up, piss, and shit.

After he saw the pictures of Taylor's Christmas, Jasper went crazy. He couldn't believe her family was sitting there drinking and chopping it up with Rahlo in a manner they never did with him. They looked like one big happy family and it angered him to know it. Blinded by rage, Jasper ruined Christmas for his son without a second thought. He started throwing things, including food, gifts, and even the tree. Sherri grabbed her kids and ran out of the house. Jalen texted Taylor and she forwarded it to Rahlo.

"Wake up, shitty." Bruce kicked him. Jasper stirred in his sleep and slowly opened his eyes. When they focused on the barrel of the gun, he jumped up.

"W-what's going on?" he stuttered.

"Why you mess up Christmas like this for them kids?" Rahlo quizzed. Jasper squinted and slowly glanced around the living room. His stomach flipped at the mess he didn't remember making, and his nose burned at the vile smell.

"Oh shit, you don't remember this, do you?" Bruce laughed. "That's fucked up. You should stop drinking."

"Why are yall here?" Jasper questioned again.

"Because you can't seem to let go of something you never should have had in the first place," Rahlo spoke up. "Why you keep bothering my girl?"

"Your girl," he snorted. "She's only yours until the next man comes along."

"Nah, I promise you she's all mine. I knew she was mine the minute I laid eyes on her, but I needed her to drop the extra baggage. Now that I have her, I'm never coming up off that ass. I love shorty and I'm in it for life, which is why my seeds found a new home."

"You got her pregnant?" Jasper gasped.

"I did, busted walnuts all in that fat ass pussy," Rahlo bragged.

"Arggggh!" Jasper ran toward him but was met with Bruce's foot in his chest. The kick sent Jasper flying back, putting a dent in the wall.

"I had it." Rahlo frowned.

"The correct response is thank you. This nigga just charged you smelling like a pig's pen and horse shit."

"The old nigga looking like he can't breathe and shit. How the fuck am I supposed to reason with a dead man?"

"Nigga, I can't fucking breathe! Say what the fuck you gotta say so I can go take a shower." Bruce snapped his fingers. "Terri would be real disappointed."

"Terri ain't gone find out." Rahlo shot him a look. "Look, I'm only going to say this once. Stay the fuck away from my girl, stop calling her, and stop following her around on Instagram. Move the fuck on and live the rest of your life before you end up in an early grave."

"Fuck you," Jasper wheezed. "You and that fat bitch can suck my-"

Whap whap whap whap!

Rahlo's fists tattooed the front of Jasper's face, knocking his teeth to the side. With every punch, Rahlo felt exhilarated, so he knocked Jasper around until Bruce snatched him back. All the frustration he felt exited his throbbing fists and entered Jasper's face as he held on for dear life.

"That's enough, nigga! You trying to go to jail." Bruce released him.

"Nah, that shit just felt good. I might need to hit the gym or something." Rahlo glanced down at his handiwork. Jasper's face was bleeding and his eyes were swollen shut. "Call your son, bitch ass nigga. Maybe your face will make him feel better."

"Take a shower though, you smell bad as fuck," Bruce uttered, covering his nose and mouth. "Did you even try to make it to the bathroom?"

"G-g-get out," Jasper hissed through his busted lip.

"We leaving, but take heed to my warning. The next time you get a visit from me, it won't be to beat your old ass. When I leave you won't be breathing," Rahlo promised, stepping over Jasper.   Once they were outside, Bruce stared Rahlo up and down with a disgusted look on his face.

"The fuck is you looking at?"

"You, nigga." Bruce pointed to his shirt. "I think you have shit on your shirt."

"Fuck, take me by the crib. I need to change before I go meet Terri."

"I think you should take the bus since you was in there tussling in that man's bodily fluids."

"Bruce, just shut up and drive." Rahlo hopped in the passenger seat.

"Damn, can you at least sit in the trunk? I don't think I can drive with you smelling like this."

"Fuck you," he chortled. "Damn, I do stank though."

"Duh, nigga." Bruce plugged his nose.

∞∞∞

Later that evening, Taylor woke up to the sounds of someone picking at the front door. The last thing she remembered was Rahlo kissing her on the cheek before he left the house for the second time. He wanted her to ride with him, but Taylor declined, telling him she was still tired. Glancing out the window, she noticed that it was getting dark. Getting up, she tiptoed to the front door but stopped when she heard voices. The hairs on the back of her neck stood up as the person on the other side started wiggling the knob.

"Ain't nobody here," the voice whispered.

"I told you, I've been watching it all day. The nigga left and ain't nobody been back," someone else said.

Taylor backpedaled to the room and snatched her cell phone off the bed. As the front door opened, she slipped into the bathroom and hid in the tub. From where she was, she could hear the voices moving about the house, knocking over everything in their path. Thinking quickly, Taylor called Rahlo.

"T-baby, you finally up?" He answered on the first ring.

"Somebody is in the house," she whispered.

"What?" Rahlo sat up, alarming Bruce. "Where you at?"

"In the bathroom next to your room."

"Lock the door and don't make a sound. I'm about to call the police."

"Noooo, don't hang up," she pleaded, hearing the voices get a little closer.

"Fuck!" Rahlo cursed, hitting the steering wheel. "Bruce, send the police to my house. I'm five minutes away, baby. I need you to be strong. Get some kinda of cleaner and a lighter. If they open the bathroom door, set them muthafuckas on fire."

"Oh shit! Grab that watch, get them earrings and shoes over there too," the intruder demanded on the other side of the door.

"We gone have to make another trip, this bag full," the other person said.

"The police are 3 minutes out. Tell Tay to hold tight," Bruce told Rahlo.

"You hear him, baby?"

"Yes," she whispered, hearing the door rattle. "Oh nooo," she cried, getting out of the tub.

"Do what I said, Taylor. I'm right here," Rahlo coached her.

Doing as she was told, Tayor grabbed the oil sheen and lighter from under the sink. Removing the top, she aimed the spray toward the door. A couple of kicks later, the door flew open, and she was face-to-face with the masked intruder.

"Ahhhh," Taylor screamed while pressing the nozzle on the oil sheen.

"The fuck?" The intruder backhanded her, sending her body crashing against the door.

"Baby!" Rahlo called over the phone. "Taylor!"

"You ain't so mighty now nigga," the intruder chuckled. "I'm about to fuck yo bitch, and you better hope she don't get pregnant," he taunted, throwing the phone to the ground.

Taylor took the opportunity to make a run for it. She got halfway out the door before the masked man grabbed her by the shirt and flung her to the bed. Climbing on top of her, he groped her breast.

"The fuck is you doing?" The other intruder asked, running back in the house and seeing his counterpart kneeling over Taylor.

"Might as well fuck his bitch too." He continued roughly pulling at Taylor's shirt, trying to pull it over her neck. She fought him with all of her might before his fist went across her face. Dazed, Taylor's head fell against the bed as blood leaked from her nose.

"Hurry up," the man grunted, not wanting to take part in a rape but he also wanted to keep him distracted so he could skim off the top. "I'm going to grab some mo' shit."

Using his legs, the burglar dug his knees into Taylor's thighs until they opened. He couldn't care less about the tears running down her face. His anger was beyond her.

"That's right, let me in." He grinned, grabbing at the hem of her panties. "Damn, look at this fat muthafucka. Bro, you sure you don't want to hit it?" he called out.

Panicking, Taylor gripped the lighter in her hand and prayed that it would still work. There was no way she was about to willingly let him take something that didn't belong to him. Striking the lighter, she pressed it to his mask and watched it go up in flames. Taylor then raised her knee to hit him in the balls, causing a loud scream to echo off the walls.

"My face," he cried, rolling to the floor. "My fucking face!"

"Sick ass bastard!" Taylor screamed, hopping over the man, who was doing a poor job of stop, drop, and roll.

Taylor ran to the bathroom and grabbed the oil sheen. Dousing him with more, she watched the flames spread over his hands and neck.

Boom!

The front door flew off the hinges and officers stormed the loft. The burglar in the living room was thrown to the ground.

The burning man was running around trying to remove the mask, but it melted to his skin and facial hair. One of the officers tripped him so they could put the fire out.

"My face," he thundered as the officer patted the flames out on his head.

"Are you Taylor?" Another officer asked, walking into the room with a phone pressed to his ear.

"Y-y-es," she stuttered, still shaken up.

"Come on, let me have someone check you out." He held his hand out to help her off the bed.

The officer led her to the living room, where one of the intruders was being led out of the house. Taylor took a look at his face but couldn't remember if she had ever seen him before. She felt like she was in a twilight zone as paramedics bypassed them, going into the bedroom to help the burn victim before they took him to the precinct.

"T-baby," Rahlo hollered, causing her head to snap in his direction.

"Sir, you can't go in there." An officer tried to stop him, but Rahlo pushed past him. At the sight of him, Taylor jumped up and ran into his arms. Smothering her with kisses, he held her tight, thanking God for sparing her life.

"You good?" he asked, wiping her face.

"Yes," she sniffled.

Before Rahlo could respond, the officers were escorting the second intruder from the back. Rahlo released Taylor and stepped forward. Without warning, he punched AJ dead in the face.

"You tried to fucking rob me?" Rahlo punched him again before the officers and Bruce stopped him.

"Fuck you, nigga! I almost had you, and I almost fucked your bitch," AJ grinned.

"He touched you?" Rahlo glanced at Taylor. It was then he saw the blood in her nose, hand print on her cheek, stretched out shirt, and red marks on her thighs. Taylor didn't even have to answer.

Whap whap!

Rahlo popped him in the face again.

"You know this man?" the officer asked.

"Yea, he's my bitch ass cousin," Rahlo snarled.

Shaking his head, the officer pushed AJ out of the door and asked Rahlo to follow him. Glued to his side, Taylor held his hand and walked beside him. The front of the building was surrounded by police cars and bystanders. Cameras were on them as the officer led them to another car. They asked Rahlo if he knew the other man, but he said no.

"What about her?" he asked. "We found her sitting in the getaway car."

Rahlo ducked his head into the car, and once again his heart broke. He didn't know why he was surprised, but seeing Emory sitting there hurt a little more than it should have. She hated him so much that she was about to rob his house and to make matters worse, she convinced her dumb ass nephew to help her.

"She gave birth to me," Rahlo cleared his throat. The officer's face dropped, but he quickly recovered.

"I-uh understand if you want me to look the other way, I'll let her go."

"No, charge her."

"Really, Rah? You going to send your own mother to jail? What kind of weak ass nigga are you?" Emory shouted, trying to break out of the tight cuffs that dug into her wrists. "You're a sorry excuse for a man."

"Come on, baby." Taylor rubbed his back. Rahlo took one

last look at Emory, who was calling him every despicable name she could think of.

"I hope that bitch bleeds your dumb ass dry. I hope her fat-"

Whap!

Taylor reached back and popped Emory in the mouth so fast that no one saw it coming. Hell, she didn't know she was going to do it, but the hurt in Rahlo's eyes triggered her. He was too good of a person for her to dog.

"She hit me! I want to press charges, cuff this fat hoe," Emory cried with blood dripping from her lip.

"I didn't see anything," the officer said, shutting the door. "Here, take my card and come down and give your statement when you're ready."

"Thank you." Taylor took the card.

Rahlo and Taylor walked back into the loft, where Bruce was cleaning up and on the phone with the locksmith. He could change the locks, but Rahlo's mind was already made up. They weren't going to spend another night in the loft. It amazed him how quickly things were changing in his life, and his family was the worst part.

"Rah, you good?" Bruce asked, watching him look around the loft. Broken glass, shoes, and clothes were everywhere while the smell of burnt hair lingered in the air.

"I'm straight. You ain't even gotta do all that. Text Chyna and have her book me a room." Rahlo shook his head at the mess. Besides a few things, he didn't want anything in the loft.

"I can go back home until you come back," Taylor offered, rubbing his arm.

"Nah, that ain't gone work for me. I'll have Terri send you a list. Let him know what you like and we'll go from there. Let's go to the hospital so I can have them check you out."

"I don't need to go to the hospital. He just hit me in the

face.. he didn't, ummm..." She sighed. "I just want to take a shower. I feel so dirty."

"I got it," Bruce assured them. "Go take care of T-baby."

"Nigga, don't call her that." Rahlo scowled.

"Oh, I didn't know that name was just for you."

"It is. The fuck."

Taylor snickered and thanked Bruce for all his help. Once they were out of the door, he picked up his phone and made a call. Bruce warned AJ about staying in his place, but once again, Emory had him looking stupid. This time, Bruce was going to make good on his promise. AJ behind bars simply made it a little easier.

∞∞∞

By the time they checked into the hotel, Terri had sent Taylor a list of houses and condos. He was happy that Rahlo decided to move. He was slowly but surely trying to transition him to think like a popular rapper vs a nigga with money. He now had brand deals, hosting gigs, and sold-out concerts. Rahlo's success was happening at a faster rate than either of them expected, and he needed to move a certain way. Although he was raised in the streets, they were envious and unforgiving. It didn't matter how much Rahlo gave back to the city, he'd always be a target in some people's eyes. His fame was a threat, and the sooner he learned that, the better off they would be.

"Kiki, no, you don't need to come up here," Taylor said into the phone.

"No, fuck that. I'm about to go to the jail and snatch that crusty ass lace off his mama. Tell Rah I like him, but I'm about to beat his mama up."

"Bitch, you loud," Taylor laughed. "He can hear you."

"I'm just saying, ugh. What the hell is wrong with people?" Kiki scoffed.

"Fuck if I know, but I'm about to eat and lay down. I'm tired."

"Well, feed our little pea, and I'm about to call up to the jail."

"For what, Shakia?"

"To see if his mama can have visitors."

"Shakia."

"I just want to talk to the ditzy hoe."

"Don't end up behind bars," Taylor laughed.

"That don't sound like a bad idea. Tell Rah he can post my bail. Bye."

"Bye, fool."

"Bye, boo." Kiki hung up.

Taylor put the phone on the nightstand and rolled over, placing her head on Rahlo's bare chest. In less than two seconds, his dick pitched a tent in the boxers, making her giggle.

"Why are you like this?" she asked, pointing to his dick.

"Because every time your soft ass touch me, I get excited."

"I'll take that as a compliment."

"You should." He stroked her face. "How are you feeling?"

"Better. Today was crazy."

"It was, and I'm so sorry for that shit. Emory's evil ass has no end."

"It's not your fault. I'm just happy that your cousin didn't get far."

"I would have bodied that nigga and did the time with a smile on my face."

"Then where would we be?" She touched her stomach.

"Yall would be straight."

"Hm, and I got a call from Jalen today. He said somebody beat his daddy up."

"Straight up?" Rahlo glanced down at her. "Maybe his stalking ass fucked with the wrong nigga or something."

"Or something," Taylor smirked. "Well, hopefully now we have a chance."

"A chance?" Rahlo asked, confused.

"A chance to be happy and enjoy each other."

"We do, T-baby."

"Who said?" She cocked her head to the side.

"God did."

New Years

"Over here! Rah! Tay!" Paparazzi shouted out as they walked up the red carpet.

Rahlo couldn't believe so many people came out to show him love. He simply wanted to rap, make money, and take care of the people he loved, but this was everything. All the big hitters in Detroit had come out to celebrate his major accomplishment, and it felt good. Going gold on his first album was big shit, and people wanted to give him his flowers while they could.

Now that he was walking down the red carpet with the

love of his life, Rahlo realized how blessed he was. Nothing in his life had gone according to plan, but it wasn't supposed to. Everything was already written in stone before he was ever a thought. It was always God's plan and Rahlo wouldn't change the path for anything in the world. His only wish was that Duke was there to share the moment with him.

A few days before the new year, Rahlo released a song called *A Letter to My Best Friend.* Taylor recorded him in the studio rapping it, wanting to show the world his raw emotions. Bruce gave her a few pictures from their childhood, and she made a video that went with the song. On YouTube, it surpassed 500,000 views in the first twenty-four hours and over two million views before the day was over.

"You wanna give them a show?" Rahlo whispered in Taylor's ear when they reached the top of the stairs.

In his eyes, she was the best-dressed woman in the building, and she belonged to him. A custom red strapless dress hugged her frame and fishtailed in the back. It took KiKi over a week to create the masterpiece, but it turned out to be everything Taylor wanted. Diamonds rested on her neck, ears, and wrist, and a pair of open-toed red bottoms blessed her feet. Esha gave her a light beat at Rahlo's request with a nude lip. Her signature blond cut was freshly dyed and laid to perfection. Standing there next to Rahlo, Taylor looked like a million bucks, and most importantly, she felt like it.

"You know I stay camera ready." She cheesed.

"You looking so fucking sexy, baby." He pulled her into his arms with her back resting against his chest. "I can't wait to get you out of that dress." Rahlo's breath tickled her neck as cameras continued to capture the moment. "And I can't wait to smear that lip liner shit."

"You know I love you, right?" Taylor looked up at him. Turning her around, Rahlo kissed her lips.

"I love you too, baby. You've been the peace in my most stressful days. You're the fresh breath of air I need when the world is suffocating me. You're the calm in the middle of the storm, and I want this for life. Nah, fuck that, I need this for life," he told her, planting a kiss on her lips.

On cue, Trooper approached her holding a beautiful bouquet of red roses.

"Aww, thank you, baby," she cooed, taking them from him. "What are you doing here?"

Von had told her they couldn't make it, and while she was sad, Taylor understood they already had plans of their own.

"We're all here." Trooper smiled, pointing behind him.

Confused, Taylor looked past her brother and saw Papa, Von, Kiki, Ariel, Esha, and Bruce waving at her.

"Wh-what's going on?"

"I just thought it was only right to have everyone here for this moment," Rahlo said from behind. Taylor spun around and her hand flew to her mouth. In front of the world, Rahlo was on his knee, bending his Jordans for her. The cameras around them went wild, witnessing what was taking place. Rahlo tweeted that something special would happen tonight, but they didn't expect this.

"T-baby," Rahlo called her name to bring her focus back to him.

"Hm?" she answered through teary eyes.

"Will you do me the honor of being my ride or die, the right to my wrong, the good to my bad? Will you be my wife, baby?"

"Rah, I was your wife when you made me chicken and waffles," she joked. "Yes, I'll marry you," Taylor screamed, causing a loud, thunderous round of applause to break out. Sliding the black princess-cut diamond ring on her finger, Rahlo's chest filled with pride.

"Oh my godddd," she screamed, jumping into his arms the second he stood up. "I love you, I love you, I love you!" Taylor kissed his lips.

"See, talking like that is going to have me saying fuck this party bullshit." Rahlo kissed her back.

"Period, best friend!" Kiki clapped, holding her phone on them.

Taylor looked into the crowd, flashing her ring, but the smile on her face slowly slipped from her lips. Her forehead broke out in a light sweat and her voice lodged in her throat. Even if she wanted to scream, she couldn't. It was too late. He looked different, but it was him. Jasper blew her a kiss before he pulled the trigger.

Pow!

The bullet struck her in the chest, knocking her into Rahlo.

Pow!

The second bullet hit Kiki in the shoulder, making her drop the phone.

Pow!

The third bullet pierced Rahlo's hand and entered Taylor's stomach.

Pandemonium broke out as people started to run and take cover. Bruce tried to get through the crowd, but he was moving against the current. It didn't matter how hard he pushed, he couldn't get to them. It didn't matter how loud he yelled, no one moved out of his way.

"Ah fuck!" Rahlo cried out, trying to reach for Taylor with his bloody hand. His heart broke seeing Kiki scream out in pain, but he couldn't help her. Not when his girl lay a few feet away from him choking on her own blood.

"Can we get some fucking help!" Rahlo shouted with tears

streaming down his face. "Hold tight, baby." He pressed his free hand on her chest.

"We al-al-almost had it," Taylor choked out.

"Had what, T?" He wiped her mouth.

"H-happiness." She smiled up at him. Even in distress, she couldn't get over how handsome he was. Their story was so amazing, and she hated that she couldn't see the end, but Taylor appreciated every moment they shared.

"We still got it, T-baby," Rahlo promised, looking around. "Get me some fucking help!"

Taylor could hear Trooper crying, she could hear Rahlo begging for her to stay with him, but her eyes were heavy, and the hole in her chest didn't hurt anymore. Suddenly, she felt light and dying didn't seem so bad. It was nothing but chaos around her, but Taylor felt peaceful.

"Aye, you promised!" Rahlo shook her, noticing her eyes flutter. "You fucking promised you wouldn't leave me, T-baby!" he yelled. "You said you were here to stay."

Taylor's eyes opened one last time before closing, and Rahlo lost it. The cry that escaped his lips would forever haunt the people who still lingered around watching the horrific scene. Perched beside her, Rahlo pulled Taylor's body into his arms and hugged her tight. He'd never understand how the best day of his life turned into a nightmare.

"Sir, let us help you." The first responder tried to pry his hands off Taylor, but Rahlo couldn't let go. She was gone, and he didn't need them to assess her to know it. She wasn't breathing.

"Rahlo, please let them help her," Esha begged, shedding tears of her own.

"Son, you have to let her go." Von leaned down to pick his daughter up. Only then did Rahlo release her. How could he deny her first love access to her? The man who helped shape her into everything he loved?

"I fucking love you." Rahlo kissed her once more before Von laid her on the gurney and allowed the first responders to take her away.

Epilogue

One year later

Rahlo walked onto the stage for an encore at the crowd's request. He was tired as hell, but the way they called his name warmed his heart. How could he deny them when they were the reason he was standing there? They were the reason his album was number one and had been for several months. They were the reason he went platinum, so for them, he'd shake off the exhaustion and put on for his city.

The stadium full of people chanted his name, giving him the energy he needed to perform one last song. Bruce stood off to the side with the phone trained on him. Terri wanted to be there but was in Miami with his other client. Now that Rahlo was in a position to make moves on his own, Terri was able to pick up four other clients. Rahlo was still his number one, and he'd drop everything for him, but he trusted him to make the right decisions.

"Last year was fucked up yall," Rahlo breathed into the microphone. "I lost a bunch of hating muthafuckas," he said, causing the crowd to yell out.

Emory was included in the people he lost. She was currently serving five years in Iona Prison for theft, robbery, and a slew of other petty charges. When she was booked the night she tried to rob Rahlo's house, they found stolen credit cards and fake IDs in the car. Emory was also being charged with welfare fraud. Her karma was sitting behind bars while the very son she hated toured the world and made millions off his story, a story she tried to sell from behind bars, but Terri slapped her with a gag order. If she even mentioned Rahlo's name, the story was dead before it even started.

AJ was locked up as well. His life behind bars was a lot worse than Emory's. Bruce kept good on his promise, and the same night AJ was booked, he was jumped. When the guards finally came around, AJ was barely breathing and his jaw was unhinged. Even when it healed, he couldn't open his mouth fully. On top of his armed robbery charge, AJ was slapped with an attempted rape charge and assault. His stay in prison was anything but pleasant.

"But I gained some real niggas!" Rahlo shouted, tossing a head nod to Kool, Chef, and Bruce.

After watching the shooting on live TV, Chef decided to make a change. He reasoned that no one could protect his son like him, so he dropped the pipe, cold turkey. Chef cleaned himself up, started going to NA meetings, and was able to help his son through such a difficult time in his life. Emory saw Chef and Rahlo on TV from her cell and lost her shit. They were enjoying concerts, basketball games, and getting to know each other while she was rotting in jail. Chef couldn't go back and change things, but he vowed to be there every step of the way moving forward.

Kool was along for the ride because of his loyalty to Taylor. Bruce hired Kool as a security guard for Rahlo, and he has been solid ever since. He stopped fucking with Jada after the massacre on the red carpet, and no matter how much she begged, Kool didn't go back. He couldn't. Too much blood had been shed, and he no longer had time for all the drama.

"Let me get a moment of silence for my nigga Duke." Rahlo dropped his head as the stadium joined him.

Duke's death was still hard on him, and there were plenty of nights he woke up in a cold sweat thinking about him. Mourning was weird. Some days, he was okay and able to conquer the world, but other days, he felt paralyzed by Duke's absence. In honor of his life, Rahlo was opening up a prison reform program for black men who were lost after being released back into the real world. He wanted to give them the support they needed and resources to help keep them from going back. Rahlo wanted to believe that if Duke had that support, things would have turned out a little differently.

"Aight, let's get this shit!" The beat dropped and Rahlo's dancers filed onto the stage.

Behind him, they twerked and twirled their hips to the lyrics that spewed from his lips. In the middle of the stage, Rahlo tried to rap but was caught off guard by the stadium finishing his lyrics. Chill bumps formed on his arm, and he tucked his lip, displaying the dimple in his cheek. He tried to speak, but he was choked up as they continued to rap to him. Rahlo stared at the crowd in amazement. He felt what people had been telling him all his life. He was different and had a gift the world loved. Rahlo dropped the mic and held his hands to the sky. He gave all the glory to God because, in that moment, he understood and accepted his blessing.

At three in the morning, Rahlo walked into his house and dropped his bag at the door. He was tired as shit but needed to lay eyes on his girl before climbing into the bed. Tiptoeing through the house, Rahlo bypassed Esha and Kiki, who were sleeping on the couch. He knew they were both probably wore out because his girl was a handful. She was demanding and spoiled, and when she didn't get her way, she cut up.

Rahlo was thankful for them. Esha and Kiki stepped up in a major way. Most of the time, when he was in the studio or on the road, they held him down on the home front. Since they both had booming businesses, Esha and Kiki took shifts, but they made it happen.

Walking up the stairs, Rahlo pushed the nursery door open and smiled until he heard singing. A frown covered his face as he listened closely to the worlds.

"Hush little baby please don't cry, Mama's trying not to punch you in the eye," Taylor lovingly sang to their daughter, who was whining in her arms.

"Stop playing with me." Rahlo closed the door and reached out for his daughter.

Born two months early, Riah was a force to be reckoned with. The bullet that entered Taylor's stomach missed her sac and clipped her rib. She was in the hospital most of the pregnancy, and at seven months, they delivered Riah early to reduce the chance of complications with the baby and mom. Riah was the perfect mix of him and Taylor. Instead of one dimple, she had two. She was the color of toasted almonds but turned red when she started crying, which was her favorite pastime. Taylor swore she liked to hear her own voice. The little girl was feisty and only like Rahlo and Trooper. Anybody else, she gave them hell.

"She has been whining ever since we cut the FaceTime off. Tell Bruce I said thank you too," Taylor told him. "I wish I could have come," she pouted.

"You're on bed rest." Rahlo looked over at her.

"I'm on bedrest because you can't keep your dick in your

pants," Taylor hissed, looking down at her stomach.

As soon as she gave birth to Riah, Rahlo waited two weeks before he had her bent over the hospital bed. He tried to be patient, but when her titty slipped out of the hospital gown, it was a wrap. Rahlo fucked her so good that the machine started beeping and nurses filed into the room, thinking she was having a heart attack. Her heart monitor was off the charts, and when Rahlo pulled his dick out of her, they knew why.

"You say it like it's a bad thing," Rahlo smirked, causing the dimple to sink in his face.

"It is, nigga. This is beyond ghetto." She pointed to her protruding stomach. "And now her fat self is going to sleep after she woke me up."

"Kiki and Esha didn't help?"

"They got drunk and went to sleep," Taylor ratted. She was low-key jealous and couldn't wait to have the baby so she could drink. In fact, she told Esha and Kiki to make sure she had a bottle of wine in her hand as soon as the baby's shoulders were out. Esha said no, but Kiki was a real one. She bought Taylor a bracelet that doubled as a flask.

Rahlo stood up from the floor and placed a sleeping Riah in her crib. After cutting on her monitor, he put the other one in his pocket and turned to face his yawning wife.

"What?" Taylor blushed under his gaze.

"I love you, T-baby."

"I love you, too."

"Come on, let me put you to bed." Rahlo picked her up as if she were light as a feather. Taylor had lost a lot of weight, but Rahlo had plans of getting her back together, and if this pregnancy didn't do it, he was going to try again.

The night Taylor was shot, Rahlo nearly lost his mind. There was so much blood, and even when he thought they had

LADII NESHA

stopped it, more seeped from the hole in her stomach. Taylor's heart stopped beating twice on the way to the hospital, and she swore it was Duke who kept telling her to take her bald-headed ass back. The doctors removed the bullets from her chest and stomach, but the rest was up to her. Rahlo prayed over her day and night. By the grace of God, she pulled through, and Rahlo was forever in debt to the man above.

After opening fire into the crowd, Jasper turned the gun on himself. He pulled the trigger but missed due to someone bumping into him. Von tackled Jasper to the ground and beat the shit out of him. When the police pulled Von off Japer, he was toothless and his head was dented in. EMS took Jasper to the hospital and he was later transferred to jail. With multiple attempted murder charges, stalking, and other charges, Jasper would be old and gray before he ever saw the light of day again.

The news saddened Sherri, and her heart broke even more because the massacre was online, and her son would one day see his father throw his life away. After the sentencing, Sherri secretly aborted the baby she was carrying and moved her kids out of Michigan. So many of Rahlo's fans had found her home and egged it numerous times. For the safety of her babies, she packed up her life and left.

"How do you feel?" Taylor asked when Rahlo placed her on the bed.

"I'm good."

"I saw you crying on stage again. They started another hashtag. **#fineasscrybaby.**"

"They were happy tears." Rahlo laughed. The internet was undefeated. "I'm just so fucking grateful for my family." He kissed her stomach.

"Awe, we love you too." She rubbed the top of his head.

"Let me go get the drunks up from downstairs."

"Can you bring me back some ice cream and chips?"

"Yea." He leaned up and kissed her lips.

"Oh, and I need you to pick up Trooper tomorrow. My daddy found Ariel's nightgown cut up and stuffed in the bottom of the garbage." Taylor shook her head.

"Nah, Edward Scissorhands can keep his bad ass right there."

"Leave my baby alone," she snickered.

Six months ago, Von moved Ariel in with them, and Trooper was still struggling to accept it. Some days he liked her, and other days he was looking up magic spells to make her disappear.

"Hurry back so we can cuddle."

"You sound pressed," Rahlo grinned.

"Like the First Lady's hair on Easter Sunday," Taylor admitted, pulling her lip into her mouth.

"Keep talking like I won't put them soup coolers to work."

"Don't threaten me with a good time." Taylor wiggled her tongue at him.

"Fuck them snacks." He closed the bedroom door and dropped his pants.

The End

GQ Couples Quiz Interview

"Hey yall, it's Tay!" Taylor waved at the camera.

"And Southwest Rah," Rahlo threw up his set, making Taylor snicker.

"You can take the boy out of the hood, but can't take the hood out of the boy," she joked.

"But you knew that," he cockily grinned, "Southwest til the death of me."

"Anyway, this is the **GQ Couples Quiz**," Taylor announced, shifting in the big pink chair.

"You ok?" Rahlo asked, concerned. The camera panned in on his face, catching the worry lines that creased his forehead. In seconds he was on his feet and at her side.

"I'm ok, baby," she assured him, rubbing her round stomach.

Rahlo was against her getting out of the bed to do the show, but the doctors confirmed she was out of the danger zone. Sitting in the bed was driving her stir-crazy, and Taylor jumped at the opportunity to move around. After discovering she was pregnant for the second time, Rahlo put Taylor on bedrest before the doctors did. If she wasn't sitting at home in the bed or on their couch, she was on his line crying right next to their daughter.

"Ok, let's get this party started." Taylor clapped her hands. Rahlo leaned in and kissed her lips before retaking his seat.

"Let's go, baby, and don't be cheating," he teased.

"Hush," she giggled. "What's my favorite sport?"

"Football," Rahlo answered with ease.

"Good, you get two points, and I'll give you another one if you can say why?"

Rahlo gave her a knowing look before stroking his chin.

"You like them tight ass shorts," he mumbled. This was one of the reasons he couldn't watch the game with her. He'd cheer for touchdowns, and she'd cheer when somebody's ass jiggled.

"Ding ding ding!" Taylor giggled and turned to face the camera. "Ladies, yall feel me." She winked.

"Yea aight, next question."

"What is my dream vacation?"

"Easy," Rahlo snorted. "Camping in Alaska. You are fascinated with the Northern Lights."

"Correct," Taylor grinned.

"Come on, T-baby, this is light work." He cockily rubbed his hands together. "Challenge me."

"Ok, smarty pants. Who's my favorite rapper?"

"Me, the –bleep-"

"Watch your mouth," Taylor laughed. "And be serious, you're my favorite rapper now, but before you it was Weezy F. baby."

"You heard what I said. Next question," Rahlo waved her off. "Nah, matter fact, it's my turn. What side is my dimple on?" Rah covered his face with his hand, making Taylor laugh out loud.

"How are you just going to highjack my questions?"

"Because I can, now answer."

The people standing in the room smiled at the banter between them. They argued like best friends but stared into each other's eyes like long-lost lovers. They admired how attentive Rahlo was to her needs. He anticipated when she wanted water, when her back was hurting, or when he thought she needed a kiss. Taylor, in return, picked lint from his shirt, brushed her hand across his waves, and stroked his cheek lovingly. Their love for one another could be felt in the room and it had them all swooning.

"It's on your left side." Taylor playfully rolled her eyes.

"Why?" He licked his lips, flexing the dimple.

"Because the left side is the best side."

"That's what they better know." Rahlo leaned in and kissed her lips. "Aight, that's all yall getting. Bruce bring the car around so we can take my baby home."

"No, I have more," Taylor whined.

"Your favorite food is tacos, your favorite color is black. You don't like to sleep with the lights off, your favorite season is fall, and-"

"You are so irritating," Taylor pouted, but he told no lies. "Who made you the boss of me?"

"God did." He kissed her lips.

Thank You!

I hope you enjoyed Rahlo and Taylor's story as much as I enjoyed creating it. I hope you laughed, cursed and shed a tear or two. If you did, then I did my job!

Thank you to all my readers! Yall ROCK and I'm grateful for each and every one of you. The TikTok's, Instagram post, Facebook shoutouts and everything else makes my heart so full! Thank you for rocking with me!

My test readers, ARC reviewers...yall are helping me grow. I appreciate your honesty and I'm thankful to have you ladies in my corner.

Thank you to my brother! He helped me out alot with writing 'Bars' and allowed me to pick his brain with all my questions.

Read. Rate. Review

Made in the USA
Monee, IL
14 November 2023